D1099472

06

Got You Back

JANE FALLON

PENGUIN BOOKS

PENGUIN BOOKS

Published by the Penguin Group
Penguin Books Ltd, 80 Strand, London WC2R ORL, England
Penguin Group (USA) Inc., 375 Hudson Street, New York, New York 10014, USA
Penguin Group (Canada), 90 Eglinton Avenue East, Suite 700, Toronto, Ontario, Canada M4P 2Y3
(a division of Pearson Penguin Canada Inc.)
Penguin Ireland, 25 St Stephen's Green, Dublin 2, Ireland
(a division of Penguin Books Ltd)
Penguin Group (Australia), 250 Camberwell Road, Camberwell, Victoria 3124, Australia
(a division of Pearson Australia Group Pty Ltd)
Penguin Books India Pvt Ltd, 11 Community Centre, Panchsheel Park, New Delhi – 110 017, India
Penguin Group (NZ), 67 Apollo Drive, Rosedale, North Shore 0632, New Zealand
(a division of Pearson New Zealand Ltd)
Penguin Books (South Africa) (Pty) Ltd, 24 Sturdee Avenue, Rosebank, Johannesburg 2196, South Africa

Penguin Books Ltd, Registered Offices: 80 Strand, London WC2R ORL, England

www.penguin.com

First published 2008
2

Set in 12.5/14.75 pt Monotype Garamond
Typeset by Rowland Phototypesetting Ltd, Bury St Edmunds, Suffolk
Printed in England by Clays Ltd, St Ives plc

ISBN: 978-0-141-03440-9

www.greenpenguin.co.uk

Stephanie closed her eyes and held out her hands, her son's almost uncontrollable excitement rubbing off on her and making her feel like a child again herself. It was hard to believe it had been nine years. Nine years ago today she had been shivering because of the cold, and crying because it was raining and her hair was going to get ruined, and James had burst into the hotel room where she had been getting ready, ignoring all the voices telling him it was bad luck for him to see his bride before the ceremony, because he had known she would be nervous and that she would care about seeing him more than she would worry about breaking with tradition.

'You're going to have to wear a mac,' he'd said, 'and galoshes. Oh, and maybe a rain bonnet. That'll look nice,' and despite her nerves Stephanie had laughed.

'I mean, I can't marry you if you look like a drowned rat – it'd be bad for my reputation.'

Stephanie's mother, who had been helping her squeeze into her untraditional grey satin dress and who had never quite got James's sense of humour, had tutted and tried to usher him out of the room, but James had flung himself into an armchair in the corner and refused to budge. By the time they had had to leave for the register office Stephanie had felt relaxed and in control, secure that this was going to be the happiest day of her life, just as it was meant to be.

In the end her hair had lain plastered to her head like wet string, and James had told her that she'd never looked so beautiful and he'd said it with such conviction that she'd actually believed him.

Every year since he had made a big fuss on their anniversary, surprising her with cleverly chosen gifts: a pair of heavily decorated designer wellingtons the first year, a reference to the weather on their wedding day but also, as it turned out, something she now treasured for a different reason – a reminder of their last weekend spent stomping around in the mud at Glastonbury before she'd found out she was pregnant with Finn; a night away at a B-and-B, complete with his parents' offer of babysitting when Finn was two, and Stephanie was at the furthest edge of her rationality; last year a flowery tin watering-can he had known she had her eye on.

Fired up by his enthusiasm, she had planned surprises for him too, something her family had never really gone in for, Christmas being more a time for 'What do you want? A new blender? Fine, that's what I'll get you.' Over the years she had bought him books and gadgets and once, when she was feeling particularly sentimental, a photograph of the three of them in a silver frame. The rule was that the gifts had to remain secret until the big day, something which Finn, confidant of both parents in the planning stages, always struggled with.

This year Stephanie had bought James a fish-shaped corkscrew, which Finn had insisted his father had been admiring in a shop window, although she'd had her doubts. He had opened it eagerly, tearing off the paper, and had certainly seemed delighted, although Stephanie knew he would never have given away that he wasn't. Now it was her turn and the suspense was killing her.

'Come on.' She laughed. She could hear Finn giggling with excitement.

'Don't open your eyes,' James said, and she felt a small light square box drop into her outstretched hands. She had suspected that he was going to buy her the new Jamie Oliver – in fact, she had been hinting heavily to Finn that that was what she wanted. This didn't feel like the new Jamie Oliver. 'OK, you can open them now.'

She did as she was told. In her hand was a small but distinctive red box. This wasn't right. They weren't meant to spend a lot: the presents were a token, a bit of fun. It was most definitely the thought that counted. OK, she thought, I'll open it and inside there'll be a plastic necklace from Camden Market. That'll be the joke.

Finn was jumping up and down. 'Open it.'

She arranged her face into what she thought was a look of genuine expectation – James had done this before: once he had wrapped a huge box in beautiful flock paper, and when she had unwrapped it there was another and then another until finally all that was left was an empty matchbox. Then he had produced her real gift from behind the sofa. Finn had thought it was the funniest thing he had ever witnessed.

She opened the box. Inside was something that seemed to be doing a very passable imitation of a silver bracelet inlaid with pink stones. Stephanie looked at James quizzically. He raised his eyebrows as if to say, 'Well, what did you expect?' She picked the bracelet out of its white satin bed. It was most definitely not plastic. 'James?'

'Don't you like it?' Finn was saying.

'Of course I do, I love it, but it's too much. Since when did we do this? Spend fortunes on each other, I mean. This *must* have cost a fortune.'

'I wanted to get you something nice, something proper for a change. To show you how much I appreciate you. Well, how much I love you, really.'

'Yuk,' Finn said, and made a face as if he was going to be sick.

'It's beautiful. I don't know what to say.' She looked at him, her head on one side.

'Well, "Thank you, James, for your amazing kindness and generosity," would be a start,' he said, trying to look serious.

She smiled. 'Thank you, James, for your amazing . . . What was it?'

'Kindness and generosity.'

'Yes, that, exactly, whatever you just said.'

'And for being such a wonderful, not to mention handsome and intelligent, some would say genius, husband.'

Stephanie laughed. 'Oh, no, you'll have to buy me more than a Cartier bracelet to get me to say all that.'

'Just remember this next year,' James said, laughing too, 'when you're out shopping.'

Stephanie slipped the bracelet on to her wrist. It was perfect, exactly the one she would have chosen for herself, except that she probably would have decided it was too expensive and ended up settling for something far less special. James, when he wanted to, could still surprise her. She slipped her arms round his neck and hugged him. 'Thank you.'

I

Five days later

It wasn't the words that upset her particularly: it was the kisses that followed them. That and the fact that the message was signed with an initial, not even a name. As if there was no question in the writer's mind that he would know who it was from. As if he received texts like this every day. Perhaps he did, Stephanie thought sadly.

Stephanie had been married to James for nine years, most of them blissfully happy, at least as far as she knew, although suddenly nothing felt that certain. They had one child, seven-year-old Finn, who was bright and funny and, above all, healthy, a black and white cat called Sebastian, who seemed to share all those qualities, and a goldfish named Goldie, who was, well, a fish. They had forty-two and a half thousand pounds left to pay on their mortgage, eleven thousand three hundred in their joint savings account, two thousand two hundred and thirty-eight pounds and seventy-two pence worth of credit-card debt, and a joint inheritance of about thirty-five thousand on its way once both sets of elderly parents died – although it wasn't looking like that would be any time soon: longevity ran in both their families.

In the years that they had been together James had lost his appendix while Stephanie had gained and, thankfully, lost a handful of kidney stones. James had put on about two stone in weight, mostly around the middle, while Stephanie's valiant efforts in the gym meant that she was only a few pounds heavier than when they had met. She had, of course, acquired a few stretchmarks, but along with them had come Finn, so on balance she thought they were a price worth paying. They were both, still, without a doubt, on the plus side of attractive for their combined age of seventy-seven.

I'm really missing you. K xxx

She thought back over the previous night. James had arrived home at about six thirty as usual. He had seemed completely himself, tired but happy to be back. He had gone through his usual after-work routine; getting changed, spending half an hour or so playing with Finn in the garden, reading the paper, dinner, TV then bed. It hadn't exactly been a scintillating evening, the conversation had hardly rivalled the round table at the Algonquin, but it had been . . . normal. An evening exactly like a thousand other evenings they had spent together.

James had told her and Finn a story at dinner, she remembered. A funny story about how he had managed to successfully remove a splinter from the paw of an Afghan hound despite the fact that the family's python was working its way up the inside of his trouser leg. He had acted out the whole scene, putting on a gruff voice to portray the bemused thoughts of the dog, which had had Finn creasing up. He had a tendency to make himself the hero of his stories – there was usually an underlying message of 'Look how great I am' – however entertaining and hilarious he made them. But that was just James. He had grown a little pompous over the years, a little too pleased with himself, but she had always put that down to insecurity, had even found it quite endearing. He was so transparent, she'd thought fondly. Apparently that was not the case.

The way it usually went was like this: James would say something self-aggrandizing, Stephanie would make fun of him, he would laugh and admit to exaggerating his part in whatever story he was telling. It was like role-play: they each knew what was expected of them and what their boundaries were. They enjoyed it, or so she had thought. They would argue about anything, however trivial or taboo – politics, religion, who had had the better voice, Nathan from Brother Beyond or Limahl from Kaja-googoo. It was what they did. Last night had been no exception. James had been trying to insist that *ER* gave a more realistic portrayal of life in an American hospital than *Grey's Anatomy*.

'You might be right,' Stephanie had said. 'I'm just saying you don't know.'

James had puffed up in that half-serious, half-ironic way he had. 'I do work in the medical profession.'

Stephanie had snorted indignantly. 'James, you're a vet. You know nothing about hospitals, apart from the eighteen hours you spent sitting in the waiting room being sick into a bag when I was in labour. I can't even get you to go to the doctor when you're ill.'

'Did you know,' James had said, ignoring her last

comment, 'that in some countries it's legal for a vet to practise on a human but not the other way round?'

'Your point being?'

'I'm just saying that what I do and what a doctor does are very closely related.'

'And that makes you an expert on life in an inner-city American hospital?'

'Well, more so than you, anyway. You know that I'd defer to you if we were having an argument about ... ooh, I don't know ... *What Not to Wear* or *The Clothes Show*.' He'd smiled at her smugly as if to say, 'Got you.'

Stephanie had picked up a cushion, aiming it at his head. 'Patronizing git,' she'd said, laughing, and his self-important front had dissolved.

'Hit a nerve, did I?' he'd said, laughing along with her. 'Upset because you know I'm right?'

Stephanie stared at the four words – actually, four words and a letter – and the three kisses. She hadn't meant to look. She wasn't the sort of woman who trawled through the messages on her husband's mobile phone while he was in the bath but today; when she had realized that he'd left his phone at home and had been scrolling through trying to find a number for the surgery's receptionist, Jackie, she'd found herself idly flicking through his texts looking for, well, nothing really, just looking. She had felt all the blood rush from her head as she'd looked to see who the message was from. 'K', it said. Just 'K'. No Karen or Kirsty or Kylie to give her a clue. No Kimberley, Katrina or Kristen. Just 'I'm really missing you. K xxx', like there was only one person in the world whose name began with a K and James would know exactly who that was. She was fumbling about for the phone's address book, trying to see if the person listed as 'K' had a number she recognized, when she heard the bang of the front door closing. Stephanie dropped the phone hurriedly, jumping away from it as if she'd been stung. She plunged her hands into the too-hot washing-up water in the sink and tried to look casual as James strode into the room.

'Have you seen my phone?' he asked, not even stopping to say hello.

'No,' Stephanie said and then she'd wondered why she hadn't just said, 'Yes, it's over there.' Because he might have noticed she'd been looking through his address book, that was why.

He cast a cursory glance round the room, rushed out again, and then she heard him running up the stairs. She grabbed the phone from under the chair where she'd dropped it, stabbed at the buttons till the main screen returned, then ran out into the hall.

'James, I've found it. It's here,' she shouted.

'Thanks.' He pecked her on the cheek as he took it from her. 'I'd got as far as Primrose Hill,' he said, rolling his eyes and heading out of the front door again.

''Bye,' she said sadly to his back. She closed the door behind him and sat down heavily on the stairs.

OK, she thought, I have to think about this rationally. I mustn't jump to conclusions. But it was the language, the over-familiarity, the three kisses rather than the routine one that everybody seemed to deem suitable on even the most official piece of office communication, these days. And why would he have a number in his phone identifiable only as 'K'? Because he didn't want her to know who it was, she thought.

She was tempted to look on James's computer, to go through his emails to see if she could find any clues, any hints of who K might be, but she knew she mustn't turn into one of those people. You'd start by glancing through his emails, next thing you knew you'd be steaming open his post or sniffing his shirt collars every time he came home, like a lovestruck dog. She had to give James the benefit of the doubt. The truth was that even though her marriage wasn't perfect, even though they didn't see enough of each other these days and when they did the routine of running a family seemed to get in the way of everything else, she would still never have thought he would turn to another woman. Not in a thousand years.

She just couldn't imagine he would have it in him, that, even if he was bored with her and tired of their marriage – and she had no real reason to believe that either of these things was true – he would do this to their child. Neither, if she was honest, could she imagine that another woman would throw herself at him, with his self-importance and his habit of poking about in his ears with a cotton bud while he was watching the TV. But maybe she'd got things completely wrong. She had to get out of the house before the lure of his computer became too much for her to resist. She had to get to the office and speak to Natasha. Natasha would know what she should do.

'Don't do anything,' Natasha said, when Stephanie had told her the whole story. 'It'll turn out to be nothing and then he'll just resent you for going through his texts. Why were you going through his texts anyway?'

'I wasn't . . . I have no idea.'

'Maybe it's from a bloke. Kevin or Kelvin or Keith?'

'With three kisses?'

'A metrosexual,' Natasha persisted. 'They're very free with their emotions. Or a gay admirer? Kieron? Kiefer?'

'I don't think it's from a bloke.'

'Or an aunt?'

'No.'

'Someone from work?'

'Three kisses.'

'I agree it doesn't look good. Just don't do anything in a hurry, OK? Sleep on it.'

'OK,' Stephanie said reluctantly. She always took Natasha's advice.

'Shit,' she said, five minutes later. 'I've just realized. That bracelet he gave me for our anniversary – he's feeling guilty. That's why he spent so much. It wasn't an expression of love, it was an apology.'

2

Stephanie couldn't get James out of her head all day. Since they'd moved to London three years ago it had felt like they had hardly seen each other. The deal was that he would only put up with living in the city if he could split his week between his old rural practice near Lincoln and his new job, declawing Bengal cats and devising diets for overweight dogs in rarefied St John's Wood. He didn't want to give up his work with farm animals, he'd said. That was what he'd trained for. To work with real live-stock, working animals, not the pampered pets of the upper-middle classes. Dairy cows and abattoir-bound lambs, not Fluffy and Precious and Mr Paws. So now he left for the country every Sunday morning and returned to London on Wednesday evenings, tired and irritable from all the upheaval. He had a whole other life up there, she thought miserably. Why had she always thought it so unlikely that there could be another woman up there too? He had means, opportunity, motive. It was the perfect crime.

In the early days she had thought she might travel up and down with him sometimes, but as soon as Finn had settled into his primary school it had seemed ridiculous to uproot him every few weeks. And, besides, it had actually felt like a relief to have one less person to worry about for a few days at a time. It was inevitable, though, that with so much time spent apart their close ties would start to unravel. That their two worlds would overlap less and less. He had never been very interested in her job anyway, not fully understanding how life-threateningly crucial it was that the new face of *Holby City* didn't turn up to an awards do wearing the same dress as one of Girls Aloud.

When she'd first met James she had moved back home to her parents' house in Bath to save money. She had accidentally run over a neighbour's cat in her Citroën and, traumatized, had taken it straight to the local vet where James was, at the time, doing some on-the-job training. The cat, sadly, had failed to pull through, despite James's best efforts, but somewhere in the middle of the blood, guts and tears he had asked Stephanie out for a drink and she had agreed. Tiddles's loss had been her gain.

James, it seemed, had been as wowed by her ambition and skill as she had been by his. It was love at first sight. Well, lust and a bit of a rapport, which was all you could realistically hope for. But, somewhere along the line – somewhere, that was, around the time she had found she was pregnant with Finn – James had persuaded her to give up her lofty dream to be the new Vivienne Westwood and move into something less all-consuming, something which would allow her to spend time with the baby.

At first he had been supportive – it had been his idea, after all – encouraging her move into freelance dress-making and enjoying all the extra home comforts her working part-time – and in the spare room – afforded him. But then, three years ago when she had decided she wanted more, that she wanted to get back on the path to having a career rather than just a job, and had persuaded him to buy the house in London so that she could be near the young women with too much money and little enough style of their own that they were happy to employ someone to find their clothes for them, she had soon realized that he was actually a little embarrassed by her work.

'Stephanie dresses people who can't dress themselves,' he would say to their friends, finding himself hilarious. 'No, she's not a carer, nothing so worthy.'

Remembering this, Stephanie flung a pile of dresses, which had just been sent over from La Petite Salope, on to the sofa just as Natasha came in from the tiny room next door holding up a red shift. 'Is Shannon Fearon a size sixteen?' she asked, mentioning a young ex-soap opera actress who had recently shot back into the public eye by winning a celebrity singing competition, and who Stephanie was dressing for a photo shoot that afternoon.

'Really or officially?'

'Really.'

'She is.'

'OK, well, this might do.' Natasha started to unpick the size sixteen label in the neck of the dress, then rooted through a small metal box and found a label marked 'size ten' to replace it. It was always good to make the client feel skinny and confident. That way, if a journalist asked how big they were, they could reply that they were well under the average size for a British woman, without giving away that they were clearly talking rubbish with a sub-conscious downward flick of the eyes.

'Fine,' Stephanie said, without looking.

Natasha sat down, moving the crumpled pile of dresses out of the way. 'Stop dwelling on it,' she said, 'because you'll turn it into something even if it's nothing. Don't worry about things before you have to. That's my motto.'

'One of them,' Stephanie said.

Natasha had worked alongside Stephanie as a pattern cutter when Stephanie was still in her dress-maker phase and then had readily agreed to come along in the role of assistant when Stephanie had set herself up as a stylist five years later. She didn't want any responsibility, she'd said. Work, to Natasha, was something you did during the day. Then you went home and forgot about it. Natasha had a lovely home with a husband who worshipped her and three well-behaved, neat children. She had never had to worry about random text messages or what Martin was up to for half the week. Consequently her face was almost free of lines and she looked at least five years younger than the forty-one it said on her birth certificate. Over the years she had become much more friend than colleague. 'Mock if you want but you know I'm always right,' she said now.

'Of course you are,' Stephanie said fondly. 'I'll try. It just makes me so angry that some silly cow might have turned his head, tried to steal my husband from under my nose without even thinking about me and my life. And my son.'

'You don't know that.'

'No,' Stephanie said. 'I don't know that.'

But the thought wouldn't leave her head. What else could it mean, after all? I'm really missing you. Kiss. Kiss. Kiss.

She couldn't concentrate at the photo shoot and found herself snapping at Shannon when she'd complained that a particular dress made her look fat. 'That's because you are fat,' Stephanie had wanted to scream, although that would have been unfair. Shannon was most definitely not fat but she was short and disastrously proportioned so she had a tendency to look dumpy. In the end Natasha had suggested that Stephanie go home early before a fight broke out.

Luckily Finn was already there, playing ball in the tiny garden with Cassie, the nanny, so Stephanie could occupy herself with making him snacks.

Finn, at seven, could still be cajoled into keeping her company, and even though usually she would be cross with him for playing his favourite new game of rolling cherry tomatoes off the kitchen table and trying to make them land in the cat's bowl (one point if they went in the water, two if they landed in the Whiskas), she was so grateful to have a distraction that she just let him get on with it. Just after six she heard the front door open and slam shut again.

'Hello,' she heard James call.

'Hi,' she managed to shout back, weakly

He headed straight upstairs without stopping by the kitchen to see her. Not that this surprised her: he usually went up to the bedroom and changed out of his work clothes then settled down with the newspaper till dinnertime. He rarely asked her what she had done at work, and if he did, she normally didn't answer truthfully because he would only roll his eyes or make some sarcastic remark that he thought passed as a joke. If she was being honest with herself she would have realized she hardly ever asked him what had happened at the surgery either. She loved animals but she couldn't rustle up much interest in stories about their ingrowing claws or dodgy hips. But Stephanie had always believed that all marriages went through this stage when there were young children around. There were simply more things to worry about, other considerations that were more important than 'Did you have a good day at work?' She had thought they would come out the other side of it once Finn was a bit older, and live out a blissful old age together, with all the time in the world to indulge in idle chat. She'd obviously been delusional, she thought now, pounding a chicken breast until it was nearly see-through. She stopped when she saw Finn, white-faced, at her elbow.

'Are you OK?' he asked, in his best grown-up voice, a mimic of the way she said it to him several times a day.

She bent down and kissed the top of his head. 'I'm fine, darling.'

'You don't look OK,' he said stubbornly.

His face was creased with worry, and Stephanie felt guilty for having allowed her mood to affect him. She picked up a tomato and rolled it along the table from which it dropped on to the head of a startled Sebastian and bounced off his ear, into his organic chicken in gravy.

Try as he might, Finn couldn't hold back a smile. 'Excellent,' he said.

3

If you had asked James Mortimer how his life was – and if he had been in the mood to tell you the truth, because, actually, he had confided in no one over the last year, knowing that to tell one person would be to tell the world – he would have told you it was complicated. That he loved his wife Stephanie, deep down, but that somewhere along the line it had all got a bit safe and maybe even a little dull; that he adored his son and would never want to hurt him; that he had feelings for Katie that bordered on love, and that when he was with her he felt alive and invigorated in a way that routine family life no longer had the power to make him feel.

He wouldn't have admitted that what he was doing was wrong because he was trying to convince himself that there was no harm in it. He believed he was happy, Stephanie, he believed, was happy, and Katie certainly was. OK, so it was a bit of a ticking time-bomb waiting to explode. One of these days he knew he'd have to make a decision, plump for one life or the other. One day either Stephanie was going to insist that he gave up his life in Lincolnshire and moved to London full-time or Katie would grow tired of waiting for him to settle in the country. But until that happened his life suited him. As long as he didn't think about what he was doing too much.

James, if he had been being honest, would probably have said that the easiest, most carefree times of his double existence were the long journeys each week between London and Lincoln, Lincoln and London. He took his time in the car, listening to music, singing along. He would stop several times, not just at service stations but occasionally veering off into Bedfordshire or Hertfordshire to visit a quiet pub or a Michelin-starred restaurant, an anonymous man taking time out between his two lives.

He had never deliberately set out to create a double life for himself. When he had first met Katie he had been feeling particularly low, particularly hard-done-by by Stephanie. He had felt sorry for himself – poor James, working so hard and slogging up and down the country because his wife had insisted that was what he do. He was tired from the travelling and lonely on his nights away from home, holed up in the flat above the surgery eating microwave meals and drinking beer out of the can. He missed the day-to-day dramas of family life, the way his routine had been so entwined with his wife and son's that he had always felt part of a team. He was miserable. Katie was sweet and pretty and vulnerable and crying, and it had seemed like the most natural thing in the world to put his arm round her. And then, of course, one thing had led to another. It wasn't the first time his head had been turned by an attractive woman since he'd got married, it was just the first time he'd acted on it. He had thought it was the textbook 'bit of fun', the classic 'What she doesn't know won't hurt her', the clichéd 'It's different for men, sex is just sex – it doesn't mean we love our wives any less.'

He had invited Katie out to dinner and she had said yes, and he had found himself trotting out the story he had prepared in advance, that his marriage was over and that the only reason he travelled to London every weekend was to see his son. Because Lower Shippingham was such a small place, the news had got round and he was now having to keep up the lie with colleagues and friends too. Lucky for him that there was no one Stephanie had kept in touch with. As she never tired of telling him, she hated Lower Shippingham and everybody in it, so there was little chance of her ever coming for a visit.

Katie had eaten mussels and oysters and prawns with her fingers, and he had laughed at her and said she reminded him of Daryl Hannah in *Splash*, which she had taken as a compliment. He had been charmed by her sweetness, her hopeful – some would have said naïve – view of the world. He had always found Stephanie's dry cynicism funny, they had always shared a rather cruel sense of humour, but Katie's optimism was so . . . unchallenging. It was relaxing to spend an evening with someone who wasn't looking for ways to contest everything you said for comic effect.

The other thing Katie did, which ensured that James would want to see her again, was say no. He had walked her home to her little cottage, buying condoms from the machine in the restaurant toilet before they left. On the doorstep she had thanked him for a lovely evening and had allowed him to kiss her just enough to let him know she was interested, then pushed him away and said goodnight. James was intrigued. It was that easy. He had known he had to see her again.

In the end Katie had kept him waiting for six dates before she had invited him into her bed for comfortable and undemanding sex. He had felt under no pressure to perform, so focused was she on making sure he was having a good time. By then he was hooked, having got used to the home cooking, the back rubs and the cosy, quiet life in Katie's cottage, so much more comfortable than the flat above the surgery.

Suddenly Katie was his girlfriend, not just a woman he had gone on a date with once. And he had found he liked it. It made his life in the country so much more homely. The first few times he had gone back to London for the weekend he had walked around in a cold sweat – a mixture of guilt and the fear of discovery. He had felt wretched, as if the enormity of what he was doing only became a reality when he was with his family. He promised himself he would break it off with Katie, that he would try to pretend it had never happened, make it up to Stephanie and Finn somehow. But then he would go back to Lincolnshire and Katie would be there, just wanting to look after him, and he would convince himself that he wasn't hurting anyone, he was just trying to make life away from home a little more bearable.

This evening he had arrived home from his practice in St John's Wood at the usual time, sweating and irritable after a half-hour journey in the car that anywhere else would have taken ten minutes. He felt out of place in London. He had grown up in the countryside and, although he had spent five years in Bristol studying to become a vet, he had always known he would move back out to the sticks to practise. He could understand why

Stephanie had needed to get back to work, to find a career, but there was no denying he resented the fact that this meant he had to spend half of his week in town.

He looked down at the list of tomorrow's patients, which Jackie had emailed him over, as she always did at the end of every day, all listed in that rather cutesy way that town veterinary practices often had, with the first name of the animal rather than the person who was bringing them in: Fluffy O'Leary, a Siamese cat who was having her teeth brushed, Manolito Pemberton, a Chihuahua with foot troubles – caused, James had no doubt, by the fact that his elderly owner never let his paws touch the ground – Snoopy Titchmarsh, Boots Hughes-Robertson, Socks Allardyce. The list went on and on with not a genuine problem between them. He sighed. Three days of indulged baby substitutes. When he was feeling especially hard-done-by he felt that Stephanie ought to be more grateful that he spent half of his life doing a job he hated.

Stephanie didn't know what she had been expecting when she saw James that evening – that he would come in and say, 'I've met a woman called Kathy,' or suddenly start talking about a colleague called Kitty he had never mentioned before. What she hadn't prepared herself for was that he would be the same old James.

'Did you have a good day?' she said, with as much dignity as she could muster, once they had sat down at the table.

'Great,' he said, smiling in a way that made swallowing her food impossible.

'Anything exotic?' Usually days that were described as 'great' were those on which he had carried out an intricate operation on an unusual pet. A salamander, or once, even, a small monkey. At least, that was what she had always thought. Clearly wrongly. *I'm really missing you. K. Kiss. Kiss, Kiss.*

'No,' he said, stuffing a huge piece of chicken into his mouth. She waited to see if he would elaborate. He didn't.

'Jonas has got a puppy,' Finn piped up, getting his father off the hook.

Stephanie had no idea who Jonas was, but she knew where this was going. 'No, Finn, no puppies.'

'That's so unfair. Jonas is a year younger than me and he's allowed a puppy so why aren't I?'

'Who is Jonas anyway?' Stephanie asked, not really caring what the answer was.

'Oh, Mum, you're so stupid.' Finn sighed and turned back to his food.

James was humming to himself between mouthfuls, something he often did and which Stephanie had always found irritating, but today it seemed to have taken on a new significance. It was as if he was saying, 'Look how happy I am. Look what a great week I've had, shagging Katherine.'

Stephanie looked at him across the table. I have to get a grip, she thought. One text does not mean he's having an affair. He smiled an I-haven't-a-care-in-the-world smile at her, and she turned away.

'Eat your peas,' she said to Finn, trying to sound like her normal self.

'I already have, stupid,' Finn said, picking up his plate

and turning it upside-down to demonstrate his point. 'See?'

Once Finn had been persuaded to go to sleep, at about eight thirty, Stephanie had claimed a headache and announced she was going to bed. James had stretched out a hand to touch hers as she walked past him, eyes still glued to the TV.

'Night, darling,' he'd said. 'Hope you feel better.' His phone, which was lying on the coffee-table, had beeped to announce a message coming through.

'That'll be Karmen,' Stephanie had wanted to say, but instead she'd huffed out of the room. Or maybe it's Kara or Kayla or Katie, she thought, accidentally hitting on the right name finally, although, of course, she didn't know that yet.

4

Katie Cartwright was in love, she was sure of it. She didn't know where it had come from, this sudden, overwhelming attraction to James, but come it had and now it was all she could think about. She had been in love before – or, at least, had thought she was. She was thirty-eight years old, after all. It would be strange if this was the first time. In fact, she had never been without a man in tow her whole adult life. As soon as one disappeared over the horizon another had always popped round the corner. But she had never felt like this. She had known James for almost exactly a year, she thought now. Nearly a year to the day since her dog Stanley had had to have corrective surgery on his leg and she had cried because she was so scared something might go wrong, and, next thing she knew, the kindly (not to mention handsome) vet had his arm round her shoulders and the rest was history, as they say.

They took it slowly at first. James was separated from his wife and he had told her he wanted to give this new relationship the best possible chance, to do everything right, which included taking their time. They had to make sure they were doing what was best for both of them before they took any big steps. Katie had found this a little difficult, not to mention unnerving, at first but she knew it meant James was taking their affair seriously, that he was considering her as someone he could spend his life with. So she accepted it when he had to leave to go down to London on Wednesday mornings and didn't return until Sunday nights. She had never questioned why he didn't invite her to go with him: she knew that while he was away he was having to lodge with friends until he found a permanent base, and that their small flat was barely big enough for the two of them, let alone James as well.

After a couple of months he had moved his toothbrush and a few other bits and pieces into her tiny girly bathroom. Gradually his clothes had begun to take up space in her wardrobe and his books and papers crept across the dining-table. She loved the feeling that his possessions were enveloping her, marking out his territory like he was a tom cat spraying the boundaries. She lived for the Sundays, Mondays and Tuesdays when his belongings were joined by their owner. She understood why he couldn't be with her all the time – he had his practice in the city to think about – but he had recently begun to hint that one of these days he might give up his London work altogether and she thought there was a promise in there somewhere that the two of them might live out their happy-ever-after in the countryside together.

Katie had had a series of careers and had never found the one that totally suited her. Recently, following a couple of years of night classes, she had set herself up practising acupuncture and aromatherapy massage, seeing clients several times a week in her house. The fact that more often than not the appointments turned into *ad hoc* therapy sessions suited her. She loved to feel she was helping people. She knew she was a good listener and she had a positive outlook on life that her clients found uplifting. It was taking a while to establish some regulars but she had known it would, alternative therapies not being something which the locals took to easily.

Ironically, if Katie had ever trained in the psychological therapy she now found herself having to practise on others, she would almost certainly have deduced that her behaviour, passively accepting that she was in a relationship with a commitment-phobe who seemed happy to keep their liaison a part-time venture, stemmed from her rather low self-esteem. That this made it impossible for her to risk confronting James or even suggesting that she move all her clients to the beginning of the week so that she could spend the latter part in London with him. That, deep down, she knew that the fact that he was a lodger in his friends' flat was just an excuse. Rather, she had convinced herself she was the victim of an irresistible force, hopelessly ensnared by love. Like Juliet with her Romeo or Cathy and her Heathcliff, she was powerless to stop what was happening. She was happy to wait it out. James was a careful man. He needed to make sure that the time was right before he made any big gestures.

5

The following morning Stephanie's alarm woke her at six forty-five. For a moment she didn't know why she had set it for such a ridiculous hour and she nearly turned over and settled back down to sleep, but then her heart plummeted as she remembered what had happened.

'Turn it off – turn it off!' James was flapping an arm in her direction, eyes still closed. He hated early mornings.

She crawled out of bed. It was nearly light outside and it was promising to be a beautiful spring day, not that she cared. She went into the bathroom down the hall, plucked, shaved and exfoliated, then buffed with the spiky body brush that had been hanging redundantly on the back of the bathroom door for months and which, she thought now, she may have used to clean the grime off the sink once. Then she carefully made up her face – not the usual wave of the mascara wand that was all her everyday routine consisted of but the full deal, from foundation to shimmering highlights on her browbones. It seemed important for her self-esteem that she look her best today. She was dressed and ready by the time she heard Finn moving about. She fed Sebastian some grey-looking cod out of a foil tray, gave Goldie his unappetizing brown pellets and tried not to think about why she was doing this, trying to leave the house an hour earlier than usual to avoid seeing her husband.

'Wow, you look amazing,' Cassie exclaimed, when Stephanie opened the front door to her at ten to eight. 'Important day?'

'Something like that,' she said, trying to smile.

'What's happening?' Finn demanded.

Stephanie ruffled his hair. 'Nothing.'

'But Cassie just asked you if you had an important day and you said yes. Why is it important?'

'It just is, that's all.'

'But why?' Finn never rested until he had answers to his many questions.

'Have you got your lunch?' Stephanie said, trying to distract him.

'Stop changing the subject. Why is today an important day?'

Stephanie was at a loss for words. She just wanted to get out of the front door and go before James's alarm clock woke him at eight.

Luckily Cassie came to her rescue. 'Every day's an important day,' she said, steering Finn away from the front door so Stephanie could leave.

'Exactly,' Stephanie said, picking up her bag and starting to go through the routine check list. Phone, keys, money. It was all there.

'That's stupid,' Stephanie heard Finn say as she went down the steps. She realized she hadn't kissed him goodbye and ran back up.

She turned to leave again, waving to Cassie who was herding Finn towards the kitchen. Just as she was going out of the front door James appeared at the foot of the stairs. Stephanie tried to make it look as if she hadn't noticed him, but in her panic she dropped her bag and half the contents spilled out on to the hall floor.

'Morning,' James said, rubbing his eyes. He shuffled sleepily towards the kitchen, then did a double-take.

He'd noticed how good she looked. She'd still got it. She put on her huskiest voice – why would he want to look at another woman? 'Morning.'

He looked her slowly up and down. 'What are you all made up for?' he asked, smiling. 'You look like you're going to stand in a shop window in Amsterdam.'

She knew he was expecting her to laugh, to come back with something equally biting, but she just couldn't. Couldn't, or couldn't be bothered? She wasn't sure. 'Right,' she said. 'Good, well, I'll see you later.'

''Bye, love,' he called, as she left the house.

'OK, so you have two options.'

'If I'm right.'

Stephanie and Natasha were spending the morning browsing the womenswear floors at Selfridges to get ideas for the three customers they had agreed to dress for the BAFTAs (would-be film actress who wanted to look as if she had her own style, ageing soap star who was worried the press had guessed she was a lesbian and wanted to look as feminine as possible, and a reality star who hadn't yet managed to secure an invitation but who wanted to guarantee getting her picture in the morning papers by showing as much flesh as possible, even if she had to go and stand in the street outside naked).

'If you're right, which, of course, you need to establish

first. But if you are, you have two options. Either you confront him or you don't. That's it.'

'And if I don't? Then what?'

'I don't know. You bury your head in the sand and hope it'll go away.'

Stephanie sighed. 'What do you think I should do?'

'If it was me I'd cut his bollocks off then ask questions later.'

'It has to be someone in Lincoln.'

'What about the people he works with up there? Any idea what they're called?'

'I think the receptionist is called Sally. I remember her from before we moved. I never speak to her, though. I just call his mobile if I need to get hold of him. And there's a veterinary nurse called Judy, who's been there for ever.'

'Who else?'

'The other vets are both blokes, I think. Simon and Malcolm . . . Something like that anyway,' she said, realizing she wasn't entirely sure she knew who James worked with, these days. 'Simon has a wife called Maria. We think Malcolm's gay.'

'And where does he stay when he's up there? No landlady called Krystal or Kira?'

'No landlady at all. There's a flat above the practice. He gets it for nothing.' She stopped suddenly, causing a young mother with a baby in a buggy and several bags of shopping to narrowly avoid crashing into her. 'Sorry,' she said to the woman, who tutted loudly and made a big show of walking around her.

'This is crazy.' Stephanie turned back to Natasha. 'It's

33

one text. Since when did I become the sort of woman who assumes her husband's having an affair just because he's got one strange text? It's probably just someone having a joke.'

Natasha exhaled loudly. 'Can you honestly tell me you don't think he's capable of it?'

For a moment Stephanie felt as if she was going to cry. 'You obviously think it's possible.'

'I just don't think it's *im*possible, that's all.'

'If it's true, there's no way I can pretend everything's OK. There's no way I'm going to let him get away with it.'

'You need to find out for sure what's going on first,' Natasha said. 'Then we'll work out what to do.'

So, that night Stephanie waited till James was asleep. Till his familiar rattling snore filled the bedroom. She tiptoed round to his side of the bed and gently lifted his mobile from the table. Pausing briefly to check that he was still oblivious, she crept out of the bedroom and down the stairs to the kitchen. There, she thought about putting the kettle on, delaying the awful moment when she would have to stoop to spying, when the bond of trust between her and James would be damaged for ever. But she knew she had to do this quickly, before he rolled over on to his side and her absence woke him.

She turned on the phone and immediately the new-message-received light came on, with its accompanying beep. Stephanie's fingers hovered over the 'read' button. Did she really want to do this? Open this Pandora's box? But she was certain that this message – which could only have been sent after James had turned off his mobile as they'd climbed into bed at nearly midnight – must have been sent by someone with a more than professional interest in her husband. She held her breath. Fuck it. Here goes.

Night night my lovely boy. Sweet dreams xxx

She looked to see who the message was from. K.

Stephanie nearly gagged, she wasn't sure whether from the trauma of having her suspicions confirmed or from the nauseating cuteness of the text. James had always been the kind of person to hate the soppy, twee language of couples in full romantic mode, as was she. It had been one of the things they'd had in common, the way they would mock their friends who gave each other pet names and exchanged baby talk. For a while, a few years back, they had started to call each other 'Snookie' and 'Cuddles' for their own ironic amusement but after a few weeks Stephanie had realized that if they weren't careful those names might stick and they would inadvertently have become the people they were mocking, so they'd stopped. She scrolled through James's contacts until she reached 'K'. The number was for a mobile and not one that Stephanie thought she had ever seen before. She had no idea who this woman was – except that, whoever she was, she was happy to steal someone else's husband.

Stephanie turned the mobile off before she succumbed to the urge to trawl back through the old messages to see what other exchanges there had been. She had all the evidence she needed. Looking for more would be like poking a stick into an already painful wound. She waited for the tears to come. She'd seen this kind of thing happen to women on TV, and they invariably broke down, weeping and wailing and then eventually beating their husbands on the chest with their fists. But, she felt bizarrely calm. She had thought about leaving James before, of course, in the way that all halves of couples sometimes do, trying to imagine themselves being reinvented, starting again and not making the same mistakes, but she had always known she couldn't have gone through with it. She would never have hurt him like that.

Natasha hadn't even protested when her phone had rung at one thirty in the morning.

'It'll be Stephanie,' she'd said to Martin, and she'd taken the handset downstairs so as not to disturb him too much. She knew that Stephanie calling at this hour meant only one thing – she had her proof.

'So?' she said, not bothering with 'hello'.

'Well, I wasn't imagining things.'

'Oh, Steph, I'm so sorry.'

'I just . . . I . . .' Stephanie said, and then her voice cracked and she stopped as if she didn't know what to say next.

'It's OK,' Natasha said, knowing it was anything but. 'It'll be OK. It's better you know. At least you can make plans now, decide what to do next.'

'I just don't know how he could do this to us.'

'Because he's a bastard. What other explanation can there be? You have to remember it's nothing to do with you and it's everything to do with him, OK?'

'What am I going to do?'

'Honestly?' Natasha said, warming to her theme. 'You have to make him suffer.'

'What's the point, though?'

'The point is that you get to feel better while he gets to feel like shit. Come on, you must be able to think of something that'd hit him where it hurts.' Natasha was a firm believer in not letting people get away with things – shopkeepers who gave you change for a fiver instead of ten pounds, men who tried to grope you on the tube, queue-jumpers, errant husbands.

'Like what? Cut the sleeves off his suits, something like that? He's only got three, it would hardly ruin his life.'

'Way too unoriginal. It's been done before, as has distributing his vintage-wine collection to the neighbours with their morning milk and leaving his mobile plugged into a premium-rate sex chatline all night. You need something much bigger. Much more real.'

'This is crazy.' Stephanie sat down miserably. 'I'm not going to play games.'

'Well, whatever you do you can't just sit back and let it happen.'

'I need to find out who she is,' Stephanie said. 'That's what I need to do first.'

On Sunday morning she helped James pack his bag as usual for the three nights he would be away, finding him ironed T-shirts and clean socks, checking whether he had his iPod and razor. She had studied him closely while they'd had breakfast, but he'd seemed exactly the same as ever. He was nearly always distracted these days so she didn't know what change she had expected to see in him.

It was a glorious day, sunny and breezy, and they had agreed to walk through the park and past the zoo before he left, so that Finn could see the wolves and the wallabies and, in the distance, the heads of the giraffes. She watched James walking ahead, talking animatedly with Finn, and couldn't imagine why he would be doing what he was doing and risk losing his life with his son.

The answer, of course, though Stephanie didn't know it, was that James had never for a moment imagined he might be discovered. Such was the gulf between his life with Stephanie and his life with Katie that it had never crossed his mind that they might collide. He had no intention of leaving his wife, just as he had no intention of giving up his girlfriend. It wasn't his fault that Stephanie had grown bored of their life in the country and that she sometimes worked late, and he found Katie's dogged devotion and non-judgemental outlook relaxing. Sometimes he thought his life had become over-complicated, that the effort of having to remember to make up stories about his time in Lincoln and his exploits in London was a bit of a strain, but all in all he wouldn't have changed it. It suited him.

Given his time again – and the ability to consider his behaviour with rational foresight – of course he wouldn't have made the same choices. Whatever he had done in his life he would never have set out consciously to hurt Stephanie and Finn. But life didn't work like that, allowing you to jump cut to the future and witness the consequences of your actions. Things just happened and you made your choices as you went along, hoping blindly that everything would turn out OK. And, on balance, he thought it had.

Just before one James kissed Stephanie goodbye, got into the car and began the long drive up to Lincolnshire.

6

On Sunday evenings Katie always had a welcoming hot dinner waiting for James. A homemade lasagne or a chicken and mushroom pie. She thought it was important to make home as homely as possible, to make it a retreat, a sanctuary that James would yearn to escape to after the stresses of city life. Once the food was under control she bathed and redid her makeup, lit candles and plumped cushions. On warmish nights, like this one, she laid the table in the garden, lit the gas heater and put a bottle of white wine in the cooler. She hated that one of James's two days off was always given over to travelling. He worked too hard. Life, in Katie's opinion, should not be all about work.

Down in London he lodged with his friends Peter and Abi, and would always come home with funny stories about their latest row or some culinary disaster Abi had had. She was a terrible cook but, James said, she liked to believe she was an earth mother, nourishing those around her. He slept on the put-me-up in Peter's study and one night it had collapsed underneath him, he'd told her, waking the whole household. In the past Katie had tried to persuade him to drive home on a Saturday but it was the only day he got to see his son, Finn, who, she thought, was seven — or was it eight? She'd seen photos of him, an adorable boy with a gappy-toothed smile. Dark-haired and brown-eyed which he must get from his mother because James was fair. She loved that James wanted to spend whatever time he could with his son.

James's ex-wife Stephanie lived in London now – it was the move down there that had put the final nail in the coffin that was their marriage, he always said. He hated having to spend time away from the fresh air and the farming people he felt most comfortable with. They had had an acrimonious divorce, which had left James with no money to live anywhere other than the smelly old flat above the vet's. Stephanie had kept their lovely London home, as far as Katie knew. James rarely talked about her. When he went to pick up Finn on a Saturday Stephanie was always out, leaving Finn in the care of the nanny, Cassie, so they rarely even exchanged a few words these days apparently. Any news of his son was passed via notes or using Cassie as a go-between. Katie was hoping that James would soon think the time was right for Finn to come up for a visit. She loved kids and was dying to meet him, knowing he'd fall in love with her instantly because children always did, and James would see what a happy family they'd make. One day, she thought, maybe she and James could have a baby of their own. She was only thirty-eight. She still had time. Just.

At five to six she heard the car pull up outside. The door to her cottage was right on the road and opened straight into the tiny living room. The pavement was almost non-existent so it was just about possible to step straight from car to house without touching anything in between. Katie flung open the door dramatically and threw her arms round James, swamping him as he came in. 'Good journey?' she asked finally, disengaging herself.

James kissed the top of her head. 'Fine,' he said, throwing down his bag on the sofa. Stanley jumped up to greet him.

'And Finn? How was he yesterday?'

'Great,' he said. 'I took him to the zoo.' He sniffed the air noisily, feeling the need to change the subject, perhaps because the exaggeration was making him uncomfortable. 'Smells good. What is it?'

'Guess,' Katie said playfully, a habit she had. She would ask him to guess the most ridiculous things, things he could have no way of knowing. 'Guess who I saw today,' she'd say, or 'Guess what Mum said.' 'Guess what I read in the paper.'

'Stuffed baby octopus and Jerusalem artichokes,' James said.

'No, silly, it's *coq au vin*. Do you remember? We had it the second time we went out. Both of us ordered the exact same thing on the menu, *coq au vin*, mashed potatoes and cheesecake to follow. Straight from the 1980s.'

'Well, I'm starving,' James said, picking her up and twirling her round. Stanley let out a frenzied bark.

'Oh, I forgot. Sally left a message for you,' Katie said, as they shared a glass of Pinot Noir on the small patio. 'Can you go straight to Carson's farm in the morning? Simon'll meet you there.'

'Did she say why?'

'Erm . . . immunization, inoculation, incubation, something like that. Cows, I think. She said it wasn't anything worrying.' She noticed that James was looking at her. 'Oh, God, I should start writing things down, shouldn't I?'

'It's OK.' He smiled, taking her hand. 'You wouldn't be you if you did.'

James rarely spoke to Sally, the country practice's receptionist, unless he had to. She had an over-familiar manner that he found irritating and which made him feel uncomfortable, as if she was trying to catch him out in a lie. 'Good weekend with Finn?' she said now, once he had said hello.

James ignored the question. 'Could you just tell me what my first appointment is in the morning?' he said. 'Katie got a bit confused.'

He could hear the sigh in Sally's voice. 'Carson's, nine o'clock. Routine inoculation for the whole dairy herd. Simon will meet you there. I *told* Katie all this.'

'And now you've told me,' James said sarcastically. 'Thank you so much, Sally.'

'God, that girl's awful,' he said, as he put the phone down. He had a vague memory that he had once tried to snog Sally at a Christmas party a couple of years ago, before he had met Katie. He had a blurry vision in his head of her pushing him away and telling him he was a ridiculous old lech. It wasn't something he liked to dwell on.

'It's my fault,' Katie said. 'If I'd written down what she said you wouldn't have had to call her in the first place.'

James scooped Katie on to his lap. 'You're too nice,' he said. 'You see the good in everyone.' He nuzzled her neck and simultaneously slipped a hand on to her right breast. Foreplay disguised as positive affirmation: always a good move.

'If you look for the good in people you'll always be rewarded,' she said, and James wished she wouldn't always kill the moment with her cod New Age philosophy.

7

Sunday nights for Stephanie were very different. After the rush of getting together Finn's things for school next day, a hopeless ritual which played out in pretty much the same way every week –

'Where are your trainers?'

'Don't know.'

'Where did you have them last?'

'Don't know.'

'Did you wear them over the weekend?'

'Can't remember.'

'Where's your gym bag?'

'Arun Simpson has got a hamster. It's called Spike.'

– and the fight to get him to go to bed by eight thirty, she usually sat on the sofa staring vacantly at the TV until it was time to go to bed herself.

Tonight, though, she couldn't even concentrate on *Ugly Betty*. Her mind was racing. She had finally given in to her worst urges and scrolled through James's emails, but had found nothing. Of course he wouldn't be that stupid. In for a penny, she had rifled through his desk and his bedside table. She had no idea what she could do next. She could ring Sally at the surgery, she supposed, but what would she say? 'I think James might be having it away with a woman whose name begins with K. What d'you reckon?' How humiliating was that? She could go to Lincoln and poke about, hiding behind bushes and hoping not to be seen by James. She could get hold of the local phone book and call every woman whose first name began with a K. She didn't know why it was so important to know who K was, but without that she felt there would be no closure. She would feel like she'd been taken for a fool, losing her man to the invisible woman.

Natasha was not happy. She waved at Stephanie to move into the smaller office next door. She certainly couldn't do this if she was being watched. She looked around for a place to sit but, as usual, all the available surfaces were covered with the dresses, bags and shoes that were sent over regularly for their clients to pick from. She moved a pile of fashion magazines from Stephanie's chair and plonked herself at the desk, then took a deep breath, checked the number written on a scrap of paper, pressed the buttons to withhold her own and dialled.

'Hi, this is Katie,' a recorded voice sang out at the other end of the line. 'I'm not available right now, so please leave a message after the tone.' Natasha hung up, breathing a sigh of relief that she didn't have to go through with the conversation she and Stephanie had planned ('Hi, I'm from Paddy Paws Pet Medical Supplies and I'm trying to get hold of Mr James Mortimer. The clinic gave me this number.' Pause for K to say, 'Oh, no, sorry, this is Katie [as it now turned out],' and then her surname, hopefully, and maybe that she could get a message to James or pass on his number, then Natasha would hang up as politely as she could). Well, she had her first name. She was halfway there.

'Well?' Stephanie said, coming back in after Natasha had called her.

'She's called Katie.' Natasha shrugged. 'I didn't speak to her. It went straight to voicemail.'

'What did she sound like?' Stephanie flung herself down on the sofa in the corner of the room. 'Young? Old?'

'Hard to tell. Youngish, I guess,' Natasha said nervously.

'How young? Thirty-two? Fifteen?'

'I don't know, just not . . . old.'

Stephanie rolled her eyes. 'Figures. Accent?'

'God, I couldn't tell. Just, you know, normal.'

'Normal south or normal north? Or normal Scottish?'

Natasha sighed. 'Just normal. Tell you what, you ring her. She's obviously got her phone turned off. You can listen to her message and decide what she sounds like for yourself.'

'What if she answers?'

'She won't.'

'But what if she does?'

'You hang up. Here.' She picked up the phone and redialled, handing the receiver to Stephanie, who held it away from her as if it were a bomb.

'Listen,' Natasha hissed. Stephanie put the phone to her ear just as Katie's voice started up again. Stephanie closed her eyes and listened intently, as if hearing the voice would give her a picture of the woman. When the message ended she slammed the receiver down quickly and sat down again, clearly depressed.

'So . . . ?' Natasha said tentatively.

'She just sounds like a woman,' Stephanie said, rubbing her eyes with the back of her hand.

'What do you want to do now?'

Stephanie looked at her watch. 'We're late for Meredith. We need to go.'

Meredith Barnard, soap-opera harridan (one dead husband, two failed love affairs, one with a man who had turned out to be her brother, and a prison sentence for grievous bodily harm, all behind her in her fictional life), was not in the mood for trying on BAFTA frocks. She was angry that Stephanie had turned up late and distracted, and she didn't try to disguise it. The dresses they had brought her, she said, made her feel like a transvestite.

Stephanie and Natasha flattered and cajoled but she wouldn't budge, refusing even to step into the red number with the bustier top and fishtail skirt.

The truth was, thought Stephanie, feeling a bit sorry for her despite the rudeness, that she *did* look like a transvestite in the dresses – in any dress for that matter – but it was her who had said she wanted a more feminine image. Left to their own devices, Stephanie and Natasha would have got her into a tuxedo and a flattering pair of black trousers, gone for the whole Marlene Dietrich thing. Maybe added a false moustache and a top hat and had done with it.

'You just haven't understood the brief I gave you,' Meredith said now. 'If I wanted to look like Shirley Bassey then that's what I would have said.'

Stephanie restrained herself from saying that if they

could have made Meredith look even half as good as Shirley Bassey it would have been a miracle. 'I just wanted to accentuate your curves. You have great curves,' she said instead. Too many of them and in all the wrong places, she thought, and nearly laughed.

'There's a fine line between feminine and tarty, that's all I'm saying. And I really think you've crossed it with this dress.'

Stephanie knew there was no point in fighting with her. 'Well, I'm really sorry, Meredith, if you feel that way. We'll keep looking. Trust me, we'll find you something perfect.'

'I certainly hope so,' Meredith said. 'I'm paying you enough.'

By six fifteen they had reached a stand-off. Stephanie refused Natasha's offer of a drink on the way home – as she always did on the evenings James was away because she liked to be home to put Finn to bed – and flagged down a taxi, which would drop her off in Belsize Park, then continue on to Natasha's cosy house in Muswell Hill.

'I'm going to talk to her,' she said ominously, as they sped up Chalk Farm Road.

'Meredith?' said Natasha, whose mind was still on the dramas of the afternoon.

'Katie. I've decided I'm going to ring her and tell her I know and see what she says.'

Natasha exhaled loudly. 'Maybe it would be better just to tell James you've found out what he's up to.'

'No. He'll lie to me and say it's not true and then coach her not to give anything away either. I'll never find out the truth about what's been going on.'

'OK,' said Natasha, although she didn't sound as if she meant it.

'When I know he'll be at work,' Stephanie said decisively, hugging her friend as she got out of the cab.

8

Katie never looked forward to Wednesday mornings. For a start it meant saying goodbye to James until the following Sunday. His Wednesday routine was always the same; he would go into work early, see patients till one, have a quick lunch, then get on the motorway for the long drive to London. He worked in his London practice on Thursdays and Fridays, had Saturday off and repeated the journey in reverse on Sundays. This morning she had got up early – ordinarily she liked to lie in bed till nine drinking the tea that James always brought her before he left for work – and helped him sort out his bag for the next few days. She enjoyed the domesticity, the simple pleasure of handing him a pile of clean, well-ironed clothes and cooking him a hearty breakfast in case an emergency meant he had to skip lunch. This morning she'd made him eggs, bacon and mushrooms with a mountain of toast and a cafetière of freshly ground French-roast coffee. She hovered round him as he ate, refilling his cup and offering to butter his toast.

James would never have said so but he found all the attention, fussing and pampering rather oppressive. By Wednesday morning he invariably found himself looking forward to the rest of the week, the more mature exchanges between himself and Stephanie, two adults negotiating the day-to-day dealings of their lives rather than the carer/child—adult relationship he sometimes felt he had with Katie. He loved Katie's helplessness, her childlike wonder at the world, her naïve optimism but sometimes it grated on him. Sometimes he didn't want to engage in baby talk and adolescent play-acting. Sometimes he just wanted to eat his breakfast.

Besides, by Wednesday his desire to see his son had always engulfed him. He spoke to him every day, of course, as he did Stephanie, although that often became quite stressful, having to find a quiet corner where Katie wouldn't hear what he was saying whenever she rang, pretending it was Simon or Malcolm. He would roll his eyes, mouth, 'Work,' and back off into the bathroom or the bedroom. Katie never seemed to doubt that he was telling the truth. It wasn't in her nature.

This morning, like any other Wednesday morning, Katie stood at the front door and waved him off, sniffling back a tear and trying to put on a brave face so as not to upset him. He, after all, was the one who had to lead the unsettled life. She might be a bit lonely on the days when he was away but she had Stanley and her friends and her lovely little home. She wasn't having to sleep on a put-me-up and eat Abi's badly cooked food. As soon as he'd left she texted him one of the many loving messages she always sent to keep him company on the journey. Later that day, unbeknownst to her, James would sit at a motorway service station, trying frantically to erase them before he got home.

Once he'd left, the other reason Katie dreaded Wednesdays crashed down on her. Every Wednesday morning for the past three months she had been seeing a regular client, Owen, for an acupuncture session. Generally Katie loved all her clients. She believed that everybody was, by nature, good and that it was only circumstance that forced people to behave badly. And it wasn't that she disliked Owen. She felt desperately sorry for him. His life was a mess: his wife had left him and moved into the house next door with their neighbour. Lying in his bed at night, Owen had told her, he could hear Miriam and his former friend Ted having energetic sex in the adjoining room. Consequently he now slept on an air-bed in the living room and used his bedroom only for storage. He had lost his job at the local butcher's because he had been caught rubbing spittle (or at least he claimed it was spittle but, who knew?, it could have been any bodily fluid, no one wanted to look too closely) into a loin of pork that was earmarked for delivery to Miriam and Ted. Lower Shippingham wasn't a village with an abundance of job opportunities so he was now languishing on the dole, sitting in his terraced cottage day in day out, occasionally shouting loudly that Miriam was a whore when he knew she was in earshot next door.

Katie had begun by feeling she could definitely help Owen. He clearly had self-esteem issues and she wanted to do all she could to enable him to regain his confidence. Besides, the twenty-five pounds he paid her for each session came in handy. Although he hadn't actually paid her anything for a good few weeks now. Feeling sorry for him, she had agreed they could set up a tab and he could pay her once he had got back on his feet. The bill now ran to more than a hundred pounds.

Gradually, though, Owen had begun to worry her. She

would catch him gazing at her trustingly, hanging on her every word. Once, he had got up the courage to ask her out for a meal and she had had to let him down gently. Let him know that, as his – what would she call herself? – complementary therapist, it would be unethical. That, even if that wasn't the case, she had a boyfriend. He had been very sweet about it, told her that one of the things he liked most about her was the fact that she was loyal to James. For weeks afterwards, though, he had spent the sessions discussing his inadequacy with women, his hurt and anger that life had dealt him a bad hand, his deep-rooted feelings of worthlessness while she slipped needles into his scalp. Truthfully, although Katie wasn't afraid of Owen – she didn't feel like he was about to pounce on her or make inappropriate suggestions – she had started to feel out of her depth. She wasn't qualified to handle his genuine emotional problems. Owen, she had come to understand, needed proper help. She had tried to raise this with him, had suggested he see his GP and get referred to someone who had a degree and some clinical experience, but he had got upset. He hadn't wanted to listen.

This morning's session hadn't been any better. They had talked about the usual things, Owen's loneliness, his lack of self-worth, and Katie had suggested burning ylang-ylang oil to elevate his mood. 'I know I keep saying this,' she had said, 'but why don't you think again about moving? It's unhealthy living so close to something that makes you unhappy.'

'Why should I be driven out by them?' he'd said as he'd said several times before.

'You mustn't look at it like that. You've got to think about what's best for you.'

'If I move out they've won,' Owen had said huffily.

'It's not a game, Owen. There's no question of anyone winning or anyone losing for that matter.'

'You don't understand.'

'Do you know what?' she'd said gently. 'I don't, I really don't. That's why maybe it'd be better if I just left you to relax. Let the needles do their work.'

'No. Don't go. I feel better when we chat about stuff.'

'You know I'm not a real therapist,' she'd said, laughing, 'and I might be giving you all the wrong advice.'

'That's OK,' he'd said, smiling back. 'I ignore it all anyway.'

So she'd stayed, although she had felt distracted, not in the mood to listen to Owen's self-pity, because of the phone call she had received just before he had arrived.

James had been gone for about an hour and Katie had been tidying the house, trying to make it look like a professional, calming space where she could receive her clients. She was lighting the burners to rid the spare room of the Stanley smell when her mobile had rung. She had looked at the screen, she didn't recognize the number — it could have been anyone — but Katie always saw her phone ringing as an opportunity. You never knew what life might throw at you, her mother had always said. Grasp everything by the throat and make the most of it. It would never have occurred to her not to answer.

'Hello,' she'd said, in her most positive voice. She had read somewhere that because of the lack of visual clues people sounded more bored and disconnected on the phone than they actually were. It was important to project positivity. Smile while you talk, the article had said, and the person at the other end will pick up on it.

There was a moment's silence, then a voice had said, 'Is that Katie?'

'It is,' she'd said cheerfully.

'This is Stephanie Mortimer.'

Katie had thought quickly. Stephanie, that was the name of James's wife. They had never spoken before but, she'd thought nervously, Stephanie didn't sound as if she was brimming with friendliness.

'Hi, Stephanie. How nice to talk to you finally.'

There had been a long silence. Katie had grown anxious. 'There's nothing wrong, is there? James hasn't had an accident or anything?'

'Do you know who I am?' Stephanie had said. 'I'm James's wife.'

'Of course I know who you are –' Katie had said, and then the doorbell had rung. Owen, bang on time for his appointment as ever. 'Stephanie, I'm really sorry but I have to go. Can I call you back later? On the number that came up?'

'OK.' Stephanie had sounded taken aback. 'I'm around all morning.'

So now Katie couldn't concentrate. This was an event, a milestone. OK, so Stephanie didn't sound like a barrel of laughs but once they'd started to talk she knew they'd get on fine. Katie got on with everyone. And then it would be only a matter of time before Stephanie suggested that James bring Finn up for a couple of days and they could all start to play Happy Families.

9

Stephanie put the phone down and wondered if she had imagined what had just happened. It had taken her two or three false starts before she had been able to go through with dialling Katie's number. She had sent Natasha off window-shopping around Sloane Street, armed with Meredith's measurements, a Polaroid camera and a note-book. She knew that even if she'd got her to sit in the room next door Natasha wouldn't have been able to resist putting her ear to the door and listening in to her conversation, and Stephanie didn't think she could perform with an audience.

She had gone over and over in her head what she planned to say to Katie. She would announce herself with dignity – she was determined not to get hysterical, she didn't want to give Katie the excuse to think, Oh, I can see why he wouldn't want to be with her. 'I am Stephanie, James's wife,' she intended to say but then it was hard to imagine how things might go after that because Katie might either deny all knowledge of James or she might break down remorsefully and beg forgiveness. Stephanie was hoping it would be the latter – not because she intended to forgive her, far from it, but because an out-and-out denial would be so hard to deal with: she would feel that Katie had the upper hand. What she certainly hadn't been prepared for was the easy friendliness of

Katie's 'Hi, Stephanie', the confidence of her 'How nice to talk to you finally.'

She had no idea what to do now. The next move was Katie's and that made Stephanie feel very uncomfortable. If she hadn't heard Katie's doorbell ring for herself she would have thought she was making up the interruption to get off the phone, giving herself the psychological advantage. I mustn't get any more paranoid than I already am, she reproached herself. All she could do now was sit and wait. If Katie didn't call her back she would try again and then again and again until she got her. She wasn't going to let her get away with it that easily.

James will soon be on his way back to London, she thought, dreading his arrival. She wanted to be fully appraised of what was going on before he got home. Forewarned is forearmed and all that bollocks. She tried to call Natasha, but her phone went straight to voicemail meaning she was probably on the tube, so she rang Cassie and listened gratefully as she rambled on about a conversation she had had with one of the other nannies on the school run.

She looked at her watch; ten fifteen. She was scared to move from her desk, even to go to the bathroom, in case Katie rang and she missed the call. Why hadn't she rung her from her mobile? She decided she needed a displacement activity and that tidying the office might be just the thing. It was about forty-five minutes later, while she was knee-deep in a selection of this season's belts and clutch bags, that the telephone rang. She almost fell flat on her face running to answer it.

'Stephanie Mortimer,' she said, trying not to sound out

of breath, which could be misinterpreted as nervousness and therefore weakness.

'Stephanie, hi, it's Katie.'

There it was again, that unrepentant tone. What was wrong with the woman? Didn't she feel the tiniest bit ashamed of what she'd done – what she was still doing? 'Hello,' Stephanie said evenly. 'Thank you for calling back.'

'That's OK. So . . . erm . . . it's great to talk to you.'

Maybe there's something wrong with her, Stephanie thought. She's bipolar or amnesiac or something. 'Katie, maybe you didn't hear what I said before. I'm James's *wife*. I know about the two of you.'

She thought she heard Katie gulp. In fact she did but not for the reason she thought. Katie was, in fact, swigging from a bottle of Evian water as she spoke.

'Of course you do. James told me he'd told you.'

Now Stephanie was really confused. And, what was more, she was growing irritated. This wasn't playing out in any of the ways she'd imagined. 'James didn't tell me. I saw one of your text messages. Accidentally. I wasn't looking or anything.' She didn't want this woman to think she was the jealous, irrational type.

Now it was Katie's turn to sound confused. 'Well, maybe I've got it wrong. I thought he told me he'd told you himself because he didn't want you to hear anything on the grapevine, you know. In case you bumped into anybody you knew from up here and it was a bit awkward.' Katie was beginning to wish she hadn't called back without talking to James first. Clearly Stephanie had issues. Maybe the break-up hadn't been as amicable as James had made out. In fact, she *had* tried to ring him, once Owen had left, but James, who must have had his hand up in the inside of a cow somewhere, hadn't answered. 'Either way, I'm glad you do know. It's much more civilized that way, don't you think? Everything out in the open.'

'That's all you can say? "I'm glad you do know,"' Stephanie snapped. 'How about "sorry" or that you feel ashamed of yourself or something? You're fucking my husband after all.'

Katie flinched, as much from the language as from the implication behind Stephanie's accusation. She rarely swore. She didn't believe it was necessary or, at least, only as a last resort. 'Ex-husband,' she said cautiously. Clearly Stephanie was a bit unhinged.

Stephanie stopped dead in her tracks. 'What did you say?'

'I said he's your ex-husband. The man I'm . . . the man I'm going out with. If you have a problem with that, then that's between you and him.'

'He told you we're separated?'

'Of course,' Katie said anxiously. 'You are, aren't you?'

'No,' Stephanie said. 'Not the last time I looked, anyway.'

Katie felt as if she were falling down a rabbit hole. Wind rushed past her ears and the floor seemed to be slipping away from her. 'What about Peter and Abi?' she said, quietly.

'Who?'

'Peter and Abi. The people he lodges with when he's

in London. What about the put-me-up and Abi's bad cooking and Peter's terrible jokes?'

'I have no idea what you're talking about,' Stephanie said. 'When James is in London he lives with me. In our house. With our son.'

Katie knew all about denial. It was a defence mechanism that protected the deluded person from having to deal with the gravity of something that had happened to them, hopefully until they were strong enough to take the consequences. A year and a half seemed like a long time to still not be acknowledging that your husband had moved out though. She was sure she read somewhere in one of her many self-help books that you shouldn't indulge deluded people in their fantasies. She took a deep breath. 'I'm really sorry, Stephanie, and know this must be hard for you to accept but James is with me now. There's nothing you can do to change what's happened. You have to move on.'

Stephanie felt a shot of adrenalin-fuelled oxygen flood her brain. This was like a bad dream. She had thought Katie might deny her involvement with James but what she had never – could never have – imagined was that Katie would actually deny Stephanie's relationship with him. She knew though, as soon as Katie spoke to her in that rather patronizing way, that Katie believed she was telling the truth. There was no doubt in Stephanie's mind that James had convinced his mistress that his marriage was over.

'Katie,' she said, trying to stay calm, 'I don't know what James has told you . . . Well, actually I do. He's clearly told you that we're no longer together – but the truth is he's lying. He's deceiving me and he's clearly deceiving you . . .'

She stopped as Katie interrupted, her voice a little wobbly: 'I have to go, Stephanie, I'm afraid. I have another client. It was nice to talk to you and I'm really sorry, I am, that you're finding it so hard.'

Katie had said goodbye and put the phone down before Stephanie had a chance to respond. She put her head in her hands. Now what?

IO

Once she had ended the call Katie started to shake. She had so often fantasized about finally getting to speak to Stephanie and consolidating her new little family, but in none of those fantasies had it ever turned out like this. Stephanie had sounded, well, crazy; deluded and angry and accusatory all at the same time. Poor woman, Katie thought. I had no idea she was this unhappy. James had always made it sound as if Stephanie had been behind the split, as if she'd put her ambition before her marriage without a second thought.

I have to speak to James, she thought, picking up the phone again and calling his mobile. The call went straight to voicemail, as it so often did when he was working. She panicked a bit about leaving him a message, not wanting to worry him, so she settled for a warm, calm 'Hello, lovely,' followed by 'Give me a ring if you get a moment,' and left it at that. Hopefully he would call her back before he left for London because once he was there communication was always a bit more hit-and-miss. James had always told her that his phone got no reception at Peter and Abi's flat in Swiss Cottage and that in order to call her he had to risk life and limb climbing out on to their first-floor flat roof. There was no point her ever phoning him in the evenings therefore, and he had never got round to giving her Peter and Abi's home number. A hot arrow shot through her. She didn't even know their surname, she realized now, she had never thought to ask – why would she? – so she couldn't even ring 118118 and get their number for herself.

She reminded herself to breathe. Surely there couldn't be any truth in what Stephanie had been saying. No way was James living a double life. Hadn't he and Katie talked about the importance of honesty and respecting your partner, and hadn't he seemed as adamant as she was?

She jumped as her mobile rang. James. She hesitated for a moment before answering, not quite knowing what to say.

'Did you call?' he shouted, when she finally said hello. He sounded as if he was out in a field somewhere.

'Oh, yes,' she said, as if she'd forgotten. 'I just wanted to tell you to drive carefully.'

'I always do,' he said softly. 'I'll call you when I get there.'

'James,' Katie said, before he could hang up, 'I was wondering if you'd got Peter and Abi's home number yet. Do you remember I asked you for it before and you said you'd get it for me? Only it seems crazy that I can't call you in the evenings and I worry about you clambering around on that roof in the dark.'

'God, I'm useless,' he said convincingly. 'I forgot. I'll try to remember tonight. But, you know, I don't really want to be disturbing them every five minutes with the phone going. They're putting themselves out for me enough already.'

'Well, just for emergencies, then. Don't you think I

should have a number for emergencies, you know, given your mobile reception's so bad?'

'Of course. Look, I've got to go. I'll call you later.' He hung up before she could say anything else.

Katie, who was unused to mistrusting people, who never questioned that what you saw on the surface was a true reflection of what was going on underneath, felt her legs go weak and sat down heavily at the table. Something wasn't right.

Later, when James phoned to say he had arrived safely, and then again that he was going to bed, she'd reminded him gently about getting her the number and he had swiftly changed the subject. She wondered how long he could keep this up. If she asked him every time they spoke, what excuse could he come up with over and over again? She wanted to think she was overreacting, that everything was fine, nothing to worry about, but it was beginning to seem unlikely.

'What's Peter and Abi's surname?' she asked him out of nowhere, trying to sound casual, when he called for the second time.

He answered without missing a beat: 'Smith. Why do you keep asking me about them?'

'Smith. Peter and Abi Smith. Or did she keep her own name?'

'I'm going to bed now, goodnight.'

'Night, darling,' Katie said sadly. 'Sleep well.'

'Do you have an address?' the friendly sounding man at 118118 asked her. 'Only there are a lot of Smiths.'

'Swiss Cottage somewhere, I don't know.'

'Postcode?'

'Sorry. NW something, I suppose.'

He sighed. 'I have seventy-six P. Smiths in north-west London. Plus eighteen Peters. What would you like to do?'

Katie knew she was defeated. 'Nothing. Thank you.'

Smith, thought James, had been a stroke of genius. He had no idea why Katie was suddenly so interested in Peter and Abi but he also knew she didn't have a suspicious cell in her body. She had never been one of those women who asked where you'd been if you were home five minutes late, or quizzed you about what you got up to when you were away. Come to think of it, Stephanie was the same, he realized, and felt a rarely acknowledged spasm of guilt. There was no getting away from it: he couldn't take any pleasure in deceiving two women who were so easily deceived, who loved him enough to truly trust him.

He pushed the thought from his mind. He felt confident that Katie wasn't trying to catch him out. He could come up with a plausible reason why Peter and Abi didn't want him to give out their number to anyone even for emergencies. They were on witness protection? Hiding from debt collectors? Had recently changed their number to avoid nuisance calls from violent ex-lovers and been advised by the police not to give it out to anyone, whoever they were? No, it would have to be more prosaic than that, but he would come up with something and fortunately –

or maybe unfortunately – Katie being Katie would believe whatever he told her.

In fact Katie was struggling to decide just what to believe. There was no doubt that James was hiding something from her. She just wasn't sure she wanted to accept exactly what that something was. Maybe she should have heard Stephanie out at least, given her the benefit of the doubt. She wondered whether she should call her back, although it was hard to imagine what she could say: 'OK, so I know I basically accused you of being delusional but now I'd like to indulge you in that delusion for a while, then decide once and for all whether or not I believe you,' was hardly going to win Stephanie round. And, anyway, it was half past ten at night: she couldn't call her now and risk waking her up. Stephanie had a young son – presumably she had to be up at the crack of dawn to get him off to school so she was bound to go to bed early. It would have to wait until morning. That gave her the whole night to decide exactly how she felt. James would ring her as soon as he got to the surgery, as he always did. She would try to think of one more way to challenge him, another question that he would struggle to answer. Then she'd know.

'I've had an idea,' she said, when she answered the phone the following morning. She had been up since six, too unhappy to sleep. 'I was thinking maybe I could come down to London tomorrow night. Book a hotel so it wouldn't be a problem for Peter and Abi. It would be like a holiday.'

She heard James gulp. 'Really? But that's crazy. I mean,

I'd hardly see you. I spend all Saturday with Finn, remember.'

Katie knew in an instant that what Stephanie had told her was the truth. She tried one last shot. 'But we'd have the evenings and Sunday morning –'

'It's a lovely idea,' James said, cutting her off, 'but by the time I've spent Saturday running round the zoo or the aquarium or whatever I just want to go to bed and sleep. I wouldn't be very good company. Sorry, love. Another time, maybe. And, you know, one of these days Stephanie will say it's OK for me to introduce you to Finn and then you can come down every weekend.'

'OK,' she said quietly. 'Whatever you want.'

Katie put the phone down. She felt sick. She knew what she had to do.

11

When her phone rang Stephanie was in the middle of a rant to Natasha about James and the fact that he had seemed blithely happy when he got home last night, blissfully unaware as he was that Stephanie had finally unearthed the scale of his deception.

'And as for Katie,' she was saying for, perhaps, the twelfth time in the past two days. She hardly noticed that Natasha rolled her eyes, and was about to launch into another retelling of her bizarre exchange with her husband's mistress when she checked the caller ID and saw that it was, in fact, that very husband's mistress who was calling her now.

'It's her,' she said, in a pointless stage-whisper.

'Well, answer it, then,' Natasha said impatiently.

Stephanie did as she was told. 'Hello,' she said, in as neutral a way as she could manage.

'Stephanie,' Katie's now familiar voice said, 'it's Katie.'

'Mmm-hmm.' Stephanie couldn't trust herself with any actual words until she had heard what Katie had to say.

'I'm . . . I think we got off on the wrong foot and that maybe it was my fault.'

'Well, yes, screwing someone's husband will sometimes do that,' Stephanie said, before she could stop herself.

She heard Katie inhale sharply as if she was composing herself before she spoke.

'I know this must have been a shock to you,' Katie said, 'but you have to believe it was as much of a shock to me. When James told me you were divorced I had no reason not to believe him. And now ... now I don't know what to believe.'

'So you thought you'd ring up and accuse me of being a fantasist again?' Stop it, Stephanie, she thought.

Katie didn't seem to be responding to Stephanie's offers of a fight. 'No,' she said. 'I wanted to say sorry for not listening to you. And that I know he's been lying to me now. I think. To be absolutely honest, Stephanie, I don't know what I think.' Katie's voice cracked and Stephanie realized she was trying not to cry.

'OK,' she said, more kindly, waving a hand at Natasha, who was leaving. 'Let's pretend we're starting again. I've rung you to tell you the man you're having a relationship with is my husband and you believe me. I accept that you thought he was unattached. What do we do now?'

Nearly an hour later Stephanie and Katie were still talking. Katie, Stephanie had discovered, had been seeing her husband for a year. It wasn't as if she and James had hidden their relationship from anyone: she had never seen the necessity because she had had no idea that they might be doing anything worthy of being hidden.

Katie, meanwhile, had discovered that her boyfriend still very much lived with his wife, and that although the past few years since the move to London had been fraught sometimes, they were still very definitely married. She had learned that Finn had been happily spared the traumas caused by warring parents, and that rather than just seeing his father for a few hours on Saturdays he spent half of every week with him and the other half looking forward to seeing him again. She had learned that, just as she had trusted that James was buried in his work and sacrificing comfort and home life on the days when he was in London, so Stephanie had believed he was doing the same when he was in Lincolnshire.

Both had had to acknowledge to themselves that he had been living a lie. Stephanie, who had had a few days to get used to the idea, was trying to reprogramme her anger so that its focus was firmly channelled at James rather than at Katie. Try as she might to hate Katie, it was hard to keep it up once she knew that Katie had been duped as much as she had.

'So, where do we go from here?' she asked eventually.

'I'm going to ring him and tell him not to bother coming back,' said Katie, tearfully. Katie, who had never been hurt before, had taken it badly. 'I would never go with another woman's husband. I mean never, Stephanie. You have to believe me. I'm going to kill him, honestly I am. I'll pack his stuff up and drop it round to the surgery and then I'll never see him again.'

'I don't know,' Stephanie said. 'We shouldn't rush into anything. We shouldn't tell him what we know yet, not till we've decided if that's the best thing to do. Don't show your hand too early, my friend Natasha always says. You can always play it later, but once you've shown it there's no taking it back.'

Stephanie didn't know why she wanted to put off the confrontation with James. Partly, she thought, because she was afraid that if she told him she knew about Katie he would look relieved, throw his hands in the air and say, 'Hallelujah. At last I don't have to live a lie. I can leave you and live with the woman I love.' She didn't think she could take the humiliation. 'I know it's a strange thing to ask,' she continued, 'but let's sleep on it at least. Another twenty-four hours isn't going to make any difference.'

'OK,' Katie said reluctantly. 'When he calls me tonight I'll try and pretend that everything's OK.'

'Just turn your phone off,' Stephanie said. 'Let him worry about what you're up to.'

Katie wiped her hand across her brow and leaned on the kitchen table for support. Of course she would wait to see what Stephanie wanted to do. After all, Stephanie had a far greater claim on James than she did – even Katie had to acknowledge that now. She might be losing a boyfriend but Stephanie was in danger of losing a husband, the father of her child. Still, the way she felt at the moment it was hard to imagine Stephanie was feeling any worse. Could it really be true? James – nice, funny, loving James? Katie had always believed that people who were treated badly in relationships had somehow brought it on themselves. That wasn't the same as thinking they deserved it, certainly not, but she trusted that if you behaved well, if you gave someone all your support, allowed them their freedom, they would repay you by being honest and straightforward. It wasn't as if she had ever asked James to lie. He was the one who had made the move on her in the first place. He could have just left her alone to get on with her life, which she had been enjoying perfectly well, thank you very much.

She barely moved all morning. James still married? She could hardly take it in. It seemed so surreal. And all those things he'd said about Stephanie. How she tried to stop him seeing his son, how she'd bled him dry in the divorce, how they barely even exchanged pleasantries these days. All lies. The whole of him was a lie, everything she had believed about him, everything on which she'd based her love for him. It was all untrue. And poor Stephanie. Stephanie who had believed she was happily married until a couple of days ago . . .

She finally gave in to the tears that had been threatening to come ever since she had picked up the phone. Big, heaving sobs, which took over her whole body and which made Stanley come and stand beside her, looking at her sadly, unsure of what to do.

As the morning wore on the tears were replaced with angry thoughts – something alien to Katie: she liked to put a positive spin on things, to see the good in every situation. Twice she had begun to dial James's number. She wanted him to know that she knew. She wanted him to know he wasn't going to get away with it any more. But she had promised Stephanie she would sit tight for now. And if that was what Stephanie wanted, it was the least Katie could do. She got up and wiped her eyes, then lit some candles – geranium to lift the spirits. She was strong, she would cope.

'Bastard,' she said out loud, to no one in particular.

12

They had agreed to speak again the following morning. Meanwhile Stephanie called Natasha to fill her in on what had happened and to ask her what she thought they should do next.

'You need to think it through carefully. Don't show your hand too early,' Natasha said, when Stephanie had finished.

'I know, I know. Haven't you got any new sayings?'

'Funnily enough, I've never discovered that my best friend's husband is a bigamist before, or as good as, so forgive me if I don't immediately know what to say.'

'But I need your advice, though,' Stephanie pleaded. 'I don't know what to do.'

'Do nothing.'

'You always say that.'

'Well, this time I mean it. Do nothing and we'll try to come up with a plan. You think Katie will go along with whatever you suggest?'

'I think so. Actually, she sounded nice.'

'OK,' Natasha said. 'Now this is getting weird.'

'She did, though. And I think she feels as bad for me as she does for herself.'

'I'll see you in the café at Harvey Nichols at two,' Natasha said, and rang off.

Stephanie ran herself a bath, then lay in it, staring up

at the ceiling, thinking over her conversation with Katie. She had meant it when she'd said Katie sounded nice. There had been genuine shock in her voice when she'd tried to take on board what Stephanie had been saying to her, but once she had absorbed it her concern had been all for Stephanie. From what she had said it was obvious that she loved James and had thought they had a future together, but Stephanie had no doubt that the relationship was over now – at least as far as Katie was concerned. She had said she wasn't the sort of woman to steal another woman's man and Stephanie believed her.

James, meanwhile, pulled into the car park of a pub called the Jolly Boatman in a little village just outside Stevenage, got out and stretched exaggeratedly. It was a beautiful day and he fancied a half of bitter, sitting in the pub's spring-flower-filled garden. He would spend a blissful half-hour taking in the countryside, then get on his way again. He didn't want to be too late getting home, Finn had football club on a Wednesday afternoon and usually got in around five thirty. James liked to be there to meet him but he also wanted to avoid getting back too much before that. Sometimes he didn't know what to do with himself in his own house when his son wasn't there.

The barmaid definitely twinkled at him as she pulled his drink, and ordinarily James would have responded, sitting up at the bar having a harmless flirtation, chatting about his job and the weather. Today, though, he didn't have the heart for it. It felt like an effort and he preferred to sit on his own, everything peaceful around him, just 'experiencing the moment', as Katie would have said. He took his beer out to the large garden at the back, which overlooked the river with its neat little families of ducks, and sat contentedly at a table away from anyone else.

It was unexpectedly warm for March, so he took off his jacket and rolled up his shirt sleeves, basking in the sun like a lion smug in the knowledge that it's the undisputed king of the jungle. This is the life, he thought, swatting an insect away from his face. He really could have no complaints. In fact, he thought now, most men would envy him. What full-blooded male hadn't fantasized about having two women on the go? Of course, he couldn't imagine that many of those men were actually dreaming about having two full-time relationships. Two sets of responsibilities and double the squabbling over whether or not to buy a new ironing-board. Sometimes he wondered if, rather than living an enviable life, he was actually living a lot of men's twin-headed nightmare. It was hardly the carefree sex-filled romp one might think. It was two lots of 'Have you put the rubbish out?' and 'Should we have the Martins round? After all, they had us over last time and we don't want it to look like we're not good hosts.' Double 'You never talk to me properly any more' and 'Which looks better, the blue one with the tan belt, or the stripy one?'

James rubbed the back of his hand over his forehead. He was starting to sweat a little. He downed the last inch of his half-pint and took the empty glass back to the bar on his way out.

''Bye, love,' the barmaid called. She really was quite attractive, he thought, and she was definitely giving him the eye.

He put on his best, most dazzling smile. 'See you soon,' he shouted, thinking, I must remember where this place is.

He had no idea, of course, that his life as he knew it was about to take a drastic turn.

13

Something Natasha had said to Stephanie a few days earlier had lodged in her brain and wouldn't go away: 'You have to make him suffer. The point is you get to feel better while he gets to feel like shit.' It made a kind of perverse sense. Why should James escape without any punishment for his crime? OK, so losing both of the women he professed to love might hurt him a little but she doubted now that he would care for long. He clearly had no respect, no real feelings for either of them. He'd just find another woman – maybe even two – to fall for his stories. The question was, what form the punishment should take.

Natasha's suggestions all seemed to involve some form of physical violence so, for the first time, Stephanie decided to ignore her friend's advice and work this one out for herself. She dug her phone out of her bag. 'I think we should meet,' she said, when Katie answered.

There was a moment's silence as Katie, on the other end of the line, took this in. 'Really?' she said, sounding nervous.

'I just think there are things we need to talk about and we should do that face to face. Besides, I'm curious.'

Stephanie heard Katie's inhalation, could feel her weighing up the idea in her head. She waited.

'All right,' Katie said finally. 'Let's do it. I'm curious too.'

*

They had arranged to meet in the bar of a hotel near Peterborough, halfway between Lincoln and London. Stephanie's plan was to leave as soon as James had gone to work in the morning, but by the time she had agonized over what to wear (jeans and a figure-hugging T-shirt with heels that would have been too high for her to drive in – even though she knew Katie was blameless she still wanted to show her that she was in good shape, not the stereotype of the little woman left at home) and whether to wear her hair up or down (up, in a low ponytail), she was about an hour late leaving. She rang Katie to tell her, only to discover that Katie had been in the same dilemma and was running late herself.

'I didn't ask,' Stephanie said, 'but what do you look like? You know, so I recognize you.' She was feeling a bit sick. The reality of what was happening to her was just beginning to sink in. What if the woman her husband had been having an affair with was stunning? She wasn't sure if she could cope with that.

'Well, I'm wearing a turquoise skirt, sort of a long skirt, and a white vest with a light blue cardigan. And I'm about five foot two,' Katie said, which wasn't the answer Stephanie had been looking for. Was she thin? Fat? Plain? Gorgeous? Twenty-five? Fifty?

Katie, too, had procrastinated in front of her wardrobe. She wanted to look good but not threatening. She didn't know why but she wanted Stephanie to like her, to forgive her, even though in reality there was nothing to forgive. She had decided to go with pretty but not too much flesh. Flattering, but not too young. She had formed a picture in her head of what Stephanie might look like based on the photos she had seen of Finn. A good-looking brunette with brown eyes, maybe with the slightly lopsided smile Finn had and his turned-up nose. She imagined she would be . . . attractive. Why else would James have been – still be – married to her?

Every now and then an image came into her mind of the woman she had conjured up and James wrapped round each other naked under the sheets. As hard as she would try to push it away it would push back, threatening to block out all possibility of ever thinking about anything else. She tried to conjure up positive thoughts but her old standbys – images of herself on a sun-drenched beach in Thailand, a memory of a particularly happy Christmas when she was a child – weren't strong enough to overpower the negative ones that had taken root. She reached into her cupboard for the Rescue Remedy.

As the taxi pulled into the hotel car park, she ran her fingers through her hair and checked herself in a small mirror. She felt sick with nerves. She had never been good with confrontation – she always tried to give people what they wanted, to go out of her way to make them happy, and she had a lurking fear that Stephanie might want to pick a fight.

She took a deep breath and walked into the hotel foyer, looking around for the bar. There were a few people in there. She scanned the room for a woman on her own. No one. She must have got there first. She settled at a table near the window and ordered a glass of mineral water. She wasn't really a drinker, but she was dying for a vodka and tonic. Sipping her drink, Katie stared out of the window. She was beginning to sweat.

No more than a couple of minutes later she heard a small cough and looked round to see a tall, slim woman, with long, dark red hair tied away from her face, standing beside her. She stood up awkwardly. Stephanie in the flesh was quite an imposing prospect. She had somehow bypassed pretty and gone straight for beautiful, and looked nothing like Katie's comforting mental picture. Her skin, which was an iridescent white, was straight out of a Pre-Raphaelite painting. Katie's own shiny tanned glow seemed cheap in comparison. She smiled nervously.

Stephanie nearly laughed out loud when she saw Katie. Not because she was relieved to find that Katie wasn't pretty because there was no denying that she was. She was maybe somewhere in her late thirties, Stephanie thought, thankful that at least they were the same age, but that was where the similarities ended. The thing that had struck Stephanie as soon as she had seen her was that they were such complete opposites. It was such a cliché that James had felt the need to seek out everything he didn't have at home. She was tall; Katie was short. She had deep red, poker-straight hair; Katie was all blonde curls. She was slim and athletic; Katie was soft and feminine. Her eyes were brown, Katie's were blue.

'God, you certainly couldn't say he has a type,' she said, and Katie laughed, although it seemed a little forced. 'I'm Stephanie,' Stephanie said, and held out a hand.

Katie shook it weakly, as if she wasn't used to shaking hands. 'Katie,' she said. 'Obviously.'

They sat down, and the silence seemed to go on for ever before Stephanie thought I really must say something, otherwise she'll think she has to take charge of the situation. Stephanie liked to be in control. In fact, James had once accused her of being a control freak and she had annoyed him by taking it as a compliment. 'Why wouldn't I want to be in charge of my own life?' she'd shouted at him. 'What kind of an idiot lets someone else run their life?'

'So,' she said eventually. 'I just wanted to see you for myself, really. I'm still trying to take all this in.'

'Me too,' Katie said, sipping her water.

There was another awkward silence.

'Did you have a good journey?' Katie asked.

'Fine, thanks. I came on the train. You?' Stephanie could hardly believe they were having such a banal conversation but she didn't know how to turn it round. She was finding it hard to concentrate, looking at Katie's little rosebud mouth and having to fight off pictures in her mind of James transfixed by it, getting closer and closer . . .

'Me too. Yes,' Katie was saying.

Silence. Stephanie fiddled about in her handbag, looking for something. Or pretended to. Now she was here she didn't know what to do. She had no idea why she had suggested this, why she had thought it might be a good idea.

'Stephanie, you do believe I didn't know, don't you?' Katie blurted out. Clearly she couldn't stand the quiet any longer.

Stephanie nodded. 'I think so. Yes . . . yes, I do. I just

don't understand how he thought he could get away with it.'

'I never suspected anything. Did you?'

'Never. Does that make us both stupid?'

'No. It just means James is a very good actor.'

Stephanie found that hard to believe. She'd once seen him giving his Third Peasant From the Left in an amateur production of *Joseph* and hadn't been convinced. Peasant One and Peasant Two had looked worn out, stooping beneath the weight of the sacks they were carrying. James had strutted along as if he was going for a picnic. 'Why did he tell you that you couldn't come down to London?'

'Because he was staying with Peter and Abi. He said it was awkward enough him staying there. It sounded really plausible.'

Stephanie forced out a laugh. 'Where do Peter and Abi live?'

'Swiss Cottage. Peter's a teacher and Abi's in IT. They live in a flat and James sleeps on a put-me-up in Peter's study. Abi's a terrible cook.'

'I hate to break it to you but I don't think Peter and Abi exist. I've never heard of them,' Stephanie said.

Katie smiled half-heartedly. 'How about you? How come you never came up to Lincolnshire?'

'Do you know what? He never told me not to. In fact, when we first moved down to London he used to keep begging me to go up there with him. But I didn't want to. And, after a while, I guess, we just got into a pattern. I didn't want to keep uprooting Finn, you know, and I had my job. And then he stopped asking – because he'd met you probably . . .' she added sadly. 'And I didn't really even notice.'

'Don't make it sound like any of this is your fault. It's all him. He's the one who's behaved badly. Not us. Not either of us.'

'Oh, fuck. What are we going to do?' Stephanie said.

'Let's have a drink,' Katie said, waving at a waitress. 'Then we'll decide.'

Three vodka and tonics (Katie) and white wines (Stephanie) later they had filled each other in with the details of their relationships with James. They decided that they had to be absolutely candid, that they needed to share everything without worrying whether it might hurt the other's feelings. So Stephanie learned that the sex was good but that James had refused to discuss having children, saying he felt he had already messed up one young life and didn't want to risk doing the same thing again, while Katie discovered that for Stephanie the sex was near non-existent but that James had recently been suggesting that another baby might be a good idea. The more they talked (and, to an extent, the more they drank), the angrier both women became at the way James had treated them. By five past three they were ready to hang him.

'So,' Stephanie said finally, 'I think we should punish him.'

'Too right we should,' agreed Katie, who, unused to feeling badly about anyone, had come over slightly heady with the whole experience.

'I just don't know how.'

Katie thought hard. Her brain was befuddled but it made sense. What goes around comes around. It would be karma, just karma, with a little outside help.

'What does he care about most?' Stephanie was saying. 'Not me or you obviously.'

'What people think of him,' Katie said, without hesitation, then wondered why she had said it. Was it true? She wished she could think more clearly. She really shouldn't drink in the day.

Stephanie laughed. 'That's probably right.'

'Like he's asked me to order caviar for his birthday party so that our friends will be impressed. I mean, caviar, can you imagine?'

'His birthday party? How do you know about that?' Stephanie asked, sounding confused.

'I'm arranging it,' Katie said. 'On the Sunday night. Everyone's coming.'

Stephanie was looking dazed. 'So he's having a fortieth birthday party on the Saturday night, which I'm saddled with arranging, and another on the Sunday, courtesy of you. He's unbefuckinglievable.'

Katie, who had been planning James's party for months and who had been really looking forward to making sure it was the best birthday he'd ever had, felt sick. 'I even asked him if I should invite his family and he said no, he'd be having a quiet dinner with a few close friends and their children on the Saturday. And that Finn would be there, and he was the only family James cared about.'

Stephanie laughed. 'And about forty other people. He told me not to bother inviting people from Lincoln because it'd be too far for them to travel and, anyway, they wouldn't enjoy it.'

'So, who's coming?' Katie said.

'Well, his friends – he was telling the truth about that. People from work, neighbours, parents of Finn's friends.'

'I wonder if Peter and Abi will show up.'

'Oh, I do hope so.' Stephanie smiled. 'I'm dying to meet them.'

'Me too. Maybe I should suggest inviting them up to Lincoln. See what he says.'

Stephanie took a deep breath. 'Maybe that's it. Maybe we tell him we know what he's been up to in the middle of one of his birthday parties – in front of all his friends and colleagues. Public humiliation, that might work.'

Katie nodded. Her heart was racing. She couldn't be sure if it was from the alcohol or the excitement. 'OK,' she said.

'Are you sure you're up for it?' Stephanie asked. 'I'd understand if you weren't.'

'Are you joking?' Katie said, slurring slightly. 'I'm looking forward to it,' she added, not completely convincingly.

'We need to plan it carefully. Work out exactly what we're going to do.'

'And what do we do in the meantime?'

'In the meantime he mustn't guess that anything's wrong so we carry on as normal. Make him feel loved. That way it'll be even more of a shock. The more he thinks he needs us, the harder it'll hit him.'

When they stood up to say goodbye Stephanie was aware that she was tottering a little. Katie reached out to give her a hug and she reciprocated awkwardly;

neither really knowing if it was the appropriate thing to do. Then there was an uncomfortable moment when they realized they were both headed for the station and they decided to share a taxi. On the platform they hugged again. Natasha was right, Stephanie thought. This was getting weird.

14

By the time James's car pulled into the drive of 79 Belsize Avenue at six forty-five, Stephanie was home and drinking coffee to disguise the smell of all the wine she had consumed. She was feeling slightly woozy, not being used to drinking in the day, and the train journey home had gone by in a blur. By the time she had left, she and Katie had the first stages of Operation Get Revenge On the Two-timing Shit all planned out. Katie was going to continue being sweet and unassuming and nurturing and unchallenging, while Stephanie was going to try to remould herself into the woman James had once been passionately in love with – if only she could remember who that woman had been, that was. She had no idea, really, if it would even be possible to win him over once more, the gulf between them having, as she saw it now, grown so wide, but if the plan was to have maximum impact then he needed to want both women equally.

'I always give him a massage,' Katie had said, 'when he arrives on a Sunday. To help him relax after the long drive. He says it destresses him.'

'Oh, God,' Stephanie had said. 'OK.'

James had come in, claiming tiredness from a stressful day at work (exhaustion from leading a double life, Stephanie had thought), and gone straight up to have a bath, stopping briefly on the way to say hello to Finn and hear about what had happened at school today ('Nothing'), what Sebastian the cat had eaten for breakfast (tuna and smoked trout), and about Arun Simpson's hamster's untimely demise.

'And then it lay on the floor all twitching with its eyes going open and shut,' Finn had said, relishing the goriness of the moment. 'And Arun said that it was making a noise like this,' he'd added, making a guttural sound from the back of his throat and lolling his tongue out of his mouth for added effect.

'How sad,' James had managed to reply without laughing. 'Poor Arun.'

He'd kissed Stephanie (now in a swirly-patterned blue and green wraparound dress that James had once said he liked and impractical high heels) perfunctorily as he passed.

'Tired?' she'd said to his retreating back, hoping she wasn't slurring.

'Knackered,' he'd called.

'Shall I bring you up a glass of wine?' she'd shouted up the stairs.

'When I get out,' he had shouted back. 'You have one if you can't wait,' he'd added, making her feel like an alcoholic. Stephanie had sighed and retreated to the kitchen where she was preparing Thai chicken curry.

She always cooked but ordinarily she would have got the sauce from a jar, adding organic chicken, but today she was making it from scratch, stirring peanut butter and coconut milk in a wok with chillies and garlic. She had no idea, really, what she needed to do to make James notice her again, but looking nice and cooking him a homemade meal wouldn't hurt. When he came down from his bath she could hear him on the PlayStation with Finn. There was no doubting he loved his son, she thought sadly, then forced herself to remember what the task at hand was. He might be a good father but she deserved better.

Once she had served up the food (plus fish fingers for Finn who might be middle class but he wasn't yet *that* middle class), Stephanie steeled herself and then moved round to the back of James's chair and began to massage his shoulders.

'What are you doing?' He laughed.

'I thought you might feel a bit tense, you know, working all day. I thought this might help.' God, she felt stupid.

He squirmed away playfully. 'OK, Finn, something's up. Has Mummy crashed the car?'

'I just thought you might like it,' Stephanie said, somewhat desperately.

Finn was laughing too, now. 'Did you crash the car, Mum?' he said delightedly.

'No,' said Stephanie, giving up and sitting at the table. 'I didn't.'

'Silly Mummy,' James said patronizingly, and she wanted to hit him.

'The thing is,' Stephanie said to Natasha on the phone later, up in the bedroom with the door shut, 'that's just not how we are. Not any more, anyway.'

'Exactly,' said Natasha. 'He's got Katie for sex and fun, and you for raising his child.'

'Great,' Stephanie said, more demoralized than ever.

'That came out wrong. What I mean is that they're probably still in that phase, you know, when it's all about the physical stuff. Your relationship's more real.'

'Less exciting, you mean.'

'No. More meaningful.'

'Well, apparently meaningful's not enough. Sex and fun win.'

Natasha tutted. 'Steph, you have to keep in your head that what James is doing isn't a criticism of you. It's all about him. It's his mid-life crisis, not your failure as a wife.'

'It doesn't feel like that.'

Natasha wasn't giving up. 'That's because he's made you feel like this. Isn't that why you're doing what you're doing?'

Stephanie sighed. 'You're right. Of course you are. You're always right. It's just hard, that's all.'

'I know it is but it'll get easier, I promise.'

'If you say so then it must be true,' Stephanie said, smiling a little. 'Night.'

Five minutes later her mobile rang.

'He just called me,' Katie's voice said. They had agreed to keep each other appraised of James's movements.

'And?'

'He said Abi's out for the evening so it's just him and Peter. Apparently they're thinking about going to the pub. What's he really doing?'

'Reading to Finn. He loves James to read to him before he goes to sleep. *Robinson Crusoe*, I think. It's one of his favourites.'

'Right.'

'What else did he say?'

'That he misses me.' She paused. 'That he loves me, you know, all the usual.'

'Are you feeling OK?' Stephanie asked, not a question she had ever imagined herself putting to a mistress of her husband's.

'I guess so. How about you?'

'Better since this afternoon,' Stephanie said.

'Me too. Oh, and he said he'll call me back later to say goodnight.'

'Excellent. I might see if I can get in the way, just to amuse myself. If we're going to do this we might as well try to enjoy it.'

'I'll text you if he manages to get through,' Katie said, and rang off.

James was watching TV in the living room, Sebastian purring on his lap. Finn was in bed. Stephanie automatically went to sit on the small sofa – her usual spot – while James sprawled on the three-seater. As soon as she'd sat down she thought that maybe she should have wedged herself on there with him, tried to force some physical closeness.

'Another drink?' he asked, standing up.

'Lovely,' she said, thinking, Well, if all else fails I'll just get pissed and jump on him. That should get his attention. She tried to think when they had last had sex. She had a horrible feeling it might have been before the move to London. Surely they must have done it since. Of course, *he*'d had lots of sex in the meantime. Just not with her.

They watched *Project Catwalk* and *Ramsay's Kitchen*

Nightmares in a quite companionable way. They'd always bonded over reality TV, laughing at the people, the unspoken relief that they weren't like them, that they were superior somehow. At ten past ten James stood up and walked towards the door. 'Just got to ring Malcolm,' he said.

Stephanie stood up too. She waited for him to go upstairs, then followed him, picking up clothes off the floor as if she was randomly tidying up. James looked a bit edgy and put his phone back into his pocket.

'Oh, sorry,' Stephanie said. 'Do you need me to get out of the way?'

'No, no, of course not,' he said. 'I just need to ask him how the Collinses' foal's getting on. It was colicky.'

Stephanie smiled at him. 'Well, go ahead.'

'Actually,' he said, 'I've just remembered he had a date this evening. I'll try him later.'

'Oh, OK,' she said. 'Has he finally admitted he's gay, then?'

James laughed. 'No chance.' He put the phone into his pocket and wandered down the stairs again. Stephanie followed, chatting away about nothing in particular. It was amazing, she thought, how cheered she felt by this tiny victory. Maybe Natasha was right. Maybe there was fun to be had in watching James squirm.

An hour later, at about a quarter past eleven, James stood up for a second time. 'I'm going to try Malcolm again,' he announced, and moved towards the door.

'Oh, I don't think you should. It's too late,' Stephanie said. 'What if you were wrong about him having a date and he's gone to bed already?'

She could have sworn she saw James blush. 'Well, he'll have turned his phone off if he's gone to bed, won't he?'

'Not if the Collinses' foal is sick,' Stephanie said. 'He's probably on call this evening. It would be a shame to disturb him if you don't have to.'

'It's fine,' James said firmly. 'He asked me to ring him.'

He left the room and Stephanie smiled. He was rattled. He would be trying to think of an excuse to give Katie as to why he hadn't called her earlier in the evening.

Katie was sitting in front of late-night TV, although she wasn't watching it. She had got home from meeting Stephanie in a kind of alcoholic daze. She'd fallen asleep on the train and nearly missed her stop, waking only when the person next to her had tapped her on the shoulder because they wanted to get off. It had gone well, she thought. Stephanie had been friendly enough, and Katie thought she had certainly seemed to accept that Katie hadn't set out to hurt her and that was the important thing.

She was trying to work out if they would have had anything in common if it hadn't been for James. They would have got on, she was sure, but she wasn't certain they would have been friends. Their personalities seemed as different as their looks. Stephanie was . . . what was the word? . . . measured. Cool and cynical and pessimistic. Katie was a passionate, glass-half-full kind of woman, or at least she liked to think so. She was so deep in thought that she jumped when her phone rang. She yawned to get herself into the right mood, then muted the television.

'Mmm . . . hello?' she said, in her best just-been-woken-up voice.

It was James, as she had known it would be.

'Shit, sorry. Were you asleep?'

'Mmmm . . .'

'Sorry. We went to the pub and I lost track of time,' he said all too convincingly.

'Just you and Peter?' Katie said.

'Abi met us there for last orders. She'd been to the theatre. *Sound of Music*,' he added, as an afterthought.

'Really? Who with?'

'No idea. Friends, I guess.'

'And did she enjoy it?'

'I think so. Listen, love, I just called to say goodnight, that's all.'

'Who was playing Maria?' Katie asked, nearly laughing although she didn't know why. It was unbelievable, the ease with which he could lie.

'I didn't ask. Look, I have to get up in the morning.'

'Was it that girl who won the TV programme?'

'Like I said, I didn't ask,' James said tetchily. 'I really have to go.'

'OK,' Katie said. 'Night, then.'

'Night, night,' he said, and made the little kissy noises that were part of their nightly ritual. Katie forced herself to do the same.

Two minutes later, as James was coming down the stairs, now changed for bed, Stephanie got a text:

James just called

it said.

95

Apparently has been in pub all evening with Peter. Abi at Sound of Music.

How ironic, Stephanie thought, that I'm the one getting late-night texts from K now.

'How was he?' she asked James, as he came in and crossed to the sideboard to pour himself a whisky. He seemed a little stressed.

'Oh, fine, false alarm. The foal is as right as rain, apparently.'

'And how did his date go?'

'I didn't ask. None of my business.' He wiped his brow as if he was feeling hot, which, of course, he must be. Ordinarily Stephanie wasn't so interested in the goings-on in Lincolnshire.

'Strange, isn't it, that he told you he had a date if you think he wouldn't want you to know who with?' Stephanie said.

'Yes, I suppose so.'

'It's almost like he wants it to get out. Maybe you should talk to him about it. Ask him straight out. He probably hates living a lie. I mean, it must be so exhausting.'

'Yes,' James said cautiously. 'Mustn't it?'

15

James had noticed that Stephanie was looking good. Gone were the sweatpants and Juicy Couture zip-up tops she usually wore round the house, an antidote to her work self, which, she said, she felt had to be faultlessly turned out in whatever fashions were prevalent, however unflattering and ridiculous they might be. In their place she had taken to wearing a flippy little A-line skirt that grazed her knees and a vest top with stringy straps – 'spaghetti straps', he thought they were called – which looked both respectable and sexy and which, he had decided, made him feel distinctly uneasy. It wasn't that he had forgotten how good his wife could look. It was just that he wasn't used to being made so aware of it any more.

He called Katie as soon as he arrived at the surgery in the morning. He knew what she would be doing: she always got up slowly, sitting at the kitchen table drinking tea and reading the papers before she could face doing anything else. He liked to think about her twirling the pencil in her hair as she tried to do the crossword. He imagined her stretching out her hand to find the phone when it rang, smiling when she looked at the caller ID. She always looked a bit like a bushbaby when she woke up, wide-eyed and vulnerable with her honey-coloured curls in an unruly mess round her face. She didn't answer till the phone had rung six times.

'Oh, God,' James said. 'I didn't wake you up again, did I?'

'No,' said Katie, who had been standing over the phone trying to decide whether to answer or not. 'I was upstairs.'

'Did you sleep OK?'

'Perfect. How about you?'

'Peter and Abi had a row so that kept me awake for a bit.'

'Oh, gosh, you poor thing,' Katie said, with all the fake sympathy she could muster. 'You must feel terrible. Tell me all about it.'

'Oh, it was nothing, really, just the usual. Domestic. "You never do the washing-up", that kind of thing.'

'Really? They argue about who does the washing-up?'

'Something like that. To be honest, I couldn't hear the details.'

'How long have they been married? Ten years? And they still argue about who does the washing-up?'

'Listen, Katie,' James said, 'I've got surgery, I'd better go.'

Despite her unhappiness, Katie smiled as she put the phone down.

Natasha and Stephanie were trying to persuade *ingénue* actress Santana Alberta (real name Susan Anderson, but she had decided early on that she needed to stand out and thought her dark, exotic looks demanded a dark, exotic name) that wearing the sheer halter-neck chiffon number they had all agreed on without any underwear was a foolish career move. Santana had worked hard to be taken seriously after forcing her way into the public's attention through a series of relationships with much older (and therefore very grateful) well-known men.

The truth was, she wasn't a great actress, she would never have stood out from the crowd of other pretty but uninspiring young hopefuls if the histrionics of her private life hadn't guaranteed her a regular place in the tabloid press. There was the time she had left her ageing actor boyfriend's house after a huge row, wearing nothing but one of his tuxedos and a pair of Jimmy Choos. Luckily the paparazzi were there to capture the moment because she had had her manager tip them off earlier in the day that this might happen. Or the time she and her music impresario lover had had a fierce argument in the street, conveniently outside the cinema where a big film première was taking place and where the photographers were trying to fill the couple of hours between capturing the arrivals and departures. Fortunately Santana had been wearing a skimpy new dress from the latest Julien Macdonald collection (which Stephanie had found for her) that perfectly complemented the black eye she was left with, and looked great splashed across the front page of the *Sun*.

With Stephanie's help Santana had gained something of a reputation for herself as a trendsetter. Unfortunately she was starting to believe what she read about herself, so she no longer silently accepted that, when it came to style, Stephanie knew best. She had recently made her first film – a low-budget biopic that had passed audiences by with barely a mention, but she had spent a lot of money having her PR people place stories with the gossip mags: 'Santana in line for BAFTA nomination', that sort of thing. 'An insider says that Santana Alberta's performance is being hotly tipped to win awards,' they went on to say, although luckily they never actually revealed that the insider was, in fact, her mum. She had hoped that if it was said often enough then people might start to believe it, and somehow it might actually turn out to be true. Of course, she hadn't actually been nominated for anything, or even short-listed for that matter. But the extra hype had meant that BAFTA had asked her to present an award and she was damn well going to make sure she got noticed.

'It's sexy,' she whined now. 'And it's important I look sexy. Otherwise they'll just print pictures of Helen Mirren again and I won't get a look-in.'

'It's tacky,' Stephanie said, losing patience with her. 'If you want to look like a stripper that's up to you. I'm not going to tell you you look good because you don't. And if you'd rather find another stylist who'll tell you exactly what you want to hear, that's fine too.'

Natasha shot her a glance that said they couldn't afford to lose Santana as a client. Few other people required their services on such a regular basis. 'Tell you what,' Natasha said, 'why don't I sew in an extra layer? Just to cover up you know, your actual . . . bits. It's much sexier to give them a hint of something rather than the whole meat and potatoes.'

Santana pouted sulkily. 'OK,' she said. 'As long as it'll still get me in the papers.'

*

'What's up with you now?' Natasha hissed at Stephanie, while Santana was in the toilet, changing back into her own clothes.

'Oh, sorry,' Stephanie said sarcastically. 'My life's falling apart, that's all.'

'Listen,' Natasha said, 'I'd have thought it was more important now than ever that you concentrate on work. You're about to become a single mum.'

'Thanks. I needed reminding of that.'

'I'm just saying, don't let this thing with James mess your life up. If you do he's won. What's the point of teaching him a lesson if you're in as bad a way as he is when it all comes to a head? You need to be looking fabulous and happy and successful while he's trying to crawl his way out of the gutter.'

Stephanie managed a half-smile. 'You're right. I know you're right.'

When Santana came back into the room, now in skinny jeans, with an ill-advised man's shirt, waistcoat and hound's-tooth-check flat cap of her own choosing, Stephanie went over and gave her a hug. 'Sorry, Santana,' she said. 'My husband's being a prick and I shouldn't take it out on you. You go to the BAFTAs with your bits on show if you want to. Dangle baubles off it if it makes you happy. It's up to you.'

Santana, who was by nature a kind girl, hugged her back. 'It's OK,' she said. 'I know you only have my best interests at heart.'

Katie was uneasy. After the initial excitement (not to mention the effects of the alcohol) had worn off she had started to question whether or not she was doing the right thing. Whatever James had done didn't justify what she and Stephanie were about to do. Two wrongs most definitely didn't make a right. It felt mean-spirited, lying and deceiving and scheming just like he had been. But she also couldn't deny that there was a satisfaction in knowing that he was oblivious to their plans. It made her feel as if she had some power, that he hadn't managed to completely ruin her life.

'Are we doing the right thing?' she said to Stephanie, almost every time they spoke.

'I have no idea,' Stephanie always said, which didn't help much but she always asked Katie to stick to the plan, and for reasons she didn't quite understand, Katie always agreed.

So far, Stephanie and Katie's plan hadn't progressed much beyond the initial decision that D-Day was James's fortieth birthday weekend. They had decided that Stephanie would throw his party in London as if nothing was wrong, then turn up at the Lincolnshire party the next day where the two women would confront him together in front of his colleagues and friends. That was as far as they had got. It needed another element, and when they were having one of their surreptitious phone conversations, a week or so later, to compare notes, Katie inadvertently said something that sparked off a whole other chain of events.

'Did you know he takes payment in cash off most of the farmers up here? Keeps it out of the books altogether. I just thought you ought to know because of . . . well . . . you know . . . alimony and all that. When it comes to it.'

'Really?' Stephanie said, suddenly interested. 'He's never mentioned it. I wonder what the tax people would say about that.'

Katie gasped. 'We can't!'

'No, you're right. We can't. Shame, though.' I wonder what else there is about him that we don't know. Maybe it's time we tried to find out.'

16

James, it turned out, had several more secrets. Some were easier to discover than others.

He was widely known in their little village community, Katie told Stephanie, for his dinner parties, at which he produced ever more complicated and sophisticated dishes for admiring groups of local dignitaries.

'Dinner parties?' Stephanie had said, incredulous. 'He can't even boil an egg.'

'Exactly,' Katie said. 'He goes into Lincoln, buys all the food pre-prepared, then passes it off as his own.'

'Hilarious,' Stephanie had replied, trying to imagine a version of James who would give a shit about people thinking he could cook. 'You should get him to organize a dinner party soon. For some of the people he wants to impress most.'

'Do you really think so?'

'Let's live a little.'

Katie laughed. 'OK.'

His parents, Stephanie told Katie, were not estranged from him as he had told her, but loved to come for the weekend whenever they could. 'I'm sure they'd love to meet you,' she said. 'Maybe I'll suggest they pay James a surprise visit in Lincoln.'

'I'll clear out the spare room,' Katie laughed. Maybe

Stephanie was right and there was some fun to be had in getting back at James.

None of these were big things – the one major skeleton in James's closet already took up most of the space – but they could be tiny mosquito bites, little parcels of humiliation on the way to the big prize. To James, his public image was everything. If they chipped away at that then he would need them – the two women who, he believed, loved him unconditionally – more than ever. Perfect.

James had been looking forward to his latest social gathering for weeks. He had suffered undercooked pork at the Selby-Algernons', dog hair in the soup at the McNeils', a two-and-a-half-hour wait for dessert at the Knightlys', and now it was his turn to shine again. He liked all of his dinner party hosts, the conversation always flowed along with the wine, but mostly they were the sort of people he felt he *ought* to be friendly with.

Hugh and Alison Selby-Algernon were the alphas on Lower Shippingham's social list. They lived in the biggest, most impressive house in the village and Hugh was something big in investment banking. In James's Top Trumps of Lower Shippingham's A-list, Hugh and Alison could beat pretty much every other resident in every category.

Close behind came Sam and Geoff McNeil, who had lived in Lower Shippingham for thirty-five years. Sam held an influential position on the local council while Geoff was something big or other in the Rotary Club. Then there was Richard Knightly, a partner in a local firm of solicitors, and his wife Simone, a journalist on the *Lincoln Chronicle*.

OK, so it wasn't exactly a cutting-edge social circle – Sam and Geoff had a tendency to steer the conversation round to the Church whenever they could – but it didn't hurt to be in with the right people. Stephanie would never go along with what she called his 'social-climbing ways', but Katie understood how important it was to make an effort.

The four couples met once a fortnight and took it in turns to host a dinner at home. The first time it had been James and Katie's turn James had got into a last-minute panic about Katie's somewhat rustic cooking. He loved her food, he really did, but it wasn't exactly Cordon Bleu. So, he'd persuaded her that he should go into Lincoln and pick up something freshly prepared from the big deli in the town centre. He'd bought dressed lobster to start, beef Wellington that simply needed heating up and a *tarte Tatin* with 'homemade' custard. The Selby-Algernons, the McNeils and the Knightlys had gone into raptures as they tucked into the starter, and the moment for James to come clean and admit that the food was shop-bought had passed. Worse, he had found himself taking the credit and elaborating on the details of the afternoon he had spent slaving away over a hot stove.

'But, James, I never knew you had such hidden talent,' Alison had cooed. 'Hugh, why can't you cook like this?' she'd asked.

'Why can't you?' Hugh had replied.

James had seen Katie shoot him a look and had had a brief moment of panic that she was going to give the game away. He'd raised his eyebrows slightly, in a way that said, 'Please don't,' and she'd obliged, as she always did, with a smile. 'Aren't I lucky?' she'd said, placing her hand over his.

'Too right,' Simone had agreed, and she'd given James a look he would have sworn was flirtatious. Simone, of all the women in their little social circle, was the only one he would have considered going to bed with. Alison was, frankly, too shapeless, with her saggy breasts swaying somewhere down around her middle where her waist should have been, and Sam too neurotic – she always looked as if she had put her makeup on in the dark but it was probably because she had the shakes. Simone, on the other hand, was slim and shapely, even if her face did have a certain horsiness. Unable to help himself, he'd tried a little wink on her and she'd smiled girlishly. Since then there had been an added frisson at the dinner parties, which had made them far more enjoyable. He was certainly never going to act on his suspicion that Simone had the hots for him and he had no reason to believe that she would either. He just liked to know that he'd still got it. Whatever 'it' was.

Since that night, word of his culinary expertise had spread. Malcolm at the clinic had remarked on it and one of the local farmers had good-naturedly called him 'Delia', after Delia Smith. James rather liked that he had gained a nickname. It made him feel as if he was back in the playground, part of a gang. He mentioned it to Malcolm and Simon in the hope that they'd pick up on it and start to use it themselves.

'Hi, it's Delia here,' he'd say, with a mock self-conscious chuckle when he had to call one of them. For a while he'd signed it on Post-it notes whenever he had to leave a message for either of them. He'd persevered for a week or so but, sadly, it had never caught on and he'd started to worry that Malcolm would think he was making some kind of statement, like those camp men who find it hilarious to refer to other men as 'she', so he had stopped.

The next eight weeks had been agonizing, waiting for it to be his and Katie's turn again and wondering if he could pull off the same trick twice. This time he'd bought goat's-cheese tartlets, venison pie and figs ready for baking, to be served with 'homemade' whisky ice-cream. There had been a hairy moment when Sam had asked where on earth he had bought the venison because she could never find any when she wanted it, and he had had to bluster something about Kent and Sons in St John's Wood, knowing she would never be able to check up on him. James had felt the glow of the praise and had almost started to believe that he deserved it.

Tonight's meal would be his fifth. He was starting to worry that he had exhausted the repertoire of the Le Joli Poulet Delicatessen and Gourmet Food Store. He had served up their rack of lamb, their monkfish and squid kebabs and their roast partridge all to great acclaim, but poking about now in the pre-prepared dinner-party food section, he was struggling to find anything new. It was too soon to start repeating himself. He was going to have to talk to the owner about broadening their stock.

He managed to find a starter of bouillabaisse and an entrée of cassoulet, which he'd always dismissed before as being a bit low-rent. There were no new desserts so he went for the *tarte Tatin* again, deciding he could claim to be doing a French-themed evening. He had a quick word with Guy, who owned the shop, but it was difficult to get his point across without explaining the whole charade and why it was so important to him to produce something different each time so he left it.

By the time he got back to the cottage Katie had made the place spotless and Stanley had been banished to the spare bedroom. The warm spell wasn't showing any signs of letting up so she had pulled the table over to the open patio doors so that they could at least start the evening with cool fresh air flowing in from the back garden.

James unpacked his goodies, checked the reheating instructions on each, then carefully hid the packaging in a plastic bag buried at the bottom of the bin. The cassoulet he transferred to a large casserole dish, and as soon as the bottom oven pinged to let him know it had reached the right temperature he put it on the middle shelf and checked his watch. He poured the bouillabaisse into a pan and left it on the side. The *tarte Tatin*, which he was going to serve cold with cream, he placed in the fridge.

'You've just about got time to have a bath,' Katie said, kissing him on the forehead and handing him a large glass of red wine. 'Anything I need to do?'

'All under control,' he told her. 'Just remind me to put the soup on at about ten past. Mmm ... you smell gorgeous,' he added, nuzzling her hair.

Katie laughed and pushed him off. 'Go and get ready,' she said.

Katie watched as James went up to the bathroom,

humming to himself. After she had heard the door shut and the thunder of running water, she lifted the lid of the bin and began to rummage around among the debris.

Sam, Katie thought, looked like a ventriloquist's dummy when she opened the front door to find her and Geoff brandishing a bottle of Merlot. She was wearing bright red lipstick that might have been applied with a paintbrush, so little notice did it take of the contours of her lips. Her short hair stood up in clumpy peaks that made her seem as if she had just received an enormous electric shock.

Geoff was his usual dour self, dressed in the kind of hand-me-down shabby clothes that only the truly rich could get away with. On several occasions, Katie had suggested to James that they might try and socialize with people more like them, more their own age, more spiritual and less . . . establishment, but he had lectured her on the importance of being in with the right people and that had been that really. It wasn't that she didn't like Sam and Geoff, it was just that it was a bit like having your dis-approving aunt and uncle over sometimes.

'Something smells good,' Geoff said, sniffing the air as he walked in. 'What's he got lined up this time?'

Katie rattled off the menu, and Sam and Geoff made approving noises. She was just offering them a drink when James burst out of the kitchen, wearing a ridiculous stripy apron and wielding a spatula. The apron, Katie noticed, had streaks of red sauce down the front, no doubt care-fully placed there just minutes ago. She sometimes thought he took the whole performance too far, putting flour in his hair and smudges of balsamic on his cheeks, but it made him happy and she had never been able to see the harm in it. Now, looking at him, it struck her that he was a pathetic man, puffed up with self-importance, obsessed by appearance and status. 'Hungry?' he said now.

'Ravenous,' Geoff replied. 'We've been looking forward to this for weeks.'

The doorbell rang again, and Hugh, Alison, Richard and Simone were huddled on the doorstep where they had bumped into one another. There were air kisses and hugs all round.

'Shall we have an aperitif before we eat?' James said, with the air of someone who knew he was about to impress.

Stephanie had not been able to get to sleep. In fact, she had given up trying and resigned herself to a night spent with her mind racing and a day feeling like shit at work tomorrow. She ran through Katie's version of events in her head again, alternately delighted and appalled. Poor James. No, fuck it, he'd asked for it.

The six guests and James had apparently started on their favourite topic, the need to elect a 'parish council' for the village to lobby on affairs like unsightly planning applications and the banning of loitering by the three teenage hoodies who occasionally hurled insults at passers-by from their post on the bench by the duck pond. All three were harmless, Katie had told her. In fact, she had once been struggling home with a bag of shopping from the village store and they'd taken it in turns to carry it for her, then refused to accept a pound each for their trouble. But, Sam, Geoff, Alison, Hugh and James loved to over-dramatize the situation to one another, imagining crack being smoked and an onslaught of muggings on the horizon. Richard and Simone were slightly more forgiving, having a teenage son themselves, but the mention of a uPVC conservatory could send them both into spasms. All seven, James included, Katie told Stephanie, believed they were the chosen few to run such a council and each was secretly hoping to head it.

'By the way,' Katie had said, as an aside, 'did you know he built the extension at the back of the surgery without planning permission? He figured no one could see it so it didn't really count. Plus he thought there was a good chance it'd be turned down. He used new brick too, in a conservation area. I bet Richard and Simone would love that.'

Stephanie remembered James telling her about his plans for expanding the practice and the subsequent trials and tribulations he had had with the builders. She had never thought to ask him whether he'd done it by the book; she had just assumed he had. He was James, after all.

Anyway, Katie told her, the bouillabaisse had been received with oohs and aahs, and several of the guests had gone for seconds even though two more courses were coming up.

'I don't know how you have the patience,' Alison had said, 'shelling all those prawns and scraping beards off mussels.'

'He probably buys them ready cleaned – don't you, James?' Geoff had offered. 'Much less hassle.'

'God, no,' James had said, puffing up with self-righteousness. 'You can never be sure they've been washed properly. Or that they haven't forced open a few bad ones. I like to do it all myself. It's therapeutic, tell you the truth. I stick on Radio 4 and I'm happy.'

Katie, she had told Stephanie, had felt a little jolt of excitement as she'd watched him dig his own grave.

The cassoulet had been praised as 'delicious' and 'simply stunning'. By now the conversation had moved on to the shortcomings of the village's other residents, especially those who were new money.

'But James is new money,' Stephanie had interjected at this point.

'I know that now,' Katie had said, 'but for some reason he likes everyone to think he's not.'

'So then what happened?' Stephanie was both impatient to get to the end of the story and dreading hearing it. She could feel her heart beating up in her throat, and she couldn't imagine how Katie – who had told her she was now locked in the downstairs bathroom to make the call in private – must be feeling.

'Then,' Katie had said dramatically, 'then it was time for dessert.'

Katie told her how James, face now rosy with a combination of wine and pride, had announced he had prepared his famous *tarte Tatin*. 'I thought about doing something new but I decided that as the whole flavour of the evening was French my old stand-by would be rather appropriate.' He'd carried it in from the kitchen on a serving dish, as if he was presenting the world with his newborn child.

'Where do you get the apples from at this time of year?'

Simone had asked. 'I always find they're really watery and tasteless.'

'Ah,' James had said. 'That'd be telling.'

He'd cut the first slice and Katie had sworn she saw him blanch as he'd lifted it up and noticed what seemed to be part of a sheet of paper stuck to the bottom. He went to drop the slice on the serving plate but, as he did so, Sam had leaned forward and whipped the paper off.

'There you go,' she'd said brightly, screwing it up and putting it by her plate. James, Katie had said, looked as if all the blood had left his body.

'Looks like I've stood it on something,' he had said, laughing nervously. 'I'll just go into the kitchen and sort it out.'

Katie had held her breath. There was nothing she could do. She couldn't be the one to reveal what it was that was stuck to the base of the *tarte*. All she could do was wait, fingers crossed. James, it had seemed, was about to get away with it. He had put down his knife and was about to lift the plate when Hugh had clumsily reached forward and grabbed a corner of the rest of the paper, which was poking out from under the *tarte*, and pulled it. 'No need to bother, old man. See? I've got it.'

'What is it?' Simone had said. There had been an almost comedy moment when James had reached out his hand to take the piece of paper just as Geoff had beaten him to it.

'Looks like a receipt,' Geoff had said, and had been about to discard it when Sam – thank God for Sam and her nosiness, Katie had said – who was looking over his shoulder, had exclaimed: 'It says "*tarte Tatin*" here.'

The others had laughed, not realizing the momentousness of the discovery they were about to make. Richard had even said jokingly, 'Don't tell me you buy the ready-made stuff when we're not here.'

Then Sam had taken a sharp breath. 'Gosh, James, it says "bouillabaisse" and "cassoulet" too. How funny.'

The room, Katie had said, had gone suddenly silent.

17

James woke up with a head that felt as if it was full of cotton wool. He groaned, feeling the paper dryness of his mouth. He'd drunk too much. He rolled over, gingerly opening one eye, flinching as the light hit his retina. Katie must be up already. He peered at the clock beside the bed. It looked like . . . No, it couldn't say ten to eleven. Wasn't he meant to be at the surgery this morning?

He became aware of a noise downstairs. The radio and something that sounded like plates being scraped. Katie must be doing the washing-up. Then a thought struck him from out of nowhere and he laid his head back on the pillow. Oh, shit. Oh, God. Oh, fuck.

He could remember the embarrassed silence after Sam had read out the receipt from the Joli Poulet. He'd tried to laugh it off at first, his brain scrabbling around for something – anything – he could say to cover his tracks. Then he had tried to imply that what he had bought were actually the raw materials for each dish, packaged up together for ease, so while he had told a little fib about cleaning the shellfish and picking out apples he had still cooked each dish from scratch.

But Richard, damn him, had laughed that annoying braying laugh of his and said he had seen whole meals being sold ready-prepared in Le Joli Poulet and had James really been fooling them all along? He had had no choice but to come clean.

His guests had been very sweet – after all, he hadn't killed anyone or done anything illegal – but it was the polite understanding of their words that had floored him. He knew they were all thinking he was a bit sad, a bit untrustworthy, that the whole thing wasn't cricket. No one was ever going to say anything damning to his face, but the minute they left he knew they would all go on somewhere else – Sam and Geoff's house maybe, that was nearby – and dissect his character over brandy. They would throw in anecdotes of times when they thought he had behaved oddly or said something embarrassing. The bond between the six of them would grow stronger as they united in laughing at him. He knew, without it ever needing to be said, that their little dinner-party circle was over. They would claim diary clashes or family commitments, and the weeks would go by until they stopped even trying to find a date. Maybe the six of them would go on meeting up regularly without him and Katie, chuckling over his ridiculousness as they ate burned duck and soapy potatoes.

He gulped heavily from the glass of water Katie had left by the bed. He remembered now that after they had gone he and Katie had had a huge row because he had somehow felt the need to blame anyone but himself for the débâcle. Then he had downed most of a bottle of whisky before finally coming to bed in the small hours.

He groaned audibly. He felt like the worst kind of fool.

Why had he allowed himself to get into this position in the first place? None of the others could cook and that had never seemed to matter. He should have just owned up that first time. The minute they had started praising his food he should have said, 'Actually, I bought it all, I'm a useless chef,' and they would have laughed and that would have been that. But he'd enjoyed the attention. He'd always felt intimidated by 'posh people', as his mother would have called them. Always felt a bit resentful about his comprehensive-school background and his lack of an inheritance. Always secretly wanted to be considered one of them. As the local vet he had managed to ingratiate himself into the community, make himself feel like an integral and indispensable part of it, but he also liked to feel he was important. Forging friendships with the local bigwigs had fed his need for status. He was ridiculous.

The first thing he had to do was to make it up with Katie. None of this was her fault and, what was more, he had put her in the awkward position of having to go along with his pretence for all these months. God, she must think he was an idiot. He slid out of bed, feeling a jolt as his feet touched the floor and he tried to stand upright. He might just have to go and be sick first.

Ten minutes later, after he'd brushed his teeth and splashed cold water on his face, he made his way gingerly down to the kitchen where Katie was scrubbing down the granite surfaces. He felt her stiffen as he slid his arms round her from behind.

'Sorry, sorry,' he said, nuzzling into her neck. 'I shouldn't have taken it out on you.'

'That's OK,' Katie said kindly. 'I understand.'

Katie, bless her, had called Malcolm and told him that James would not be at work today because he was unwell.

She had thrown away all evidence of the disastrous meal, all the leftovers and the empty bottles and the clam shells had already gone into the bin outside and been taken away by the refuse collectors. She seemed happy to pretend that nothing had happened and fussed around him as usual, making him coffee and offering him toast, which made him gag.

James felt like he needed a debrief, though, a trawl through the evening's horrors to confront head on what the worst-case scenario might be. But that, he knew, was pointless. If he tried to talk about what had happened Katie would just insist that everything was fine and that it was unhealthy to dwell on negative things that had happened in the past, even if the past was only last night.

Stephanie would have indulged him, he thought. Indeed, Stephanie would have been only too happy to pick over the excruciating details. Somehow they would have found something funny in the retelling – the look on Sam's face, lipstick askew, as she'd read the receipt; how slow Hugh had been to catch on, the extent to which Alison had had to spell it out to him ('James has been buying the food all this time, dear, not cooking it himself. That was a lie'), so that eventually they would have found themselves helpless with laughter and that would have made the whole thing so much easier to bear. He thought about reminding Katie about the way Sam had tripped over the front step in her haste to get away from the source of the embarrassment and her skirt had ridden up to reveal hairy legs and alarmingly skimpy underwear, but he knew she wouldn't crack a smile. Instead she would probably say something like 'Oh, poor Sam. Well, it's all forgotten now,' so he decided to go back to bed instead.

'That's perfect,' Meredith announced, via her reflection in the mirror, and Stephanie wondered whether she shouldn't give up altogether. Meredith was wearing an emerald-green creation that looked like something a Disney princess might aspire to. The plunging neckline showed off her crêpy cleavage, while the low waist made her broad hips seem even more substantial. They were in the changing rooms at Selfridges, and Stephanie had only allowed her to try on the dress to prove a point about how bad it would look.

'Meredith, it really does nothing for your figure,' she said now, as diplomatically as she could. 'Does it?' she added, looking piercingly at Natasha for support.

'Er, no, not really,' Natasha said. Natasha was terrified of Meredith.

'This is the one I feel comfortable in, and as you have failed so far to come up with anything better, then this is the one it shall be.'

Stephanie flinched at the insult in Meredith's comment. 'I think you should wait. We still have a few weeks to go and we're bound to find something we can all agree on.'

'And what if this one's sold out by then? What if you haven't managed to show me anything else I like and this one's no longer available?'

Stephanie looked at the shiny pea-coloured monstrosity. It was hard to imagine there would be a rush on bright green flouncy dresses. 'Tell you what,' she said, 'we'll buy this anyway and bring it back when we find something better.'

'*If* you find something better,' Meredith said frostily.

'Yes, of course, if,' Stephanie managed an insincere smile.

She glanced at her watch when Meredith wasn't looking. She was both looking forward to and dreading having to go home this evening. James was due back and Stephanie would get to see how their first tiny arrow had wounded him. Of course he wouldn't be able to tell her about his trauma, but Katie had said enough for her to know that he must be feeling humiliated and more than a bit foolish. Apparently he had gone back to work yesterday and had come home fuming because Malcolm had been called out to see Richard and Simone's retriever, which had an ear infection, and Simone had told him the whole story. In turn, Malcolm had told Simon and Sally, and James had been subjected to merciless – but, Katie had said she was sure, affectionate – teasing for the rest of the day.

'He's furious with Simone,' Katie had said. 'Which is hilarious because I think he always thought she fancied him.'

'Didn't she?' Stephanie interrupted, laughing.

'No, I don't think so. Richard's gorgeous and he dotes on her. I think she was just being polite.'

'And,' Stephanie said, 'how do you feel?'

'I know it's awful to admit it but I actually feel good. Serves him right,' Katie said, with conviction.

Stephanie wondered whether James was looking forward more than usual to his few days in London because he hadn't made an idiot of himself in front of anyone down there. She was planning to be extra nice to him this evening, the calm before the storm as it were, while she and Katie tried to decide what their next move should be.

By five to five she and Natasha were heading north in a cab, the hideous green creation in the distinctive yellow carrier-bag between them. Katie had told her that James usually left for London at about one but, Stephanie had said, he never arrived home until gone five thirty or so. Neither of them had any idea why his journey seemed to take so long.

'Remember,' Natasha said, hugging her as the cab turned the corner into Belsize Avenue, 'just grit your teeth and smile.'

James's car was parked in the street, she noticed, as the cab pulled up. He was early. Stephanie smiled to herself. They'd rattled him.

'Hi,' she called, as she opened the front door. Finn dived on her from out of nowhere and then James appeared from the living room and swept her up in a bear-hug. 'You're earlier than usual,' she said breathlessly, when he'd put her down.

'I wanted to get home. I missed you both.'

'Excellent.' Stephanie prised his arms off her. 'You can help Finn with his homework.'

'So', she said, once they were sitting down to dinner, 'how was your week?'

'Yes, good, fine,' he said, giving nothing away. 'How about you? Meredith still being a nightmare?'

Stephanie wondered if she'd heard correctly. James never asked about her work. Never. The fact that he even remembered that she had a client called Meredith was an event in itself.

'Don't get me started on Meredith.'

James smiled. 'No, go on, I want to hear about her. Has she made a pass at you yet?'

God, Stephanie thought, he must be really desperate to keep the conversation away from himself.

So, she told him about the green dress – even producing it from its carrier-bag to illustrate her point – and he laughed and said that Meredith must look like a small hillock in it. For a split second Stephanie had forgotten what was happening to them, and then she was stung with the realization of how easy it seemed to be for him to pretend that everything was normal, that they were a happy couple relaxing after a day at work, that he didn't, in fact, have a mistress squirrelled away in the countryside, that his whole existence wasn't a lie.

'Well, anyway,' she said, putting the dress back in its bag, 'I'd better not get it creased in case I have to take it back.'

18

Katie was having a good day.

It had started off badly. She had been buoyed up by the events at the dinner party, which had gone like a dream. Seeing James upset and embarrassed had given her an unexpected rush of pleasure, which had made her feel both guilty and elated. She had thought that maybe she would feel sorry for him or be tempted to own up to her part in his tragi-comic humiliation, but she had discovered a well-hidden core of steel inside her when it came to it, and she had watched him, moping about miserably, unmoved. This morning, though, as they had said goodbye for another three days, the reality that her relationship – which up until a couple of weeks ago, she had thought was perfect – was over had hit her full on. She had found herself crying on his shoulder and he, stupid man, had thought it was because she was going to miss him, although in a roundabout way maybe it was.

He had kissed the top of her head. 'I'll be back on Sunday, silly girl,' he'd said, and Katie had thought how patronizing he sounded and that had made her stop crying and remember what she was doing and why.

Once he'd gone, she had flicked half-heartedly through the post, which contained cards from Hugh and Alison ('What a lovely evening. Do let's do it again soon') and

Sam and Geoff ('Thanks muchly as always!'). Neither of them made any mention of the awkward end to the dinner and she knew that none of their friends ever would. They would just fade into the distance and eventually include some other poor couple in their exclusive dinner-party circle. With luck she'd never have to bother trying to make polite conversation with any of them again, beyond a hello in the post office.

She would miss Richard and Simone more – at least they were nearer her age and they had things in common – but then they would probably have thought the whole thing was hilarious and Katie was sure that if she rang Simone up and asked her if she wanted to go for a drink, once this was all over, she would say yes. Meanwhile she had no intention of making contact now because she knew James would be too embarrassed to make the first move and she wanted him to have to suffer the loss of his friends.

She looked round her little cottage and thought how nice it would be to reclaim it as her own. She could get some lilac paint or a pale pink, maybe, and freshen up the living room by painting one wall in a colour James would never have put up with. She could burn candles all day if she wanted to, without him commenting that the place smelt like a church. Stanley would be allowed to sit on the sofa. By the time her doorbell rang, a couple of minutes before ten, she had mentally redecorated the whole house and had forgotten all about Owen's appointment again.

She was going through the motions ('How are you sleeping', 'Can I look at your tongue?'), dreading the hour ahead listening to Owen rehash the same old story, when he surprised her. 'I'm moving,' he said, out of nowhere.

'Really? Good for you.' Owen had always been so adamant that he wouldn't be driven out of his home despite the impossibility of the situation.

'I've got a little house on Springfield Lane. Only renting but it's a start.'

'What's brought this on?' Katie asked.

'What you said to me last week. About negative energy destroying you if you're not careful.'

'I've been saying that to you for months.'

Owen ran a hand through his hair. 'I think I just started listening. Anyway, I should thank you. As soon as I made the decision I started to feel much more positive. Just like you said I would. Like I was taking control.'

Katie felt like she imagined a proud mother must feel watching her infant cycling without the training wheels on for the first time. 'Gosh,' she said. 'Well done.' It was amazing to think she might have made a difference to someone's life, however small.

She managed to hold on to that feeling even when Owen went on to tell her that while packing up the house he had thrown every one of his wife's possessions over the garden wall, mostly after defacing or damaging them in some way. One of them, a small Moorcroft vase that Miriam's mother had given her when she was first married, and which he had found in a box in the attic, had smashed through her and Ted's conservatory window.

'Wasn't it worth rather a lot?' Katie asked, not quite knowing what to say.

'Serves them right. I saw them snogging in there one

night when I looked over the wall. Bold as anything, didn't care that the blinds weren't drawn,' Owen said, through gritted teeth.

Katie laughed. 'I meant the vase.'

'Oh, probably.'

Despite Owen's declaration that he had moved on, it looked as if they were going to go back along the same well-trodden path they always did ('She's a bitch, he's a bastard'), but when Katie asked him to describe his new home and what he was intending to do with it, Owen's mood changed and his new-found optimism returned. They spent the rest of the hour discussing colours and flooring, and even though Katie would still rather have retired to the other room while the needles worked their magic, as she did with her other clients, the hour passed much more pleasantly than usual.

'Maybe,' Katie ventured, when the session was over, 'once you're settled into your new place you'll be able to find a job.' She didn't say what she really wanted to say, which was 'And then you can pay me back all the money you owe me,' but the thought was implicit.

'Yes,' Owen said, smiling. 'Who knows? Maybe I will.'

After he had left, she put on her jacket and drove to Homebase on the outskirts of Lincoln where she picked up swatch cards for pastel paints, then went to the newsagent where she bought several interior-design magazines. No harm in getting a few ideas.

'I'm tired. Maybe we should just skip it – have an early night.'

'But I've got the tickets,' Stephanie said, smiling

innocently. 'You've been going on about wanting to see it for ages. I thought it'd be a surprise.'

'It is. It was a really nice thought but I don't think I can face it. Tell you what, why don't you see if they'll exchange them for another night?'

Stephanie forced herself to pull a hurt expression. 'But Cassie's coming over to babysit. Come on, James, I hardly ever go out these days.'

James rubbed a hand across his forehead. 'OK,' he said. 'What time does it start?'

Victory. What James couldn't know, of course, was that Stephanie was fully aware that he had already sat through the new Will Smith blockbuster earlier that week with Katie because Katie had mentioned in one of her phone calls that they had gone to the cinema to take his mind off the dinner-party débâcle and had added that James had said afterwards that he would rather slit his eyes with razor blades than sit through that shit again.

'Excellent,' Stephanie had said. 'I'll book tickets.'

'You know,' he said now, as he and Stephanie were about to leave home, 'I've heard it's not as good as it looks.'

'Where did you hear that?' Stephanie said.

'Oh, I just read a bad review somewhere. I don't remember where.'

'Well, everything gets a few bad reviews. When can you last remember a film that only got good reviews?'

She knew he was dying to say, 'It's shit, OK? I've seen it,' but that he couldn't because then he'd have to explain why he hadn't mentioned to her on the phone during the week that he'd been to the cinema and then make up a story about who he'd gone with. James always affected to have no social life in Lower Shippingham, beyond a quick pint in the pub with Malcolm or Simon. Instead he grunted an 'I suppose so,' and shuffled his arm into his jacket sleeve reluctantly.

Once there, Stephanie wondered if she was punishing herself more than she was him. The film was interminable. Only James's fidgeting and sighing kept her spirits up. At one point, about an hour and a half in, he leaned over and whispered in her ear that maybe they should cut their losses and go for a pizza, but she had said no, she wanted to stay and see the end 'in case it gets any better'.

'It's not going to get any better now,' he said huffily.

'How do you know that?' she said. 'It might.'

'Oh, well,' she said once the film had finished and they were in a taxi on the way home, 'who could have known it would be so bad?'

James said nothing.

'And then he rolled his eyes all back in his head.'

Stephanie could hear Finn talking into the telephone as she ran down the stairs. She had heard it ring from the bathroom and had shouted, 'It's OK, I'll get it,' but to no avail. She had no idea who he was talking to – it was as likely to be a telesales representative as anyone he knew: he was happy to regale anyone who'd listen with the gory details of Spike's untimely end.

'His tongue hanged out,' he was saying, as she took the receiver out of his hand.

'Who is it?' she hissed.

'Granny,' Finn said, rolling his eyes as if to say who else would it be.

'Go and start that project you've got to do on the Vikings. I'll come and help you in a minute,' Stephanie said, her hand over the mouthpiece. 'Hi, Pauline, how are you?'

'Oh, all the better for hearing about Finn's friend's hamster,' her mother-in-law said, laughing.

Stephanie, flying in the face of cliché, was fond of her husband's parents. The first time she had gone home with James — months after they had started seeing each other and after a lot of protesting from James that he didn't really 'do family' — he had been apologetic on the way down, telling her that the house was small and his mother and father's tastes parochial. She'd laughed at him; he hadn't yet met her family and he seemed to have decided they must be upper-middle class and wealthy. He was wrong, as it happened, they were lower-middle class and impoverished, but she had later come to realize that his assumptions said more about him than they did about her. He was ashamed of where he came from.

Such was the vibrancy of the picture James had painted that when they pulled up outside the neat little semi-detached house Stephanie had thought they must be in the wrong place. OK, so it was on an estate where all the houses were the same, but they were well cared-for. She looked round for the graffiti, the feral children, the drug pushers she had thought were implicit in James's descriptions of where he had grown up, but all she saw was the odd garden gnome and a bit of stone cladding. James's mother Pauline and his father John had flung open the front door, then almost suffocated their only son with hugs, and had welcomed Stephanie as if she was the daughter they had always wanted.

'They're small people,' James had said to her, in the car on the way home. 'Small people with small lives.'

'They're nice,' she'd said, feeling suddenly protective of Pauline in particular. 'They're really proud of you, you know.'

'I know they are,' he'd said, mellowing slightly. 'I'm the only one of their friends' kids to go to university. It gives them something to boast about.'

'Well, I thought they were lovely,' she'd said, and turned up the radio, indicating that the conversation was over.

In the years that followed Stephanie would seize every opportunity to spend time with her in-laws. Pauline was so exactly like a mother should be, warm and caring and nurturing, always hovering in the background with a teapot and a plate of biscuits, ready to spoil you. Stephanie had no doubt that her own parents loved her but they were undemonstrative. Interested, but emotionally distant. Pauline was all hugs and kisses and endearments, soft and cuddly like a giant walking, talking teddy bear.

John wasn't much different. He was totally sentimental, instantly moved to tears by a story in the paper about a lost child or an abandoned puppy, an attribute James found embarrassing but which made Stephanie want to get him in a bear-hug.

When Finn was born John was inconsolable, holding his first grandson and sobbing and laughing at the same time. Stephanie's parents, drowning in an abundance of grandchildren already provided by her older brother and sisters were there, too, but they chatted to Finn dispassionately, as if they were calling him up for mortgage advice. Stephanie had always longed for a bit more unbridled emotion in her life. And now she had it.

The last thing she wanted to have to do now was to break it to Pauline and John that her and James's relationship was over, although she supposed they would have to know some time. Meanwhile she knew Pauline was hurt that James had never invited them up to see him in Lincolnshire and she had decided the time had come to put that right. She felt uncomfortable using them as pawns in her campaign against their son but she would make sure they never found out – in fact, she was determined to try to make sure they had a good time.

'I've had an idea,' she said now, into the telephone. 'James is always saying how nice it'd be if you went up to see him in the country . . .'

'Is he really?' Pauline said, and the note of pleasure in her voice sent a shard of guilt through Stephanie. She wondered if she could go through with this. She wished she could be certain that James would be kind to his parents when they turned up. She made an on-the-spot decision that it would be too cruel having them show up as a surprise, even though that would give James the biggest headache. But she knew too that if she told him they were coming he would ring them and tell them he was too busy and that they should come up to London one weekend instead.

'So,' she said, thinking on her feet, 'maybe you and John would fancy a couple of days in Lincoln. We'd book you into a nice hotel in the city centre, because, you know, the flat above the surgery is a bit small. That way, when James is working you wouldn't be stuck in Lower Shippingham, you could have a look round the cathedral and the old town. It'd be like a holiday.' Perfect. They'd be close enough to James to make him uneasy but not so close that he would ever think they'd come into contact with Katie. Obviously, the truth was that Katie would make sure they did but, of course, James shouldn't know that.

'Will you and Finn be there?' Pauline asked hopefully.

Stephanie had often wondered if Pauline thought she was a bad wife, abandoning James for half the week, but if she did she would never have said so. 'Finn has to be at school.'

'Maybe we should wait until the holidays – then we could all go together.'

'Tell you what,' Stephanie said, 'why don't you come on here afterwards? James can drive you down and you could stay for a couple of days. We'd all love that. We could do it next week.'

'Gosh,' Pauline said, sounding like an excitable school-girl. 'It sounds lovely. Let me just talk to John and I'll ring you back.'

Stephanie put the phone down. It had been almost too easy.

19

'What do you mean they're coming up on Monday?'

James knew that he was shouting and he knew that Stephanie must be thinking his reaction was a bit over the top but he couldn't help himself. This couldn't be happening. Stephanie had told him his mother had brought up the fact that he never invited them up to see him and that she had felt so sorry for her she had suggested they go up to Lincoln this week.

'What else could I have done?' she said. 'I think she thinks you're ashamed of her and she just seemed so down about it all. It won't hurt you, will it, having them around for a few days?'

'But I'm working,' he replied, clutching at straws. 'I don't have time to worry about entertaining people.'

'Exactly,' Stephanie said. 'That's why I've booked them into a hotel in Lincoln. They can potter around and amuse themselves. If you're working in the evenings there are loads of restaurants they can go to, or the theatre. It'll make them feel wanted and you'll probably only have to see them once. Then they can come down here and I can make a fuss of them.'

'I suppose,' James said grudgingly. He could see that Stephanie was right. Plus, doing it that way would mean he wouldn't have to worry about them fishing for an invitation again for years. He sometimes felt bad about the way he was with his parents. He loved them, he really did, and over the years he had come to appreciate how much they had tried to do for him. But, somehow, whenever he saw them he found himself reverting to being a sullen teenager, snapping at his mother's attempts to talk to him about his work and snootily putting her right whenever she used a word incorrectly. He was much better at loving them from a distance. If he allowed Stephanie to go ahead with her plan it was a win-win situation all round: his parents could tell their friends that their prodigal son had invited them up to stay for a few days and he could feel good about the gesture while claiming work commitments prevented him from meeting up with them in the evenings. Actually, the more he thought about it, the more this idea of Steph's seemed like genius.

'You're right,' he said, smiling for the first time since she had broken the news. 'It's a great idea.'

Katie spent Saturday doing things for herself. That was how it was going to be from now on, she had decided. Herself first and everyone else could wait. She had always put the needs of other people before her own – James, her friends, her clients, someone she'd met in the bank once. It didn't matter who they were, her natural instinct was to help them. 'You're a pushover,' her mother had said to her, after she had lent some money she really couldn't spare to a neighbour who, she knew deep down, was never going to even think about paying it back. Well, not any more.

She started off by having her hair coloured and

straightened. James adored her long blonde curls. They were the first thing he had noticed about her, he had told her. He loved winding them round his fingers and would spend what seemed like hours absorbed in them. The chemicals hurt like hell but it would be worth it to see the look on his face. To be honest the poker-straight look really didn't suit her but she didn't care. It was only hair. It would grow out in a couple of months. She had considered going black – she had always wanted to be dark and mysterious – but that was probably a step too far. She didn't want to repel James before she was ready. So she let the hairstylist persuade her that a deep red tint, a fiery-goddess look, as he had put it, was the right thing to do. Straight red hair, just like Stephanie's. She laughed when she saw her reflection in the mirror. That'd freak him out.

Once her hair was finished she was exhausted by the effort of sitting still for so many hours, so she went downstairs to the beauty salon and was lucky enough to find there had been a cancellation. She treated herself to a massage and a glycolic facial, which left her skin rosy and glowing like a baby's. On the way home she bought magazines – trash about celebrities and their weight problems and who was going out with who – and organic sausages with ready-made mash for dinner. She texted James to say she was going over to her mother's, then took the phone out of its socket and turned off her mobile. She poured herself a glass of wine, fed Stanley a piece of steak that James had put in the freezer for himself, and which she had defrosted this morning, then curled up in the big armchair in the living room.

Stephanie had called earlier to unveil the next step in the plan. Katie could remember the day James had told her he no longer had any contact with his parents. They hadn't been seeing each other long and she had been touched by how much the estrangement seemed to pain him. He had tried everything, he'd said, to patch things up, but his mother and father wouldn't relent so he had had to give up. He had had to let it go, he'd said, looking saddened, otherwise it would have eaten him up. When she had pressed him to tell her exactly what the fall-out had been about he had concocted an elaborate story about his mother having taken Stephanie's side in the divorce because she felt he had been selfish to insist on spending half the week up north. 'She said she thought I cared more about my career than my family.'

'But the only reason you moved to London in the first place was for *Stephanie's* career!' Katie had exclaimed indignantly.

'Exactly,' James had said. 'I thought about saying that to her but I didn't want to look like I was trying to blame the whole thing on Steph. It was both our fault, we were equally to blame.'

'You're such a nice person,' Katie had said, and thinking about that now she laughed out loud.

'So, we ended up having a flaming row. Mum told me what a disappointment I was, and Dad joined in, saying I'd let everyone down by allowing my marriage to break up. I left before I said something I regretted and I haven't spoken to them since.'

Katie had stroked his hair. 'You poor thing.'

'As long as Finn can see his grandparents, that's all I

care about now. I'm a grown-up. I can live without my parents.'

'I couldn't stand not to see my mum,' Katie had said. 'I hope Stephanie appreciates what you did for her.'

James had laughed a forced laugh which, she had thought at the time, was tinged with sadness. 'Oh, I doubt it.'

On a couple of other occasions when he had mentioned his childhood or his family she had got the distinct impression that his parents were very demanding, that he'd always felt their expectations had not been fulfilled.

'But you're a vet,' she'd said. 'It doesn't get much more impressive than that.'

'They don't think so. To be honest, I don't know what I'd have to do to impress them, really.'

So, when Stephanie had told her that James had a long conversation with both his doting parents at least once a week and that Pauline, his mother, always referred to him proudly as 'my son the vet' to anyone who would listen, she had been a little taken aback. She could understand now how important it was to him that his parents never came up to visit: it would blow apart his double life – but it had been such an elaborate lie, and he had told it with such relish. Stephanie had said they were good people, that they had to stage-manage next week very carefully to avoid Pauline and John getting hurt, and Katie was more than happy to go along with that. She had no desire to be mean to people she didn't even know and it seemed to her that they were just two more victims of James's deception. She felt sorry for them.

20

Fluffy O'Leary was pegged out on the operating table, tongue flopping out of the side her mouth while the anaesthetic did its work. It was a routine operation and one that James had performed hundreds of times before. Admittedly Fluffy was older than the average cat who came in to be spayed, but her owner, Amanda O'Leary, had felt strongly that she had to indulge Fluffy's natural female urges and allow her to have at least one litter of kittens before her womanhood was cruelly stripped away from her. Fluffy had duly been mated with some close male relative who was deemed to be worthy and had produced a brood of underweight sickly-looking kittens with red squinty eyes and runny noses, a symptom, no doubt, of too much inbreeding.

James had never been overly fond of Fluffy, who was about as unfluffy a cat as you could get and who had a tendency to bite and scratch whenever he went near her, but he couldn't help admiring how lithe her muscular form was so soon after having had five babies. Pity women aren't like that, he caught himself thinking, then chastised himself. Had he really become that shallow? Yes, probably, he told himself.

He had never quite got used to Steph's stretchmarks and the soft pouchiness of her stomach since she had had Finn. God, it would be so much easier being an animal. You rarely saw a male dog who didn't feel like mating because the female had a bit of cellulite on her haunches. Mostly, with Steph, though, things had changed because she had suddenly seemed so aware of what he might be thinking. She had taken to getting changed with her back to him or even in the bathroom with the door closed. It was her self-consciousness he found offputting, not the changes to her body. It had made his arousal seem dirty and unwanted, something she was embarrassed by. Katie, on the other hand, was still uninhibited. A female dog, he thought, wouldn't bat an eyelid if her mate shagged half the bitches in the country. Animals so often got it right where humans failed.

He often found his mind wandering in this way during procedures and would suddenly realize that the nurse was handing him the suture to sew up the incision and the whole thing was over without him really even noticing. The first time it had happened he had worried for days about what might have gone wrong. Now he just accepted that this was his way of getting through the tedium. He scrubbed his hands, checked that Fluffy was coming round satisfactorily and headed upstairs to Reception to make a phone call before he had to greet his next patient.

His parents were arriving on Monday afternoon and he needed to ring Sally at the other surgery and get her to cancel his appointments so that he could go over and see them and still get home early enough so that Katie wouldn't wonder where he was. He had booked them tickets to see *The Importance of Being Earnest* at the Theatre Royal for Monday evening, and had told them he was on call so he wouldn't be able to join them. Of course, they understood that it wouldn't do to have his beeper go off in the middle of the performance. Now he just had to think of some way to get out of seeing them on Tuesday evening and he was in the clear. He would take a long lunch break on Tuesday and drive them to a pub somewhere, then on Wednesday he would pick them up at their hotel and ferry them down to London. He knew they'd be disappointed at not being taken to Lower Shippingham to see where he worked and meet his colleagues, but that would quickly be outweighed by their delight at seeing him at all and the knowledge that he'd made an effort to spend time with them. He was almost looking forward to it.

'I just saw Sam McNeil,' Sally said, as soon as she realized who she was talking to. 'She's still going on about you buying the food for your dinner party from Le Joli Poulet and pretending you'd cooked it. God, what did you feel like when they found out?'

James remembered why he didn't really like Sally and why he must get round to replacing her. 'Can you cancel everything I've got on Monday afternoon? See if Simon or Malcolm can handle any appointments that are hard to reschedule.'

'Why? What are you doing?' she said, and he thought, no, I really *must* sack this girl, she's awful.

'That's none of your business,' he snapped. 'Just do it.'

He put down the phone without saying goodbye, his good mood punctured.

Stephanie and Natasha's dealings with Mandee Martin had so far proved to be much more straightforward than those with their other two clients for the BAFTA awards. Mandee had lost the *y* and added the two *e*s so as to differentiate herself from another girl called Mandy who was also famous for no one knew quite what. Both girls were trying to lose their surnames and become known by their first name alone. At present Mandy with a *y* was winning having gained two headlines in the last few weeks: 'Mandy's Randy' above a story in which she bemoaned her lack of a boyfriend and 'Handy Mandy', in which she had dressed up in dungarees and very little else and gone to the shop to buy some paint. Mandee could see that there was still potential for 'Mandee's Dandy' if she could get herself photographed with a dapper young man on her arm, or maybe 'Bandy Mandee' although that didn't sound like it would be too flattering. Neither Natasha nor Stephanie could understand why she was paying for the advice of a stylist but Mandy with a *y* apparently had one, so that was probably the reason. Mandee's brief was that she needed to wear something that would get her in the papers. It didn't matter what it was (a balaclava and a bowling ball with a sparkler sticking out of the top and 'BOMB' written on the side, Natasha had suggested laughing, but Mandee didn't get it). Stephanie wasn't really comfortable with having Mandee as a client, but Natasha had assured her there was no danger of any journalist ever asking Mandee who her stylist was so they should just take the money and run.

Currently they were in Agent Provocateur trying to find the smallest piece of underwear that could be worn on its own without Mandee getting arrested. Stephanie was hoping that when Finn grew up no one would tell him his mother had once encouraged a nineteen-year-old girl to go out for the evening more or less naked.

'Maybe you should buy some of this stuff,' Natasha said, holding up an admittedly very pretty thong and balcony-bra combination. 'That'd give James something to think about.'

'He probably wouldn't notice,' Stephanie said glumly.

'Apparently,' Mandee piped up, 'you should never let your man leave home without giving him a blow-job first. That way, even if he meets a gorgeous woman, he's not going to stray because he'll be thinking about what he's got at home.'

'You really should be a marriage-guidance counsellor,' Stephanie said. 'Men'd be queuing up to take their wives to Relate if they thought you were going to give them advice like that.'

'Well, that's according to some magazine I read.'

'Let's have this conversation again a few years down the line when you've got a couple of kids and your husband's idea of grooming is pulling the hairs out of his nostrils with your tweezers.'

'He doesn't?' Natasha looked at Stephanie aghast.

'You know Martin does it too. Your relationship just hasn't degenerated far enough for him to do it in front of you yet.'

'You have to work at relationships. Make an effort.' Mandee stood hands on hips, oblivious to the fact that passers-by in the street outside could get a great view of her standing there in her underwear.

Stephanie bristled. 'Exactly how many relationships have you been in, Mandee? And I mean relationships, not a quick one with some bloke whose name you haven't even bothered to ask.'

'Steph.' Natasha shot her a warning look.

Mandee was looking unfazed. 'No, it's OK,' she said. 'Actually, I've been with my boyfriend since I was fourteen. I've never slept with anyone else.'

'Really?' Stephanie flushed. 'Shit, sorry.'

'Don't worry. Everyone just assumes I'm a slapper. I'm used to it.'

'And do you . . . you know . . . every time, before he goes out?' Natasha asked.

'God, no. I was just telling you what I read in a magazine.'

'Mandee, do you really want to go out dressed like that? I mean, can't we find you a nice dress or something?' Stephanie rubbed her eyes. They were going to have no clients left soon if she kept on offending them all.

'Do you think maybe you should take a couple of weeks off?' Natasha asked tentatively as their taxi sped up Camden High Street.

'And do what?' Stephanie snapped.

'I just think maybe you need a holiday, that's all.'

'You mean you're worried I'm upsetting our clients?'

'Well,' Natasha said, 'there is that, yes.'

'I don't need to be lectured on relationships by a nineteen-year-old girl.'

'I know. She was just trying to be nice. And, even if she wasn't, she's paying us so we can't start picking fights with her.'

Stephanie knew she was behaving like a sulky child

but she couldn't help herself. 'By "we" you mean me, I take it?'

'I mean both of us,' Natasha said diplomatically. 'I know they're annoying, Mandee and Santana and Meredith, but it's only a few weeks till the BAFTAs so we should just think of the money and bite our tongues.'

Stephanie exhaled loudly. 'I know you're right but the last thing I need is time off now, OK? Maybe it was a mistake, dragging this thing with James out like this. Maybe I should just have told him to get out the minute I found out.'

'Are you telling me you didn't get a tiny bit of pleasure from the dinner-party fiasco?'

Stephanie managed a smile. 'Well, maybe a little.'

'Just imagine his face when what's-her-name – Sam – read out what was on the receipt.'

Stephanie laughed. 'Katie said he looked like a dog who'd been caught red-handed, eating someone's birthday cake.'

'I love that he tried to deny it at first.'

'Poor James,' Stephanie said, without feeling. 'And it's only going to get worse.'

21

James had found the past few days almost therapeutic. Away from the humiliating scene of the food incident – and, indeed, anyone who knew about it – it had been almost possible to forget that it had ever happened. He could go about his normal day-to-day business in London without having to listen to people's jovial comments about what to him was a major source of embarrassment. That was the trouble with living in a small village: everyone knew everyone else's business. It would be forgotten soon, some other piece of local gossip would rise up to eclipse it, but for now it felt painful being the butt of the joke. He had never been any good at laughing at himself.

Following his conversation with Sally, he had called Malcolm and then Simon, and told them he had decided to get rid of her. They had each protested that he had no grounds to do so. Besides, she worked hard and was invaluably reliable. 'She even came in on Christmas Day last year when we had that emergency,' Malcolm had said angrily.

James, irritated by their lack of support, had dug his heels in even further. It was his practice, he said imperiously. He was the one with the power to hire and fire.

'So why did you bother to ask my opinion?' Simon had said.

'You can't just sack people randomly,' Malcolm had

continued to object. 'There are procedures. Verbal and written warnings, that kind of thing.'

'Don't be ridiculous,' James had replied. 'This isn't Goldman Sachs.'

Sally, when he'd called her to break the bad news, had been incredulous. 'You're kidding, right?' she'd said, seemingly thinking at first that maybe this was some kind of bizarre practical joke. When it had become obvious that James was, in fact, deadly serious, she had given way to tears of indignation. 'But what have I done wrong?' she'd cried. 'Just tell me what it is and I can try to put it right.'

James had stuck to his guns. It wasn't her work so much, it was her attitude. He had received several complaints from clients, he'd said, thinking on his feet. This wasn't true, of course. Sally was generally well thought-of in the local community.

'From who?' she'd asked.

'I can't tell you that. It's confidential.'

'But it's so unfair,' Sally had wailed. 'Do Malcolm and Simon know?'

'We're all in agreement about this, I'm afraid. You can work out a month's notice, obviously, to give you time to look for another job.'

Once off the phone Sally had stormed into Malcolm's room. Before she'd had a chance to say anything he'd put his hands in the air to stop her. 'It's nothing to do with me or Simon. I'd sue him for unfair dismissal, if I were you. There are laws about this kind of thing.'

'I would never do that,' Sally had said. 'I'll just look for another job and then go quietly. I just wish I understood what I'm meant to have done.'

'You and me both,' Malcolm had said, giving her a hug.

Half an hour after he'd made the phone call James was feeling like he might have overreacted a little. After all, Sally had only been having a joke with him: she wasn't to know she'd hit a raw nerve. He considered calling her back and telling her that he hadn't meant it, or that he'd found out the complaints had been made up so, of course, he had changed his mind, but he felt like he had gone past the point of no return when he'd said her attitude stank so he decided he was better off just leaving things be. He would give her a good reference and he was sure she'd have no trouble finding another job. Besides, he would look weak in front of Malcolm and Simon if he backed down and that would never do.

With the twin horrors of both Sally and the dinner-party fall-out, not to mention his visiting parents, James felt a sense of impending doom on Saturday that threatened to completely overshadow his precious day off. It was a feeling he didn't think he had experienced since school when the last few glorious days of the summer holidays would be wasted, given over to depression at the thought of the new term.

He ended up staying in bed far too late, like a sullen teenager, emerging from the bedroom at eleven thirty to find Finn sitting huffily on the top step of the stairs, just outside the bedroom door. 'I thought you were taking me to the park,' he said accusingly. 'I've been waiting here for one hour and eleven minutes . . .' he looked at his watch. '. . . and twenty-seven seconds.'

James felt a rush of guilt. He saw Finn little enough as it was and he had indeed promised to play football with him in Regent's Park if the weather was fine. 'Well, why didn't you wake me up?' he said, ruffling Finn's hair.

Finn squirmed out of reach. 'Because Mum told me not to. She said you must be tired if you were sleeping in this late so I should leave you alone.'

'Tell you what,' James said, 'next time you wake me up anyway. I promise I won't be cross, however tired I am. OK?'

Finn tried to stay looking angry. 'OK,' he said.

'Now, let's go and find Mummy and see if she'll let us take a picnic. What do you think?'

'Just me and you,' said Finn, who loved his mother but was desperate for a bit of father-son bonding . . .

'Of course,' James said, confident that he had won his son back over. 'Just us.'

22

The journey from Cheltenham to Lincoln by train took three and a half hours and involved a change at Nottingham. Pauline had studied the timetable and there didn't seem to be any quicker or easier way to do it so she had stocked up on sandwiches and bottles of water for emergencies and made sure John had kept the review and sports sections from the day before's papers to keep him occupied. She was intending to finish the Maeve Binchy she had started a couple of days ago. They would get a cab from home to the station, which was a bit of an unnecessary expense but John couldn't really manage the bus these days with his knee. They would get there in good time to buy their tickets and find the platform without needing to panic. It would be an adventure.

They were seasoned travellers on the route up to London. They visited James, Stephanie and their grandson maybe three or four times a year, usually spending one night in the guest room. It was years since they had stayed away from home for any longer – Stephanie had persuaded them to have two nights in London this time because she was worried they'd be tired out after the long car journey from Lincoln. That along with the two nights they were going to spend at the hotel in Lincoln added up to four nights away, almost a proper holiday. Jean from next door was going to go in and feed the canary.

Stephanie had found the hotel – typical Stephanie that she had wanted to book it for them to save them the bother. Pauline considered herself very lucky with her daughter-in-law. She had friends who had barely managed to sustain a relationship with their sons once they had got married, but Pauline had liked Steph from the first moment they'd met, and fortunately that affection had always been reciprocated.

Indeed, Pauline sometimes felt that Stephanie was keener on her company than James was. She could understand why James had never invited them up to Lincolnshire before – although, obviously, they had been up there several times when the whole family was still living there, and stayed in the large, rambling house in a village near to where James's practice was. Now that that house had been sold to pay for the London home, half the size and without the land, James was having to live in the flat above the surgery and, of course, there was no room to put his parents up. The hotel idea really was a stroke of genius, and Steph and James had been so generous offering to pay for it because there was no way Pauline and John could have paid for it themselves. Plus he'd bought them seats at the theatre. She really was very fortunate.

When James had arrived home on Sunday night Katie had made sure she was standing in the doorway to greet him looking sweet and soft and unthreatening.

'What have you done to your hair?' he'd said, looking horrified.

Katie, who had had a few days to get used to it, had

almost forgotten what a shock it would be to him. 'I just fancied a change,' she'd said.

'But why red? I love your blonde hair.'

'You'll get used to it,' she'd said lightly, and he had been huffy and said he didn't want to get used to it, he had liked her as she was. 'Don't you like red hair?' she'd asked, and he'd changed the subject.

'That top, on the other hand', he'd said, slipping his hand up inside the new low-cut floaty thing she'd bought earlier that day, 'is driving me crazy.'

She'd pushed him away, laughing. 'Later,' she'd said, hoping that, in fact, he might be too tired later. She'd asked him about his week while she poured him a glass of wine and stirred a sweet-potato casserole. She'd quizzed him about what the coming few days held in store for him and he'd said, 'Oh, you know, the usual,' and, of course, had failed to mention his parents' upcoming visit.

Katie had decided she wanted to expand the range of services she offered to her clients and so had signed up for a reflexology evening class at a college in Lincoln. She had been wanting to do something like this for ages but the classes were held on Tuesday nights and James had always persuaded her it would be a shame – 'unfair', she thought she remembered him saying – for her to be out on one of their few evenings together. Now she had decided she was going to do it anyway. She no longer cared what he thought.

James, after making a couple of disgruntled noises ('Really? On Tuesdays? I thought we'd agreed our time together was precious') and having realized she wasn't about to give in as she usually did, had suddenly changed tack. 'It starts this week?' he'd said. 'This Tuesday?'

She'd told him it did, and then he'd asked, 'What time?' and it had occurred to her that he was thinking maybe he could see his parents for dinner, after all. She told him the class began at seven and ended at nine thirty. It was a small white lie. In fact, the session was due to start at seven thirty but she could explain to him later that she'd made a mistake.

They had had an early night and by-numbers sex, and Katie had found herself thinking how strange it was that you could love someone one day and then the next you found it impossible to imagine what you had ever seen in them in the first place. It was like you had been wearing blinkers, and suddenly they were removed, leaving you completely exposed to all your loved one's unattractive and even faintly repugnant qualities.

James, of course, had to face Sally when he arrived at the practice bright and early next morning. He had been mulling over how he would handle it and had decided to be friendly but business-like. He wouldn't be apologetic for the decision he had made. He was expecting Sally to be belligerent, to confront him about the unfairness of it all, but she just looked at him with sad, reproachful eyes and said, 'Good morning,' which was much more unsettling. James's guilt factor edged up a few notches.

He was thankful that his first couple of appointments were home visits. The atmosphere at the surgery was a little tense and it was a relief to get out of there and remind himself why he did this job in the first place.

Malcolm and Simon had been shut away in their rooms when he'd arrived, which was just as well because he had a feeling that they both – Malcolm especially – were upset with him. He would get an advert in for a new receptionist-cum-would-be-veterinary-nurse as soon as possible. Once Sally had gone and a new girl had settled in, things would quickly go back to normal. He had no idea, though, what the etiquette was for asking someone to arrange for an ad to be placed looking for their own replacement. Maybe he could ask Katie to do it as a favour, he thought.

At about ten past one he set off for Lincoln. He had arranged to meet his mum and dad in a small café in the city centre for a late lunch, and then he was intending to take them round the cathedral. An hour or so spent pottering round and then a pot of afternoon tea before he made his excuses and said he had to head back. That should do it.

His mother spotted him before he'd even got his hand on the door handle and was standing up waving frantically as he entered the café. Every time he'd seen her recently she had seemed to be growing smaller. Now, as she rushed over to hug him, she looked minute, a small child in a Marks & Spencer trouser suit. He bent down and kissed the top of her head then held out his hand for his father to shake. John was wearing his age better than his wife. He still looked like the big strong man James remembered from his childhood only with less hair and all of it grey.

'You look tired, love,' Pauline said. Pauline always said this whenever she saw him. Later she would almost certainly ask him whether he was eating enough and whether he shouldn't think about moving down to London permanently to be with Stephanie and Finn. 'You're a family, you should stick together,' she would say, and he would have to stop himself saying, 'Well, tell her she should have stayed up here, then.'

They managed to keep the conversation on neutral and non-confrontational ground throughout their lunch of lasagne and chips: work, the garden, Jimmy the canary ('I wish you could have a look at him, he's gone bald all down one side'). Pauline expressed a desire to come over to Lower Shippingham to give the flat a good clean, which gave him an anxious moment, but he managed to convince her that time wouldn't allow it.

'Oh, I've managed to get out of working tomorrow night, so I've booked us a table at Le Château,' he said, naming one of Lincoln's most fashionable and expensive restaurants. He regretted it immediately. He'd never get a table at such short notice, but he had wanted to make it sound as if the arrangements were already made so that his mother wouldn't suggest eating at the Cross Keys in Lower Shippingham where they were bound to bump into someone he knew who would give the game away about Katie.

'How lovely,' Pauline said, her face lighting up. 'Are you sure you can spare the time?' she added in that irritating way mothers have of making you feel guilty all over again that you were usually too busy to see them.

'I'm looking forward to it,' he said, squeezing her hand. Shit, fuck, bollocks. Who did he know who could pull a favour at Le Château? He had no doubt that Hugh and

Alison Selby-Algernon would be friends with the restaurant's owners, they seemed to be on first-name terms with most of the local movers and shakers, but he couldn't bring himself to call them and ask for help. He hadn't spoken to either them or the others since the fateful dinner party, and although he knew that if he didn't make contact soon the friendships, such as they were, would fizzle out, he couldn't face the teasing to which they would undoubtedly subject him. Plus he couldn't ask anyone who might later bump into Katie and ask her how she'd enjoyed her meal. He would have to take a chance and call the restaurant himself as soon as he was alone.

After a fight over who was paying for lunch (Pauline and John won once James realized that they would be offended if he didn't let them), they ambled over to the cathedral and spent a perfectly pleasant hour looking at the tombs and the frescos, and then had tea in the Cloisters Refectory. At four o'clock James made a show of looking at his watch and said he ought to be hitting the road. The table for the following night, he told them, was booked for seven thirty. He would meet them at their hotel at seven and they could have a drink at the restaurant before they sat down to eat. He feigned disappointment that he wouldn't be able to see them during the day on Tuesday (he had, he told them, agreed to cover some of Simon's appointments in exchange for having the evening free) and left them deciding what they were going to do with the next few hours before *The Importance of Being Earnest* began at seven thirty.

Back at his car he pulled out his mobile phone and

called directory enquiries, who put him straight through to the reservations desk at Le Château.

'I'm sorry, sir, we're fully booked in the evenings for the next two weeks,' the supercilious man, with what James strongly suspected was a fake French accent, said when he had put in his request.

'But it's for my parents. They're elderly. Tomorrow is the only night they can do.'

'May I suggest you bring them in to lunch? We have a table at three.'

'No, it has to be the evening. Oh, forget it,' he said, and rang off. He'd just have to book somewhere else. It didn't matter where, as long as it was far enough away from Lower Shippingham. He'd just tell his parents when he picked them up that there had been a change of plan.

'So apparently he's booked a table at somewhere called Sorrento for seven thirty. It's right by the hotel, he said. Do you know it?' Stephanie had sneaked out to the kitchen to call Katie while Finn was watching CBBC. She couldn't risk saying anything in front of Finn, who had an antenna for secrets. He hated to be left out.

'Never heard of it,' Katie said.

'Well, he's meeting them at the hotel first so they shouldn't be too hard to find. Are you scared?'

'Terrified,' Katie said convincingly.

'Just remember, don't give too much away and don't say anything that'll upset Pauline and John.'

'I know, I know. Just him seeing me ought to be enough to give him a coronary.'

'Exactly,' Stephanie said emphatically. 'And call me when it's over.'

The next day Katie cooked James a large early dinner of chicken wrapped in Parma ham with Jersey Royal potatoes and asparagus. He had almost given himself away when he'd got home from work to find her standing over the stove. 'It's a bit early for me,' he'd said. 'Will it keep warm? Maybe I can eat it later, after you've gone out.'

'Not really,' Katie had said. 'Besides, it's six o'clock. We often eat at this time. And I didn't like to think of you sat here all on your own having beans on toast.'

She plonked the dishes on the table.

'Maybe I'll just have a shower first,' James had said, clearly thinking that if he delayed the start of the meal she would have to leave to get to her class on time, never knowing if he'd finished it or not.

Katie hugged him, steering him towards the table as she did so. 'You've got all evening to have a shower. Sit down with me for a bit.' She watched as he picked at the food on his plate. She pulled a disappointed face. 'Don't you like it?'

'It's great. I told you, I'm not very hungry yet. I had a late lunch.'

At six thirty James was still pushing his food round, eating the occasional small mouthful. Katie cleared away her plate, picked up her bag, kissed him lightly on the forehead and said, 'I have to go. I'll be back by ten at the latest. Are you sure you'll be OK?'

'I was thinking I might go down to the pub for one.'

'Good idea,' she said, and as she left she realized that he hadn't even wished her luck with her class.

She drove into Lincoln and parked up near the hotel. Sorrento was a couple of doors down, a sad-looking Italian with torn tablecloths and half-dead flowers in jars on the tables, their brown leaves drooping into the sugar bowls. A distraught fly buzzed around in the window, trying to find a way out. James had obviously struggled to get a table anywhere decent so last minute.

She sat in the car waiting for him to arrive, trying to go over in her head what she was meant to be doing. She needed James to see her and to see that she had seen him. Ideally she wanted to put him in a position where he'd have to admit that these people were his parents without, of course, anyone giving away the fact that he was still married to Stephanie. They didn't want to blow the major surprise this early on.

She looked at her watch. It was five to seven. Assuming that James had rushed out of the house almost as soon as she had left – pausing only to throw his uneaten dinner in the bin, of course, and to cover it up with other bits of rubbish so that Katie would never guess he hadn't eaten it – then he should be here any minute. She sat low in her seat. She didn't want him to spot her on the way in.

A few moments later and there he was, striding into the hotel foyer with all the confidence in the world. He was still in his work clothes so he had obviously left home in a hurry. Katie waited until he had gone in, then got out of her car and stood pretending to look in the window of a shop fifty metres or so along the street. Her heart was pounding and she felt sick with anticipation. She stood there for what seemed like an age, and then he emerged with two old people in tow, a tiny woman who looked sweet and friendly, and a distinguished, white-haired man. Katie took a deep breath and walked forward: she had to reach them before they got to the restaurant.

23

James thought he was hallucinating at first. He was trying to explain to his parents how the reservation at Le Château had fallen through ('Trouble in the kitchen, they've had to close down for the night' was the best that he could do) and why, instead of just taking them over to the pub in Lower Shippingham, they were now going to eat at what looked like a greasy spoon.

'What kind of trouble?' his mother was saying. 'Hygiene?'

'I've no idea. Probably,' he said, slandering Le Château even further.

'What, though?' Pauline persisted. 'Rats? Cockroaches? It doesn't bear thinking about, really, does it?'

'Well, anyway,' James was saying, 'this place is meant to be very good. Their chef came from Rome,' he added, making things up off the top of his head. 'He's well known in . . .'

A woman who looked just like Katie was walking towards them. Paranoia, he thought, was making him see things. The woman was staring straight at him. She really did look a lot like Katie and, of course, Katie was in Lincoln this evening, although her class would be under way by now. Nevertheless he tried to usher Pauline and John along but he couldn't seem to get them to move at more than a snail's pace.

'In where, dear?' Pauline was saying.

The woman was still heading his way. She had Katie's newly dyed red hair – which, by the way, was still making him feel rather unsettled. When he'd woken up this morning she had had her back to him and he had thought she was Stephanie, and it had taken him a moment to work out where he was and who he was with. She was wearing the clothes Katie had been wearing when she'd left the house, the flowing pink skirt and the white T-shirt with the soft baby pink mohair hoodie over the top. Shit, he thought. It's Katie.

There was a moment before she spoke when he felt as if he was moving very fast in a tunnel. He could hear the blood whooshing round in his head and he wondered, briefly, if he might black out. His mother was wittering on, something about Italian food and how you couldn't go wrong with it, except for sometimes when they got a bit carried away with the garlic, and he thought briefly about turning round and simply walking off in the other direction before Katie could catch him.

'James?'

Too late.

He raised his eyebrows at her as if she might somehow understand telepathically what he was asking her to do. This was it. This was the moment when both Katie and his parents would find out about his double life.

'Hello,' he said, in a voice so falsely jovial he sounded a little insane. 'What are you doing here?'

His parents had stopped and were smiling at this woman, who was obviously a friend of their son's.

'I've got my evening class, remember?' Katie said, in a

tone that gave nothing away. 'Only I got the time wrong. It starts at seven thirty, not seven. So, I was just walking around, killing time.'

He waited for her to say more, to say, 'What the hell are you doing here when I just left you at home eating dinner?' but for some reason she didn't.

'I'm just having a quick dinner with Pauline and John here,' he said, gesturing towards the restaurant. If he could just get in there, away from her, everything might be OK. He would have time to conjure up a plausible story. Something about old family friends and phoning out of the blue. He started to move away, hoping his parents would take the hint and follow, but his mother, of course, was not going to miss an opportunity to say hello to one of his friends.

'I'm Pauline,' she said, 'James's mum, and this is John, his dad.'

Katie just stood there looking at them all. There was still time to save the situation. OK, so he had lied to her about being estranged from his parents but he'd think of something. Just as long as she didn't say, 'Hi, I'm Katie, I'm his girlfriend.'

'This is Katie,' he blurted out. 'She lives in the village.' He looked at Katie and gave an almost imperceptible shake of his head. She would know what it meant – don't say anything – and, hopefully, sweet, unsuspecting Katie would still trust him enough to give him the benefit of the doubt. She wasn't the sort of woman who would ever have a public confrontation.

Luckily, she said nothing. She just smiled sweetly at his mother.

'Right,' he said, clapping his hands. 'We'd better go – don't want to be late for our table. 'Bye, Katie, nice to see you.'

He moved off towards the restaurant praying that she would just go away. If she did, if she was really that loving and innocent and generous that she would let him get away with whatever he was getting away with and be content to wait until later to hear an explanation, he swore to himself that he would make it up to her. He would never deceive her again. He kept his fingers crossed as he walked away and then he heard: 'Well, it was nice to meet you.'

'You too, dear,' his mother said.

James dared to look round just as Katie was walking off. She looked back briefly and frowned at him, out of sight of his mum and dad, as if to say, 'What's going on?', and he pulled what he hoped was a 'trust-me' face before ushering his parents through the door of Sorrento.

'She seemed nice. Who was she again?'

'Oh, just some woman from the village. She brings her dog into the surgery sometimes.'

James could feel that his heart was still on overdrive. Jesus, that had been close.

Concentrating on Reflexology Class One had not been easy. Katie had arrived a few minutes late, having got lost trying to find the college. Her head was all over the place, and she had turned left instead of right and by the time she had worked out where she'd gone wrong, she had been on the dual carriageway heading out of the city.

Once she'd reached the classroom she had muttered apologies to the lecturer, who was already in full flow with his introductory speech, smiled hesitantly at her new classmates and taken a seat at the back. She'd felt elated in one way, that she had pulled it off, that she had put James on the back foot and left him stewing about how he was going to handle the consequences, but at the same time the whole thing had made her uneasy. If their meeting had been truly accidental, if she hadn't known what she knew, then she had no doubt she would have introduced herself to Pauline and John as James's girl-friend and the whole sorry story would have come out. She couldn't believe James was stupid enough to have woven this elaborate web of lies in the first place. How could he ever have thought it would have a happy ending for any of the parties concerned? The truth was, she knew now, he had never been thinking about anyone other than himself. Well, she'd unsettled him now. That was a good thing.

She'd tried to concentrate on what the lecturer was saying and on the complicated diagrams of the human anatomy that had accompanied his talk. She had to keep her wits about her for her confrontation with James when she got home. She needed to be indignant about the way he had lied to her, to press for a satisfactory explanation without even giving a hint that she was aware of what was really going on. The one thing she knew was that he would never offer up the truth unless she actually presented him with it.

By the time she got home James was already there. He leaped out of his armchair before she had even had time to close the front door behind her. 'I can explain,' he said.

Remember, Katie thought, be sweet, innocent Katie. Don't push it too far. 'Go on,' she said. 'I'm listening.'

James had obviously been planning his speech and she decided to let him deliver it uninterrupted.

'I couldn't tell you,' he said. 'I wanted to, but I couldn't. The truth, the absolute truth, is that my mum got in touch with me recently. She said she was sorry about how she'd been, and she wanted us to try and put it behind us. I invited them up to see if we could sort things out.'

He paused, and Katie wasn't sure if he had finished or not. He seemed to be waiting for her to say something.

'But that's great. I just don't understand what all the secrecy was about.'

'Because I haven't told them about you. That's why I had them stay in Lincoln, not over here. You see, I think it's a big step for them to accept that it's not my fault my marriage is over. I don't think in a million years they could cope with me telling them I was already with someone new. Not yet, anyway. They'd always be thinking that maybe we'd got together before Steph and I split up, that maybe you were the cause. And I'd really hate for them to have bad feelings towards you.'

She had to give it to him, he was good. Katie put a hand on his forearm. 'But why didn't you just tell me that? I would have understood. I'd just have been happy for you that you were patching things up with them.'

James looked at her like a grateful puppy. 'Yes, you would have, wouldn't you? I'm so sorry, darling. I under-estimate you. It's just ... well, it's just that I'm not used to being with someone who's so supportive and kind.'

'But I thought we didn't have secrets from each other,' Katie just about managed to say, without a hint of sarcasm.

'I know, I know, you're right. But sometimes I forget how amazing you are. You know, after all those years with Steph. She would never have been so understanding.'

'Well, I think it's great,' Katie said. 'And one day you'll feel able to tell them and we can have them to stay and start being a real family.'

'Definitely,' James said, putting his arms round her. She could feel through his shirt that he was dripping with sweat.

24

Pauline and John's visit to London was over, Stephanie felt, too soon. As she put them in a taxi to Paddington on Friday morning she found herself thinking how sad it was that she was going to lose them as in-laws and she felt her eyes well up as she hugged Pauline goodbye. Pull yourself together, she thought. They'll still be Finn's grandparents; you'll see them just as much as you ever did.

Pauline, especially, had been full of their trip to Lincoln, how kind James had been, and how much time he'd been able to spend with them despite being so busy. Stephanie was a little disappointed that she didn't mention the nice ladyfriend of James's that they had met so that she could have quizzed James about who it was just to put him on the spot. She had heard all the details of the meeting, and James's subsequent cover-up, from Katie, of course.

Finn had been spoilt rotten for two days and was hyper with sugar and attention overload. He had somehow persuaded his grandparents to buy him a guinea pig on the way home from school. Now it sat sulkily in the garden, in a corner of a large cage that James had brought home from work after Stephanie had phoned him in a panic because it was running round the kitchen. Finn had named it David, somewhat prosaically, after his favourite Doctor Who.

James, Stephanie thought, had been on his best behaviour, indulging his parents with their long and rambling reminiscences about his childhood. She wished they didn't have to leave. Having them around had taken the pressure off somehow. It was much easier to deal with James when she didn't have to be alone with him. He had also seemed tired and, maybe, a little subdued, hopefully because the stress of his double life was starting to get to him.

'Why should we make it easy for him?' she said to Katie, on the phone on Monday afternoon.

'Too right,' Katie said.

By the time James arrived home again on Wednesday Stephanie had been out shopping and purchased the low-cut, floaty top which Katie had sent her a photo of. 'Only £9.99 in New Look!' the accompanying text had declared. 'It'll be worth it.' It was a mixture of pinks and purples in an abstract pattern that, Stephanie thought, she would never have chosen, with her colouring, but it was certainly distinctive enough that there was little chance of James failing to remember it. It had been a good idea of Katie's, and Stephanie was pleased that she seemed to be getting into the plan properly at last, looking for ways to have fun at James's expense.

Stephanie was at home when James arrived and she rushed to the door, flinging it open enthusiastically and beaming at him as if he were a brandy-bearing St Bernard in a snowstorm. His face reflected her warmth momentarily – there was no doubt he was pleased to see her – but then she had noticed his eyes flick down and a look of confusion replaced his smile for a second. Stephanie nearly laughed but instead she looked down at her top and said, as innocently as she could, 'Oh, do you like it? I bought it today.'

James, who was definitely looking pale, managed to say, 'Mmm, yes, nice.' He didn't, she noticed, tell her it was driving him crazy.

On Friday evening she asked him to get home from work early so she could have a drink with Natasha. It felt like an age since she had been out for anything other than a swift glass of wine after work. James usually moaned if she asked him to do babysitting duty. 'I hardly see you as it is,' he would say, and she had always used to think it was sweet that he didn't want to spend any more evenings away from her than he had to. Now she knew it was because he didn't want the hassle of trying to convince Finn to go to bed on time.

This time, though, he agreed without complaint, and Stephanie got enjoyably pissed in the pub with Natasha and felt almost generous towards him when she got home.

On Saturday Finn was in heaven because James had got up early and spent most of the day in the back garden with him, creating an appropriate home for David. They built an Addams Family hutch out of wood and then James took Finn to B&Q where they bought chicken wire to make a run. Stephanie could hear them chatting away happily outside. Above all else, Finn loved to spend time with his father.

'You have to remember to feed him every single day, and to change his water and let him have a little run around,' James was saying.

Stephanie peered through the slats in the blind. She could see that Finn was hanging on his every word.

'And you know that Sebastian will eat him, given half a chance?'

Finn nodded, deadly serious.

'And you have to make sure he's shut in the little house bit before you go to bed so the foxes don't get him.'

She took them out sandwiches and Coke for lunch, and watched them eat, sitting side by side on the grass. At four o'clock she went out to watch as David was transferred from his cage to his palatial new home where he immediately edged his way to the corner and resumed his sulky position.

'That was my best day ever,' Finn said later, as she was tucking him up in bed.

Stephanie and James shared a bottle of wine in front of the TV. It felt relaxed, they felt like a family, they even had quite a jolly conversation, and then at about ten thirty, he had picked up his mobile and left the room.

A few minutes later she got a text: 'Said he's been to dinner with two of Abi and Peter's friends in Vauxhall. Said it was boring.'

'I'm going to bed,' Stephanie said, when he came back in. 'Night.'

She left the room without bothering to kiss him goodnight.

There was a letter waiting for James when he got to the country practice on Monday morning. 'It has been brought to our attention that there may be some irregularities in your tax returns for 2005/2006 and 2006/2007.

Please be aware that one of our inspectors will be carrying out a full audit of your accounts in the coming weeks,' it said.

Fucking Sally, James thought. Fucking bitch. No wonder she hadn't confronted him since he'd sacked her. She'd obviously got straight on the phone to the Inland Revenue. He knew he should never have been so open at work about the fact that he was often paid in cash, but that was him, he was too trusting, he had assumed that he had loyalty from his staff. Besides, everyone did it in the country. It was just a version of the barter system. If he'd let the farmers pay him in pigs, it would probably have been OK, but what would he have done with a freezer full of pork chops and ham hocks?

His head was starting to pound. This was all he needed. He slammed a few things around on his desk, upsetting his coffee all over some papers.

'Bollocks,' he shouted. 'Shit and bollocks.'

Sally had opened his door at just that moment and he was about to lay into her when he saw that she was closely followed by his first client, Sharon Collins and her elderly border collie, Rex, so he tried to look as if everything was normal. Like shouting 'shit and bollocks' loudly and dabbing angrily at your papers with a wadge of Kleenex was common practice for vets first thing in the morning.

'Sorry,' he said, smiling through his teeth, 'I spilled my coffee.'

By the time Sharon had left, he was feeling more rational if no less angry. What had the country come to that the tax people would take the word of any old disgruntled employee? Was this how the world worked now? That if you were fed up with someone you could just ring the authorities and make life hell for them? Well, he thought, it'll be my word against hers and who are they more likely to take notice of? As long as none of the farmers corroborated what she'd said, and he couldn't imagine that they would, it wouldn't look good for them either.

'You have no evidence that this has anything to do with Sally,' Malcolm said, when James had filled him in. 'It might not even be about the taking-payment-in-cash thing. You could have just filled your form out wrong.'

'It's Sally,' James was adamant. 'Otherwise the whole thing's a bit of a coincidence, don't you think?' He had known Malcolm and Simon wouldn't be sympathetic. Malcolm shook his head at him in a way that made James want to slap him. He knew that what he was really saying was 'Well, if you hadn't taken cash payments in the first place and you hadn't treated Sally so badly then this wouldn't be happening.' Malcolm's view – and Simon's too – would be that he had brought it on himself.

'She's got to go,' James said angrily.

'She already is going. Isn't that what this is about?'

'I mean, she's got to go now. Today. I don't want her in the office a moment longer.'

'Oh, for God's sake, James,' Malcolm said wearily. 'Grow up.'

But James was having none of it. There was no reason to go easy on Sally now. The damage had been done. She couldn't undo it. He wanted her as far away from him as possible as quickly as possible.

Sally was chatting on the phone when he went out to reception to look for her. A woman he didn't recognize was sitting on one of the chairs with a mournful-looking cat in a basket. James stared at Sally until she looked up and acknowledged him.

'I need a word,' he said, not caring who she was speaking to.

'I'd like you to pack up your stuff and go,' he said, when she came through to his room a couple of minutes later.

'I don't understand.' Sally looked as if she was going to cry, which made him uneasy, but she had brought this on herself.

'Oh, I think you do. Don't think I haven't worked out that it was you who tipped off the Inland Revenue.'

'What?'

He had to admit she was a good actress. She looked genuinely taken aback.

'You know I'd never do a thing like that,' Sally was saying.

'I tell you you're fired one day and a couple of days later this happens. Come on.'

'James,' Sally was crying properly now, 'whatever's happened is nothing to do with me. I swear.'

God, he hated it when women cried in front of him. It always made him lose his resolve. Well, not this time.

'I'd like you to leave now, please,' he said, and then he left the room before he changed his mind. Once Sally had gone, the tax people could investigate all they liked. They wouldn't find anything to corroborate her story. He had had to do what he had done. He'd been given no choice.

What James hadn't thought through when he'd ordered Sally to pack her bags and go, he thought later, was who was going to run the surgery in the meantime. He'd have to get Katie to help him out, she always seemed to have all the time in the world and she was always ready to do anything for him if it would make him happy.

'I can't,' Katie said, when he told her why he was calling. 'I've got clients this afternoon.'

'Well, can't you cancel them? This is an emergency.'

'No, James, I can't.'

'Oh, for God's sake,' he said, and put the phone down. Well, they'd just have to muddle through. Between him, Simon, Malcolm and Judy, the veterinary nurse, they'd have to manage.

There was something up with Katie, James thought, once he'd rung off. She wasn't being her usual sweet, compliant self. It would be this thing with his parents – she was still pissed off that he had lied to her about it, that would be it, although she would never have said so. He resolved to be extra nice to her. He had had a good weekend at home – he had felt closer to Stephanie than he had allowed himself to feel for a long time, once he had got over the shock of her in that top, that was. What was it with women that they all wanted to wear the same thing? Actually, she had looked gorgeous in it and he had wanted to take her in his arms and tell her so, but that wasn't really how they were with each other, these days. They had got out of the habit. He felt bad now that maybe he had been neglecting Katie a little, but the harsh truth was that as much as he believed he loved her he would have preferred to be down south with his family right now. Life was simpler there.

25

Stephanie could hardly believe it when Katie called to tell her what she'd done. 'You tipped off the Inland Revenue? God, Katie, maybe we should have talked about it first.'

Katie had been unrepentant. 'He's asked for it. Anyway, I thought that was the point, we were meant to be doing stuff to him to make ourselves feel better. That's what you said.'

'It's just that this is so ... huge,' Stephanie said. 'I mean, it's one thing to upset him a bit, make him feel like he's not so invincible after all but this is a whole other area. This could have serious consequences for him.'

'And?' Katie said, and Stephanie started to wonder if she was speaking to the right person.

'I don't know. I just feel a bit uncomfortable, that's all.'

'What's the worst that can happen? They'll ask him if it's true and he'll say no. Even if they somehow stumbled across the truth he'd just have to pay the back tax and maybe a fine. Come on, Steph, it'll give him a few sleepless nights, that's all.'

She was right. Stephanie could see that. It was just, well, she didn't like the idea of Katie acting without discussing it with her first. If she were being honest that was what was really bothering her. 'OK,' she said. 'You're right. Poor Sally, though.'

Katie laughed. 'I know. At least he'd already fired her because if he'd just told her to leave on the strength of this I would have had to do something to change his mind. She'll be OK.'

Stephanie was running late. By the time she'd finished talking to Katie and slapped her makeup on it was ten past ten and she was due at a private members' club in Manchester Square at ten thirty for a magazine shoot. She called Natasha to tell her to try and hold the fort without her. The subject today was a young writer who had been showered with awards for her first TV piece, which dramatized her own abusive marriage. She was telling her life story to one of the weekly glossy magazines and Stephanie and Natasha were providing the outfits for the pictures. Luckily Natasha had had time to go into the office first thing this morning to pick up the two suitcases of clothes they had chosen.

By the time she arrived at the Georgian building, which was so discreet there wasn't even a sign on the door – Stephanie had had to go twice round the square before she figured out where it must be – she was red in the face and looking anything other than a glamorous stylist. Natasha had everything under control. The writer, a sweet nervous girl called Caroline, had been cajoled into a sleek black dress and was looking gorgeous.

'Sorry, sorry,' Stephanie muttered, as she climbed over the mess of lights and reflectors and made her way through to the side room, where Natasha was sifting through the cases looking for something or other. 'How's it going?' she asked breathlessly.

'Fine. Calm down,' Natasha said. 'The clothes fit, she looks great in them and everyone's happy. Plus the photographer's quite cute.'

Stephanie peered round the door. Natasha was right, she thought, looking at the photographer, who was at that moment standing on a chair to get a shot of Caroline gazing up at him. Oh, well, that would make the day go faster. 'What's his name?' she said to Natasha, retreating behind the door before he looked over and saw her staring.

'Mark or Michael, something like that. I can't remember.'

'Michael Sotheby,' Michael, not Mark, said, as he held out a hand. Caroline had been sent off to try on another outfit.

Stephanie smiled. He really was quite good-looking. Late forties, maybe. Brown eyes. Crinkly smile. 'Stephanie Mortimer. Sorry I was late.' His name rang a bell. She had seen it in magazines, probably. She always looked at photograph captions to see if they credited the stylist. They almost never did.

They chatted about nothing in particular – editors and makeup people they both knew, and an exhibition of pictures by the controversial photographer Ian Hoskins, which catalogued his father's descent into alcoholism and which was opening in Hoxton in a few days' time.

'That's amazing,' Stephanie said. 'I absolutely love him and you're the first person I've met who's even heard of him.'

'When are you thinking of going?' Michael asked, and

Stephanie realized she was blushing, as if he'd invited her out on a date.

'Oh, you know, I'm not sure so —'

'Well, maybe I'll bump into you. Stranger things have happened.'

Stephanie laughed as if he'd made a fantastically witty pronouncement. Then she realized that she was being a little bit flirtatious — a reaction, she was sure, to the fact that Michael was doing the same. Immediately she became self-conscious and awkward and the moment passed.

Caroline came back in wearing a knee-length royal blue dress from Diane von Furstenberg and Stephanie fussed around her, pinning up the hem and feeling ridiculous. It was so long since she had flirted with anyone that she had forgotten how to do it and, anyway, strictly speaking, she was still married — at least for the next few weeks — so it was probably highly inappropriate. James may have ditched his morals but I still have mine, she thought self-righteously.

'He fancied you,' Natasha said, in the cab on the way home.

'Don't be stupid.' Stephanie blushed, giving away the fact that she had noticed it herself.

Katie was drawing up a list of things to do and people to invite to James's fortieth, which was now only a couple of weeks away in early May. So far, the list of guests ran to nearly fifty. James was well known and well liked in the village, where most people had needed his services at one time or another. She had put Hugh, Alison, Sam, Geoff, Richard and Simone on the list because she knew that, although their little dinner-party circle was history, James would still think it was important that they were there and, more importantly, she didn't want them to miss the big showdown, which she and Stephanie were planning for around ten o'clock.

'Anyone I've missed?' she asked, handing him the list. She had hired the village hall, her cottage being way too small, and James had suggested they serve lavish canapés and champagne followed by dancing.

'How about the McIntyres?' he said, mentioning a couple who had recently moved into the village. The wife, so Katie had heard, was distantly related to royalty, which would be right up James's street. 'Have you ever even spoken to them?' she asked now.

'No, but it would be neighbourly,' James said, and Katie had to stop herself from asking if he would be being so neighbourly if the McIntyres weren't so well connected.

'How about that couple who've moved into number twenty-six?' she said, knowing what the answer would be. The couple who had moved into number twenty-six had five kids and three dogs and four old cars in their front garden. Neither of them seemed to have a job.

'Oh, no, I don't think so,' he said. 'They don't seem like our kind of people.'

What 'our kind of people' were, Katie wasn't entirely sure, but she'd had a pretty good idea that the couple at number twenty-six wouldn't qualify. 'We'll invite whoever you want,' she said now, leaning over to kiss him. 'It's your party and I'm going to make sure it's exactly what you deserve.'

'Actually, stuff it,' said James, who, she imagined, was starting to feel as if he wasn't quite as popular now as he'd once thought. 'Ask them. They might turn out to be nice.'

Katie had felt a rush unlike any other she had ever experienced when she had picked up the phone and asked to be put through to the local tax office. It had taken a few minutes to get through to the right person, and while she was hanging on, she had wondered whether she could really go through with what she was about to do. She had decided to put on an accent, suddenly afraid that they might one day play James a recording of his accuser, but as soon as she had started to speak and the officious woman at the other end had asked her to talk more slowly because she couldn't understand her she had dropped it. She was a former employee, she told the woman, and she had left because she had been shocked by James's business practices. When asked to give her name she had claimed to be Sylvia Morrison – the first name that had popped into her head, presumably because her mother was called Sylvia and Morrison was the name of the man who ran the local fruit and veg shop where she had done her shopping that morning.

The woman hadn't been at all friendly and had, in fact, sounded very sceptical. It didn't seem to Katie as if she was taking the accusation seriously. When it was over Katie had had to sit down with a stiff brandy, which was what people always claimed they did in these kinds of situations. After that she'd felt sick, a mixture of the drink and the excitement. She couldn't believe what she had just done. She felt scared and elated, guilty and shocked by what she was capable of. She didn't know whether to feel relieved that almost certainly nothing would come of it or disappointed. Most of all she felt alive.

When James had come home a week or so later and had told her about the letter, she had been afraid she would smirk and give herself away but she'd managed to be all sympathy and understanding. It frightened her how naturally it had come.

26

When the phone rang on Tuesday evening Stephanie nearly didn't answer it because Finn was moaning about having been given broad beans, which he 'hated', with his homemade chicken nuggets, and she knew that if she took her eyes off him for even a second he would scrape them into the bin. She'd picked up her mobile, intending to turn it off, but when she saw that it was a number she didn't recognize her curiosity took over and she found herself pressing the green button to accept the call.

'Hi,' a man's voice said. 'It's Michael.'

Stephanie racked her brain. Did she know a Michael? He sounded vaguely familiar. Before she could answer he, obviously having picked up on her hesitation, added, 'From the shoot yesterday. Michael Sotheby.'

Michael the photographer. Nice Michael who had made her blush. 'Hi!' she said, a little confused. 'How did you get my number?'

'It was on the call sheet,' he said. 'Is this OK, me ringing you?'

'Yes. God, yes, of course.' Stop gabbling, Stephanie.

She remembered Finn, who she had momentarily forgotten about. She glanced over at him and saw that he was looking very pleased with himself, a clean plate in front of him. She smiled at him and moved through to the hall, pulling the door shut behind her. 'So . . .' she said, trying to ignore the fact that her heart had gone a little racy. What was wrong with her? 'What can I do for you?'

'I just wondered,' Michael said, and she was sure he sounded like he was wishing he hadn't rung, 'if you wanted to go to that Ian Hoskins exhibition with me. You know – we were talking about it.'

Stephanie took a deep breath. Was he asking her out on a date? She hadn't mentioned she had a husband yesterday, but then they had been working, why would she have? But she had been flirting with him, she thought now. She must have given him the impression she was interested.

Her silence had obviously made him nervous. 'It was just a thought. But if you're too busy or whatever then that's –'

'No,' Stephanie heard herself say. 'I'd love to. But it couldn't be till next week and I'd have to get someone to babysit my son. I have a son,' she added breathlessly – what was she doing? 'And a husband, but we're separating, except he doesn't know that yet. You see, he has a girlfriend, up in Lincoln. I only just found out. Well, a few weeks ago. He doesn't know that I know yet either. He only lives in London a few days a week. To see Finn. That's my son's name.'

'Stephanie, calm down.' Michael laughed. 'All I'm asking is if you'd like to go and look at some photographs. If you'd rather not, then that's fine.'

'No,' Stephanie said, collecting herself. 'I just wanted to be straight with you. It's a bit of an issue with me, honesty, after what's happened to my marriage. I just wanted you to know exactly what the situation is so that there are no nasty surprises lurking.'

'OK. Well, I was married for fifteen years until last year when my wife decided she wanted out. No one else involved, as far as I know. No children. I own a flat in Docklands and I have all my own teeth except for one which I knocked out in a cycling accident and which is a fake. I once dressed up as a lobster for a school play, but otherwise no embarrassing skeletons in my closet.'

Stephanie laughed. 'Well, in that case I'd love to go to the show with you.' She was doing nothing wrong. Certainly nothing that matched up to what James had been doing to her.

'How does next Monday evening sound?' he asked, and she said that would be lovely and that she'd see him there, at the gallery, at seven.

Once she'd hung up she stood in the hall for a moment, trying to work out how she felt and whether or not she had done the right thing. Finn appeared at the kitchen doorway. 'What are you doing?'

'Nothing. Did you eat your broad beans?'

'Yes. Who was that on the phone?'

'Just someone from work. You don't know them. Did you really eat your beans?'

'You saw I did. All of them.'

Stephanie knew that if she looked in the kitchen waste bin the broad beans would be sitting in a neat pile on top of the rest of the rubbish but she decided not to push it. She had a date. Someone thought she was attractive enough to ask out. She'd make sure Finn ate his vegetables tomorrow.

*

Despite feeling like she was doing nothing wrong by accepting Michael's invitation – looking at a few photographs hardly rivalled pretending you were single and setting up home with someone else on the infidelity scale after all – Stephanie didn't mention it to Natasha the following morning. She kept wanting to. She and Natasha had never had a secret as far as she was aware.

At one point she even mentioned his name in passing, during a conversation Natasha began about when they were intending to return the dresses lent to them for Caroline's photo shoot. 'Michael seemed pleased with how she looked,' Stephanie had said.

'He spent most of his time looking at you. I don't think he even noticed her,' Natasha had replied, laughing, and Stephanie had thought, Now's the moment to casually drop it in that he had called and then, if that went down well, to add that they were meeting up on Monday. But something had held her back. She felt foolish, talking about going on a date like a teenager. And, anyway, there was nothing to tell as yet: they were just going to look at some photographs, Stephanie reminded herself.

By the time the following Monday came round she was wishing she hadn't agreed to go out at all. It just felt too much like hard work, worrying about what she looked like and trying to think up interesting and witty things to say in advance. It was a rainy evening, and more than anything she wanted to go home and curl up on the sofa in front of the TV. She thought about calling Michael with an excuse – an illness or, even better, a childcare problem – but she knew he would probably try to rearrange for another evening and there were only so many personal problems she could pull out of the bag to bat him away with. So she had resolved to make the evening as brief as she could. Be polite, a quick look at the photographs and home by nine, nine thirty at the latest.

Finn was going straight from school to spend the night with Arun's family, so she had plenty of time to lie in the bath and to fret about exactly what image of herself she wanted to portray through what she was wearing. She settled eventually on a fairly conservative but youthful Pucci rip-off patterned top and a pair of fitted-but-not-too-tight jeans with her favourite too-high-to-walk-in boots. She was checking her makeup for the fifth time when her mobile rang. Katie.

They hadn't spoken for a few days. The initial excitement of texting each other whenever James said or did anything newsworthy had died down and they had fallen into a routine of a quick catch-up after each of his visits. Stephanie knew she should have called Katie yesterday, once James had hit the road to head back up to Lincoln, but she had found she didn't feel like it. They had actually had quite a pleasant few days. Stephanie, nurturing the secret of her upcoming date, had felt less resentful of his presence than usual and he, in turn, happy, she had guessed, to be away from the recent pressures of his country life, had seemed relaxed and glad to be there. They had got through the whole time without arguing once and, although there was no doubt in Stephanie's mind that things would be easier once he wasn't there at all any more, she had almost managed to forget her anger and hurt and the feeling of betrayal his double life had caused her and pretend that things were normal. It was easier now that she truly believed she didn't want him any more.

The only awkward moment had been when James had brought up his birthday party and asked her what she was planning. They were having it at the house and Stephanie had gone through the list of the people she was intending to invite: family, friends, colleagues. They were going to have catering, with the teenage children of various friends earning a few pounds each by working as waiters. The music would be provided by James, who was intending to sit down and make playlists on his iPod that would take them right through from eight in the evening until about four in the morning, with several changes of mood scheduled along the way. One of the first-floor bedrooms was to be turned into a giant playroom for their friends' younger children.

'I can't wait,' James had said, and Stephanie, in turn apprehensive, excited and uneasy, had said nothing.

Michael was waiting for her outside the gallery when Stephanie arrived, sheltering from the drizzle under an awning. He looked good, she thought, relieved, because she had been worrying that her memory of him might have been coloured slightly rosy by the fact that he had liked her. He waved as she got close and did the crinkly-eyed smile thing that had made her notice him in the first place. He was wearing baggy combat trousers and a long-sleeved T-shirt under a shorter-sleeved, contrasting-coloured one. His thick hair, which was a dirty blond colour, was just the right amount of ruffled. He looked totally at home in the urban chic Hoxton surroundings in a way that James could never have pulled off. He looked, maybe, a bit too much of a *type* for Stephanie's usual taste, a bit like he spent longer than he should thinking about the impression he was going to make. But he definitely looked good.

'Am I late?' she said breathlessly, as she got within speaking distance. She was always late. It was one of the things she liked least about herself and something which she seemed to be powerless to change. The time just went, no matter how organized she tried to be. She put it down to the fact that, to all intents and purposes, she was a single mother – well, for most of the week.

'No,' he said, smiling. 'Not at all. I wanted to be here early in case you couldn't find the place. It's not really an area you want to get lost in.'

He held the door open for her and they went into the stark white space. The photographs, no holds barred, warts and all depictions of underprivileged family life, were both shocking and moving and, best of all, Stephanie thought, conversation starters. By the time they reached the end, almost an hour and a half later, she felt as if she and Michael knew all about each other's backgrounds and upbringings and their views on family life and relationships. She felt like she hadn't talked so much in years, certainly not to someone who had at least given such a good impression of being interested in what she had to say. Michael's family, like hers, came from the stifling corridor between city and suburbia. 'Neither gritty nor idyllic,' he'd said, and she had laughed, knowing exactly what he meant. 'Just ordinary. Really, really boringly ordinary.'

By the time they stepped out into the damp evening again it was eight thirty and Stephanie knew that if she was going to stick to her plan then she should make her excuses now and head straight home, but when Michael asked if she wanted to go for a drink she heard herself say yes.

They walked round the corner to an achingly self-consciously cool space with an eclectic mix of armchairs and mismatched tables where they squeezed themselves into a corner and drank beer out of the bottle. Just as Stephanie was beginning to feel completely out of place in the crowd of young men with sticky-up hairdos and courier bags slung across their chests and the girls in their vintage dresses, and was starting to think she might just drink up and go home after all, Michael leaned over and touched her arm. 'I can tell this isn't your sort of place,' he said. 'Let's go somewhere else.'

They found a tapas restaurant, which was quiet and candlelit and sat and talked more and shared a bottle of red wine. At a quarter past eleven Michael suggested they share a taxi and Stephanie agreed, half wondering if, in fact, they were both going to end up at his place and not minding in the least if they did. As they pulled up outside his flat in Islington, however, Michael kissed her on the cheek. 'Can we do this again some time?' he said.

'Definitely,' Stephanie said, wondering if he was waiting for her to suggest that she come in for a nightcap.

'I'll call you tomorrow,' he said, as he got out and slammed the door behind him. 'Belsize Park,' she heard him say to the driver, and then he turned to wave as he went up the steps to his front door. Stephanie sat back in her seat. Michael, it seemed, was a gentleman.

27

James's Monday had been equally eventful. A cow with mastitis, a sheep with an infected cut on its leg, and another with an eye infection. In between he had manned the phones at the surgery and badgered the temp agency in Lincoln to give him an answer about when they would be able to send someone to cover reception – no time soon, it seemed. There weren't many girls in Lincoln who were prepared to travel out to the village for the small wage the agency was able to offer. At ten past one, just as he was wondering if he could lock up for an hour while he sneaked out to get a sandwich – Simon and Malcolm having breezed off to the pub without asking if he needed assistance or even if he wanted to come with them – a woman in a dark blue suit, slight and rather attractive, had come through the front door. Unlike most people who called she wasn't accompanied by an animal but was holding a handful of papers. James had smiled hello, wondering whether she was lost.

'Is James Mortimer here?' the woman had asked.

'That's me,' James had said, standing up behind the reception desk. 'What can I do for you?'

The woman had consulted her papers briefly. 'I'm from the planning department,' she said. 'We've been led to understand you've had an extension built which we don't seem to have any paperwork for.'

James had swallowed his smile and then forced it back on to his face again. 'I'm sorry, there must be some mistake. Who did you say had told you this?'

The woman hadn't smiled back. 'I didn't. I'm afraid that's confidential. Now, if you could just show me round.'

James had noticed that the woman was holding a floor plan of the building, among other things. There was no way he was going to be able to avoid her seeing the extension. He'd run through in his head what the possible consequences might be. A fine? Nothing more serious, surely? Fucking Sally. She wasn't going to get away with it. OK, he had thought, there was only one way to deal with this. Bluff.

He'd led the woman, who had told him her name was Jennifer Cooper, towards the extension, which was currently housing a convalescent sheepdog and a post-operative cat.

'I wonder if you mean this,' he'd said, gesturing at the large room. To the side, through a door, was the small operating theatre. Jennifer was studying her floor plan. 'I had it put up two years ago but the architect told me it was small enough not to need permission.' He'd been aware that he was sweating. 'Ten per cent, isn't it? Of the overall size?' Jesus, what was he saying? Surely the worst thing you could do was lie to these people.

Jennifer had looked round, taking in the size of the room. Then she'd walked over to the theatre and had a good look in there too. And in the cupboards. She had returned to her floor plan. 'You're saying that this addition is less than ten per cent of the original size of the whole

194

building?' The way she had looked at him when she'd said this had made his heart sink.

'Well, that's what I was told anyway,' James had said, looking at his shoes.

Jennifer had produced a pen from somewhere. 'Well, if you could just give me the name of your architect then.'

James had taken a deep breath. This was ridiculous. He hadn't, in fact, used an architect when he had put up the extension because he had known they would insist on going to the council for permission and that would have taken months. In fact, it would almost certainly have been refused, as almost any application for building works in the village was. Especially once Richard and Simone got to hear of it. Unless, of course, it was built from reclaimed stone and lime plaster and fashioned to look as if it had been there since the sixteen hundreds, which would, frankly, have cost him a fortune. He should just come clean with this woman, tell her the truth. Plead naïvety or ignorance. What was the worst she could do?

'OK,' he had said, trying to put on his most charming expression. Maybe she was flirtable with. 'You've got me. I can't lie to that sweet face. Nobody told me it was OK to put the extension up without permission. I took a chance. I figured it wasn't huge and it was out the back where nobody could see it –'

'This is a conservation area,' Jennifer had interrupted. 'You can't just go putting up buildings left, right and centre without permission, whatever size they are.'

His fabled charm definitely wasn't working. 'So what happens now?' he'd said. 'Do I get a fine?'

'What happens now,' Jennifer had said, 'is that you apply for retrospective planning permission.'

'And?'

'And if it fulfils all the criteria it's granted.'

'And if it doesn't?' James had said, knowing what the answer would be.

'Then you have to knock it down.'

'You are joking? If I knock it down the practice will have to move. There's no way the building's big enough without it.'

'Well, maybe you should have moved to larger premises in the first place,' Jennifer had said, smiling for the first time. 'You have sixty days in which to apply. Goodbye now.'

When she had left, James sat on the floor, absent-mindedly stroking the ears of the sleeping sheepdog through the mesh of its cage. What was happening to him?

Half an hour later he was outside Sally's house, finger jammed on the doorbell. This had gone far enough. It was understandable that she was angry and he could see she might feel she wanted to get some small revenge. She hadn't yet managed to find another job, as far as he knew, because the village was small and there simply weren't that many opportunities. Maybe he had been a bit hasty, getting rid of her like that. After all, he was starting to realize that it was impossible to keep the surgery going with no one to man the desk. Then he thought about the letter from the tax people and Jennifer's quiet officiousness. Fuck it. He would rather spend all day answering the phones himself than have that girl work for him.

He heard a dog barking behind the door and heavy footsteps coming along the hall. Sally's father, Jim O'Connell, a red-veined-faced, usually genial man, appeared in the doorway. He frowned when he saw James. 'Yes?' he said curtly.

James hesitated. He tried to weigh up whether Jim could take him in a fight or not and decided that, if he put his mind to it, he definitely could but that he probably wasn't the fighting sort. 'I'd like to see Sally for a minute, please,' he said, smiling nervously. 'If she's in.'

He stood on the doorstep for a few moments waiting, wondering whether he should leave and come back later when Sally might be on her own. He couldn't really shout at the girl while her father was lurking around in the background. In fact, he now wasn't sure why he had thought shouting at her at all would be a good idea. It was just that it might make him feel better.

Sally, when she eventually came down the stairs into the hall, was looking at him defiantly, he thought, and all his anger came flooding back. What right did she have to pick apart his life like this? He spoke in a low voice, hoping Jim wasn't in earshot. 'Well, I hope you're proud of yourself.'

Sally's confident mask dropped. Her face, if only he had been able to read it, was registering utter confusion. 'What are you talking about?'

'You know what I'm talking about. Bit convenient that that woman from the planning department turns up out of the blue after all these years.'

Sally, who, although James couldn't know it, had been thinking that maybe he had come round to tell her it had all been a big misunderstanding and did she want her job back — in fact, on the short walk from her room to the front door she had decided that she would give him a hard time for a few minutes and then accept graciously — put her hand on the door frame to steady herself. 'The planning department?'

'Don't try and play the innocent with me,' James hissed, and he had a fleeting out-of-body experience in which he saw himself, a middle-aged, slightly greying man, standing on a doorstep bullying a young girl and using language that sounded as if it came from a bad police drama. 'It's enough, OK? The tax people, the planning people . . . You've got your own back, if that's what you were trying to do. I'm sorry if you feel hard-done-by but let's just call it quits now.'

He turned to walk away. There was nothing else he could say, really. There was no point pushing her even further. Who knew what else she had up her sleeve?

28

Katie had taken to going for a drink with her fellow students after her reflexology class. They were a nice bunch – mostly women, which suited her at the moment because her faith in men had been completely shattered. There was a pub just round the corner from the college where they could always get a table, have a couple of glasses of wine and chat through what they had just learned or, more and more, as the weeks went on, about their lives. Then she would drive home – very carefully because usually she knew that she was slightly tipsy – to an increasingly moany James.

The sense of freedom those few short hours gave her was immense. She felt as if she was getting her life back, preparing for when she was soon to be single again. And if James didn't like it that she would rather spend time drinking with her new friends than rushing home to see him, well, sod him. She no longer cared what he thought. On a couple of occasions he had suggested that he could drive over to Lincoln and join them in the pub, but that was the last thing she wanted. These were her friends, it was her social life and she didn't want to share it.

He had been hurt and confused and once, when he'd had a few drinks, he had had the cheek to ask if there were any men in their little after-college drinking group.

She had wanted to say, 'We're not all like you. Not everything's about sex,' but instead she had bitten her tongue and reassured him sweetly that the only men present were gay or astonishingly unattractive. 'You wouldn't like them,' she had said, of her new friends, by way of explanation. 'They're all very spiritual people, New Age. You'd get into an argument straight away.'

For the first couple of weeks James had taken himself down to the local pub for his dinner and a couple of pints, but lately whenever she'd got home he was sitting on the sofa resentfully, like a grumpy toddler. She had decided to ignore it, to breeze around as if everything was fine. It was unbelievably hypocritical of him to begrudge her one independent night out a week when he was living a whole double life.

Through her new friends – some of whom already practised complementary skills and others of whom were novices in the world of alternative therapies – Katie had acquired several new clients and had taken to visiting them in their homes with her portable massage table, rather than expecting them to travel to her. It meant longer days and less free time but she was starting to feel that this was actually a good way of making a living. She could support herself comfortably if this kept up. People would pay handsomely for someone to treat them in the comfort and privacy of their own home, even in the countryside, and she was able to almost double her prices. Even taking into account the petrol and her travelling time, she was doing well. People who worked were willing to pay a small bonus for a visit in the evenings and at weekends, and soon her Sunday and Monday nights were filled with appointments and James was starting to complain that he never saw her at all.

Just when she had started to think she might stop treating Owen – she was beginning to feel that he was taking her for a ride, despite his recent progress, and the days of her seeing any clients for free were most definitely over – he turned up one morning with three manky ten-pound notes in an envelope and explained to her that he had got a new job and was able to start paying her back. 'It's only in the hospital, as a porter, but I'm earning, that's the point.'

Katie was overwhelmed. 'Owen, that's great. That's such a positive step. I'm really pleased for you. And you wait, other good things will follow. They always do.'

'I'm going to pay you back. It'll only be a bit a week but I'll do it. Eventually,' he laughed.

In fact, he had come straight from work to tell her he would no longer be able to keep his Wednesday-morning appointments. It was a luxury he simply couldn't afford any more and he was no longer prepared to keep taking something for nothing. He owed it all to her, he said, this new change of outlook. Maybe, once he had paid off his debt to her and saved up some money, she would rethink his invitation to take her out to dinner. Katie, delighted though she was by the proof that what she did could make a difference, had no intention of saying yes. The last thing she needed was to hook up with another man, especially one whose insecurities and failings she already knew intimately.

'You really don't have to,' she said now, politely. 'But it's very kind of you to ask.'

Owen flushed red. 'I didn't mean like a date or anything. The invitation's for both of you, you and James,' he stuttered.

'Honestly, Owen, save your money. Thank you, though. It's a really lovely thought.' She kissed him on the cheek as if to signal that their chat was over. 'Good luck,' she said, 'with everything.'

Sally O'Connell's uncle, Paul Goddard, had always had an amiable working relationship with the local vet. He found James to be reliable and prompt, even when called out in an emergency. There was no doubting his sensitivity and compassion when it came to handling animals but with none of the sentimentality that Paul had no time for. If you were a farmer you had to believe your livestock were a commodity. Treat them well, by all means – a happy cow was a healthy cow after all, and healthy cows produced superior milk, in Paul's mind – but remember that they were, above all, your livelihood.

He had always sent round a bottle of whisky for James on Christmas Eve, in appreciation of his services and because they came cheap due to the arrangement they had whereby Paul would pay James in cash. This had always seemed like a sensible way to do business to Paul: there were no losers, both parties came away up and, besides, everybody did it. He barely even gave it a second thought.

When the man from the Inland Revenue turned up at his front door one afternoon and started asking questions, Paul's first instinct was to deny everything. After all, if he didn't admit to it and neither did James then no one would ever be able to prove them wrong. Then he remembered the look on his niece's tear-stained face the night before, when she had told him about her visit from her old boss and the accusations he had thrown her way, and suddenly he didn't feel like protecting this man.

'It's easier for me to pay him in cash,' he found himself saying to the suited man with the clipboard. 'That way I know exactly where I am. I don't like bank accounts,' he added, playing the role of simple farmer to perfection. In fact, Paul not only had a healthy bank balance but also an ISA, which he topped up once a year. Since he'd turned the farm organic, things had really started to look up financially.

'What he does with it then is his business, isn't that right? Whether he tells you lot about it or not, well, that's nothing to do with me.'

The man had thanked him for his time and his candid answers and had gone off happy. That'll teach the fucker, Paul thought. Sally had always been his favourite niece.

By the time James got back to London on Wednesday afternoon he felt like he wanted to go into the bedroom, close the curtains, crawl into bed, pull the covers over his head and never come out again. He was feeling besieged, run ragged by trying to keep the surgery going without a receptionist and sure they were losing custom. He had heard on the grapevine that when one of Paul Goddard's cows had calved in the middle of the night Paul had called in a vet from the next village over. James, who had had his phone turned on as always, waiting for Paul's call, which he knew was imminent, had been both bemused and hurt in equal measures.

He had barely seen Katie in the evenings because of all her new work, and her little cottage had started to feel like a prison, no longer a place where two people were content to ignore the fact that it was tiny and poky because they were so happy to be playing house together. It struck him now as a ridiculous place for a man of his age to be living. If you stood in the living room and turned round you could touch all four walls. Was this what he had worked hard for all his adult life? To live in a Wendy house with a woman who was hardly ever there?

And then, of course, there was this business with Sally and the Inland Revenue and the planning department. Plus the fact that Malcolm and Simon hardly seemed to be talking to him any more. When he had tried to confide in Katie about his worries she had blithely told him that everything happened for a reason, it would all work out for the best in the end, and he had found himself cutting the conversation short. What was the point in talking to someone who was only ever going to tell you what they thought you wanted to hear?

London, by contrast, held no terrors. He could do his job and then spend quiet evenings with Stephanie and Finn. He could relax and not feel as if everyone was out to get him. He could just be at home. When he first walked through the door at five past four – he no longer bothered to stop off on his journey down, he just wanted to get to Belsize Park as early as he could – and smelt the familiar smell, a mixture of coffee and polish and Finn's particular small boy odour that mixed shampoo and guinea pigs and trainers, he felt a lump come into his throat. This was his real life. This was his family.

Finn came bowling out to meet him, full of stories of school and David and his friends, and things that James, away half the week and, he thought now, absent in his head much of the time when he was physically there, couldn't make head or tail of but the details of which made him laugh. His son had a great sense of drama when he was telling a story.

He had found Stephanie in the kitchen and, as she turned to greet him, he was struck by the distance that had sprung up between them. When they had first come down to London she would throw herself into his arms whenever he walked through the door on a Wednesday evening and then, on Saturday nights when they were curled up in bed, she would cry about the fact that he had to leave again the next day. It had got on his nerves at the time. He so resented the fact that he had been forced into this dual existence that he had been sceptical about her tears – if she cared that much then surely she would give up her work again and move back to Lincolnshire. Now, as she smiled coolly and asked politely how his journey had been, he felt he would have given anything for an indication that she was happy to see him.

She looked beautiful, he thought with a jolt. Well, he had always known she was stunning physically, but in the past few years Katie's earthy softness had seemed so much more arousing than Stephanie's willowy angles. Katie's need for protection had drawn him in whereas Stephanie's independence had pushed him away. He went to hug her and felt her stiffen for a split second before she relaxed and, half-heartedly, patted him on the back. A wave of utter misery swept over him and he squeezed her tighter, burying his head in the silkiness of her hair. She allowed him to stay there for a second before she gently pushed him away and turned back to the vegetables she was chopping.

'Finn, come and sit down and do your homework,' she called, effectively cutting short any moment of intimacy they might have had.

29

With the BAFTAs only a few days away Stephanie hadn't really been putting the effort into planning James's party that she should have. She had sent out the invitations, and received mostly acceptances, and had hired the caterers – a Japanese firm who would come to your house with their bags of big scary knives and prepare sashimi in the kitchen while the guests stood around, admiring their skill – but that was about it. She decided to phone Katie to see how her preparations were coming along. At least, that was the pretext for her call. In reality, she was starting to worry about Katie. James had told her that Sally had tipped off the planning department about the extension he had had built at the back of the surgery but she had her suspicions. Katie seemed to have had some kind of epiphany since they had first met and agreed on their plans. As if she was transforming from a sweet, hurt woman into some kind of vengeful crusader. Stephanie, who knew that the whole idea of their taking revenge had come from her, was now afraid that she had created a monster she couldn't contain.

Katie answered on the second ring. Her voice, Stephanie thought, sounded as sweet and unthreatening as ever.

'Stephanie, hi, how's it going?'

'Good,' Stephanie said. 'I just wondered where you were, you know, with the party and stuff.'

Katie told her about the decorations she had planned for the village hall, the yards of white muslin that would transform the inside into a kind of Bedouin tent and the white tablecloths and crockery offset by the green foliage of the white lilies she had selected. It all sounded a bit like a wedding, Stephanie thought, hardly James's taste at all. She realized she had stopped listening when she suddenly heard Katie laugh and say, 'Mind you, I doubt he'll have any friends left to invite by then.'

'What do you mean?' Stephanie said.

So, Katie told her the full story about Sally and her uncle Paul, and how, now, James had got to have a meeting with the Inland Revenue to explain himself and would probably be facing a fine or, at the very least, would have to pay what he owed. And how he had gone to see Sam McNeil to ask if, in her capacity at the planning department, she could give him some advice as to how to handle the retrospective permission for the extension and how she had gone ballistic and accused him of trying to get her to pull some strings for him and get him some kind of special treatment. And how even Simon and Malcolm were barely speaking to James now and several of the surgery's customers had chosen to move their business to the vets in the next village over. And Stephanie listened to it all and found that she was starting to feel sorry for him, despite everything he had done to her.

'How did the planning people find out about the extension?' she asked, knowing what the answer would be.

'I told them,' Katie said, sounding like a two-year-old who thought she was about to be congratulated for going to the toilet on the laminate instead of the carpet. 'Anonymously, of course.'

Stephanie sighed. 'I thought we'd agreed not to do anything without discussing it first,' she said lamely.

'I know. I did try to ring you. It's funny, though, isn't it?'

'It's just that we don't want to blow everything before the party. Isn't that the point?' Stephanie said, although she no longer felt her heart was in this plan at all.

'Well, he deserves it,' Katie said, with venom. 'And he's so arrogant, he'll never think it's anything to do with me. So what if a few people don't come to his party? He'll still get what he deserves.'

'Maybe we should forget the whole thing,' Stephanie said. 'We've given him a few things to worry about. We should just dump him and move on.'

'Hold on,' Katie said. 'Wasn't it you who said it would be a travesty if he got away scot-free?'

'I know. But now I'm not so sure. It all feels a bit . . . I don't know . . . over the top.'

'Stephanie, you need to do this for your self-esteem after everything he did to you. And so do I. Besides what would be the point in backing out now?'

'OK,' Stephanie said, without enthusiasm, 'but no more surprises.'

'I promise,' Katie said. 'It's only two weeks. We have to stay strong.'

Stephanie found herself agreeing reluctantly. The truth was that lately she had stopped caring whether or not James got his comeuppance. She just wanted to move on.

*

Luckily for Stephanie, Natasha was in the mood for giving one of her pep talks when she saw her later that day. It was Meredith's last free time before the event at the weekend so she was in the office trying on shoes to go with the hideous green dress, which she was still insisting on wearing. Because no designer in their right mind would have manufactured anything which remotely matched the nauseating bright green of the dress, Stephanie had reluctantly promised that they would dye Meredith's favourites in time for Sunday. She was trying to steer Meredith away from a beautiful pair of off-white Jimmy Choos, which she didn't have it in her to ruin, and towards a much cheaper high-street pair. Meredith, however, was having none of it and, cramming her blistery feet into the exquisite open-toed sandals, declared that these were the ones she wanted.

'They're three hundred pounds,' Natasha said, trying to put her off.

Meredith scowled. 'Won't they lend them to us? I am a nominee after all.'

Stephanie shook her head, trying not to laugh. She couldn't imagine the conversation she might have to have with the Jimmy Choo press office, offering up Meredith as a walking fat-footed advertisement for their delicate shoes. 'Not if we dye them, no.'

In the end Meredith, who was always money-conscious and was, Stephanie knew, already resentful of the fee she was having to pay to be styled at all, had plumped for the cheaper option. Stephanie had confirmed with her all the details of the car for Sunday that would bring her to the office to get ready. Ordinarily either Stephanie or

Natasha would have gone to her house, but with three clients to dress the practicalities meant that that wasn't possible.

Once Meredith had left, Stephanie and Natasha flopped down on the sofa and resumed the conversation they had been having before she arrived.

'The point is,' Natasha began, as if they had never been interrupted, 'just because you're feeling a bit better doesn't mean you should lose sight of the original objective.'

'It just feels really petty suddenly,' Stephanie said, leaning her head back against the sofa's cushions. 'The grown-up thing to do would be to tell him I know and that it's all over between us, and then we can separate with dignity. And that's got to be better for Finn, surely.'

'OK, so you're feeling positive because you've been on a date with someone else . . .' Stephanie had finally got up the courage to confide in her friend about Michael. Natasha's response had been to hug her happily.

'Two dates, actually,' Stephanie interrupted. 'But I'll tell you about that in a minute.'

'Really?' Natasha's eyes widened. 'Anyway, so you're feeling positive because you've been on *two* dates with someone else, even though you didn't tell me about the second one till now and I'm supposed to be your best friend, but . . . you're not assuming you're going to run off and marry Michael,' she looked at Stephanie enquiringly, 'or are you?'

Stephanie laughed. 'Obviously not.'

'Exactly. So, while you may not care about getting back at James now because you've got Michael as a bit of a distraction, that doesn't mean you'll feel like that for ever. You have to remember how important it felt to you that you make him suffer like he'd made you suffer. All I'm saying is that it's still important, for your long-term well-being and all that. At least, *I* think it is. There! Speech over.'

'OK, OK, I'll stick to the plan. Just so long as Katie does. Happy now?'

Natasha nodded. 'Extremely. Now, tell me about Michael. I can't believe you saw him again and didn't mention it.'

So, Stephanie told her how Michael had called her on Tuesday morning and that they had ended up agreeing to meet up for dinner that evening. He had booked a table at the Wolseley, which was somewhere Stephanie had casually mentioned to him that she had always meant to go but had never got around to. They had talked about real stuff, she told Natasha, a proper grown-up conversation. Michael had opened up about his ex-wife and how she had announced out of the blue that she had been feeling resentful and taken for granted for years and that she wasn't going to put up with it any longer, which meant that he had very strong views on honesty in relationships. Views that coincided exactly with Stephanie's own. It had been a thoroughly enjoyable evening, and there was nothing else to report.

'No kiss goodnight?'

'I told you,' Stephanie said defensively. 'Michael's got principles and so have I. As long as James and I are still together nothing's going to happen. But I am going to see him again next week.'

'So you've told James about your little dates?'

'Of course not. He'd go crazy.'

'So Michael's OK about going out for secret evenings with you behind your husband's back as long as you don't kiss?'

'What are you saying?' Stephanie said, irritated. 'Are you implying I'm doing something wrong after everything James has done to me?'

Natasha cut in, laughing. 'Calm down! Of course I'm not saying you're doing anything wrong. I'm saying in for a penny ... If you're seeing him behind James's back anyway you might as well jump him. What's the difference?'

'The difference,' Stephanie said, 'is that I don't want to be like James. I want to be able to look back and say I behaved impeccably. OK?'

30

It was a weekend that ordinarily James would have dreaded. Stephanie had to be at work all day on Saturday, buying last-minute bits and pieces and making sure her three clients were happy with their manicures and pedicures and whatever else they needed to have done before a big occasion like the BAFTAs and then, of course, she would be out on the big day itself. James had agreed to stay until she returned once her clients were safely in their cars and off to the event, probably at about four o'clock.

He found, when he went to bed the night before, that he was actually looking forward to it. He could take Finn to the zoo – not just past it this time but actually inside. Finn, used to only ever seeing the wallabies and a few other random things that could be viewed for free from the park, would think all his Christmases had come at once. Or they could go on the Eye or maybe to the Tower. Or perhaps, James thought, it would be better to stay at home playing games on the computer or in the garden. Whatever Finn wanted to do.

He had got up early and made Stephanie tea and toast before she had to leave. From the look on her face when he gave it to her, it was obvious that this was an unexpected gesture. He tried to remember the last time he had made her breakfast and, of course, couldn't because it would have been a long time ago. A time when he had just had Stephanie in his life and no one else.

Finn had declared that the morning was to be spent cleaning out David's cage, then Goldie's tank and Sebastian's litter tray. The meticulous attention to detail that his son showed when he was caring for his animals reminded James of how he had been as a child. 'You should become a vet,' he said to Finn, as he laid new straw in the bottom of David's hutch.

'That's what I'm going to do. Obviously,' Finn replied, with a serious look on his face, and James had felt as if he'd stumbled on to the set of some kind of schmaltzy Children's Film Foundation film. He felt his eyes brim with tears and had to stop himself hugging his son and ruining the moment.

In the end they had gone to the zoo in the afternoon, with Finn exclaiming over everything from the pygmy shrews to the mountain gorillas and then had dropped in at the surgery in St John's Wood to pet the animals who were being kept in over the weekend. By the time Stephanie got home at about five thirty they were both lying exhausted on the sofa in front of the TV.

'You have to do it all again tomorrow.' Stephanie had laughed when she saw him.

They had had dinner and Stephanie had told them about her day and how Santana had still been in bed when the beauty therapist had turned up at her flat at two o'clock, and had refused to get up so the poor girl had had to do her toenails while she lay there with her filthy feet poking out from under the covers. Finn had laughed and said girls were 'stupid' and Stephanie had said, 'But

I'm a girl, does that make me stupid?' and Finn had said, 'You're not a girl, you're a mum. There's a difference,' and James had laughed and laughed, and the evening had passed so quickly that he hadn't once thought about phoning Katie.

Stephanie wanted this weekend to be over. It was the same every year: no matter how much preparation you did, the day itself was always chaos. Natasha, thankfully, was dealing with Santana, who had refused to come to the office to get ready because she was hoping the paparazzi might be outside her house in the afternoon, waiting for her to be picked up. If she left too early they might not know where to find her.

Stephanie was trying to get the ambience right before her other two clients arrived. She liked people to feel relaxed while they were having their hair and makeup done but she couldn't think what kind of music she could put on that would suit both Meredith and Mandee. In the end she plumped for James Morrison, who was both inoffensive but just hip enough, she hoped. She lit a few candles and scattered a few magazines around. Never assume that your clients want to chat was rule number one and she always impressed it on any hair and makeup people she booked for events.

The two makeup and hair designers, as they insisted on being called, arrived promptly at one. They set up their two stations at opposite corners of the room so that Meredith and Mandee could chat or not as they wished. Stephanie ran through the clothes on the rack in the other room, the makeshift changing room. As well as Meredith's green dress there was one other option Stephanie was keen for her to try on, along with an alternative pair of shoes. Mandee's Agent Provocateur outfit was there but so was a very cute mini-dress from Chloé in case she could be persuaded to change her mind. There was an array of Spanx industrial-force underwear for Meredith to pick from, still in its boxes so that what she didn't choose could be sent back to the shop. Both women had been lent a few pieces of not very impressive jewellery, which Stephanie had sorted through, picking out one suitable item for each.

At one twenty-five she answered a panicked call from Natasha, who was standing on the steps of Santana's apartment block with the makeup girl. They had been ringing the bell for five minutes straight but there was no reply. Stephanie told them just to wait it out. They weren't Santana's babysitters, and if she had decided to go out somewhere the night before and not come home, then that was her problem. Likewise, if she missed her hard-fought-for presenting slot this afternoon, that wasn't their problem either.

Stephanie, meanwhile, managed to get her two charges settled with lattes and some magazines and the soothing sound of two hairdryers. She did a final check through of the clothes in the other room and then sat down on the sofa, thinking she might just close her eyes for a moment. The occasional fragment of conversation broke through from the other room but the heat from the dryers ensured that she dropped off into a deep sleep.

Her alarm rang. No, wait, it was the doorbell. Stephanie sat up with a jolt. Where was she? Someone was calling from the other room, 'Do you want me to get that?' and Stephanie called back, 'Yes, please,' before she could even remember who that someone was. OK, she was in the office. Shit, it was BAFTA day. She looked at her watch: three forty. She must have been asleep for an hour. There was a tiny stream of dribble coming from the side of her mouth. She wiped it away. She looked at herself in the mirror on the wall. One side of her face had the imprint of a flock-covered cushion in bold red down her cheek. She rubbed at it furiously. What if any of them had looked in and seen her lying there, dead to the world? God, that was unprofessional. And who was that at the door? She wasn't expecting anyone. She heard a man's voice. Shit. Fuck. Yes, she was. She had asked Michael to come and take some photos.

It had been a moment of madness. She usually took pictures herself for her records, once her clients were all dolled up to go to an event. It was mostly for reference but sometimes she would send them to the designer if the clothes looked particularly good in the hope that they would then offer that client an outfit for free. On Friday, though, she had wanted an excuse to ring Michael – they had arranged to see each other again on Monday night – and so she had asked him if she could hire his services on Sunday for an hour or so, as if that was the most normal thing in the world to be asking. He, of course, had said he would do it for free and now here he was, in her office, and she was looking like death warmed up.

'Stephanie,' someone was calling from the other room, 'there's someone here to see you.'

She wiped the stray mascara from under her eyes and

dragged her fingers through her hair. Oh, well, he would have to see her at her worst some time.

'Michael, hi,' she said confidently – or at least as confidently as she could manage – as she went through the door. His face definitely lit up when he saw her, she noted. OK, so maybe she didn't look so bad.

'This is Michael, our photographer,' she said to the others in the room. Luckily she had never dressed either Meredith or Mandee before so they wouldn't realize this was an unusual event. One of the makeup girls, Davina or Davinia, everyone had such stupid names these days, was looking at her, confused.

'I didn't know this was a photo session,' she said now. 'I haven't done photographic makeup. I've gone for the natural look. You didn't say anything about this,' she added accusingly.

Stephanie forced a smile. 'It's not for editorial, don't worry about it. Now,' she said, wanting to get off the subject, 'you both look beautiful. Let's get you dressed while Michael sets up.'

She looked across at Michael, and he shot her a sympathetic smile. God, what was she doing? She hadn't even told Natasha because she knew that Natasha would see through her right away and know that she just wanted an excuse to see him again. Luckily Natasha, who was across London hopefully dealing with Santana by now, would never have to know.

Meredith and Mandee were both adamant about sticking to their original outfits and Stephanie was grateful that, at least, she had filled Michael in with the fact that the clothes weren't her choice but that her clients had mutinied and overruled her. By five to four they were ready.

Meredith, with her industrial underwear under her lurid green concoction, actually looked as if she had a figure for once. Her enormous breasts, which she usually hid in an ill-fitting saggy bra under a succession of baggy shapeless tops, had been hoicked up and pushed out and looked magnificent. Stephanie was hoping that any of the weekly magazine editors would be so blinded by the acres of white cleavage that they wouldn't notice how awful the dress was and feature Meredith on the worst-dressed list.

Mandee was a study in the use of tit-tape, which was gluing her skimpy two-piece to her body and hopefully keeping all her bits and pieces in check. If she looked like she was dressed for a photo shoot in *Nuts* rather than to go out, at least she had the figure to carry it off. They would have to do.

She could have sworn she heard Michael stifle a laugh when she led her two *protégées* into the next room. The makeup women gave them a quick touch-up and Michael tweaked the lighting to be a bit kinder, then rattled off a couple of shots of each of the women.

'Have you got any other outfits while I'm here anyway?' he said, in his most charming voice. 'Seems a shame to waste the film.'

'Yes. Good idea.' Stephanie jumped in. He was trying to help her out, that was so sweet of him. 'Treat it like a free photo session. That way, if you like any of the pictures you can get copies. You never know when they might come in useful.' She looked at her watch. 'We've got time.' Actually, they didn't really, the cars had been due five minutes ago, but it was worth a try.

She helped as Meredith squeezed herself into the black number with the drop-shouldered top and watched Mandee transform from a hooker into a pretty, trendy young woman in the Chloé dress. 'Wow, you both look great,' she said, and the pair of them looked at her unimpressed.

'Now that is sexy,' she heard Michael say, as Mandee went through to the next room. Meredith rolled her eyes. 'You could be a model,' he went on. 'I couldn't see it, how you were dressed before, but everyone's going to want to photograph you now.'

'Do you think?' Mandee said. 'Really?'

Stephanie smiled a conspiratorial smile at him as she entered the room and he allowed a hint of a smirk to get through. He turned his attention to Meredith as she came in. 'Great dress,' he said. 'Very flattering.' Meredith who was a much harder proposition than Mandee, snorted.

'It does look much better than the other one,' Stephanie added, but Meredith was having none of it. She allowed Michael to take a couple of shots and then announced her intention to change again.

'I'm going to wear this one, I've decided,' Mandee said, and Stephanie could have kissed her. She looked at Michael, who seemed to be trying to signal something to her while Meredith wasn't looking. He was jerking his head in the direction of the other room and rolling his eyes. He looked like he might be having a fit. He stopped abruptly as Meredith turned round. 'Just a couple more, Meredith. The last ones were a bit out of focus. My fault.'

Meredith agreed reluctantly and Michael gave Stephanie an intent stare that meant . . . Well, she didn't know what it meant. Suddenly she was struck with inspiration. She moved through to the adjoining room, picked up Meredith's latte and threw it over the hideous green dress. 'Oh, God!' she called, trying not to laugh. This was ridiculous. 'Oh, fuck! Meredith, I'm so sorry, I've spilled coffee all over your dress.'

Meredith came barging through the door. 'Well, wipe it off – quickly for God's sake!'

'It's no good,' Stephanie said, picking up the dress quickly. 'It's all soaking in. It'll stink of milk, apart from anything else.'

'Well, what do you suggest I do now?' Meredith said, smoke practically coming out of her nostrils.

'Well . . .' Stephanie said and then the doorbell rang. Thank God, it was the cars they had booked to take Meredith and Mandee to the ceremony. 'I guess you'll have to wear what you've got on. There's no choice really. I'm sorry, Meredith.'

Meredith looked as if she was ready to explode. Michael swept in holding handbags and wraps and tickets. 'Come along, ladies. You don't want to be late,' he said, and ushered them towards the door. 'You both look beautiful.'

'Right,' Stephanie was saying. 'I've put lipstick and gloss in both your bags. Touch it up just before you get out of the cars. And have a great time,' she added, ignoring the furious look on Meredith's face.

She thanked the two hair and makeup girls and promised she would use them again, then shut the door behind them, leaning back against it and putting her hand over her mouth to stifle her laughter until the women were out of earshot. Michael was laughing, too, and he threw an arm round her neck and pulled her towards him.

'We must be telepathic,' he said.

Stephanie looked up at him. 'You're not trying to tell me that that's what you were saying, with all those nods and meaningful looks – "Go and pour coffee over her dress."'

'That's exactly what I was trying to say,' he said, smiling and he leaned down to kiss the top of her head but next thing she knew they were in a full-blown kiss, hidden there in the tiny hallway of her offices.

Stephanie couldn't remember the last time she had kissed someone who wasn't James. In fact, she couldn't even remember the last time she had kissed James in anything other than a 'Say thank you to your uncle for his Christmas present' kind of way. She was aware of Michael's hand holding the back of her head and the weight of his body as he pressed her against the wall. Then he stopped as abruptly as he had started, took her by the hand and led her through to the sofa in the main office. She wondered vaguely whether she should remind him that they had been going to wait until she was offi-cially single, but seeing as it had been him who had made that resolution in the first place, then who was she to hold him to it? Fuck it, it was only a week till she was free. In fact, she knew really that this was what she had been hoping would happen when she had invited him over. James would be waiting for her to get home so that he could be on the road up to Lincolnshire but she felt no guilt. She was only doing what he had been doing himself for the past year.

Michael pulled his head away again and looked at her. 'Is this OK?' he said, and the tone of his voice, the way that he said it, made her feel weak.

'Yes,' she replied. 'Definitely.'

The next part was a bit of a blur of arms and legs and items of clothing coming off and she was just thinking, OK, this is it, when she heard a noise. The click of the front door, footsteps maybe, and then a voice, a woman's voice, saying, 'Oh, whoops. Excuse me.' She pushed Michael away and saw Natasha's retreating back going towards the front door.

'Natasha,' Stephanie said, sitting up and trying to pull odd bits of clothing round herself. 'Hold on a second.'

Michael had sat bolt upright and was trying to behave as though this was just an ordinary day, move along, nothing to see here.

Natasha was still facing the door and obviously not about to turn around. She held out a suit-carrier of clothes behind her at arm's length. 'I was just bringing Santana's clothes back. She never turned up, you see. Sorry, I wouldn't have, you know . . . if I'd known.'

'It's fine,' Stephanie said, clutching around for something to say. How undignified was this, caught fumbling around like a pair of teenagers in the classroom stationery cupboard? 'We were just, erm . . . I asked Michael to come over and photograph Meredith and Mandee and we just . . .' She ran out of steam. 'Oh, God, this is so embarrassing.'

'Well, anyway,' Natasha was saying, 'I'd better go. You

just carry on or . . . whatever. Nice to see you again, Michael.' She dropped the suit-carrier over a chair. ''Bye then. See you tomorrow, Steph.'

Stephanie and Michael sat side by side on the sofa watching as Natasha left and closed the door behind her. The mood was most definitely broken.

'Sorry,' Michael said. 'That was my fault, I just got a bit carried away.'

'No, no,' Stephanie said. 'It was both of us. And how were we to know that she'd come back? It's fine. It's just a bit . . . awkward, that's all.'

'Well,' Michael said, standing up, 'I should go. I mean, you probably have to get home.'

'Yes, I suppose I should.' Stephanie got to her feet, wondering how in the space of a couple of minutes they had gone from the throes of passion to acting like two people who barely knew each other. They finished getting dressed awkwardly, avoiding looking at each other.

'Are we still on for tomorrow night?' Stephanie asked, as they left the office without even having kissed one another goodbye.

Michael stuck out his arm to flag down a taxi. 'Sure,' he said. 'I'll ring you in the afternoon and we'll make a plan.'

She thought he might get into the cab with her but instead he slammed the door shut, raising his hand in a wave as it pulled away. She turned on her phone. There was a frantic message from Natasha: 'Oh, God, Steph, I'm so, so sorry for barging in on you like that. Why didn't you tell me he was coming over? Then I could have taken the clothes back to mine. You looked like you were getting on rather well, by the way. Hopefully you picked up where you left off once I'd gone. Good for you. You deserve a bit of fun. But I'm still really sorry I walked in and ruined it.'

Stephanie looked out of the window. Now that the feelings of embarrassment were fading she just felt a bit sad that the whole thing had put up some kind of a barrier between her and Michael. There was an awkwardness there now that hadn't been there before. Maybe they'd tried to move things on too fast. It was fine for her: she knew Natasha and she knew that Natasha would never disapprove of what she had been doing, but Michael would be worried about how unprofessional it had looked, she thought, managing a smile. Hopefully they could regain their old ease with one another tomorrow, maybe even laugh about it because, to be honest, once you got past the initial embarrassment it was funny. She just wished she could be certain that he would call her tomorrow as he had promised. She had a feeling he might not.

James was doing some serious thinking on the drive back to Lincoln. Stephanie had got home just after six, looking stressed and dishevelled. He had been tempted to stay, to say, 'Sod work on Monday morning, let Malcolm or Simon worry about the surgery for once,' but he didn't know how to broach it without Stephanie thinking he was behaving oddly. And the truth was he was *feeling* odd. It was as if he had been asleep for a year and had only now woken up and realized exactly what it was he had been doing all that time. What had he been thinking? More to the point, how had he ever thought he could get away with it? He had dug himself into so deep a mess that he couldn't imagine there was a way to dig himself out again without losing everything. He had thought he could keep the situation going indefinitely, that both women would remain contentedly in possession of half of him, and that his feelings towards both of them would always be such that he would never feel the need to jump one way or the other. Now he had started to wonder if he had been wrong.

When he got home around nine forty-five Katie was out. She had left him a note saying she had a client and that she had left him some dinner in the oven. He petted Stanley and then ate, sitting at the tiny table in the kitchen. He looked around at the Thai statues on the shelves and the framed photos of Katie's holidays in the East before she had met him, on the walls. There was nothing of him in the room, he thought, nothing really to say that he had been living here for the past year. Even the colour, a bright, sea turquoise, wasn't one he would have chosen himself.

The doorbell rang.

James looked at his watch. Five past ten. It was late for someone to be calling unannounced. He opened the door cautiously to find Simone standing there. 'Is Katie in?' she asked, before he could even say hello.

'Erm . . . no, she's working,' he said. Something about Simone seemed a little manic.

'Good. It's you I wanted to see. Can I come in?' Simone was already halfway through the door as she said this. 'Do you have any wine? I'm desperate for a drink.' She had clearly had a couple already.

James poured her a small glass. 'Are you OK?' he asked.

'I'm fine – why wouldn't I be? I just heard you were having trouble with the planning department and I thought I might be able to help, that's all.'

James was having trouble believing that Simone had come round at five past ten in the evening to discuss his extension.

'I could put in a word with the Conservation Area Group. They have a big influence on the council, you know. If I could get a consensus that there's no objection to the building . . .'

James interrupted her – this really was very strange: 'Simone, that's really very kind of you, but I can't see the Conservation Area Group agreeing that my breeze-block and uPVC extension is an asset to the area. And, besides, I wouldn't want to put you to any trouble.'

Simone, who had been sitting in one of the little arm-chairs, stood up and moved on to the sofa next to James. He shuffled along awkwardly.

'It's no trouble,' she said, and gave him a look which made him realize exactly why she was there. She was trying to seduce him. For a split second he toyed with the idea of calling her bluff, but he knew that whatever the solution to his problems might be, shagging one of his neighbours wasn't it.

'Actually, Simone, I've decided to do the right thing for once. I'll apply for the permission and if I don't get it, well, then, it serves me right. But thank you for your offer. I really appreciate it. You're a good friend.' He stood up as if to say that it was time for her to go, but Simone didn't move.

'Could I have another glass of wine?' she asked, in what she clearly thought was a come-on voice.

James looked at his watch. 'To be honest, I was hoping for an early night,' he said, but before he had finished getting the words out, Simone had stood too and was making a grab for him. He pulled his head back, avoiding her kiss. 'Come on, Simone,' he tried to laugh it off, 'we can't be doing this. Katie will be back any minute, and what about Richard?'

'Richard can fuck off,' Simone said viciously.

'Ah,' James said. 'You've had a row with Richard.' That would explain it. She was looking for a way to get back at Richard and she clearly thought that James would never turn down the offer of a quickie.

'So what if I have?'

James took the glass out of her hand and set it on the table. 'Simone, I think you should go home. You can sort things out with Richard in the morning. What do you say?'

Simone was starting to look angry. 'You've been flirting away with me for months and now you're going to humiliate me by saying no? What, do you think I'm the sort of woman who goes round flinging herself at any old man? No,' she said, answering her own question. 'I came to you because you have always made it very clear that you fancied me.'

She was shouting, and James couldn't help worrying what the neighbours might think. 'I'm sorry if I gave you that impression,' he said. There was no doubt in his mind that if this had happened a couple of weeks ago he would have been tempted to go for it and sod the consequences. He had never been one to turn down an invitation for sex, however complicated. Now he just wanted her out of his house. He was in enough trouble already. 'I did flirt with you, it's true, but I never meant anything by it. I'd never have acted on it. I thought you felt the same, that we were just having a laugh.'

He realized immediately that this had been the wrong thing to say. Simone's face contorted into an angry sneer. 'Having a laugh? Do you think I'd be here cheating on my husband if I thought we were just having a laugh?'

God, he wished she'd stop shouting. She really was very drunk. 'Let's get this straight,' James said, his tone more serious now. 'You are not here cheating on your husband. You and Richard had a fight and you came over here wanting to get back at him but that's not going to happen, OK? Now, why don't you just go home and sort things out with him?'

'What's wrong with me? Don't you like me?' Suddenly big wet tears were running down her face.

Oh, great, James thought, now what do I do? Next thing she'd be passing out on the sofa and then he'd never get rid of her. The truth was, he had let her think he liked her. He'd amused himself by flirting and enjoying the feeling that he was getting one over on Richard. He was that pathetic, he thought now, that he had needed to think his friends' wives fancied him, that they would all jump into bed with him if he said the word.

There was only one thing for it. He had to get Simone to go home, whatever it took. He put his arms round her. 'Of course I do,' he said. 'You know I do. It's just that we can't do anything about it because of Richard and Katie. I want to, I really do,' he added, looking down at her tear-stained face. He didn't fancy her in the least, he saw now. It had all been a big game. 'But we can't. We've both got too much to lose.'

Simone was looking up at him calmly, blinking through her tears, her pride intact. They were the same, he thought. They just wanted to be the one everyone desired.

'Now, you should go home before we do something we'll regret.'

She leaned up to kiss him again and he pushed her away gently. 'No, if we start we'll never be able to stop.' He couldn't believe he was able to trot out these clichés so easily, or that she was lapping them up.

'OK,' she said. 'You're right.'

James untangled himself as quickly as he could, without appearing rude, then steered her towards the front door. He wondered if he should walk with her, she had had way too much to drink, but decided that that would be asking for trouble. 'Goodnight, then,' he called, as she tottered off into the night. He wanted the neighbours to know she was leaving, that way, there would be no nasty rumours.

Half an hour later when Katie got home he told her the whole story. He was through with keeping secrets. Well, almost.

32

The newspapers on Monday morning were full of pictures from the BAFTAs, the winners, the losers, the people who had got drunk at the party and fallen over in the street outside. Stephanie had bought them all on the way into work and was now leafing through them as she drank a giant latte.

Natasha wasn't in yet, having arranged to pick up Meredith and Mandee's accessories on the way in – somewhere around midday to allow them to sleep off their hangovers – and sort them out ready to return to the stores who had lent them, more as a favour to Stephanie than because they wanted Mandee or Meredith to be seen in them. Neither Mandee nor Meredith had been loaned a dress because neither was considered someone the clothing designers wanted to be associated with. Santana's dress, although it could be returned unworn, would be cleaned and pressed first.

Stephanie was dreading seeing Natasha, knowing she would want to know all the gory details and probably spend the day teasing her about being caught out having sex on the sofa like a teenager. Worse, she would think that the only reason Stephanie had hired Michael was so that she could jump him. Which was true, of course, but she had been trying to convince herself it wasn't.

She forced herself to scour the broadsheets first, knowing it was unlikely that any of her three clients would feature there. She had watched the awards on TV last night, after James had left. Santana had been there, in the end, to present her award but looked like she had just turned up in whatever she had been wearing the night before, having partied all day and all night. In fact, that was probably exactly what she had done. She had slurred incoherently through the presentation, occasionally running a hand through her matted hair A couple of the papers carried pictures of her, with comments saying she looked like she was in the middle of a massive bender and, in fact, one had printed pictures of her out the night before in the same outfit and Stephanie's initial fears that she would feature in one of the weekly magazines under the heading 'Sack the Stylist!' immediately dissipated. Hopefully, some smart journalist would string together a few pictures to make the point that Santana was clueless when left to her own devices.

Meredith's soap had won the 'Best Continuing Series' category and Stephanie had seen Meredith up there in the throng of cast members who went on stage to collect the trophy and, indeed, there she was on page five of the *Sun* with a caption that said how well she had scrubbed up. 'Is it my imagination or is Meredith Barnard actually *sexy*?' the male reporter had written. Stephanie allowed herself a little smile. One up to her.

In the *Mirror* there was a picture of a popular young TV heart-throb leaving the party with Mandee in tow. They had got into the same taxi, the report said, and didn't Mandee look lovely with her clothes on for once?

There didn't seem to be any shots of Mandy-with-a-*y* anywhere.

Stephanie clipped the two cuttings out, it was a much better result than she had been hoping for and, really, it was all down to Michael. She wondered about phoning him to say thank you, but she felt like if he wanted to talk to her then he would make the call. It had all ended so awkwardly and she knew he was mortified that Natasha had walked in. As was she, of course, but Natasha was her friend. Michael had only met her once. He was probably worried that she would think he was a wife-stealer or a sleaze. He couldn't know, of course, that Natasha had been encouraging her to go out and find another man for weeks now.

She decided to call Meredith and Mandee with the good news, to take her mind off things. Meredith, who had already been out and bought the papers, couldn't have been nicer.

'I was so wrong about the dress and you were so right,' she said graciously, sounding as though she really meant it. She had already had two phone calls from magazines this morning, asking who had dressed her, and she had happily said to them that Stephanie Mortimer was a wonderful and talented stylist and that she would be recommending her to all her colleagues. This, Stephanie thought, as she put the phone down after promising to dress Meredith for the annual cast and crew party, is why I do what I do. She just wished she could feel more excited about it.

Mandee's phone went straight to voicemail. No doubt she was still holed up somewhere with Mr TV

Heart-throb. Stephanie left a message telling her to buy the *Mirror* and hung up.

She looked at her watch. She had a consultation with a potential new client at their home in Holland Park at twelve. It was only ten thirty but she wanted to get out of the office before Natasha showed up so she decided to leave early. She could browse a few shops on the way, get some ideas. She left the clippings on Natasha's desk, where she would see them, and went out.

'I just feel it's about time, that's all,' Simon was saying.

James was trying to take it in. Simon, who had worked with him since he first set the practice up more than eight years ago, was leaving to set up on his own. Not just that, but he was staying in the village, opening a practice just along the road. And Malcolm was going with him.

'But . . .' James heard himself stutter '. . . but there's no way two vet practices can survive in a village this small. I mean, where's all the work going to come from?' This was a disaster. Simon and Malcolm were popular locally, plus they worked here full-time. Who was going to stay loyal to him when they knew that if their pet fell sick on a Wednesday afternoon, a Thursday, a Friday or even over the weekend, there would be no one to see to them? His mind was whirring; he was going to have to take someone else on, maybe just for the days when he wasn't there.

'I'm sure there'll be enough work to go round,' Simon said, with a sickening smile, and James knew he was finished. They were going to be in direct competition and he was going to lose.

When Simon had gone he sat behind his big oak desk

and put his head in his hands. He had fucked up his life well and truly. Katie would have said it was Fate, but he didn't believe in all that bollocks. There was only one person he felt like talking to about it, he realized, and that was Stephanie. Stephanie wouldn't keep trying to tell him that everything happened for a reason. Stephanie would allow him to wallow in his misery for a while, then help him laugh his way out of it. He picked up the phone.

Stephanie sounded sympathetic but distracted, telling him that she was out in the street, that her reception wasn't great. He found himself offloading about Simon and the problems he was having with the council and the planning department, not to mention some of the locals, and she listened patiently, not really saying much. When he had finished she told him she was sure it would all sort itself out in time but that she had to go because she had an appointment. After she had rung off he realized that there had only been one thing he had really been hoping she would say. He realized that he had wanted her to tell him that maybe this was a great opportunity to close down the Lincolnshire practice. That maybe now the time was right for him to move to London full-time. But she hadn't. Why hadn't she? Shit, James thought. He had always taken it for granted that Stephanie was just waiting for him to give up the country practice and move home. Maybe not.

'That's bad karma,' Katie said, as he had known she would, when he told her what Simon and Malcolm were doing. 'If you behave badly you always get your come-uppance,' she added, looking him straight in the eye in a way which made him uncomfortable. They were having a rare evening in together, sitting opposite each other at the table eating chicken and purple broccoli.

'I think we should cancel the party,' James said. He had been thinking about this for the last couple of days. What was the point of having a birthday celebration when half the people they'd invited were no longer speaking to him or, at least, that was what it felt like.

'Don't be silly,' Katie said. 'We can't cancel now, it's on Sunday, everything's ordered. Besides, there are loads of people coming.'

'Not Simon, not Sally or her family, not Malcolm.'

'OK,' Katie said, 'not Sally and her family, I'll give you that. But you wouldn't want them there, would you? Simon and Malcolm are still coming. So, you might not like what they're doing but it's only business. It's not personal.'

'Isn't it?' James said glumly.

'Of course not. Plus there's Sam and Geoff, Hugh and Alison, Richard and Simone –'

James groaned.

Katie carried on regardless, '– and all your clients.'

'The ones who aren't related to Sally or who aren't feeling guilty because they're going to go with Simon or Malcolm and not me.'

'James, stop being so negative,' Katie said. 'You're exaggerating the whole thing. It's going to be wonderful.'

Katie was worried that things had maybe gone a bit far. Not because she felt sorry for James – she could barely look at him, and when she did she had to stop herself from screaming out accusations. No, her worry was that if he was dreading the party, as he now was saying he was, then the public humiliation they were planning might not have the impact they were hoping for. Kicking a man when he was down didn't seem like half as much fun as toppling a man when he was up and then kicking him. She hadn't been able to help herself, though. All the little digs, the tiny arrows she had shot at him, had made her feel so much better. It wasn't her fault if the damage had gained its own momentum. She couldn't have known that he would sack Sally or that Simon and Malcolm would decide they'd had enough and leave. Those things were James's own fault.

She hadn't spoken to Stephanie for days now. She had had a few messages and there had been a couple of missed calls, but she hadn't got round to phoning her back. She didn't need Stephanie telling her to go easy on him. In fact, she was getting the distinct impression that Stephanie was getting cold feet about the whole plan, which, considering it had been her idea in the first place, was laughable. Without Stephanie, Katie would just have told James it was over, that she had found out he was still very much married. He would have moved out and that would have been that. But no: Stephanie had convinced her that revenge was empowering, that the punishment had to fit the crime and, let's face it, she had been right. When Katie had first found out the truth about James's double life she had felt devastated, worthless, let down. Now she was feeling stronger than she had ever felt. She was in control, and there was nothing James could do about it.

*

Stephanie still hadn't told Michael the whole truth about her situation with James. She had been as honest as she could, telling him she was still married, that she had discovered her husband's double life and that she was in the process of extricating herself from her marriage, but she had been vague about the reasons why she was still there, why she hadn't just ended it there and then when she had found out. And she knew why: it was because she had sensed that he would disapprove.

He was an adult, she was worried that it would seem like game-playing to him, making light of the fact that her marriage was over. Despite the fact that his wife had apparently been very vocal about his shortcomings with his friends, he was demonstrably proud of the fact that he had handled the situation with dignity. Retaining the moral high ground was high on Michael's list of priorities. Holding a party with the specific intention of unmasking your unfaithful spouse in front of all his friends and colleagues wouldn't have been an idea that would have entered his thought process, let alone one he would put into practice. Michael was big on doing the right thing.

It was because of this that Stephanie knew he would be feeling bad about what had happened on Sunday. They had agreed not to get too involved before Stephanie had sorted out herself and her marriage, and getting carried away in the heat of the moment, like a pair of adolescents, had never been part of the plan. Let alone getting caught doing so. He had left so quickly after Natasha had gone, as if he couldn't bear to be with her a moment longer. It had completely killed the moment. What had happened between them suddenly felt furtive and a bit tacky. A bit behind-the-bike-sheds.

Anyway, he had phoned, eventually, to confirm that they were still meeting up this evening. It had been a brief conversation, quite business-like, as if they were organizing a conference. Now she was waiting for him in the bar of the Soho Hotel, sitting up on a stool at the counter, self-consciously sipping a cocktail.

Michael, when he arrived, five minutes late and apologizing breathlessly for a hold-up on the tube, was looking good, Stephanie thought. She was feeling stupidly nervous. He put an arm round her and kissed her warmly. Her nervousness dissipated. It was going to be fine. Luckily he seemed to be doing his best to act as if nothing awkward had ever happened. He suggested trying to get tickets for the new Joe Penhall at the Royal Court and she agreed happily. Relaxed now, she suddenly let out an involuntary laugh.

'What?' Michael said.

'Sorry,' Stephanie said, colouring up a bit. 'I was just thinking what it must have looked like to Natasha.'

'Don't,' he said, grimacing.

Stephanie laughed again – she couldn't help it, it *was* funny. 'I've just remembered her saying, "Oh, whoops," like she was a member of the WI dropping some of her jam on the floor.'

Michael only managed to crack half a smile. 'I'm trying to forget about it,' he said, and changed the subject. Maybe an evening sitting in close proximity in the theatre but not actually being able to talk about what had happened was exactly what they needed.

33

The kitchen had almost disappeared under a sea of paper chains and streamers. Stephanie had told Finn he could decorate the hall for the night of his father's fortieth birthday party and he was taking his job very seriously. He had spent the last two nights making a banner with Cassie, which said, 'Happy Birthday Dad (James)' and which was decorated with a picture of James with a stethoscope round his neck, surrounded by animals that were all dying in one gory and painful way or another. There was a lot of blood and legs hanging off and even a panda impaled on a fence, its tongue lolling out of its mouth. Finn had heard Cassie telling his mum it reminded her of a painting of World War One that she had seen at the National once. He was enormously proud of it.

He was a bit fed up at having had to spend so many evenings with Cassie recently, to be honest. Not that he didn't like her. As babysitters went, she was a good one. She was funny for a start and sometimes when she leaned over his bed to kiss him goodnight he could see down her top, which he found fascinating although he didn't quite know why. Plus she always let him stay up past his bedtime and she helped him out with things like the banner and his homework. It wasn't the same as being with his mum, though. But, then, she always seemed to be working late, these days.

He had been saving his pocket money (seventy-five p a week) for weeks now to get something nice for Dad for his birthday and he had decided on a drink-holder for his car, because Dad had to do all those long drives every week and Finn thought it would be nice for him to be able to drink a hot coffee on the way. He had seen one in the garage shop down the road where Dad sometimes went to fill up the car on a Sunday morning, and his mum had promised she would take him down there after school one day to get it. The last two nights, though, she hadn't had time because she'd had to get ready to go out again. He was hoping she would take him there this afternoon before Dad got home from the country. He'd reminded her twice already.

Stephanie lay in bed, knowing she should get up and make Finn's breakfast but she was exhausted. She wasn't used to going out in the evenings. On Monday night, after the theatre, she and Michael had shared a cab home and a chaste kiss on the way. Last night they had gone for a meal at The Oxo Tower, then walked along the South Bank for a while before they realized that maybe that wasn't such a great idea after all as they ran the gauntlet of dodgy-looking boys in hoodies and homeless beggars. They had jumped into a taxi, laughing at their lucky escape, and Michael had sat with his arm around her all the way back to his place, and they'd kissed with more urgency, oblivious to the driver, who was glancing at them every now and again in his rear-view mirror.

'I wish I could ask you to stay,' Michael had said, as he'd got out.

'Next time you see me I'll be officially single,' Stephanie had said, and for the first time the whole thing had seemed real. She and James were going to split up. This weekend. In her head their relationship was so dead it almost felt like an anticlimax. As far as she was concerned it had been over weeks ago. Now she and Katie just had to go through the motions and then that was that. The start of her new life.

Ridiculously she had been agonizing over whether or not to get James a birthday present. His party was on Saturday, he would expect a gift, but she was going to need every penny she could muster once they had separated. It felt wrong to spend hundreds of pounds on him one day just to tell him she was leaving him the next. In the end she had decided to tell him she had booked them a holiday. She could make it sound as extravagant as she liked, it was never going to happen.

She forced herself to get out of bed. She could hear Finn moving around downstairs and her heart flipped as she thought about having to tell him that his dad was going to be moving out. 'It's not my fault,' she said to herself. 'None of this is my fault.'

Finn was bent over the kitchen table, working on his banner.

'It's brilliant,' Stephanie said to him, hugging him a bit too tightly so that he squirmed in her arms. 'Dad'll love it.'

It seemed impossible to grasp that James would be coming home for the last time today. Stephanie had decided that the fair thing to do after the split would be for her to remain in the house with Finn until everything was sorted out. She was sure that, however unreasonable James had been in all sorts of other ways, he would see the sense in causing as little disruption for his son as possible. She just wanted it all to be over. The whole plan seemed ridiculous now, she thought. She had even considered backing out of Sunday, letting Katie go ahead and tell him he'd been found out on her own. But Katie had called her last night – the first time they had spoken in what seemed like ages – and she had been so positive that they were doing the right thing and she'd sounded so . . . well . . . so much happier, really, than Stephanie had ever known her to be, so much more confident, that she had found herself mirroring Katie's mood and agreeing the last-minute details, like where she was going to stay and precisely what time she was going to turn up.

The exact plan was this: Stephanie would travel up to Lincoln by train on Sunday afternoon, leaving a couple of hours after James had left in his car, flushed with pride and happiness after his party the night before at which his family and close friends had made him feel important and loved. She would check into the same hotel where James's parents had stayed only a few weeks before, where she would spend time in her room, making herself look as glamorous and desirable as possible.

At exactly nine thirty she would take a taxi to the village hall in Lower Shippingham. Katie was planning on presenting James with his cake at about ten o'clock and had arranged to text Stephanie – who would be waiting in the pub next door to the hall – to let her know when it was about to happen. As Katie made a speech about how marvellous James was and what a great partner and friend, Stephanie would enter the hall. As soon as Katie saw her, the plan was that she would announce a special guest, someone who occupied a unique place in James's heart. She would look at Stephanie, James, excited, would look at Stephanie, the gathered crowd – some of whom knew her – would look at Stephanie. 'Yes,' Katie would say, 'it's his wife. No, you didn't hear me incorrectly, I said his wife, not his ex-wife.' James would be in shock. 'He still lives with her, you see, down in London for half the week,' Katie would go on. 'Here she is, my friend and *still* James's wife, Stephanie.' Stephanie would walk over, smiling at Katie, they would embrace. Cue mayhem all round and James having some kind of a heart-attack. Quite how it would go after that they couldn't be sure. But the damage would be done, James would be unmasked as a cheat and a liar, and Stephanie and Katie could go on with their lives.

It all sounded so simple.

Stephanie came out in a cold sweat. Could she really go through with this? She picked up the phone and dialled Katie's number, walking through to the living room so that Finn couldn't hear.

'We're definitely doing the right thing, aren't we?' she said, when Katie answered.

'Of course we are,' Katie said confidently. 'Stop worrying.'

James was on the motorway by twelve forty-five. He wanted to get down to London, to Stephanie and Finn. He wanted to get back to what he now thought of as his real life. He had had a meeting with the tax people first thing where he had been made to feel more like a naughty schoolboy than a criminal, but it had still been humiliating, and the fact that they were now trying to calculate the back tax he owed meant that he would soon get a pretty hefty bill, plus interest. Neither Simon nor Malcolm had been at the surgery this morning because they were out looking at their new premises – a huge barn conversion, which they were apparently buying for a pittance from Sally's cousin Kieron, a local dairy farmer. Sally, so Judy the practice nurse had told James this morning, would be working for them as their receptionist and, in fact, she, Judy, had just accepted their offer of a job too.

James had left the surgery in the incompetent hands of a temp, asking her to tell any would-be customers to come in this afternoon when there was a hope in hell that one of the vets would actually be there. He knew he should stay, that the only way to save the sinking ship that his beloved practice had become was to put all his energy into it, and simultaneously go on a charm offensive round the local area, trying to drum up custom, but he couldn't be bothered. At least, not at the moment, anyway. He wanted to get home.

He only stopped once on the way, at a service station where he used the toilets and bought himself a bottle of water. By five to four he was turning into Belsize Avenue and singing along with some banal song on the radio. He checked his phone before he got out of the car. No messages from Katie. He'd noticed she no longer sent him the barrage of miss-you-already texts that she always had done on Wednesdays until a few weeks ago. He put the phone back in his pocket, got his case from the back seat and walked up the front path.

Stephanie and Finn both jumped when he came into the kitchen, and then they scrabbled around laughing and trying to hide something – it looked like a large piece of paper – under the table. James smiled. He knew they were making some kind of a surprise for his birthday. He pretended to try and look at what it was they were doing and Finn squealed hysterically and ran to try and stop him. James looked over Finn's shoulder, laughing, and noticed that Stephanie was looking pensive, sad, even.

'Are you OK?' he said.

Stephanie smiled at him. 'Absolutely,' she said.

34

The big day had arrived. Well, the first – and slightly smaller – of the two big days, that was. Pauline and John had travelled up from Cheltenham and got to work immediately, helping to tidy and to unpack the glasses Stephanie had borrowed from the local off-licence. Finn had unveiled his banner to great applause although, privately, they all agreed it was a little disturbing and worried about whether he was harbouring psychopathic tendencies. It was now hanging proudly in the hall along with his homemade paper chains and a few bunches of balloons. In the rest of the house the decoration was much more grown-up, consisting mostly of scented red candles and red tablecloths with a few exotic floral arrangements thrown in here and there. The Japanese caterers were due to arrive at five thirty to start their preparation, and Finn was under strict instructions to keep Sebastian locked in one of the bedrooms, away from the temptations of a kitchen full of raw fish. The guests would, hopefully, start arriving at about seven thirty.

Stephanie was trying to maintain an air of excitement when, underneath it all, she actually felt sick. James was being annoyingly affectionate and kept moving in for a cuddle whenever he got the chance. She could feel herself standing limp in his embrace and it took all her willpower not to push him away. He didn't seem to notice. In fact, he seemed to be on a curious high, singing around the place and generally getting on her nerves. It was strange the way she felt now, not really angry any more, just irritated, wanting him out of the way so she could get on with her life. Wondering how she could ever have found him attractive.

At around a quarter past six she went off for a bath, deliberately leaving it late so that she had no time to lie there and think about what she was about to do. She pulled on a fitted dark red shift dress, which ought to have clashed with her hair but somehow didn't, and a pair of strappy sandals with three-and-a-half-inch heels. She could always take them off later if her feet started to ache too much. By the time she had done her makeup and come back downstairs again, there were only a few minutes left to rush around doing a last-minute check that everything was perfect.

'Wow, you look amazing,' James said, as she went back into the kitchen and she forced out a smile. Pauline, who already looked like she'd had a few, held out a glass of champagne for her. She knew she shouldn't, it was important that she keep her head clear, but she really felt like she needed it. She thanked her mother-in-law and drank it back in one go.

The doorbell rang. Stephanie looked at her watch: twenty-five past seven. It would be Natasha and her husband Martin, who had reluctantly agreed to arrive early as moral support – not that Martin was aware of Stephanie and Natasha's plan, or even James's double life for that matter. He would probably have refused to come if he'd known.

James came over and kissed Natasha on the cheek. Stephanie was sure her friend recoiled visibly. She thrust a glass of champagne into Martin's hand and grabbed Natasha's hand, pulling her out of the room. 'Sorry, Martin, I just need to borrow her for a minute.'

'So, how are you feeling?' Natasha said, in a stage-whisper, once they were in the bedroom.

'Sick, scared . . . excited, I suppose. I just want it over with.'

'He looks so relaxed, so happy,' Natasha said, with venom.

'Actually,' Stephanie said, 'he's been in a bit of a funny mood lately.'

'Maybe Katie's giving him a hard time. Whatever, he's about to get what he deserves. You have to keep remembering why you're doing this.'

'Why *am* I doing this again?' Stephanie said, and Natasha rolled her eyes.

'For your self-esteem, to make him suffer, to end things on your terms. I could go on . . .'

'Go on, then.'

Natasha thought for a moment. 'OK, so I couldn't, but aren't those reasons enough?'

Stephanie put her head in her hands. 'I know, I know. It just all seems a bit . . . pointless now.'

'Since you met Michael? How is he, by the way?'

Stephanie could feel herself blushing. 'He's fine. Let's not talk about him.'

'Nice arse,' Natasha said. 'And I should know. It was the first thing I saw when I walked into the room.'

'OK. I'm going now.' Stephanie stood up.

Natasha laughed. 'The point is, Steph, it's great about you and Michael but you mustn't lose sight of the bigger picture. It's fun and it makes you feel better and it's taken your mind off what James has been doing, which is great. It's in the exciting phase where you still feel flattered and desirable and all those things. But once it's run its course you'll need to feel confident on your own, about yourself. Not like you're someone whose husband cheated on them for a year and got away with it. Not like you're the kind of person men walk all over and you just take it.'

Stephanie smiled sadly. 'I wish you *would* write a self-help book. I'd buy it.'

'You know I'm right.'

'I do. It just feels hard to get up the energy to hate him at the moment.'

'And how does Katie feel?' Natasha had never quite got used to the fact that Stephanie bore no ill-feeling towards Katie.

'She definitely doesn't have the same problem. In fact, she thinks we're not going far enough.'

Natasha draped an arm round Stephanie's shoulders. 'Two more days, not even that, it'll all be over.'

By the time they were back downstairs several more guests had arrived. Pauline and John were doling out glasses of champagne on a one-for-me-one-for-you basis and were already a little unsteady on their feet. Finn was running excitedly from one group of people to another and generally being too loud and getting in the way, but Stephanie decided to let him enjoy himself for a while before the inevitable tears when she tried to get him to go to bed. She looked around for James and saw that he was chatting with one of his work colleagues. He smiled and waved at her, and she turned to talk to the nearest person to her and found herself embroiled in a very dull and intense discussion about the core curriculum with the father of one of Finn's friends. After a couple of minutes of nodding and trying to look like she cared, she excused herself and put the iPod in its speaker dock, setting it to quietly play one of the many playlists James had created for the occasion. Classical violins filled the room. Later, once everybody had loosened up a bit, she would switch to the eighties pop compilation and ramp up the volume in the hope that someone might start dancing. Pauline probably, if she had many more drinks, Stephanie thought fondly.

She checked on the Japanese chefs, who were entertaining a few stray guests in the dining room with their cutting techniques. 'Five minutes?' she said to one of them, indicating when they might start preparing their food in earnest, rolling *futomaki* rolls and forming tiny pats of rice to make *nigiri*. He nodded and communicated something or other with his colleagues in Japanese. The plan was that they would bang a gong in a slightly hammy fashion when they were ready to begin serving and people could go in and ask for what they wanted or just watch and try different things.

It was a beautiful May evening. The doors to the garden were open and Stephanie noticed that a few of their friends had drifted out in groups. Finn was now beside David's cage, lecturing anyone who would listen on the best way to care for a guinea pig. Stephanie smiled; he took his responsibilities so seriously. There must be forty people here by now, she thought, and then she remembered that she was the hostess and she should be making sure they were all having a good time. She moved back through to the living room, stopping to chat for a couple of minutes here and there. Everyone seemed to be enjoying themselves; no one looked left out or lost.

Before she noticed he was there she felt an arm snake round her shoulders and James was standing next to her. He kissed the top of her head and she felt herself stiffen and then forced her body to relax. 'Are you having a good time?' she asked.

'It's perfect. We're lucky we have such great friends.'

'Mmm,' Stephanie said, not quite knowing what else to say. James was looking down at her intently and she looked away, grasping around for something else to talk about.

'Finn seems to be having a good time –' she began, but then petered out as James interrupted.

'Come upstairs a minute. I have to talk to you.' He was staring her straight in the eyes, making her feel unbelievably uncomfortable.

'We've got guests, James,' Stephanie said, trying to make light of the situation. 'What will they think if we disappear upstairs?'

James wasn't loosening his grip. 'This can't wait. I have to talk to you now. Please, Steph.' His voice sounded strange. Desperate almost.

Stephanie looked round for Natasha. This wasn't part of the plan. She tried to shrug him off but he wasn't having it. Finally she gave in. 'This had better be good,' she said, as he led her up the stairs, her hand limp in his.

Once in the bedroom with the door shut firmly behind them, James put his arms round her and drew her to him. Stephanie pulled away, faking a laugh. 'We can't do this now. We're in the middle of a party. Let's go back down.'

And then James did a strange thing. James burst into tears.

He hadn't been intending to tell her. All week he had been trying to get things straight in his mind, to work out what it was he really wanted. And now he had. He knew, without a doubt, that what he wanted was Stephanie and Finn. That Katie had been a mistake – a year-long mistake. He had risked everything that was important to him because he'd felt resentful that Stephanie had wanted a career, he knew that now. The whole thing had happened because of his insecurity, his jealousy, his . . . vanity. But he had made a decision. He was going to tell Katie it was over, close down what was left of the business in Lower Shippingham and announce to Stephanie that he missed her and Finn too much, that he'd been selfish, that he'd decided it was worth living full-time in London – a city he hated, although he had told himself he mustn't rub this in – just to be with them. He wouldn't make her feel she had to be grateful or that he was making a massive sacrifice for her. No, that was the old James. This James would work on making his family happy, putting them first and trying to atone for the things he had done. He would bear the guilt on his own rather than burdening Stephanie with it.

But tonight it had all got a bit too much. Seeing all the thought and the love that Stephanie had put into the preparations for the party, watching her and Finn so excited as they tidied and decorated, he had been overwhelmed by a wave of love for the two of them. How could he keep on deceiving them? He tried to stifle the urge to come clean, to confess everything, but it wouldn't go away. He knew it might backfire, but he had to try and make a clean start and the only way that that was possible was to be completely honest.

For the first time in his life he wanted to tell the truth and take the consequences, whatever they were. He tried to stop himself, he knew deep down that it would be suicide, but as he watched Stephanie laughing with his parents, and as he received the pats on the back and hugs of his friends, he knew that he had reached the point of no return. He felt a wave of surreal calm wash over him as he went and took Stephanie by the arm and told her he needed to talk to her. This was it. He was stepping out over the precipice.

'Steph, I have to tell you something,' he managed to say through the tears that had started to run down his cheeks. Stephanie stood looking at him blankly.

'Oh, God, I don't know where to start so I'm just going to say it. I've been seeing someone else.' He took a deep breath, waiting for a reaction. 'Actually, it's worse than that. I'm living with her, in Lower Shippingham. And I have been for a year. Just over a year. I'm so sorry, Stephanie. Please say something.'

The way it played out was nothing like either of the versions he had run through in his head. Stephanie neither shouted and screamed and told him she hated him, nor did she throw her arms around him and tell him that

256

everything was going to be OK. This second was the outcome he had allowed himself to fantasize about most in the brief run-up to his confession. Bless me, Stephanie, for I have sinned, and she would absolve him, telling him he was forgiven. Instead, even after he had cried, even after he had told her the whole story, every word of it the truth, she had stood there impassive, not speaking, until he had had to say, 'Did you hear what I said?' and, despite the fact that she had nodded, he had found himself telling her all over again.

'I never meant for it to happen. It had nothing to do with how I felt about you and Finn. And, Steph, you have to believe me when I tell you how bad I feel about it. How I'd do anything to change things, but I can't. But I'm going to end it, I promise you. I'll do anything . . .'

Eventually he'd run out of steam and had sort of thrown himself at her, needing her to comfort him. Stephanie had patted his back, like she might a dog, and then she'd pushed him away. She'd looked unmoved – completely unmoved. And then she'd said coldly, 'I knew anyway. I've known for ages.'

Stephanie felt as if the wind had been taken out of her sails. The truth was, she felt sorry for him. He was so pitiful, crying and begging and wanting a reaction from her, wanting to know if it was all going to be all right, but she couldn't bring herself to comfort him. She wondered what had tipped him over the edge, made him risk everything by telling her. She tried to imagine how she might have felt if this really was the first she had heard of it, if this had happened all those weeks ago before she'd found the text message, but she wasn't that person any more. She briefly considered that maybe he had found out about their plan and that this was a pre-emptive strike, but she knew him well enough to know that what she was seeing was genuine emotion. Something had happened to James to make him want to confess. And although she felt so distant from him, so removed from the histrionics of it all, she could see that this was a big step for him and that it had taken a lot of courage. He looked so desperate, staring intently at her, willing her to say that it was going to be OK, that she had to put him out of his misery. She could hardly tell him the truth, though, that she had been conspiring with his mistress to make his life hell.

'I'm sorry, James. I think we should separate. I just wanted to wait until after your birthday to tell you . . . Finn was so excited and –'

She didn't get a chance to finish whatever it was she had been about to say because James let out a howl and grabbed on to her arms, begging to be given another chance. 'I've changed,' he was saying. 'I don't know how I can prove it to you, or make it up to you but I promise I will. Please. Please don't just finish it like this.'

She peeled him off her. 'I have to. Sorry, James, I really am. I've had a while to think it through, you see, and I know it's best that we separate. There's nothing you can say to change my mind.'

James seemed so confused. It was obvious that of all the possible outcomes he had imagined to his big confession her resigned acceptance had never been one of them.

'How did you find out?' he asked eventually.

Stephanie thought about telling him that she and Katie had met, that they spoke on the phone regularly, that his parents' unscheduled visit had actually been part of their plan. There was some joy to be had, she thought, in watching his face while she revealed to him that the way his life had been crumbling around him recently had been partly her doing. But she found she didn't feel like kicking him when he was so obviously down. 'I just did,' she said. 'You weren't as discreet as you thought you were, obviously.'

'I'm so sorry,' he said again. 'I'm so, so sorry. I'm going to tell Katie it's over tomorrow. And then, please, please, can we talk? Please don't shut me out.'

Oh, shit, Stephanie thought. Katie.

After another ten minutes, in which James continued to cry and to tell her more and more details of his deceptions, as if by burdening her with it he would leave her with no option but to forgive him, Stephanie persuaded him that she had to go downstairs to check on the guests. 'We can talk later,' she said as she went. 'Although, to be honest, I don't think there's much more to talk about.'

James had told her that Katie was planning another party for him the next day – a fact she, of course, knew already. He wasn't intending to go, he said. In fact, he wasn't intending to ever see Katie again.

'Don't be ridiculous,' Stephanie found herself saying. 'You can't just run away from the situation. You've got a business to run up there.'

James had looked at her, confused: he had clearly

thought that promising to have no further contact with Katie would have pleased Stephanie. Christ, Stephanie thought, he still thinks it's all going to be OK.

'Then you come up with me,' he was saying. 'That way you'll be able to see I'm telling you the truth when I say it's all over and done with. We can present her with a united front and then we can go to the surgery, clear my stuff out and come straight back down here.'

'James, if you want to finish things with Katie, then finish things with Katie. But don't do it for me. I've told you it's over, OK?'

There was no way James was going to be able to go down and face their guests, so when Stephanie finally made a break for freedom, she did a quick circuit, telling them he was unwell and having a lie-down. Several people cast suspicious glances at the Japanese chefs and put their plates down nervously, rubbing their stomachs and feeling their foreheads for signs of a temperature. Once she had told enough people for the word to go round, Stephanie took the phone out into the garden, found a quiet spot and called Katie.

'How's it going?' Katie squealed.

Stephanie told her the whole story, leaving out some of the more unkind things James had said about her in an effort to please Stephanie.

'Was he on to us, do you think?' Katie asked, when she had finished.

'No. Definitely not, I'd say. That's why it's so weird . . . it's genuine.'

'Shit,' Katie said. 'I was so looking forward to tomorrow night.'

Stephanie told her of James's plan to travel up early the next day to end the relationship. 'So, I guess it's all over,' she said. 'What will you do? Cancel the party?'

'No way,' Katie said, laughing. 'I'll tell everyone it's to celebrate my freedom.'

'That doesn't sound like you,' Stephanie said, thinking of the sweet, rather naïve woman she had first met all those weeks ago.

'It's the new me,' Katie said. 'The new improved no-one-messes-with-me version.'

Stephanie laughed although she wasn't entirely sure that the new Katie could be called an improvement. 'Let me know how it goes, won't you?'

'Of course.'

Back among her friends and family, Stephanie wondered whether she should stand up and make a statement: 'Thank you all for coming. James and I would like to announce our separation. He turned out to be a lying, cheating, two-timing bastard but I'm sure we'd all like to wish him a happy birthday.' She decided to leave things as they were. Everybody was having a great time and, probably, it was the last time they would all be together. Tomorrow she could start to let the truth slip. Besides, she had to tell Finn first.

35

In the end, Stephanie and James had had to share a bed on the night of the party because Pauline and John were sleeping in the spare room and one of their friends had fallen asleep on the sofa in the living room. James had taken Stephanie's reappearance in the bedroom as a signal that a thaw was approaching, and she had spent much of the night fighting off his tearful advances.

On Sunday morning he made a big show of getting up early and announcing to her that he would be back from Lincolnshire by dinnertime. Stephanie had to sit him down and tell him all over again that there was no hope.

'If you're coming back down to London tonight, then you'll need to find somewhere to stay,' she said. 'I'll start packing up your things.'

At breakfast, Finn was full of the party, and Stephanie had felt a genuine wave of pity for James while he tried manfully to join in the conversation and not give anything away to his son. They had decided that Stephanie would break the news to him once James had gone, because she would be able to do it rationally and calmly. James, on the other hand, was likely to break down.

'Let me know where you're going to be,' Stephanie said to him, as he got in the car, wanting to reinforce the idea in his head that he wasn't coming home.

'Sweetie, I've got something to say to you,' she said to

Finn, as soon as James had left. Might as well get it over with. 'Me and dad are . . . Well, we've decided to live in different houses for a bit. It's not because we don't love each other or anything like that, it's just, well, sometimes grown-ups decide to do things like that. It doesn't mean we're not a family any more . . .'

It sounded like one big cliché to her but Finn seemed to be taking it in. He was looking at her calmly.

'And it doesn't mean either of us loves you any less either. Oh, and you can see Dad whenever you want. OK?'

'OK.'

She waited for him to say something else but he had already turned back to his PlayStation. So many of his friends lived with only one parent, she thought sadly, that it probably seemed quite normal to him. Either that, or he was pretending to take it in his stride for her sake. She needed to get some advice on the best way to make sure he didn't bottle up his feelings and end up in a couple of years as a homicidal crack-taking maniac.

Katie had spent most of the night and the best part of the morning trying to decide how to react when James told her it was over. She had thought about packing up all his stuff and leaving it on the doorstep, calling out an emergency locksmith to change the locks and then watching him secretly from an upstairs window. She'd considered cooking him his favourite meal (roast lamb with broccoli, minted peas and roast potatoes), putting on her prettiest dress, making up her face and watching him squirm as he tried to get up the courage to tell her.

She'd even thought of letting out all her pent-up anger and screaming insults at him in a way she'd often fantasized about over the past couple of months. In the end, though, she decided that absolute indifference would unsettle him the most.

So, when he pulled up at about one o'clock – Stephanie had called her at ten this morning to let her know he was on his way already – she was sitting on the sofa reading the Sunday papers, legs curled under her. She had arranged herself in this casual position when she had heard his car turn into the road and she was now doing her best to look as though this was any normal Sunday morning. In fact, she was curious to see whether James had it in him to tell her the whole truth. It was hard to imagine that he would and, to be honest, she would hardly blame him if he couldn't. After all, where would you start? 'I'm sorry I forgot to mention that I was still living with my wife. Did I tell you I was separated? Really? I don't know what came over me.'

Her heart had clearly not been listening when her brain had been telling it to act as if it didn't care because it was racing now, as James got out of the car. She noticed that, of course, he didn't have any bags with him – he wasn't intending to stay. She forced herself to stare at the page of the supplement she was holding and, with her other hand, she stroked Stanley's ear, willing herself to calm down. James, when he came through the front door, looked as if he had been up crying all night, which, of course, he had, according to Stephanie, who had told Katie she had had to tell him several times to keep it down so as not to wake Finn. His hair was standing up on end and his eyes were wide and haunted. If she hadn't already known exactly what he was about to tell her she would have thought someone had died. He stood in the doorway, clearly waiting for a reaction.

'You're early,' she said. Stanley, who didn't know any better, was up on his feet and wagging his tail, happy to see his master.

'I have to talk to you,' he said dramatically. 'I have to tell you something.'

Katie knew that he wanted her to help him out, to look fearful and ask him what it was, to rise to the melodrama of the occasion. But she wouldn't.

'OK,' she said calmly.

He flung himself into the armchair, opposite. He looked as if he was going to cry some more, she thought, and that made her irritated. Just get on with it, she wanted to say.

'The truth is . . .' he started, and then paused – for effect, she thought.

'OK, I'm just going to say it. The truth is that I'm still married to Stephanie. We still live together when I'm in London and she had no idea about any of this. About you and me. I've been lying to you all this time – to both of you, actually – and I'm sorry. I'm really sorry.'

Katie was momentarily taken aback by the fact that he seemed to be being completely honest. She had to remind herself to keep her expression neutral.

James was looking at her for a reaction. When he didn't get one he took a deep breath and carried on: 'And I've realized I've made a terrible mistake. I don't know how to say this to you without it sounding cruel but I know

now that it's my family I want – even though they don't want me at the moment – but I'm going to fight to get them back. I'm sorry, Katie, I really am, but I've got to do anything I can to save my marriage. This has to be the last time we see each other . . .'

Even though she had known what was coming, this last part made her angry. He was happy just to cast her aside. Forget that she didn't want him any more, it still hurt that he seemed able to dump her so easily, so finally, and without even considering the time they'd had together as anything other than, in his own words, 'a terrible mistake'. Bastard.

She took a deep breath to try and slow her speeding pulse and spoke slowly to ensure that her voice was steady and calm. 'Good,' she said. 'I'm going to take Stanley out now. Please make sure you've packed up your stuff and gone by the time I get back. I'll give you, what, an hour? Oh, and leave your key.'

James, exhausted by his long speech, was incredulous. 'Is that all you've got to say?'

Katie forced a smile. That'd confused him. 'Good luck,' she said cheerily. She waved as she went out of the front door, not looking back. ''Bye!'

Once she was round the corner, out of sight of the cottage, Katie allowed her expression to drop. She hated him. OK, so it was to his credit that he'd actually managed to tell the truth for once in his life, but the fact he hadn't even seemed to care about sparing her feelings incensed her. He was so blinkered now that he couldn't see anyone other than himself and Stephanie. He hadn't cared that Katie might be hurt, that for all he knew he was ruining her life. She let out a shout of frustration and it echoed back across the empty field. He wasn't going to get away with it.

By the time she returned home, exhausted after walking miles through the damp grass, all trace of him had gone. She wondered, briefly, whether he had driven straight back to London or whether he would try to tie up the loose ends of his life here properly first. She shook her head, as if dismissing the thought. It was nothing to do with her any more and she had a party to get ready for.

There wasn't a great deal he wanted to take with him. As much of the equipment as he could cram into the car – that might come in useful for selling later – his personal bits and pieces and copies of the company accounts, which he imagined he might need in the future. He had already loaded the patient files into boxes and had made two trips round to Simon's house where he'd dumped them outside the front door. He couldn't face speaking to anyone. He had placed a note on top of the pile which simply said, 'I have decided to give up the business. Here are all the records. J.'

Katie's reaction had both confused and, he realized, disappointed him. He hadn't wanted to hurt her any more than necessary and he knew he should be grateful that it seemed she was going to be absolutely fine, but he didn't want to believe that she hadn't really had feelings for him. If that was the case, what had the last year been about? It wasn't so much that his ego was punctured, it was that he felt stupid. Had he risked – ruined, maybe – everything for someone who could just casually wish him good luck and take the dog for a walk when he told her it was over? He had always believed that Katie was absolutely devoted to him. Had he been completely mistaken?

He took one last look round. He would have to call a house-clearance company to take away all the things he was having to leave behind. He had already sent away the paperwork for the retrospective planning application so that was in the lap of the gods. He wondered whether, if it wasn't granted, he would have to come back and rip down the extension with his bare hands before he could sell the place. He couldn't worry about that now. The important thing was to get back to London and start trying to piece his life back together.

36

If the party guests didn't know that something was up before they reached the village hall that night, it didn't take them long to pick up on it once they arrived. Slung between two hooks above the front door was a printed banner that had once clearly read 'Happy 40TH Birthday James' but which now, with the aid of a thick black marker pen, proclaimed 'Happy Fuck You James', something which made those of the villagers who had brought their children to the party with them feel very uneasy.

Inside the room had been decorated beautifully, but there was an edgy atmosphere with people standing around in small groups, whispering about what might be going on. News of James giving up the surgery had already spread, and clearly all was not well, but Katie seemed to be smiling and laughing and all she would say to anyone who asked was that she would explain everything later. She was looking especially lovely. In a flowing floral maxi-dress, and with her hair dyed back to its former blonde self and falling in curls round her shoulders, all she needed was a bicycle to look as if she had stepped straight out of a postcard from the 1970s.

At about nine o'clock she took a deep breath and had her first swig of champagne. She had been dying for some alcohol all evening but had resisted, knowing that she wanted to be able to remember every detail of what was about to happen. Now she knocked back half a glass in one go and made her way up to the small stage at one end of the room where the Lower Shippingham Players, led by Sam and Geoff McNeil, performed their twice-yearly shows. She climbed the stairs at one side and stood in front of the patchy red velvet curtains. Before she had time to worry about how she was going to attract everyone's attention, all eyes were on her and the antici-patory buzz was almost tangible.

Katie swallowed. She had never been any good at public speaking, preferring to play the role of the quietly supportive friend rather than vying for attention. But she had thought through exactly what she was going to say and, after all, this was her night. There was no doubting that the crowd would be on her side. She cleared her throat softly.

'I expect you're all wondering what's going on,' she said, and a low murmur went round the room. She could see them all there, looking up at her expectantly: Richard and Simone, Sam and Geoff, Hugh, Alison, Simon, Malcolm, even Owen. She hadn't been able to persuade Sally or her family to come, although she had tried. She recognized countless of James's clients among the crowd and the bloke who ran Le Joli Poulet. All of them were staring at her now and she could feel herself blushing. Just get on with it, she told herself.

'I'm sure lots of you remember Stephanie, James's wife.' She watched as their expressions changed to utter bewilderment. What did Stephanie have to do with anything?

'As you know, James and Stephanie separated about

a year and a half ago. James and I got together a few months later and he moved into the cottage with me. Since then he's spent half the week living with me and the other half down at his London practice where he lodges with friends and gets to see his son Finn on a Saturday. Or . . .' she paused dramatically '. . . that's what I thought.'

The silence in the room was so intense she felt light-headed. She waited a second for her words to sink in.

'A few weeks ago I discovered that James and Stephanie have never, in fact, been separated.'

There was an audible gasp.

'In fact, as far as Stephanie was aware, they were still happily married.' The murmuring had started again. Katie wanted to laugh as she looked round at the expressions on their faces. Several people asked for quiet, eager to hear the rest of the story.

'So, you see, the truth is that I had no idea about Stephanie, and Stephanie had no idea about me. James was living a double life. Caring husband and father from Wednesday through till Sunday and loving boyfriend for the rest of the week. Until Stephanie found out, of course. Then she told me. She wanted to be here this evening, by the way, but she couldn't make it.' More confusion all round. This was perfect, Katie thought. They were hanging on her every word. She could hardly bear to leave the stage.

'So,' she said, 'to cut a long story short, James and I are finished. I told him to get out and he's gone, back to London, as far as I know, although what he's going to do there I can't imagine because Stephanie has thrown him out as well. And I don't care because I have no intention of ever speaking to him again.

'Now, I want you all to enjoy the party. The buffet will start in a minute. Let's all get drunk.'

Someone started to applaud and a few others joined in, unsure of quite what the etiquette might be. As Katie stepped down from the stage a small crowd gathered round her, hugging her and commending her on her bravery. She could do much better, they assured her. James was clearly a loser and would certainly never be made to feel welcome in Lower Shippingham again. Katie basked in the attention. OK, so it wasn't the public humiliation she and Stephanie had wanted for James, but this felt almost as good.

At about eleven, when she could finally tear herself away from the concerns of her neighbours for the first time, she went outside and called Stephanie. 'I've done it.'

'Good for you,' Stephanie said, and Katie could tell that she was smiling. 'Tell me all the details.'

After that things became a bit of a blur. Katie could remember all the kind words and how everyone seemed to want to look after her, fetching her drinks and encouraging her on to the dance-floor. She remembered crying briefly when someone – Simone, she thought, who was obviously feeling guilty for her attempted seduction of James – was especially sympathetic. What she didn't remember, though, was going home with Owen or how she had managed to end up nearly naked in his bed.

The view from the window of James's hotel room was of the air-conditioning units outside the back of the next-door restaurant and their insistent hum drowned out any hope of being able to watch the TV. He tried closing the window, but as his hotel didn't have the luxury of its own air-conditioning it quickly became unbearably hot and he had no choice other than to open it again. But he had chosen the hotel for the location, not for its facilities. He was within walking distance of Stephanie, somewhere where it wouldn't seem ridiculous for him to bump into her every now and then. He felt it was important that she couldn't just put him out of her mind completely.

He lay down on the narrow bed. He was exhausted but he knew he wouldn't be able to sleep. His head was reeling with the events of the past couple of days. He hadn't expected Stephanie to just say she forgave him and carry on as normal after he'd blurted out his secret, but her reaction had knocked him sideways. How could she have known what he was going to tell her? And how long *had* she known? He tried to think back over the last few months to see if her behaviour towards him had changed, if he could pinpoint a day or an hour when her attitude had shifted, but the truth was he hadn't been paying attention. And as for Katie . . . James rubbed his eyes. He had no idea what was going on, except that his life with Katie, indeed his whole life in Lincolnshire, was over and he didn't care. In fact, it felt good to cut off a whole portion of his existence so completely. Once he had sold the surgery he would never have to think about Lower Shippingham or the people in it again. Good riddance.

He broke out in a clammy sweat as he thought about how he was going to survive. Until he got any money from the sale of the surgery he would have to live on his savings, a big portion of which had just been wiped out by the tax people. He would call an estate agent in the morning – maybe there was a way of selling up without having to wait for the planning permission for the extension to come through. Although why anyone would want to take on that headache he couldn't imagine. The hotel was costing him seventy-five pounds a night for this little space without even a kettle or a free bottle of water. He supposed he should look for a flat although he thought it unlikely that, in London, he could afford to live alone, and the idea of having to share, like a student, with a person or people he didn't know (and who would almost certainly be at least ten years younger than him) made him want to weep. He thought of Stephanie in their cosy house just round the corner and wondered if she was thinking about him.

She wasn't.

37

On Monday morning Stephanie woke having slept rather well after talking to Katie. It was over. She couldn't help but be pleased that James had been spared the public humiliation they had had planned for him. It was strange the way he had decided to tell her, quite brave, really, she supposed, very unlike him.

Finn had been a bit tearful getting ready for school, as if the news that Stephanie had broken to him the previous day had just sunk in. She bribed him by promising to buy him a girlfriend for David, which seemed to work. Oh, God, she thought, we've only been separated for two days and I'm trying to buy my child off. But he went into school happy so it seemed worth it, even though Stephanie was now having visions of having to live in a kind of Noah's Ark just to appease her son.

After dropping Finn off she went back to the house where she was, euphemistically, 'working' from home. Things had gone a bit quiet after the BAFTAs, as they always did, but the glossy magazines had featured photos of both Meredith and Mandee, with complimentary comments, so that should guarantee some future business. She spent half an hour on the phone to Natasha filling her in, half-heartedly flicked through some magazines for inspiration, then allowed herself to think about the evening ahead.

Michael was meeting her in Nobu at seven thirty and, although he didn't know it yet, Stephanie had decided that this was the night they would take their relationship on a stage. She had arranged for Finn to sleep over at Arun Simpson's house, telling his mother that she thought an evening spent with his friend would take his mind off the trauma at home. Arun's mum, Carol, herself a single mother, had been only too happy to help.

Stephanie's plan was to break the news to Michael that her marriage was finally over for good during the starter and then have seduced him into wanting to take her home by the time they had finished their main course. She didn't, in truth, think he would take much persuading. In retrospect she felt relieved and happy that Natasha's interruption had meant they hadn't yet had sex – well, not quite, anyway. She wanted their relationship to be totally above board, with no niggling thoughts at the back of her mind that it had started before she had told James their marriage was over.

By the time it got to six o'clock and she was starting to put on her makeup she felt sick. Could she really go through with this? Forget whether it was the correct thing to do morally, she wasn't sure if she could cope with taking off her clothes in front of another man after all these years. OK, so he had pretty much seen her naked the other day, but not quite. She blushed when she remembered the way they hadn't even waited to get undressed properly, like two teenagers shagging in the park. Oh, well, she thought, if he doesn't like what he sees, then that's his problem. She tried to convince herself that she really believed this but, of course, she didn't.

It was twenty to eight by the time the cab dropped her off in Park Lane. Michael was sitting at the bar, an almost empty white wine glass in his hand. 'Dutch courage,' he said, as he saw her, and she laughed.

Of course he was nervous too. He had been married to the same woman for fifteen years, after all. Stephanie relaxed a little. 'I'd better have one too,' she said.

Four and a half hours later it was over. Well, for the first time at least. Stephanie lay back in Michael's big wooden bed while he went downstairs to fetch drinks and congratulated herself. It had been . . . well, it had been a bit awkward, like first-time sex always was. They couldn't anticipate each other's moves yet and there had been a lot of 'How does that feel?' and 'Is that good?' and 'Do you like it like that?' going on and she had had to put on a bit of a performance because otherwise they would have been there all night. But otherwise it had been good. Nice. Not earth-shattering, but nice. And nice was definitely good enough at the moment.

Katie had woken up with a dry mouth and a slightly hazy memory of the previous evening. As she'd struggled to open her eyes she'd become aware of an unfamiliar smell. Nothing unpleasant, it just wasn't her lily-scented familiar bedroom. Someone had grunted softly beside her and she'd felt wide awake in an instant. She'd forced herself to look round. Sprawled on his back, she would have sworn with a smile on his face even though he was asleep, was Owen. Surely not. She couldn't have. She'd looked under the covers: she'd seemed to still have her underwear on, that could be a good sign. Oh, God. She had no idea what had happened.

She had eased her way out from under the covers, trying not to wake him. She hadn't been able to face having to have a conversation, let alone whatever else he might have been be expecting. She had to get out of there. Owen had mumbled softly and rolled over, blissfully unaware that Katie had been standing looking down at him, horrified. She'd stopped dead in her tracks for a moment, holding her breath, and he had settled down again, like a contented baby. Katie had felt anger welling inside her. How could he sleep so happily after what had happened? Not that she knew quite what that was, of course, but she could imagine. He must have taken advantage of the fact that she had been drunk and emotional. She hadn't even been able to remember what time she had left the party or even if she had said goodbye to anyone. She'd spotted the rest of her clothes lying on a chair and had gathered them up as quietly as she could. She'd looked around for her shoes and couldn't see them anywhere. Sod it, she'd have to leave them behind.

Outside, the grass was dewy wet. She had no idea what time it was and realized, looking at her wrist, that she had left her watch behind too. It must be early, she thought, but she didn't want to risk bumping into anyone she knew so she decided to go the long way round, through the fields. She tiptoed along, occasionally stepping on something sharp or stubbing a toe on a tree root. She felt sick, too, and headachy. It was so long since she'd had a proper hangover that she'd forgotten how miserable it felt. All she wanted to do was lock herself inside her little cottage and sleep it off.

As she put the key in the lock she heard Stanley's miserable whine and realized, with a guilty pang, that she had forgotten about him. When she opened the door he shot out past her and cocked his leg against a tree and she felt terrible, knowing that he had probably been dying to go for hours but would have kept his legs tightly crossed rather than mess on the floor, which he had always been told was wrong. She made a big fuss of him and tried not to gag as she opened a can of his favourite foul-smelling food. He wagged his tail happily, the trauma of the previous night already forgotten.

Upstairs, Katie undressed and, despite her tiredness, had a shower before she crawled into bed. She wanted to wash all traces of Owen off herself.

A few hours later – she had no idea how many – she was jolted from sleep by the front-door bell. Stanley began to bark loudly, just to make sure that if the shrill peal of the bell hadn't woken her, at least he would. Without thinking, she stumbled down the stairs in her pyjamas and opened the front door. On the step sat her shoes with her watch curled up inside one of them. She picked them up quickly, looking around to check that Owen wasn't going to materialize. There was no sign of him.

She went back to bed, turned off her phone and stayed there for the rest of the day.

38

James was struggling to concentrate. He knew he should be looking for somewhere better to live but he didn't really know where to start. He spent twenty minutes or so half-heartedly looking in estate agents' windows but even the smallest flat was out of his price range. He was starting to regret leaving so many of his belongings behind; he could have done with something to sell, although what and to whom he couldn't quite work out. He bought a *Standard* and scoured it for flatmate-wanted adverts, but it seemed it was the wrong day.

Newsagents' windows, he thought, that was the answer. He couldn't remember where any newsagents actually were but he decided that if he wandered round for long enough then he was bound to bump into one.

His aimless pottering inevitably took him nearer and nearer to Belsize Avenue, and before he knew quite what he was doing he was in front of his house looking up at the windows and wondering what Stephanie and Finn were doing. Finn, of course, would be getting ready for school and Stephanie would probably be about to go to work, although she worked at home on at least a couple of days a week. He looked at his watch. Eight twenty-five. He could ring the doorbell and explain that he'd been passing and wanted to collect some more clothes. And then what? There was no point in asking her again to take him back. It had only been two days since she'd turned him down flat. She was hardly going to have changed her mind. He turned away sadly. He needed a strategy.

As he rounded the corner on to Haverstock Hill, his mission to look for room-to-let signs all but forgotten, a taxi passed him, going the other way. A woman who looked suspiciously like Stephanie was sitting in the back, gazing out of the window away from him. James did a double-take. It looked like she was heading home. At twenty-five past eight in the morning? It was too early for her to be on her way back from taking Finn to school. He turned round and walked slowly back up the road. Sure enough, the cab stopped outside his house and Stephanie got out. James found himself stepping into a neighbour's front garden and peering out from behind a tree to avoid being seen. Stephanie was dressed up as if she was going out – pencil skirt, high heels, that little Chanel jacket she loved so much. If you'd have asked him what her expression was like, he would have said that she looked like she was smiling. Smug, almost. And then it hit him: she was coming home after an evening out. Stephanie had been out all night.

Stephanie had woken early. In fact, she had only slept fitfully, waking every time Michael turned over or mumbled in his sleep. Not that he was unusually fidgety or noisy, it was just that it was unfamiliar fidgeting and unfamiliar noise. No doubt it must have been the same for him. They had woken at the same moment, at about five thirty, and they'd sleepily had sex again, this time at a more leisurely, less frenetic pace. More of an experience, less of a performance.

Afterwards Stephanie hadn't been able to go back to sleep so she'd got up and had a bath and then tried to make herself at home in the strange apartment, poking about in kitchen cupboards to find the teabags and the bread. Really, she had wanted to go back to her own home, to relax for a bit before she had to get ready for work, but she was worried it would seem she was making some kind of statement if she left before Michael had surfaced.

She had no idea if he was a late or early riser. There were a million and one things she didn't know about him, but she did know that the events of the last twelve hours had gone a long way towards giving her back her confidence. She'd decided to wait until eight, and if he wasn't up by then, she would leave him a note and go.

For the next hour and a half, while she'd drunk three more cups of tea, which made her feel slightly light-headed, she'd tried to decide what exactly the note might say. It couldn't just say 'Gone to work, love Stephanie' or he would think there was something wrong, but she didn't know whether she should be chatty ('Had a bath and then helped myself to tea and toast'), funny ('So, obviously, I've looked through all your cupboards and I've realized I've made a terrible mistake! We can never see each other again') or sexy ('What really turned me on was when you . . .' No! She couldn't go there). It had suddenly felt as if this note was the most important thing she was ever going to have to write. As if Michael's lasting memory of the night they had spent together would be dictated by the impression she left behind on paper.

She was starting to get a headache. She had just been wondering whether Natasha would be up yet and whether or not to call and ask her advice when she'd heard Michael moving around in the bathroom. She'd shot over to the cooker and tried to find a reflective surface in the stainless steel to check herself. By the time he'd come into the room she was sitting at the table, reading the paper and giving a good impression of looking casual.

'Morning,' he'd said, smiling in a way that had made her heart beat out of her ears. He'd come over and put his arms round her, leaning down to kiss her on the top of her head. 'I was worried you'd have left already.'

'I was going to leave you a note,' she'd said. 'If only I could have decided what it was going to say.'

'Well, I'm glad you're still here. Have you got time to come back to bed?' he'd said, kissing her before she had a chance to say yes.

She'd spent the rest of the morning, after having gone home to change, looking through a bag of Frost French samples with Natasha and filling her in on the details. Natasha had an almost insatiable appetite for the minutiae of other people's relationships. She claimed that living vicariously through her friends meant she was able to stay happy in her own long and completely monogamous situation. Stephanie knew that in reality Natasha and Martin didn't need any kind of outside input to keep them glued together. She had always envied her friend's seemingly idyllic relationship.

She had told Michael she couldn't see him for a couple of nights because she felt guilty about Finn and didn't want to be palming him off on his friends' parents or calling Cassie in more often than she had to. James would certainly have had him if she asked him to, but she had no idea where James had been since Sunday or where he was going to be living and, besides, she didn't really want to call him anyway. And it was way, way too soon all round to introduce her son to her new boyfriend. Michael had been understanding. They'd arranged to meet for lunch tomorrow, the only day that both of them could guarantee they would get a lunch break, and then again on Friday evening.

'That's good,' Natasha said, when she told her. 'Keeps him on his toes.' 'And how are you feeling about James?' she asked, a few minutes later.

'Do you know?' Stephanie said. 'I have no idea. Relieved it's all over, I guess.'

'Just don't forget,' Natasha said, as if she had just remembered that she was always the one with the words of wisdom, 'Michael is your transitional man. He's your rebound. Don't go taking it too seriously, whatever you do.'

'I've known him five minutes, Tash,' Stephanie said, hoping that what she was about to say was true. 'I'm just having a bit of fun.'

At about twelve o'clock her mobile rang and she saw that it was Katie. She hadn't really expected to speak to her so soon – if, indeed, ever again. Suddenly the whole scheme seemed so long ago. It felt like her life was finally starting over, she wasn't sure if she wanted to dwell on the past. It wasn't that she didn't like Katie, she did, but they didn't really have anything in common except for James. She answered hesitantly: 'Katie, hi.'

'So . . .' Katie said expectantly. 'How's it going?'

For a split second, Stephanie thought she was talking about Michael and nearly said, 'Well, we've finally slept together,' but then she remembered that she had never confided in Katie about her new relationship. She didn't know why not, she just hadn't felt like it would be the right thing to do. So, instead, she said, 'Oh, fine, I guess. He's gone. I don't know where.'

'Somewhere awful, I hope,' Katie said, laughing. 'The village is full of it, by the way, it's all anybody can talk about. I've got so many bookings – you wouldn't believe it. All because they want to hear the whole story, I think. I'm exhausted.'

'Good for you,' Stephanie said, and then couldn't think of anything else to say.

'And how has Finn taken it?'

'Oh, you know, a bit up and down. I guess things will start to get back to normal once we work out a plan for when he can see James, that kind of thing.'

'Sam McNeil told me his planning application is almost certain to be rejected, you know. She didn't admit it but I think she's going to make sure it is.'

'God, really?' Stephanie said, genuinely shocked. 'Maybe you could persuade her not to. I mean, there's no point carrying on now, is there?'

'Of course there is,' Katie said. 'It's fun.' She paused for a moment and then laughed again. 'Only joking. I'll see what I can do. Everyone's being so nice to me, Stephanie. I never knew I had so many friends here.'

'Great,' Stephanie said. 'I'm pleased for you.' But she felt uneasy. Katie, she thought, didn't believe that the game was over.

39

It was James's first day back at work since his life had begun to unravel. He had been late for his surgery because he had no clock and the hotel had forgotten to give him the alarm call he had booked the night before. He had finally got to sleep at about five, then had tossed and turned feverishly until a car horn woke him at about twenty past nine. He hadn't known where he was at first and, for a brief moment, had been afraid that he'd got himself into some kind of seedy encounter with a stranger, until he'd remembered, bad as that might be, the truth was much, much worse.

He had been intending to walk to work to save money but the fact that he was so late meant that he had had to take a taxi he couldn't afford, which then got stuck in traffic and caused him to be later still. He arrived at the Abbey Road Veterinary Clinic out of breath and sweating at a quarter past ten. There had been times in the past few years when James had enjoyed the fact that, in the London surgery, he wasn't the boss; he didn't have the responsibilities of hiring and firing or balancing the books. But today was not one of those times.

'Harry's spitting blood,' Jackie the receptionist said to him, the minute he walked through the door. 'I've been trying to ring you to find out where you were.'

James could picture his mobile phone lying on the

bedside table at the house he no longer lived in, where he'd accidentally left it. Great.

'I rang Stephanie but she said she had no idea.' James noticed she was looking at him as if she sensed something was going on and he tried to keep his face neutral. Jackie continued, 'Is everything all right?'

'So where is Harry?' James asked, ignoring her question. Harry, the owner of the Abbey Road Veterinary Clinic, had a notorious temper and was always fond of reminding James that, skilled and qualified he might be, the fact that he was head of his own practice in the countryside notwithstanding, in London Harry was the boss.

'He's removing a splinter from Barney MacDonald's paw. Barney was booked in with you at nine forty-five,' she said ominously, 'and Harry's already done your nine-o'clock, your nine-fifteen and your nine-thirty.'

'Well, I'm here now. You can send in my ten-o'clock.'

Jackie looked down at her list. 'Alexander Hartington is next,' she said, indicating a pale, middle-aged man with a large ginger cat, either of whom might have been called Alexander. James indicated to the man that he should come on through. It hadn't been a good start to the day. He had been planning on asking Harry if there was any chance of increasing his days – ideally to five a week – but now that didn't seem such a good idea. Once Harry was in a bad mood it tended to last the whole morning.

By lunchtime he was exhausted, lack of sleep and the fact that he was running late with all his patients and so wasn't able to stop for a quick coffee to perk him up conspiring to make him feel like he was never going to make it to the end of the afternoon. Just as his twelve forty-five left and he could slump back in his chair, and maybe get in a thirty-minute power nap and still have time to eat a sandwich before his next appointment, his phone rang. He thought about not picking it up but he knew that if he didn't Jackie would walk through from Reception and tell him whatever it was she was going to say anyway.

'It's Stephanie for you,' she said, when he finally answered and his heart nearly stopped. 'OK, put her through,' he said, in what he hoped was a normal voice, but Jackie had gone. She never waited to see whether he actually wanted to take his calls or not.

'James.' Stephanie sounded business-like.

'Hi, Steph, how are you?' Maybe she was calling to see how he was getting on. Maybe she had been worrying about him.

'I just wondered whether you wanted to have Finn tomorrow night. Cassie can't make it.'

James thought of his wife, dressed for a night out, coming home at eight thirty in the morning. Unable to help himself, he said, 'Why? Where are you going?'

'I don't think that's any of your business any more, James,' Stephanie said. 'Can you have him or not?'

She's seeing someone, he thought, and forgetting that he had been living a double life for the past year and that if ever a pot really shouldn't be starting to call a kettle black it was now, he said, 'Who is he?'

Stephanie laughed. More of a snort, really, it seemed to James. 'You're unbelievable.'

James forced himself to say nothing.

'Where shall I drop him off?' Stephanie said eventually.

'I'm staying at the Chalk Farm Travel Motel in Camden,' James said. 'You can bring him there.'

'You're staying at the Travel Motel? I'm not taking him over there. What are you going to do all evening? Race cockroaches?'

'I could come to the house,' he said hopefully. If he was at the house, surely Stephanie wouldn't have the front to stay out all night.

'Actually,' she said, without missing a beat, 'that might be a good idea. It'd be less disruptive for Finn. I'll be home by midnight. I'm only going out to eat with Natasha.'

OK, he thought, maybe I was overreacting. Maybe when I saw her the other morning she had just been at Natasha's. That would make sense. It's none of your business, he told himself. You have no right to ask her questions.

'Who are you really going out with?' he said, before he could stop himself.

'That's none of your business any more,' Stephanie said pleasantly. 'See you tomorrow. If you could try and get there by six that'd be perfect.'

In actual fact Stephanie hadn't been lying when she had said she was going out to eat with Natasha on Friday. She was trying to be as truthful as she could with James without actually telling him about Michael just yet. She didn't want to get into a situation where she felt she had to mention every date she went on or every flirtation she had. It was none of his business: they were separated now. Michael was on a job in the East End all day the next day and couldn't meet her till eight. They would have about three and a half precious hours together – she didn't want to stay out all night again so soon: it wasn't fair on Finn. So Natasha had offered to have a bite to eat with her after work, which gave her a night off from cooking for the kids, then kill an hour or so with her before Stephanie headed over to Shoreditch to meet him. It wasn't ideal but it was the reality of being a single working mother and trying to have a relationship.

She and Michael were planning on going to a music event. Jazz, Stephanie thought, which didn't really fill her with excitement. She would rather have gone back to Michael's flat and spent the time with him there. It felt like a bit of a waste of a precious night out to sit in a sweaty bar listening to music she wasn't keen on. But the musicians were friends of Michael's and he had promised them he'd go.

James, when he arrived at the house on Friday, looked like he had washed in the sink, which in fact he had, having moved to a cheaper room at the Chalk Farm Travel Motel – one that had the honour of sharing bathroom facilities with three other rooms on the same floor. The bathroom never seemed to be empty so James had been forced to use the tiny basin in the corner of his bedroom to clean both himself and his clothes. He had been torn between wanting to make a good impression on his wife and wanting her to feel sorry for him. In the end, circumstances had dictated that he couldn't have made a good impression if his life had depended on it so he went for the sympathy vote. It would be the first time he and Stephanie had been face to face since she'd thrown him out. She would, he knew, be looking good for whatever assignation she had lined up. He knew he had no right to be jealous. That if she had met someone already, unlikely as that seemed, he would have to accept it and try to move on. But he just wanted there to be a level playing-field – a chance that he could win his wife back without having to worry that it was too late already because she had lost her heart to someone else. He tried to work out who it might be. It had to be someone she knew already. Someone she had had waiting in the wings. Oh, God, what if it was a friend of his? Someone who had been at the party, even. James felt sick just thinking about it.

Finn opened the door when he got there and James could have sworn that his son's expression changed from one of excitement to something like fear when he registered the Grizzly Adams lookalike standing on the doorstep. James wished he had shaved, although who would have known he could grow such a fine beard in just a week? Once Finn realized that it was, indeed, his father, he allowed himself to be hugged, pulling back after a moment to say, 'You smell funny.'

'So do you,' James replied, and Finn laughed.

James looked around for Stephanie as Finn led him through to the kitchen but there was no sign of her. He had been hoping that maybe they could have a heart-to-heart before she left. He listened as Finn told him the details of his week ('Sebastian was sick on the carpet and it was all brown with a big lump in the middle like a dead mouse'), keeping an ear open for her footsteps on the stairs. As the minutes ticked on he realized she was avoiding having to spend any more time with him than she had to.

'Where's Mum?' he said to Finn, when there was a break in his stories.

'Upstairs,' Finn said. 'She's going out.'

'Oh,' James said, trying to sound casual, knowing that this was textbook bad-fathering to involve his son in his and Stephanie's personal dramas. 'Who's she going out with?'

Luckily Finn didn't seem to understand he was being used and simply shrugged and said, 'Dunno.'

At about a quarter past six he heard her coming down from upstairs and braced himself. She was in and out before he could take her in, telling him that she would ask the taxi driver who brought her home to drop him back at the Travel Motel, thus ensuring that there was no question of them having a cosy chat later on. She had done a slight double-take when she had first seen him, but she hadn't commented on his dishevelled appearance. She kissed Finn goodbye in a blur and was out of the house in a moment. She had been looking particularly good, he had noticed. Jeans and high heels, always one of his favourite combinations, with a fitted pale blue top. He sat back as he heard the front door close behind her, deflated.

Some six hours later, having allowed Finn to stay up way beyond his eight-thirty bedtime because he wanted the company, James was dozing on the couch when he heard the front door open and shut. He sat up, bleary-eyed.

'The taxi's waiting outside,' Stephanie said, as she came into the room.

James rubbed his eyes. 'Did you have a good time?'

'Yes, thank you.'

There didn't seem to be an open door for conversation, so he just said, 'Right, well, I guess I'd better get going then,' and stood up. Stephanie was looking a little unsteady on her feet, as if she'd had one glass of wine too many.

'Any time you'd like me to do this again just let me know,' he said. 'I want to spend as much time with Finn as I can.'

'If you could smarten yourself up a bit before the next time,' Stephanie said. 'I don't think it's good for him to see you in such a mess.'

So much for sympathy, James thought, as he left.

40

In Lower Shippingham Katie was still feeling like a minor celebrity. In a village any news was a headline, and a story like this could keep the gossip machine running for weeks. Almost everyone had a connection with James, even if it was just that their neighbour had once called him out to see to their sick hamster. The general consensus now seemed to be that 'He was always a bit strange' despite the fact that if you'd asked these same people their opinion a couple of weeks ago they'd have said he was charming, helpful and reliable. Katie was relishing her status as the wronged woman ('How could he do that to her of all people? She's so sweet, so vulnerable'): old ladies came up to her in the village shop to tell her she was better off without him and that somewhere out there was a man who would treat her like a princess, as she deserved.

Her business was still thriving, both because people were booking her to help her out ('She needs to keep busy, poor thing') and because they were keen to hear her side of the story ('Did you know he tried to seduce Simone Knightly? As if two women weren't enough!'). Simone, by the way, had relished telling Katie a heavily rewritten version of the night she had thrown herself drunkenly at James, which made her look like the victim and James the predator. Richard, she told Katie, was furious, threatening to flatten James if he dared to show his face in Lower Shippingham ever again.

Sam McNeil had told Katie that the council had, indeed, decided to insist that James tear down the extension to the surgery, but that as they didn't have a forwarding address for him there was a chance he wouldn't get this news until the deadline had passed, in which case he would incur a fine as well. 'How irresponsible,' she said, 'to go off and not let anyone know where he was going to be.'

Katie had been trying to resist being taken under Sam's wing but Sam, it seemed, was determined to mother her and kept insisting that Katie stop round for a drink or dinner. While she had been wanting to fuel the fire about the extension Katie had gone along with it, but she was hoping that she could now withdraw from the suffocating blanket that was Sam's friendship. It was time for her to have some fun, to make new friends and live a little.

She had never really got to know Sally O'Connell, James's receptionist, but she had decided that now was the time to put that right. Sally had been badly treated by James too, they had something in common now and, besides, she might be a useful weapon. So, one morning, armed with a bag of home-baked biscuits, and with her biggest, most friendly smile at the ready, she knocked at the door of Sally's house and reintroduced herself. 'So, I think you really shouldn't let him get away with it,' she said, once she had a cup of tea to go with the biscuits and they were sitting at the table in Sally's parents' kitchen. 'There are laws about that kind of thing. You can't just go around sacking people on the spot, whatever you think they've done.'

'I didn't do anything wrong,' Sally said defensively.

Katie, of course, knew this but couldn't admit that she did. 'Even if you did . . .'

'I didn't,' Sally said again, and Katie thought she was going to cry.

She tried a different tack. 'I know that. I just mean that even if James has decided to blame you for everything it was still wrong of him to just get rid of you. There are *procedures*.' She had no idea what those procedures actually were, but she was pretty sure that James would get into some kind of trouble if Sally made enough fuss. 'Official warnings and stuff like that. You should go and talk to Citizens' Advice.'

Sally took a sip of her tea. 'I don't know,' she said. 'I start work for Simon and Malcolm next week. It doesn't seem worth it.'

Katie had read that apathy was rife among the younger generation these days and that they were motivated by very little except the desire to sit on their sofas and play video games all day. Looking round Sally's family's kitchen it didn't look as if they could afford many video games, let alone anything to play them on. 'You could be owed money,' she said. 'I bet they'd make him pay some kind of compensation.' She could have sworn that Sally perked up.

'So, what exactly would I have to do?' Sally asked, pouring more tea.

The only cloud on Katie's horizon was Owen. She had managed to avoid him since the night of the party – or, rather, the morning after the night of the party – but she was still smarting from the idea that he might have taken advantage of her in her vulnerable state. From now on she was intending to be completely in charge in her relationships with men. No more sitting at home waiting for them to call or spending hours making shepherd's pie just the way they liked it. Next time she went out with someone it would be on her terms, they would have to fit their lives around her.

Lower Shippingham was a small place, though, and avoiding bumping into someone for long wasn't a realistic prospect. It was inevitable, then, that a couple of weeks after the party she should spot Owen coming out of the organic farm shop as she was about to go in. He smiled when he saw her. Katie thought about blanking him, but that seemed a little extreme when he was standing right in front of her so she said hello in as flat a way as she could muster.

'How are you?' Owen said warmly.

'Fine.' Katie moved as if to pass him and go into the shop. Owen, who was now looking a little confused, she thought, didn't step out of the way as she had expected him to. 'Excuse me,' she said.

'Are you OK?' Owen asked. 'Have I done something to upset you?'

Katie snorted. 'What do you think?'

'To be honest, Katie, I have no idea, but you're definitely giving a good impression of someone who's pissed off.'

Katie was aware that the two customers already in the shop were watching them, sensing a drama. She took

Owen's arm and led him outside on to the road. 'Well, since you ask, no, I am not OK, and yes, you have done something to upset me. Don't tell me you can't imagine what that could be.'

'I can't, actually. But I'm sure you're about to tell me,' Owen said, sounding irritated.

'So you don't remember getting me into bed on the night of James's party?'

'I remember *putting* you to bed, if that's what you mean.'

'And you getting in with me.'

'I had nowhere else to sleep. What is your problem?'

Katie faltered. This didn't seem as straightforward as she had imagined. 'And you just thought you'd take all my clothes off first?'

Owen looked round as if he was checking that no one was listening in. When he spoke again it was in an angry whisper: 'No, *you* took all your clothes off. Well, not all – I managed to stop you before you took off your under-wear as well. What's up, Katie? Are you embarrassed that you tried to sleep with me, is that it? Because all I thought I was doing was helping you out. Giving you somewhere to stay, rather than letting you wander off in the state you were in.'

Katie was taken aback. She had propositioned him? Oh, God, this was so humiliating. Still, she had to find out exactly what had gone on between them. 'So . . . you didn't . . . *we* didn't . . . ?'

'Of course we didn't. You were blind drunk. God, you really have got a low opinion of me.'

'Oh, shit, Owen. I'm really sorry. I just assumed . . .' She tailed off, not knowing quite what to say.

'What? You just assumed I must be so desperate that I'd have sex with you when you were practically comatose. Thanks a lot.'

'I just couldn't remember, that's all. When I woke up and you were there, well . . .'

'Forget it,' he said, starting to walk away. 'Of course I must have taken advantage of you because I'm such a loser.'

'God, I really am sorry,' she called after him, and then she noticed Sam McNeil standing in the doorway of the shop, watching the whole drama unfold.

'Can I help you?' Katie said aggressively, and Sam tried to pretend she had been examining the baby plum tomatoes all along.

Katie turned on her heel and walked off, blushing furiously. How was she supposed to have known that Owen was the one man in a million that would have behaved impeccably?

41

James had given up looking for a flat. Everything was too expensive, too far away or just too depressing. Besides, the Travel Motel was happy to continue accepting payment by credit card, which meant he could keep his head well buried in the sand as far as his financial situation was concerned. Harry had agreed that he could do one extra day a week in the surgery and he still had some savings, which would hopefully help to keep him afloat for a while. He didn't like to think for how long. He had sold his car for a ridiculously low price, because it had already been broken into twice, sitting in the street outside his and Stephanie's house, and now he was on the phone, trying to explain to an estate agent in Lincoln exactly why it was a good idea to sell a building with a large extension attached that needed to be pulled down.

'It's hardly worth my while,' the man was saying. 'I mean, I suppose I could market it as a renovation project but then you're looking at, what?, asking about fifty per cent of its true value.'

James thought about his beautifully appointed surgery, which had only been redecorated four months ago and wanted to weep. 'And what's the alternative?' he asked, feeling angry with the estate agent for, he didn't know quite what. It wasn't his fault, after all.

'Well, you pull the extension down, make good and

then we put it on the market. It'll fetch a much better price.'

'Fine,' James said, not feeling fine at all. 'I'll get back to you.'

The one thing he knew was that he couldn't go up to Lower Shippingham himself to sort this mess out. He had no doubt he was a pariah in the village by now and he was far too much of a coward to ever want to risk bumping into Katie. Or Sally or Simone or pretty much anyone, really. He tried to think if there was anyone up there he trusted to do the work without supervision, but the only builder he had any kind of relationship with – the one who had built the extension in the first place – was Sally O'Connell's boyfriend Johnny, and he somehow didn't feel like calling him would be the best idea he'd ever had. He would have to take a chance and call one of the big firms in Lincoln and get them to do it, although God knows how much that was going to cost him.

He knew that the time had come for him to sit down and have a proper adult conversation with Stephanie about what should happen next, but he was too afraid that she was going to start talking about divorce to initiate the conversation and, besides, she seemed to be avoiding being left alone with him. Whenever he went to pick up Finn or to spend the evening with him at the house, Cassie always seemed to be there too, right up until the moment Stephanie left. And then, when Stephanie came home, she still always kept the taxi outside, engine running, to take him back to the Travel Motel. He knew she was seeing somebody. It was obvious. And he suspected that there were other nights, when either Natasha or

Cassie babysat, when she didn't come home at all. After her comment that first evening he had made a real effort to smarten himself up but he wasn't sure she'd even noticed.

He wanted to do the right thing by her. Of course he wasn't planning to try to persuade her that they should sell the family home so they could both buy somewhere smaller. He was the guilty party so he was the one who should have to make sacrifices and, besides, he wanted Finn to be able to be as settled as possible. But he was terrified that he was going to be left with nothing. That by the time he had sold the surgery for whatever fraction of its worth, he would have credit-card bills so huge that the money would simply be swallowed up and he would be left with nowhere to live and no savings left to bail himself out.

He was a vet, for God's sake, and he had trained for years so that not only could he spend his days doing something he loved but he could also earn big money. Long term, he thought, he could set up on his own down here, although for that he would need capital to fund the start-up costs. He had made half-hearted enquiries at several other practices to see if he could pick up the odd day here and there, but no one seemed interested.

He could get work a couple of days a week doing something else entirely, but what? He had no other skills. And, besides, he needed his days off so that he could keep tabs on Steph. He had taken to hanging around furtively outside the house sometimes – luckily, this being London, his old neighbours didn't bat an eyelid – and had watched her coming and going, trying to work out who it was that she was seeing, if indeed there was anyone. In the past three weeks – apart from the four evenings he had looked after Finn – she had been out at least another three times. Luckily there was a small green space almost opposite the house where he could sit with his sandwiches and his bottle of water and wait for her to return. He hadn't seen any sign of a man with her, which gave him hope. Realistically he knew there was someone, but until he saw the evidence he could convince himself that she was just out having a few drinks with the girls. He had thought about following her on her nights out – hailing a taxi and offering up the classic follow-that-cab line from the movies – but he knew that, sad as he had become, even he wasn't *that* sad. If she had met someone she liked, she would bring him home eventually. Meanwhile he needed to try and get her to see what she was losing. (And what was that? he thought. A sad unshaven man who lived in a Travel Motel and ate baked beans out of the tin in the evenings because he had nowhere to cook and no money to buy a takeaway. Worse, a man who had proved himself to be untrustworthy and not worth investing in emotionally.)

He decided to go for a walk. The four walls of his room at the Travel Motel were suffocating him and there was only so much daytime TV he could watch. He called Stephanie and left a message that he was going to pick Finn up from school. He had no idea whether or not she was working at the moment, although she always seemed to be busy when he spoke to her but, of course, that might just be an excuse to get off the phone. Then he rang Cassie, who answered, and he told her the same. She sounded delighted to have the afternoon off, as he had known she would be.

He slogged up Chalk Farm Road towards Belsize Park, puffing a bit from the effort of walking uphill. He felt at home once he got up here where the streets were greener and getting mugged was an altogether more remote prospect. These days, he was finding it hard to remember why he had always hated it so much. It seemed positively like an oasis of calm compared to the Travel Motel's surroundings. He arrived outside the gates of the little school with five minutes to spare and stood there, feeling self-conscious in among the young mums and even younger au pairs. Just a few weeks ago he would have seen this as a great opportunity, a hunting ground where he would have used the fact that he cared enough for his son to come and pick him up from school as a flirting tool. Now he couldn't have been less interested. There was only one woman he wanted to impress.

Finn's face lit up when he saw James waiting for him, and then he must have remembered that his friends were around because he rearranged his expression into something he thought was more moody, and therefore more grown-up, and said, 'What are *you* doing here?'

James laughed and, resisting ruffling his son's hair, patted him on the back instead. 'I gave Cassie the afternoon off,' he said. 'I thought we could give David's cage a good clean-out.'

And then Finn said something that made James's heart stop: 'Does Mum want you to meet Michael too?'

Michael. So that was his name. James thought for a

moment that he was going to throw up the instant noodles he had eaten for lunch into the hedge. He mentally flicked through everyone he knew, friends, fathers of Finn's classmates, people Stephanie had ever mentioned working with. He couldn't come up with a Michael. He breathed deeply. 'Who's Michael?'

Finn, oblivious to the reaction he had invoked in his father, said blithely, 'He's Mum's new boyfriend. He's coming round this evening so I can meet him.'

'Right. What time?' James was trying, and failing, to sound casual.

'Don't know,' Finn said, bored of this topic now. 'When Mum gets home probably.'

Oh, God. Having given Cassie the day off, James knew that he would have to stay with Finn until Stephanie got home. On the other hand this was just what he had been wanting – to know who Stephanie was seeing, to work out who the competition was. 'How soon after Mum gets home, do you think?' he asked. 'Will he travel home with her? Do they work near each other? What does he do?'

'Why are you asking so many questions?' Finn said grumpily. 'Don't you like Mum having a boyfriend?'

'Not much, no,' James said miserably, and then wished he hadn't.

'Mum said you've got a girlfriend.'

'I haven't. I did have but I definitely haven't any more. It was a very bad thing to do.'

'Having a girlfriend is a bad thing to do?' Finn asked, and James couldn't tell whether he was being serious or not.

'When you already have a wife it is.'

'Well, obviously,' Finn said, rolling his eyes. 'Everyone knows that.'

42

Since she had picked up James's message telling her that he was on his way to collect Finn from school, Stephanie had frantically been trying to call him back. Not today. She was always happy for Finn to see his father, just not this afternoon. It had taken her a few sleepless nights to decide that Michael was worthy of an introduction to her son. And then a few more anxious days before she could bring herself to suggest it to both Michael and Finn. A couple of weeks into her new relationship, she had started to mention Michael's name casually around the house. She had had no idea whether this was the right way to let your child know you had a new partner without traumatizing them for ever, but she didn't really know how else to do it, and to have sat Finn down and made a big announcement would have made way too big a deal out of something that was still a casual affair.

Finn had been remarkably laid-back about the whole thing which made her worry that he hadn't quite understood what her relationship with Michael was, so one day, when she was cooking him his favourite fish fingers and beans, she had said, in as *blasé* a way as she could manage, 'You know Michael is sort of like my boyfriend?'

Finn had merely rolled his eyes and had said, 'You're too old to have a boyfriend,' which hadn't made her feel any better.

Then, two days later, he had said to her out of nowhere, 'Arun's mum's got a boyfriend.'

She'd waited to see if he added anything else and, when he didn't, the only thing she could come up with was, 'Oh? Has she?'

'Like you,' he'd said, and then he'd gone off to play with Sebastian and that had been that.

Michael had been a slightly harder prospect. Not because she thought he wouldn't be interested in Finn – he always asked about him and he hadn't yet yawned when she was in the middle of a story about some cute thing or other that Finn had done and which she knew, deep down, could only be fascinating to a parent – but because asking him if he wanted to meet her son was like asking him if his intentions were serious. It felt only one step away from asking him if he wanted to settle down.

In the end, though, it had been him who had suggested it. They were at the opening of a gallery in Shoreditch, once again surrounded by the self-appointed beautiful people who lived in the surrounding area. In truth, Stephanie was getting quite worn out with the amount of culture she had been asked to ingest lately. They had been to exhibitions and concerts and installations, all of which seemed to happen within a half-mile radius of Hoxton Square and all of which seemed to attract the same thirty-five people.

Stephanie had never been comfortable with the whole Hoxton thing. It all felt a bit late-1990s and a little too self-consciously cool. Michael's friends were mostly artists or musicians, although she suspected that half of them actually had day jobs in accounts departments and the other half were squandering their wealthy families' money. They had a way of making her feel inadequate without, she was sure, meaning to, with their obscure references and their shabby couldn't-care-less chic, which, she knew, took them hours to perfect. She always felt overdressed, and overstyled and altogether too . . . conventional. Without fail, they were nice to her and made an effort to include her, but sometimes she yearned to have a conversation about something down-to-earth, like what was on the TV or a film she'd seen that didn't have subtitles.

Anyway, two of those friends had brought their children to the exhibition, a boy of six and a girl of eight. Both were precocious in the extreme and were pontificating with their parents about the meaning behind the paintings in a way that made Stephanie want to slap them. Or maybe it was the parents she had wanted to slap, she couldn't be sure. Michael had mentioned that Stephanie had a son and, somewhere in the ensuing conversation, had said he was looking forward to meeting Finn and, what was more, that it was one of his greatest regrets that he had never had children of his own. Pia, his wife, had, of course, never wanted them. Of course, the friends had said knowingly, leaving Stephanie none the wiser.

Later she had asked him what he had meant, and he had said that Pia was a model and that her foremost preoccupation had always been preserving her figure. Now Stephanie felt inadequate in two additional ways. First, his wife had been a model, a woman picked out from the crowd because of her physical perfection, which was never something that was going to make any normal woman feel great, and second, implicit in what he had said there had been the suggestion – admittedly Pia's suggestion, not Michael's – that childbirth disfigures a woman's body. She had just about managed to stop herself from sharing her paranoia with Michael, knowing that nothing was less attractive than exposing your neediness for reassurance that you were attractive, and she had steered the conversation round to the pleasure and satisfaction that came with having a child and how that made any amount of physical sacrifice worth it. She had felt a bit sorry for Michael by the time she'd finished because she'd got rather carried away and it wasn't his fault that his wife hadn't wanted to have a baby. It had suddenly seemed like the natural thing to do to ask Michael if he would like to come over and spend some time with Finn, and he had agreed readily.

The plan was that Michael would meet her at her office at the end of the day and they would travel home together. Michael and Finn could spend some bonding time together while Stephanie cooked dinner and then Finn, who would be on his best behaviour, would go to bed without moaning and leave them to enjoy each other's company. Now James's voicemail had changed all that.

Stephanie had left him four messages by the time Michael arrived to pick her up. He had obviously turned his phone off, probably precisely to avoid getting a call from her telling him to drop Finn off at Arun's or round at Cassie's. The house phone was going unanswered, which made her think they had stopped by the park on the way home. She had also tried Cassie, of course. She was loath to drag her back from her unexpected afternoon off but she thought that if she explained exactly what the situation was and promised her another free day instead, she would be sure to understand. Unfortunately she, too, seemed to have anticipated such a call and was unreachable. Now Stephanie had to decide whether to tell Michael that there was a change of plan and let Finn down, or whether she should bite the bullet and introduce her boyfriend to her ex-husband along with her son. In the end she told Michael exactly what was going on and he made the decision for her: they were all adults, Stephanie and James were separated, where was the harm in them all being in the same room together?

By the time their cab was turning into Belsize Avenue Stephanie felt sick. She couldn't imagine how James was going to react to the fact that she was about to turn up with a man in tow, but she was sure he wasn't going to take it lightly. A part of her felt like it would do him good to see that she'd moved on – and that she could attract another man, and a good-looking, successful one at that – but mostly she just wanted this to be a positive experience for Finn.

Before she'd even managed to turn the key in the lock the door swung open and there was James, big smile plastered on his face and his hand outstretched for Michael to shake. Finn must have told him what was happening, she thought gratefully.

'You must be Michael,' James said, pumping Michael's arm up and down manfully. 'Pleased to meet you. Hi, Steph, did you get my message?'

'Yes,' she managed to say hesitantly. 'I've been trying to ring you.'

James stepped back into the house to let them in. He

didn't look as though he was about to leave any time soon.

'Finn's in the kitchen, Michael,' he was saying. 'He's been dying to meet you.'

'Right,' Michael said, following him through the house.

God, James was unbelievable. He was acting like he still owned the place, which of course he partly did, but anyway. Michael looked back at her questioningly, and she pulled a face that she hoped said, 'I have no idea what to do.'

Finn was sitting expectantly at the kitchen table. James waved his hand at him, as if he was a prize exhibit. 'Finn, this is Michael. Michael, this is Finn.'

'Hi, Finn,' Michael said, and held out his hand. Finn, who had never shaken hands with anyone before, stared at him suspiciously and left his hand hanging in mid-air. His face, Stephanie thought, looked as if it had been scrubbed to within an inch of its life. As did James's, come to think of it.

'Shake hands with Michael,' James said, and Finn took Michael's hand limply. He had been eating a Marmite and cheese sandwich when they'd come in and Stephanie noticed that Michael surreptitiously (or so he thought) wiped his hand on the leg of his combat trousers after Finn let go of it. Michael, she knew, wasn't very experienced with children and she felt sorry for him, trying to find a way into conversation with her son. It would be so much easier if James would fuck off and leave them to it, but she knew what he was like: he was going to ruin it for all of them, sitting in the kitchen, monopolizing Finn's company, making little digs at Michael and showing off about how marvellous and successful he was, although she wasn't entirely sure how true that last one was any more.

In fact, she wasn't at all sure how James was surviving at the moment. She made a mental note that she must sit down with him and discuss finances; it was just that she couldn't face being on her own with him any more than was necessary, and they could hardly have that kind of a conversation in front of Finn. Anyway, he'd be showing off about something because that was what he did. So, if it wasn't work it would be his prowess on the golf course or maybe his ability to fool two women into loving him at the same time.

Her train of thought stopped abruptly as she noticed that James had stood up from the table where he had been sitting opposite Finn and Michael. 'Well,' he said jovially, 'I'd better go and leave you to get acquainted.'

He held out his hand and subjected Michael to another pumping. It was like being at a Masons' meeting, Stephanie thought, and she nearly laughed. All they needed were the rubber gloves and the feather dusters. Or was it pinnies?

'Nice to meet you, Michael,' James was saying again. 'I'm sure it won't be the last time. Finn, behave yourself. Steph, see you soon. I'll let myself out.'

And he was gone. Just like that.

'I thought you said he was difficult,' Michael said later, when they were enjoying a glass of wine on the sofa after Finn had gone to bed.

'He is. I don't know what came over him.'

In the end the whole thing had been a great success.

Michael, no animal lover, had watched as Finn put David into the closed part of his hutch for the night and had managed to look interested. They had bonded a bit over football, although some of what Michael had said about Leeds United's need for a new left-winger had gone over Finn's head and he'd started to yawn a little.

Finn, no doubt led by the mood his father had seemed to be in, had been in 'good Finn' mode, had been polite and hadn't talked incessantly or with his mouth full of carrots. He had dutifully gone off to bed at eight thirty, saying, 'Nice to meet you,' exactly as James had done, and had remained there ever since.

Stephanie snuggled up to Michael. As evenings went on which you introduced your new boyfriend to your son while your soon-to-be-ex-husband looked on, it had gone pretty well.

43

There was something cathartic about wielding a sledge-hammer, something manly, James thought, although he felt as if he was in danger of suffering a cardiac arrest at any moment. The walls of the extension were proving to be far more solid than he had imagined. Just his luck that he must have employed the services of the only local builder to have scruples about building structures made to last. The sledgehammer was barely making a dent and already he was sweating enough for four men.

James had arrived in Lower Shippingham late the previous night and had slept in the flat above the surgery. He had left Stephanie's house (as he now thought of it) in a bit of an emotional turmoil. He had felt sick about the fact that Michael was such a textbook good-looking bloke, that he was so painstakingly trendy – something which James had never been interested in being and, indeed, wouldn't have known where to start if he had been, but it seemed like a quality Stephanie, with her love of fashion, might find attractive – and that he had a job that not only sounded impressive but also cool. He wasn't sure how he could compete with a man like that, someone so fundamentally different from himself. He realized that, deep down, once he had been able to acknowledge to himself that Stephanie might indeed have hooked up with another man, he had comforted himself with the thought that that man might be fat or short or both, and maybe work in accounting or as a data systems analyst. Maybe have halitosis – although for all he knew Michael might have a breath problem: he hadn't got close enough to find out. Somehow he didn't look the type, though. The fact that Michael was artistic was the blow that had hurt him the most. James didn't have an artistic bone in his body.

On the other hand, he had felt elated that he had handled himself so well – Steph had definitely been impressed. He knew she would be feeling grateful to him for being so . . . what? Adult? . . . about it all, that she would be thinking how much he had moved on. His instincts had all been telling him to stay, not to leave the two of them together, that to do so would be giving up. But his rational head, the one he valued the most, had insisted that he do the grown-up thing.

If he was ever going to win Stephanie back – and that was feeling like a distinctly remote prospect these days – he had to let her see for herself that Michael wasn't the man for her. This meant, of course, that he had to take the not-inconsiderable risk that she might in fact come to realize that Michael actually *was* the man for her, but it was a risk he had to take. And as he had closed the front door behind him and had fought off the urge to spend the night hiding in the bushes and watching them through the windows, he had felt unbelievably proud of himself. All he could do now was behave well, do the right thing and hope that one day she would take him back. Everything else was out of his hands.

Buoyed up with this feeling, he had decided he had to

take the bull by the horns and sort out his life. He had got straight on a train to Lincoln. On the way he had remembered Jack Shirley, a lad whose cat he had once revived after it had fallen out of a tree. Jack had scooped the cat up and had run to the surgery, a gibbering wreck. Once the cat had recovered, Jack had admitted tearfully that, as an impoverished student, he couldn't afford to pay the bill. He had offered to work off the debt somehow but James, who had been touched by the boy's affection for his pet, had refused the offer. Jack, overcome with gratitude, had insisted that James take his number in case he thought of anything he could do at a later date, and James had immediately forgotten all about it. Now Jack was only too happy to be here helping out and had roped in his brother, Sean, who was staying with him for a few days too. James, who had been quoted two thousand pounds by a firm of builders, was delighted.

James's plan was this. It would take them two days to tear down the extension and make good the original outside wall of the house, he had calculated. Assuming, of course, that those two days started at seven in the morning and ended at ten in the evening. He had stocked up on Pot Rice and cans of Diet Coke and had no intention of setting foot on the streets of Lower Shippingham any more than was necessary. By the third morning he would be on his way back to London, and the surgery would be on the books of a local estate agency. Once the place was sold, James would use the money to buy a one-bedroom flat in London near to both Finn and his work, and begin his slow ascent back up the ladder.

With the help of Jack and Sean he had disconnected

the services in a slightly cavalier fashion. They were nice boys, hard-working and funny and both too interested in girls and motorbikes and beer to have absorbed the village gossip about James's fall from grace. Their conversation consisted chiefly of tales of excessive nights out, interspersed with information about bands he'd never heard of, and which got you pissed more quickly – Snakebite or vodka shots. It was quite relaxing, listening to them prattling on about nothing in particular. It reminded him of what his life had been like at their age: uncomplicated and full of possibilities. He wanted to tell them not to fuck it up, to think before they acted and to learn to value what they had, but he knew they would just think he was a dull old out-of-touch man, lecturing them, and it would go straight over their heads. That was the thing. You could only learn from your own experience. No one else's mistakes resonated with you. You had to make your own.

By lunchtime they had managed to take down most of one of the walls, and James sent the boys off for a quick lunch at the pub while he boiled a kettle for his chicken chow mein. He looked around the tiny kitchen, which was just off reception. Funny to think he had spent so many years of his life here. He had loved having his own practice. He had always thought that what he liked was the status it gave him, the fact that he was a recognized pillar of the community, but now it occurred to him that what he had really enjoyed was being the boss of his own little empire, the freedom that came with working for yourself, the camaraderie of the little team you had carefully put together. Except for Sally. Sally had clearly been a mistake. And, to be fair, Simon and Malcolm hadn't turned out to be so great in the end either. It was exciting thinking about starting again one day, taking your time and getting it right. He decided he would look on it as a challenge. A fresh start.

He boxed up the few bits and pieces that he hadn't cleared out when he'd first left, ready to go to the dump. Then he sat and waited for the boys to return, which they did after thirty-five minutes, Sean carrying a pint of lager in a glass from the pub for him. By seven fifteen that evening the whole structure was down and they loaded up the boy's dad's van with the rubble and the three of them piled in and took it to the tip a few miles up the road. James felt exhausted. He was too old for all this physical stuff.

Jack drove him back to the surgery and James waved them off after reluctantly refusing their invitation to join them at the Fox and Hounds. There was nothing to do – he had no TV or radio, not even a can of beer to drink – so he went up to the flat and lay down on the unmade bed, falling asleep almost immediately.

Next morning he woke at six, stiff and aching but eager to get on with it. He had an hour to wait till the two boys arrived, so he braved a jog round the outskirts of the village, careful not to go too near the homes of anyone he knew, although he couldn't imagine who might be up at this hour apart from the farmers. He had a cold shower – he had forgotten to turn the water on – downed a can of Diet Coke and waited. Jack and Sean turned up on the dot of seven, yawning and stretching and full of stories about the night before and seven pints and the local police officer's teenage daughter.

This time they were finished by five thirty, and apart from the tell-tale footprint of the foundations, it was as if the extension had never existed. Well, almost. It was as good as it was ever going to be anyway, James thought, without shelling out for professionals.

Once again, he was asleep the minute his head touched the space where the pillow would have been if he had had a pillow. Once again, he woke at six, went for a run, showered, and this time sat waiting for the estate agent to turn up at nine.

At about twenty to, there was a loud knocking on the front door and James, impressed by the agent's keenness, which he took as a sign that his property was desirable after all, went to answer it. Standing on the doorstep was Richard. James was momentarily taken aback by the expression on Richard's face, which definitely wasn't that of someone who had just popped round for a neighbourly cup of tea. Richard hadn't been that friendly with Katie, as far as he could remember, and hadn't they once had a drunken conversation about the impossibility of monogamy? He couldn't imagine that Richard would be angry on her behalf. He must be misreading the signs, he decided, and he forced himself to arrange his face into a welcoming smile. 'Hi, mate,' he said. 'Nice to –'

The sentence was left hanging in the air as a fist – Richard's fist – connected with his face. James fell back against the wall, sliding downwards, hand clutched to his cheek where the punch had landed.

'What the fuck? What have I done?'

'Like you don't know,' Richard said, leaving James none the wiser. James thought about hitting him back but

Richard was a good three inches taller than he was and was a regular in the Lincoln branch of Bannatyne's. He decided to stay seated on the floor. It was harder to hit a man who was down, surely.

He rubbed his cheek. The pain was unbelievable. 'What happened between me and Katie is between me and Katie. And Stephanie, obviously. It has nothing to do with you and your macho sense of justice.'

Richard laughed. The sort of scary laugh the gangland boss makes in a film, just before he rips someone's tongue out of their head with his teeth and swallows it. 'This isn't about Katie. This is about my wife.'

Oh, God, James thought. Simone. 'It's hardly my fault she threw herself at me,' he said, knowing he was doomed.

'*She* threw herself at *you*?' Richard snorted. 'Like she would ever be that desperate.'

James took a deep breath. He was going to get beaten up anyway so he had two choices: tell the truth and maybe plant a seed of doubt in Richard's mind about the state of his marriage, or lie and allow Richard and Simone to bond over their hatred of him. Reformed James, nice James, chose the latter. What did he have to gain by contributing to the break-up of Richard and Simone's marriage?

'OK,' he said, bracing himself for the onslaught. 'I'm sorry, Richard. I was drunk. That's no excuse, I know. Making a pass at Simone is one of the lowest things I've ever done. You are – you were – my mate, after all. I just wasn't thinking straight at the time.'

Richard took a step towards him and James felt himself shrinking back against the wall. He deserved this – not because of Simone, obviously, but because of how he had treated Stephanie and Katie. It didn't matter that he was going to be punished for the wrong crime. If he had murdered someone but was convicted of murdering someone else, what was the difference? He was still a murderer and he deserved to be behind bars. In a strange way he thought he might feel a bit better about himself if he took a beating. More like a man.

There was a split second when Richard hesitated and James thought that maybe he was going to get off lightly after all, and in that split second he realized he really didn't want to get beaten up, however righteous that might make him feel. Richard, clearly not a man used to fighting, swung his arm backwards, then flailed a slow, clumsy, clenched fist in James's direction. James, who saw the punch coming from half a mile away – and who had conveniently once come second in the under-15s amateur boxing tournament at his local club in Frome – instinctively sprang up and threw his own fist straight out where it connected with Richard's aquiline nose, causing it to splatter across his tanned face like a squashed strawberry. The accompanying noise, a sound effect from a cheap *kung fu* film, nearly made him laugh, it was so clichéd. Richard fell backwards and slumped to the floor, more an avoidance technique, it seemed, than from the force of the punch, which had been hard but not *that* hard. There was no question of James hitting him again. It was too ridiculous and, besides, this wasn't a fight he had ever wanted to have.

James reached down and pulled Richard upright, grabbing his reluctant fingers and shaking his hand as if to say, 'It's over.'

'Just so you know, nothing ever happened between me and Simone, whatever she's told you.'

Richard was rubbing the side of his face. 'Well, why would she make it up?' he said, his anger having apparently not completely dissipated.

'I have no idea,' James said. 'Why don't you ask her?'

There was a cough and James looked round. A man-boy in a too-big suit who could only be the estate agent was standing in the doorway, surveying the scene nervously. James wiped his slightly bloodied hand on his trousers and held it out. 'We were sparring,' he said, indicating Richard who, dressed as he was for work in a brown suit, couldn't have looked less like a man in training if he'd tried. 'We got a bit over-eager. You know how these things are.'

The estate agent, who introduced himself as Tony, nodded as if this was the most normal explanation in the world, although his wide eyes gave away the fact that he didn't believe a word of it.

The property, as it turned out, was worth some twenty-five thousand pounds less than it would have been if the extension had been allowed to stand, and some ten thousand less than if it had been taken down professionally ('. . . because they'll have the hassle of getting the concrete foundations dug up so they can have a garden . . .') so the whole trip had been a false economy. By the time he left, James was past caring. 'Stick a few plants in pots on it and tell them it's a patio,' he said, to the bemused estate agent, gesturing at the concrete rectangle that took up half of what should have been the garden.

'Oh, I couldn't do that,' the agent, who couldn't have been more than seventeen and must surely have come along with his dad on bring-your-son-to-work day, said.

'OK, just go for a quick sale,' James said, when he realized that, unlike London estate agents who thrived on hyperbole, this one actually seemed to have some kind of ethics. 'I need the money. Just get rid of it.'

44

Katie had taken to walking Stanley early in the morning past the bus stop where Owen waited for his bus to the hospital in Lincoln. If he was surprised to see her he didn't let it show but, then, he didn't let much of anything show, grunting a 'Hello' in response to her chirpy 'Hi', and then moving off in the direction of the bus as quickly as he could. It was infuriating. Part of her felt he should consider himself lucky to have someone like her paying him so much attention, while another part wanted to get him by the shoulders, shake him and scream, 'What's wrong with me?' in his face.

It annoyed her that she cared. The man was a loser, everyone knew that. She knew she was suffering the textbook reaction to being rebuffed. It was a cliché but it was irritatingly true that the minute someone started acting as if they weren't interested in you any more was the moment you started to think you might just fancy them, after all. Someone who ordinarily you would bat away without a second thought suddenly took on an aura of desirability. When she looked at him objectively she still didn't think he was good-looking, but the fact that he'd looked after her, that he hadn't taken advantage of her vulnerability had somehow rendered him attractive. He was a good man – he needed a bit of work to transform him from a slightly unhinged charity case into someone presentable admittedly – and good men were rare, as she had discovered. If she was ever going to even think about getting into another relationship she wouldn't make the mistake of going for the handsome, successful one. She would set her sights on someone who would be kind and caring. Someone who, she hoped, would treat her as well as she would treat him. And that someone, she suspected, might be Owen.

This morning, though, she had been distracted from her mission by the sight of a very familiar-looking man running red-faced across the fields near the edge of the village. Momentarily it had stopped her in her tracks. James was back. She couldn't believe he had the front to return. And so soon. She dug into her pocket for her mobile but then realized that six twenty in the morning was a bit early to be calling Stephanie.

She hadn't heard from her for a while, actually. In fact, the only times she had spoken to her since the big night were when she had made the effort to make the call herself. She knew Stephanie thought she had overstepped the mark a bit but James had deserved it after everything he had done. And, besides, it had made her feel better. She had always believed in karma. If she hadn't intervened something else would have happened to him anyway: a broken leg or a misplaced winning lottery ticket, maybe a pile-up on the A1. He should be grateful to her. He might be dead if she hadn't made sure he'd got his comeuppance in other ways.

James was far enough away and looked lost enough in his own thoughts not to notice her, for which she was grateful: she had nothing to say to him. Stanley was straining at his lead, his nose going, struggling to confirm from a field's distance away that this was indeed his former master jogging past. Katie, afraid he would bark or slip his collar and go hurtling off, tail wagging, unaware of the inappropriateness of his excitement, pulled him in the other direction and set off for home. She would have to go without stalking Owen for one morning. Maybe it was a good thing. Maybe it would make him wonder where she was.

The morning routine in Belsize Avenue now often included Michael making his gluten-free toast with organic marmalade in the kitchen as Stephanie tried to wrangle Finn into his school uniform. He stayed over on three or four nights a week and, although he had still not quite worked out how to communicate with a seven-year-old boy, he and Finn were getting used to being around each other. She knew Michael would have preferred it if they went out more and Stephanie knew she was using Finn as an excuse, but she had basically seen as many jazz combos and underground art installations as she could stomach. She wasn't sure she could live through another conversation about French cinema with Michael's friends without giving into the urge to say, 'Did anyone see *Ratatouille*?' Now that's what I call a real film.' She thought about talking to him about it, suggesting maybe they could go out for a drink, just the two of them, or to see a blockbuster, but it was hard to tell someone that you didn't like their friends or share their interests, especially when that someone was your boyfriend. She had a feeling that Michael would be a bit offended rather than finding it funny. So, for now, avoidance, not honesty, was the best policy.

On the nights they stayed in they cooked big meals together and listened to music – luckily, Stephanie thought, she didn't have any jazz on her iPod so they found common ground with Norah Jones and Seth Lakeman – and cuddled up on the sofa, talking. Unlike James, Michael was always interested in the details of her day, and even more unlike her ex-husband-to-be, he understood her job and didn't think it was trivial. They rarely ran out of stuff to talk about. Michael was passionate about so many things, and they usually stayed up far too late, which meant that she could never drag herself out of bed early enough to avoid having to do everything in a mad panic.

The last time they had gone out, three nights ago, they had been to Fifteen with Natasha and Martin, Stephanie having finally decided that it was time for her boyfriend and her best friend to get properly acquainted. Michael had been nervous, still not quite over the embarrassment of Natasha walking in on them in the office. Stephanie had told her to be on her best behaviour, but clearly Natasha had had a glass of wine before she left the house: 'Nice to see you with your clothes on,' she said, as Michael shook her hand.

Stephanie couldn't help but laugh but, when she looked at Michael he hadn't even cracked a smile. 'Oh, come on, Michael,' she'd said. 'I think we're allowed to laugh about it now.'

'I'd rather just forget about it, to be honest,' he'd replied, not in an irritated way, Michael was never anything other than reasonable and polite, but in a way that said, 'Please can we change the subject?' And so Stephanie had bailed him out by starting a conversation about something else.

The evening had gone well, though, she thought – even though they had had some pretty intense conversations about the state of the world and Michael had used a couple of obscure film references at one point, which had left Natasha and Martin looking like two rabbits caught in the headlights, not knowing what to say. Once Stephanie had jumped in, saying, 'Isn't that the one with Juliette Binoche?' and Michael had looked at her as if she had said, 'Isn't Michael Winner the greatest director ever?' and said, 'No, that was *Chocolat* and it wasn't even a French film it was just set in France. There's a big difference,' all of which she knew already: she had just taken a bullet for her friends.

But all in all they had seemed to get on. Natasha was always utterly transparent when she disliked somebody so the fact that she was smiling at Michael as she spoke to him was definitely a good sign. Michael had said afterwards that Stephanie's friends were 'very good company' and that Martin was 'knowledgeable' and 'considered', and wasn't it great that he slogged away in an inner-city state school for next to no money? All of which he made sound like a big compliment.

'Phew,' she had said. 'It's really important to me that you like my friends.'

'Well, I do,' he'd said, putting both arms round her in a gesture she loved, which made her feel safe and secure. 'I had a really good time.'

*

She had seen James several times since the day he had been there waiting for her and Michael to come home. He liked to drop round and see Finn whenever she would allow him to and, because he still seemed to be on his best behaviour, she was tending to say yes most times he asked. She would leave them to it – she still had no desire to spend any more time with him than was necessary – and the sound of Finn laughing hysterically at some stupid shared joke or other would confirm that she had done the right thing in letting James come by. Since that first time she had always made sure he had left by the time Michael was due to arrive. Not because she was worried about how James would be any more but because it was, frankly, a bit ... weird to be making polite conversation with both your husband and your new partner at the same time.

Her phone rang as she was stepping out of the shower and she thought about ignoring it, but when she looked at the caller ID and saw it was Katie her curiosity took over. They hadn't spoken for a couple of weeks. Stephanie had been meaning to call to ask how Katie was coping on her own but she could never quite get up the enthusiasm. Katie had left her a couple of messages, sounding very positive, but still keen to talk about James and what a shit he was, and was there anything else they could do to get their own back? Stephanie had tried to tell her weeks ago that she thought they should move on, get on with sorting out how their lives would be in the future, but she wasn't sure Katie had taken it in. Now, presented with a ringing phone and Katie's name flashing up, she didn't feel she could just reject the call, so she decided to keep it short and, hopefully, light.

'Katie, hi.'

Katie launched straight in. 'Guess what? I just saw James.' She paused as if waiting for Stephanie to react in amazement.

Stephanie, who had a fair idea why James was in Lower Shippingham, didn't. 'At the surgery?' Stephanie said. 'He mentioned he was going up to sort it out so he could sell it.'

Katie gasped. 'You knew and you didn't warn me? I nearly had a heart-attack when I saw him.'

'I didn't think, sorry. He's only there for two days and I knew he'd go out of his way not to bump into you. Or anyone else, for that matter.'

'How much is he selling it for?' Katie asked. She had been thinking for a while, she told Stephanie, about swapping her cottage for somewhere she could live that would also accommodate her ever-expanding business. Find somewhere with a couple of treatment rooms and maybe take someone on part-time to deal with her less-important clients. Get a much overdue foothold on the property ladder.

'No idea,' Stephanie said. 'He wants a quick sale, I think. He's nearly out of money.' As soon as she'd said it she regretted it. It was too personal, too tangible a weapon to give to someone who would have no hesitation in using it. 'What I mean is, it's all tied up in the house and I have no intention of moving.'

'Quite right too.' And then, changing the subject, Katie said kindly, 'How are you coping?'

'Oh, fine, you know,' Stephanie said, giving nothing away. 'Surprisingly well, actually. I'm over him completely.'

'God, me too,' Katie said. 'But it must be harder for you. You've got Finn, after all.'

'Finn's fine,' Stephanie said. 'We're both fine.'

45

It had been a stressful day so far. Bertie Sullivan, the much-loved pug belonging to Charles Sullivan, Tory councillor for Westminster, was having trouble breathing. He lay strung out on the operating-table, eyes rolling back in his head while James tried frantically to decide what to do for the best. It had been a routine operation. Bertie had had an abscess on one of his back teeth, which had had to be removed. It was a procedure James had done, what? Probably a thousand times over the years. Nothing had ever gone wrong.

This morning, though, he hadn't been thinking straight. Tony, the estate agent, had been on the phone to say that after several weeks of no interest they had received an offer on the surgery. A very low offer but one that, Tony said, reflected the state of the place and which he would advise James to accept, given that he was in dire need of the cash. The offer, he told James, had come from a Miss Katie Cartwright, a very nice lady who had nothing to sell and a very healthy bank balance, due to her thriving business. Maybe you know her, he said, 'Lower Shippingham being such a small place and all.' She was very pretty – James would remember if he'd ever seen her. In fact, he was thinking of asking her out himself because she'd mentioned she was single. James hadn't bothered to comment. To say now, 'Oh, yes, I used to live with her,' seemed to be extending an invitation to a conversation he didn't want to find himself having.

He had told Tony he would need to think about it, mull it over for a few hours. The offer was so low the money was hardly going to enable him to set up a whole new life, but on the other hand he could pay off his debts and put down a deposit on a tiny flat in a not-too-dodgy part of London. Somewhere that Finn could come and stay overnight, even if James had to give up his bed and sleep on the sofa. He had to get out of the Chalk Farm Travel Motel, there was no doubt about it. The longer he was there the more he could feel himself turning into one of those hopeless single men you saw in sitcoms. He felt like a 1970s travelling salesman, living out of a suitcase, wearing increasingly threadbare clothes, eating takeaways and counting the pennies. And Stephanie would never see sense and come back to him while he was living like that. There was also the Katie factor. If he sold the surgery to her at a knockdown price then maybe she would feel she had evened the score a little. Maybe he would feel a little bit better about the way he had treated her.

He was trawling through the pros and cons, and indulging himself in his usual routine of beating himself up about how he had behaved in the past, when he noticed that Bertie was choking. He poked about in the dog's mouth and could see, lodged far down in the back of Bertie's throat, a piece of cotton wool, dropped in there, no doubt, when James had been calculating how much the estate agent's fees would be or which solicitors in Lincoln were the cheapest. Amanda, the nurse, had nipped out to check on another patient while he was finishing up. After all, hadn't he done this a thousand times? He thought about calling her, then decided it was simpler and quicker if he just dealt with it himself rather than explain how he had managed to drop a swab down a valued patient's throat. He didn't need to panic, he just needed to get it out. James poked about with his fingers and then forceps, growing increasingly edgy. Before he could even think about whether he should perform an emergency tracheotomy Bertie went limp. Once he was apparently unconscious, James was able to fish out the offending swab easily. He dropped it on the floor. When Amanda breezed back in she found him trying to force oxygen by tube into a dog who, apparently, had been in perfect health until five minutes before.

'What happened?' She rushed over to the operating-table to help.

James reluctantly turned away from Bertie. 'I have no idea. He was fine a minute ago.'

He couldn't bring himself to confess. Not now – not with everything else that was happening. He had lost patients before, scores of them in different ways, of course he had, but never, as far as he knew, had he killed off an animal because he had lost his concentration. OK, so everyone made mistakes, but there was no way he could own up to the fact that he had fucked up the most basic of procedures because he was thinking about his personal life and what a mess he had made of it. It was hardly going to be a comfort to Charles Sullivan that at the moment his beloved dog had died James had been wondering whether to look for somewhere to live in Swiss Cottage or Queen's Park. Better that he never knew.

Better that they could imply that Bertie must have had an undiagnosed weak heart or dodgy bronchial system. Better that Amanda could testify to the fact that James had been desperately trying to save the dog's life, rather than that he was responsible for its death in the first place.

Charles Sullivan, when James called to give him the bad news, was distraught but grateful for the efforts that had apparently been made to keep his pet alive. He declined an investigative post-mortem, as pet owners always did, and asked instead if he could collect Bertie's body so that he could bury him in the park. When he arrived, his eyes red from crying, he gave James a manly hug and thanked him again. James, who was feeling like a prize shit, shed genuine tears when he told Charles how sorry he was.

It happened to every vet at some point in their career, death by human error, he knew that, but the guilt he felt was almost overwhelming. He thought about Finn and how he would feel if anything happened to Sebastian, and he tried not to think about Charles's ten-year-old daughter who had come with him when he had first brought Bertie in. By the time he got to Belsize Avenue at six fifteen for his prearranged visit with Finn, he was feeling thoroughly miserable.

'Hi, mate,' he said, as Finn opened the door, his face alight at the prospect of spending some time with his father.

Stephanie was in the kitchen, talking on the phone to Natasha. She had been intending to spend the evening

337

sorting out her bedroom wardrobes – one pile for charity, another for things not worn for over a year and a third of definite keeps – just to be out of James's way. Michael was working – photographing the celebrating cast at the opening night of some play or other – and with Finn being entertained by James she would have the chance to spend some time on herself, a luxury that was increasingly rare these days. It seemed only polite, though, to say hello to her husband on the way.

'How are you doing?' she asked, thinking that he didn't look as if he was doing too well but not really wanting, or expecting, any answer other than 'Fine'.

'Shit, if I'm being honest.'

Stephanie flicked her eyes towards Finn.

'Sorry,' James said. 'I mean, not too good. I had a bad day.'

She had no choice then but to sit and listen to the details of what had happened. When it became obvious it was a story that would give Finn nightmares she sent him off to brush David so that he could show James how well he was taking care of him.

Finn sighed, knowing he was going to be missing out on something. 'I don't want to,' he said petulantly.

'Tell you what,' James said. 'Give his cage a good clean-out and then I'll show you how to give him a bath.'

'Cool,' Finn said, running out into the garden.

Stephanie eyed James sceptically. 'Are you meant to bath guinea pigs?' she said.

'Not really, but it won't hurt him just once.'

By the time Finn was done James had told her everything: the fight with Richard, Katie's offer on the

338

surgery, his preoccupation with his financial worries, his part in Bertie's untimely death. Stephanie had resisted the urge to say, 'Well, you brought it all on yourself.' In fact, she'd found she was feeling a bit sorry for him.

'If I was you I'd take whatever I could get for the surgery. If you're in real trouble we could talk about selling the house, maybe. Get something smaller for me and Finn.' She had meant it. She didn't want to punish him any more.

But James wasn't having any of it. 'Absolutely not. That's not why I told you . . . I mean, I wouldn't want you to think I was trying to play the sympathy card. You and Finn have done nothing wrong. Nothing would make me take your home away from you. I just need to get back on my feet, that's all. And you're right, getting rid of the surgery is a start. And then, maybe, I can get some more work down here. Set up on my own eventually. I'll tell the agent to accept her offer.'

Stephanie realized he still felt awkward saying Katie's name in front of her. As if she still cared.

'You don't mind me selling to . . . her . . . do you?' he asked now, nervously.

'Of course not. Don't be stupid. In fact, I think it's a great idea. You owe her something too, James.'

Secretly Stephanie was hoping that Katie would think this was all the payback she needed: screw James out of a few thousand pounds and then move on. She didn't blame her, she thought. It was understandable that she wanted blood.

James put his hand on her arm and Stephanie stiffened.

She had to stop herself from pulling away abruptly, from pushing him off her.

'Thank you, Steph, for being so . . . good about everything. I don't – I mean I didn't – deserve you.'

Stephanie patted his arm half-heartedly and he took his hand away, as if he knew it had been an inappropriate gesture. 'It's fine,' she said. 'I want you to get yourself sorted as much as you do. For Finn's sake. So we can just get on with things, you know.' God, she wished he would stop giving her that look, that cross between a hurt puppy and a hopeful child. She stood up to put some physical distance between them and, thankfully, Finn burst in, David in hand. James, to give him credit, snapped out of his self-pity and into jolly-dad mode.

'OK, the first thing you have to remember is that you should only do this once a year.'

Stephanie laughed – she knew he was hoping that Finn would have forgotten all about guinea-pig baths by the time twelve months had gone by. She left them to it, hoping David wouldn't be too traumatized by the experience. James would make sure he wasn't, she knew, because, contrary to how he was feeling right now, James was both a good father and a good vet. He was just a shit husband.

46

That James accepted her offer on the surgery so quickly took Katie completely by surprise. She had expected him to hold out for more money or even to turn her down flat so that he wouldn't have to face the embarrassment of having to deal with her. She couldn't wait to get on the phone to Stephanie and tell her.

'Great,' Stephanie said, when she had broken the news. 'Well done.'

Stephanie didn't sound as delighted as Katie had anticipated, and then it hit her why that might be. 'Oh, God, Stephanie, I hope you don't think I'm doing this to try and screw you out of money as well. Shit, I hadn't even thought of that. Do you want me to go back and up my offer? I will, if you want me to.' She felt genuinely upset that it hadn't even crossed her mind that James getting a knock-down price for the surgery would have an effect on Stephanie too once they got round to sorting out a divorce settlement. She would never have wanted Stephanie to suffer any more than she already had.

'It's not that,' Stephanie said. 'That hadn't even occurred to me. It's just . . . I don't know . . . I'm feeling a bit sorry for him at the moment –'

Katie couldn't help but jump in before Stephanie had had a chance to finish her sentence. 'Sorry for him? After what he's done? Come on . . .'

And then Stephanie told her how down he had been when she'd last seen him and how he was still living in a motel, and some story about a dog dying, which, even though Katie loved dogs, seemed vaguely comical. It all seemed fairly trivial. The man wasn't dying of cancer or on Death Row, he was just feeling a little bit sorry for himself because he'd made his own bed (well, two beds to be fair) and now he was having to lie in it (them). Stephanie had mentioned that the dog had belonged to a Tory councillor, and Katie had laughed and said that must have been James's worst nightmare, a potential falling-out with such a pillar of the community, but Stephanie had said he didn't seem to care about that kind of thing any more: he was just upset that he had made such a terrible mistake and, anyway, as far as Charles Sullivan knew, Bertie had died of natural causes.

'God,' Katie heard herself say, 'if I found out something like that had happened to Stanley I'd go ballistic.'

As soon as she had told Katie about the dog Stephanie knew she shouldn't have. There had been a hint of excitement in Katie's voice when she had said goodbye and Stephanie felt as if she had loaded the gun and then handed it over. She thought about calling Katie back and saying, 'Forget what I just told you, I made it up,' or even going straight to the point and asking her not to do anything rash, but she felt like that would fan the flames. She would just have to hope that the excitement of the new premises and the satisfaction of the small victory she had won would take the edge off Katie's desire for revenge.

She was spending the day shopping with Meredith for

the upcoming soap awards. Meredith had been nominated in the best actress category specifically for a harrowing episode in which she'd learned that the man she was about to marry already had a wife and three children, who had conveniently just moved into the same area. She was up against an actress whose character had died a prolonged death from cancer (which she had been winning the battle against by all accounts, until she had asked the producers for a substantial salary increase) and another whose alter ego had recently been jailed for drug-running. There was no doubt about it, she had confided to Stephanie, death always won out at awards because the judges knew that this would be the last chance they would get to fawn over the genius of that particular actor. But, spurred on by her triumph at the BAFTAs, she was intending to go along and knock them dead in an outfit, the design of which she was happy to leave entirely to Stephanie.

Currently they were in Ronit Zilkha, Meredith in the changing room trying on one enormous creation after another while Stephanie paced outside like an expectant father. She was dreading the fact that it was nearly lunchtime and she had no doubt that she would be expected to indulge Meredith in at least two courses in the restaurant at Harvey Nichols. She was quite fond of Meredith, these days – it was easy to feel benign towards someone who followed your instructions blindly – but they didn't have much to talk about. Besides, she wanted time on her own to think about the bombshell Michael had dropped on her this morning.

Meredith, however, was having none of it, and at a

quarter to two they finally sat down to starters of scallops and butternut-squash soup, and Stephanie scoured her brain for something to talk about. Luckily Meredith blathered on for a while about some new storyline she was involved in and how unfair it was that some of the cast had been granted permission to take a break from filming for the lucrative panto season while others – herself included – had been refused. Stephanie tried to look sympathetic about the fact that Meredith would spend the next winter only making four thousand pounds a week instead of ten, but it wasn't easy. After that the conversation ground to a halt and Stephanie, desperate to fill the silence, found herself saying, 'So, my boyfriend wants us to move in together.'

'Wow,' Meredith said, putting down her fork. 'That didn't take long.'

'Nearly three months,' Stephanie said. 'Is it too soon? I think it might be too soon.' Why was she talking to Meredith about this? she thought. Mrs In-the-closet-lesbian. Probably never had a relationship in her life.

'That depends. I once moved in with someone after a week.'

Stephanie nearly choked. She resisted the urge to voice the question she was dying to ask.

Meredith was still talking: 'To be honest, it was a stupid thing to do, though. I moved out again a month later.'

Stephanie laughed. 'Well, that helps me a lot.'

'I think that if you're worried it's too soon then it's too soon.'

'That's what I think.'

If she was honest, she didn't know what she thought.

Michael had mentioned it over breakfast as if he was discussing a new kind of cereal or the state of the Dow Jones. It had come so out of nowhere that at first she'd laughed and then he'd said that he was deadly serious, and that it was crazy for them to keep two separate homes when they spent so much time together. Besides, he was serious about this relationship and he wanted to move it on to a stronger footing. It would make most sense, he'd said, if he sold his place and then, if she wanted, he could use the money to buy a half-share in her house. He knew she wouldn't want to move.

Stephanie's first thought had been Finn. He and Michael got along fine, although they didn't share much common ground and, when it got right down to it, Michael wasn't and would never be his father. And then she thought about how she felt, and how she felt was blank. She had a feeling she should have been elated. It was the promise of a whole new life with a kind, decent man, who clearly adored her. There was no chance that Michael was ever going to set up a secret life somewhere else, sneaking off to the countryside and some other poor woman he'd conned into loving him every few days. He was smart and he was talented. There was just a lingering anxiety, hovering somewhere on the periphery of her brain, that she couldn't quite put her finger on.

'Well,' Meredith continued, 'you either tell him you want to wait a bit or else you do a trial run. Move in together for a couple of weeks and then decide. But don't go promising him it's permanent before you're sure.'

Stephanie sighed. 'You're right, I know you are. But, if I'm being honest, I'm scared. What if I say no and then he never asks again?' Why was she telling Meredith all this? She really had no idea.

Meredith snorted. 'What – and then you stay as you are, just you and Finn? Is that really so bad? Come on, Stephanie, don't tell me you've turned into one of those women who'd rather live with Fred West than be on their own?'

Stephanie laughed. 'Of course not. Although he did have nice hair.'

'If he's really into you, he'll still want to move in in six months' time. And if he doesn't, it proves you were right to wait, don't you think?'

'I know that makes sense.' Stephanie ran her hand over her eyes. 'I guess I just don't understand why I'm not jumping up and down. I mean, who'd have thought six months ago that I'd meet someone else so quickly? Someone who's attractive and kind and smart and who loves me . . .' She tailed off, not knowing what else to say.

'But?' Meredith said, raising an eyebrow.

Stephanie looked at her quizzically.

Meredith continued: 'There was a "but" coming.'

'But . . . I don't know. But . . . he's a bit . . . he's not . . . He likes jazz and talking about world cinema. All his friends are artists and photographers and musicians. Or, at least, they're trying to be. Not that there's anything wrong with that, except that they take it all so seriously. And so does he.' She had no idea if Meredith understood what she was going on about. She barely understood it herself. 'I think that's what my "but" was – "But he's a bit too cool for his own good."'

Meredith nodded. 'He sounds . . .'

'Dull? He's not dull, he's really not, he's just a bit . . . serious.'

'I was actually going to say that he sounds interesting. I'm just not sure he sounds very you, if you know what I mean. Sorry if that's presumptuous.'

Stephanie sighed. 'Sometimes I do wish he'd lighten up a bit.'

'Well, if you really insist on taking the advice of an embittered old spinster who's never lived with anyone herself except for four weeks in 1989 then here's what I think . . .' Meredith, ever the actress, paused as if for effect. 'Do nothing. There's no rush. You can't lose anything by waiting, except for a bit of sleep, maybe.'

'Is that the only piece of advice anyone ever gives? Do nothing?'

'I'm naturally lazy. Doing nothing always seems like the best answer to me.'

Stephanie smiled gratefully. 'Thanks, Meredith, I appreciate you listening.'

'She's right, of course,' Natasha said smugly. 'Although why you'd be asking that dried-up old misery for advice when you could have asked me I don't know.'

'Well, she said exactly the same as you would have said, so what's the difference? Besides, I like her.'

'Since when?'

'Since she decided I was a genius. Actually, she's been very sweet lately.'

Natasha snorted. 'You'll be going out on a date with her next. No wonder she's trying to put you off Michael, she thinks she's in with a shot.'

'OK, let's move on from the 1970s.'

'Just tell me this,' Natasha said, suddenly serious. 'When was the last time you made him laugh?'

'He laughs.' Stephanie was indignant. 'What do you mean? I thought you liked him. He likes you.'

'I do like him, he's smart and thoughtful. He's just not exactly hilarious to be around, that's all I'm saying.'

'I like being with him. He's kind and clever and an adult. Plus he's never going to mess me around.'

'Great. And I can understand why that seems like the most important thing at the moment but . . . it doesn't mean you should make it permanent, that's all. Not until you're sure at least and you're clearly not sure at the moment.'

Stephanie sat down heavily on the sofa. She suddenly felt miserable. Overwhelmed by a wave of uncharacteristic self-pity, she burst into tears.

Natasha looked horrified. 'I wasn't having a go! Oh, God, sorry, Steph.'

Stephanie rarely cried and, consequently, whenever she did it was as if everything she had been bottling up since the last time saw an opportunity and came flooding out and then she couldn't stop. Now she tried to say, 'No, it's nothing to do with what you just said,' but it was too hard to speak and cry at the same time and the crying won out. She shook her head in the hope that Natasha would know what she meant. Whether she did or not, Natasha came and sat beside her and patted her leg helplessly. Stephanie knew she must be making her uneasy – she didn't think that in all their years of friendship Natasha had ever seen her cry – but she had no way of stopping. She didn't even know what she was crying *about*, just that she felt empty and hopeless and as if her whole life had gone to shit.

'It's good for you to let it all out,' Natasha was saying. 'You always put a brave face on everything. It's just not . . . natural. Look at you. Most people would have fallen apart after what happened to you but you barely missed a breath. It's not healthy.'

'What do you mean? I was trying to hold it together. I thought that was the right thing to do.'

'It's not a criticism, Steph. I'm just saying that no one could go through what you've just gone through without breaking down at some point. It's just taken you longer than most, that's all. It's a good thing. If I didn't hate everything and anything New Age I'd be saying things like "You can't start to heal until you've allowed yourself to break completely." But obviously I'm never going to say that so I'm just going to say that all those things, like getting your revenge on James –'

'Which you said was a good thing.'

'– which I said was a good thing – and Michael were like self-preservation. They helped you get through the worst of it. They gave you something to focus on. They helped put off the moment when you really took in what had happened till now, till you were strong enough to deal with it. And now that you've got it all out of your system, you can move on, that's all.'

'Me and Michael are fine, OK?' Stephanie said defensively. 'I know you don't like him but that's your problem.' She ignored Natasha's protestations. 'You never liked James and now you don't like Michael.'

She knew as soon as she said it that it was a childish thing to say. The truth was that Natasha had been right to be wary of James: she had only ever had Stephanie's best interests at heart. And if Stephanie had let herself dwell on it she would have known that she would have to agree that there was something in what Natasha had said about her relationship with Michael that was right too. But she wasn't about to let herself dwell on it.

'I'm going to let him move in,' she said, somewhat petulantly. 'He's right – we're good together.'

'Well, if that's what you want to do, then good for you,' Natasha said. 'I only wanted to make sure you were certain. I really am pleased for you, if it makes you happy.' She held out her arms to give Stephanie a hug but Stephanie was having none of it. She was sick of Natasha telling her what was right and what was wrong, what to do. She conveniently forgot that it was always she who pressed Natasha for advice, that Natasha was the person she called at one or two in the morning when she didn't know what to do, that Natasha would always drop everything and listen to her moaning on whenever she had a problem.

Stephanie stood up and reached for her coat. 'I have to go,' she said coldly, and left without saying goodbye.

47

The one professional mistake that James had made – the only one that mattered, really, when it came to it – was not to have held his hands up and taken the blame for what had happened to Bertie. Charles Sullivan might have been angry, he might have taken his custom away and entrusted the care of his cat and his one remaining dog to another vet, he might even have threatened to sue for some kind of compensation, but what he almost certainly wouldn't have done was demand that Harry get rid of James. And even in the unlikely event that he had done, had James's recent behaviour not been so erratic, his appearance so unkempt, then Harry would surely not have listened. As it was, Harry was so preoccupied with his own doubts about James's state of mind that when he got the call from the woman purporting to be Charles Sullivan's aide, and he was told that Charles had been given reason to believe that James had effectively killed Bertie through incompetence – exhibit A, the swab that had got itself lodged in Bertie's throat – he didn't think twice about calling James in to explain himself.

'It was a genuine mistake,' James said immediately, believing – wrongly, of course – that Amanda, the nurse, must have worked out what had happened and reported back.

'You're telling me that it's true? That you caused the

accidental death of Charles Sullivan's dog and then tried to cover that fact up?'

'I'm sorry,' James said. 'But you know how it is. These things happen.'

'No, no James,' Harry said. 'You misunderstand me. I'm not angry about what happened to Bertie, I'm angry that you made me look like a bloody fool. I'm angry that you put me in a situation where I had to defend your actions without knowing the facts.'

James shuffled from one foot to the other. 'Sorry,' he muttered.

'It's the deception,' Harry continued, in full flow now. 'The fact that I was put on the spot and forced to bluff my way through the conversation so it didn't look like I had no idea what was happening at my own practice. I had to tell her I was already investigating what had happened. Surely you can see how unacceptable that is?'

'It won't happen again,' James mumbled, looking at his shoes.

'I know it won't, James, because . . . and I'm sorry, I really am . . . I'm afraid I'm going to have to let you go.'

James looked up for the first time. This couldn't be happening. 'Please don't do this, Harry.'

Harry was still talking: 'We can make it official with all the attendant publicity that might bring or else you can just agree to leave at the end of the week. It's up to you to do what you think is the right thing.'

James had no doubt that the right thing to do was the thing he was going to do. It was what he should have done in the first place and then he wouldn't have been in this mess. It was what he should have done a year ago too, when Katie and Stanley first appeared in his surgery.

'Fine,' he said. 'I'll deal with any appointments that have already been made and then I'll go. Don't worry, I won't make it any more difficult for you than it already is.'

'Thank you,' Harry said, turning back to some paperwork on his desk to indicate that their chat was over.

James walked out into the corridor in a daze. This was it. He was unemployed. He had gone from having his own successful business along with a beautiful house and an equally beautiful wife (not to mention the mistress, but he was trying to gloss over that even in his private thoughts) to being out of work and living alone and unloved in a motel in the space of three short months. He had no job, no home, no partner, no money, no self-esteem. No dignity, he thought bitterly.

Next step would probably be to grow his hair long and move out on to the streets where he could sit in a cardboard box all day, maybe with a mangy-looking dog on a piece of string. He had heard you could hire them for a few hours from modern-day Fagins who kept them by the dozen. The skinnier the better. People were far more likely to give money to a homeless person's dog than to the person himself, apparently. That just about summed up the world, James thought miserably. Maybe he should become an alcoholic or get a crack habit, although how he was meant to afford to do either of those things now he didn't really know. God, he couldn't even be a proper tramp. How pitiful was that? He'd have to turn to crime to fund the drug habit he hadn't yet acquired. No wonder

Stephanie didn't want him any more. He was just considering which was more effective, pills or hanging, when his phone rang. He looked at the caller ID: Finn. Of course, Finn, he thought. Finn still loved him. Finn was a reason to carry on.

'Hi, mate,' he said, his eyes watering at the thought of his son.

'Where are you?' Finn sounded angry. 'You promised you'd be here.'

James panicked. Be where? He looked at his watch. It was five to four already. How had that happened? Shit, he thought, his heart lurching. Finn's football match. Somewhere back when he had been feeling more like a normal human being he had promised his son that of course he would be at the game and that he would arrange with Harry to have one of the other vets see his patients. The kick-off was at four. Fuck.

'I got held up. I'm leaving now. I'm so sorry, Finnster, I should have rung you.' He started stuffing things like keys and money into his pockets to make a quick getaway.

'You forgot about it,' Finn was shouting now. 'You never do anything with me. I hate you.'

James listened as Finn pressed the button to end the call. Great. He raced through reception with his head down. He could see Cheryl Marshall and her beagle Rooney, his four o'clock appointment, watching him expectantly. He was so intent on avoiding Cheryl's eye that he almost bumped into Harry, who was coming the other way, carrying a small dog that must be on its way to surgery. 'I have a family emergency,' he muttered, without stopping.

'What about your patients?' Harry protested.

'I don't work for you any more, Harry,' he shouted back as he broke into a run in the street. 'Go fuck yourself,' he added, for good measure, although he thought later this might have been overkill. So, this time doing the right thing actually meant fucking his boss over in favour of his son. God, it was complicated. They should teach stuff like this in school: 'How to have the moral high ground', 'Honesty for beginners' or 'Treading the path of righteousness 1:01'.

Stephanie hated standing on the sidelines with the other parents. Not that she didn't enjoy watching Finn play, she nearly burst with pride every time he got the ball and, on occasion, had been known to shout, 'Tackle him,' rather too over-excitedly. No, it was the forced conversation with the mothers of his team mates – it was always the mothers, except for Shannon Carling's father whose wife had died soon after Shannon was born and who worked flexi-time so that he could look after his daughter – the illusion that because they all had sons and daughters the same age they must have other things in common. Most of them were nice enough, some of them she was even friends with, but the forced jollity of the incessant banter during matches exhausted her. Plus she was in a foul mood because James hadn't turned up to watch Finn as he'd promised he would. Not that she cared one way or another if he was there but she knew her son was bitterly disappointed. And, to be fair, it wasn't like James, these days, to be so unreliable. He had been going out of his way to prove what a caring and hands-on father he was.

She checked her watch again – a quarter past four. Finn was running his heart out on the pitch, with a miserable look on his face. She glanced round to see if there was any sign of James – he had told Finn he was on his way – just as he rounded the corner of the school drive, red-faced and sweating, running as if he was being chased. All the other mothers turned to look and she knew that they were torn between thinking that they were grateful their husbands didn't go around making such twats of themselves and feeling jealous and a bit sad that Stephanie had a husband – albeit a soon-to-be-ex one – who could be bothered to come to school events.

'Did you run all the way?' Stephanie said when he had flopped down on the grass beside her.

He nodded, unable to get enough breath to speak.

'Well, better late than never,' she said, and then hated herself both for being so catty and for trotting out such a cliché.

James didn't reply. Instead, as soon as he had got his breath back, he stood up and started shouting encouragement to Finn, who turned round, beaming, when he heard his father's voice, his anger forgotten in that way children have of being able to be so instantly forgiving. They didn't speak again until the end of the match when Finn came running over – buoyant from a five to four victory – flung himself at his father and asked him if he was coming over for tea.

Stephanie noticed James cast a nervous glance her way. 'Oh, no, I don't think –' he started to say, and Stephanie interrupted. It would make Finn happy and in some way compensate for his earlier disappointment.

'I'm sure Daddy would love that, if he doesn't have anything else to do,' she said, and managed a smile.

James smiled back gratefully. 'I don't. I don't have anything to do.'

Stephanie thought he seemed rather subdued during their – very early – supper. She was hoping to have the meal over by six, and then she could hide in the living room while James and Finn chased each other round the garden for a couple of hours before he headed back to the Travel Motel. He was making jokes with Finn, going over their old rehearsed routines, which made the two of them crack up but which left pretty much everyone else cold, but it didn't seem like his heart was quite in them. Finn didn't notice, of course, so overexcited was he that his father had witnessed him deliver the crucial cross which had spawned the third goal, but Stephanie had an inkling something was wrong – something more than his usual woes, that was – and that whatever it was he was going to want to share it with her. She wasn't sure she could face dealing with whatever new problems James perceived he had: she had enough on her own plate, trying to find a suitable time and occasion to tell Michael the good news. She had been putting it off. She didn't know why.

By seven thirty Finn was exhausted and ready for bed, and it was apparent that James was going nowhere. Reluctantly she opened a bottle of Cabernet Sauvignon and offered him a glass.

'I may as well drink the whole bottle. I don't have to get up for work in the morning,' he said, with a grim laugh, and then he waited for her to ask him what he meant, which, of course, she did.

As soon as James got to the part about Charles Sullivan's aide, Stephanie knew where the story was going. 'Was it a woman?' she asked.

'Was what a woman?' James said, evidently confused by this detour.

'His aide. Was the person who phoned up a woman, do you know?'

James's brow furrowed into several long creases. 'It was, I think. What's that got to do with anything?'

Stephanie knew she couldn't tell him. Or, at least, if she ever did she needed to think it through very carefully first. 'I just wondered, that's all. Anyway, carry on.'

When he got to the point where Harry had sacked him Stephanie exhaled loudly. OK, so this had gone too far. Apart from anything else James being completely out of work would affect both her and, more importantly, Finn.

'I don't know what I'm going to do,' James said plaintively, and he looked so pathetic that all she felt for him was pity.

'I guess we'll have to sell the house after all,' she said, and James looked like he might burst into tears. 'Buy two smaller places.'

'No. I've told you that's not going to happen. That's not why I'm telling you. I'm going to sort myself out, I promise.'

He carried on with his story, getting to the part where he had shouted at Harry as he ran down the street to get to Finn's game. Stephanie couldn't help but laugh at the way he described Harry's open-mouthed stare. 'Did you really tell him to go fuck himself?'

'I did.'

'About time, I reckon.'

'He was gesticulating like he wanted to kill me but he had someone's Chihuahua in his hand, so it kind of looked less macho than he was hoping, I think,' James said, laughing himself.

'You should talk to the police. Tell them he was threatening you with it. That's a lethal weapon.'

'It had a pink jumper on,' he added, helpless now. 'And nail varnish. I distinctly saw that the dog had nail varnish on. Also pink.'

Stephanie wiped her eyes. 'It was probably going in for a nose job.'

'Breast augmentation,' James said. 'All eight of them.'

'Do you want another glass of wine?' Stephanie said, and then wondered where that had come from.

'Thank you,' he said, holding out his glass for her to fill.

As soon as James had left – nearly two and a half hours later, and for all that time they had chatted and laughed and he had exhibited a remarkable lack of self-pity – Stephanie tried to call Katie. What she had done was beyond belief. OK, so they had both agreed that James had to pay. She flushed as she reminded herself that it had all been her idea. Well, Natasha had started her off thinking that way, to be fair, and she wasn't exactly sure how she felt about Natasha and her advice at the moment. She forced herself not to think about the way she had spoken to her friend. At this rate there wouldn't be anything left she could think about that didn't make her feel uncomfortable.

Katie's mobile rang and rang, and eventually went to voicemail. Stephanie left a message, trying to sound much friendlier than she felt because she wanted to make sure that Katie called her back. 'Hi, it's Stephanie, call me! We haven't had a chat for ages.' Then she did the same with Katie's home phone. An hour later she tried both again and the same thing happened. She left more messages, this time saying Katie wasn't to worry how late it was – if she could still call Stephanie back this evening that would be wonderful, thank you. She left her mobile on her bedside table and went to bed angry.

She slept badly. She felt panicked about what Katie might do next. The woman had clearly lost her mind and had no intention of stopping. Paying James back was one thing. Completely ruining his life was quite another. Stephanie had always believed that the punishment had to fit the crime. She had wanted James humiliated, like he had made her feel humiliated. She had wanted to make him feel hurt and ashamed and regretful. But the truth was that both she and Katie had been able to pick up the pieces of their lives. Whatever he had done to them, they still had their work and their homes and their friends. They still had foundations to build on. It was simply too much to strip James of everything he'd had in his life, to leave him with nothing. Not to mention the fact that to hurt James like this would inevitably hurt Finn too. Finn, who had already all but lost his father, would probably also lose his home and the garden he loved. Of course they could manage somewhere smaller, the house was too big for the two of them really, but that wasn't the point. The point was that at the moment what Finn needed was some stability in his life.

At six thirty she got up and made herself a cup of tea and tried to find displacement activities to stop herself from dialling Katie's number too early. She made a lot of noise hoovering outside Finn's room so that he got up and came out to see what was going on. By the time she had dropped him off at school and returned home it was gone nine. A respectable hour to call someone.

Once again Katie's phones rang and rang with no response. Stephanie had convinced herself in the night that Katie was actually avoiding her and could now picture her standing, mobile in hand, checking who was calling before she decided whether or not to answer. She left two strained, polite messages, which didn't sound quite as jolly as she'd managed to sound yesterday: 'Katie, I really want to talk to you, you know, just to see how you are. Call me back.' This was crazy. Katie could avoid answering the phone to her for the rest of her life if she put her mind to it. There had to be something else she could do.

By the time James had got home – well, to the Travel Motel which was the closest thing he had to a home, these days – he'd felt a little bit worse for wear, having had four glasses of wine, but surprisingly cheerful for a man who had just lost his job. Stephanie had cheered him up, just as he had dared hope she might. A couple of hours' laughing about the tragedy of the situation he found himself in had made him feel like a different person.

48

Finally Katie could stand it no more. She was exhausted getting up at five thirty to put on her makeup and do her hair so that Owen could more or less ignore her at the bus stop. It was time to bring things to a head. Stanley, who now thought this was his permanent new routine, was waiting patiently by the front door at ten past six, lead hanging down from either side of his floppy mouth. Katie made sure she had change – eighty pence, she thought it was, and then, of course, another eighty pence for the return journey. She didn't think she would have to pay for the dog. Owen would have no escape: when he got on the bus so would she.

She picked up her mobile, which she had turned off last night, and decided not to switch it on again. Stephanie had been leaving messages for her, which had made her nervous. It wasn't what she said, all of which sounded perfectly friendly, it was the way she had said it, the strain Katie could hear in her voice, the almost imperceptible undertone of annoyance. And Katie knew why. Stephanie would be cross with her that she hadn't consulted her before she phoned the surgery. She had meant to ring her about it but when she'd had the idea she'd just had to get on and do it. She had always been impulsive. Besides, she'd had a feeling that Stephanie might disapprove and try to talk her out of it. Stephanie had been disapproving a lot lately. And, anyway, as far as Katie was concerned, Stephanie would never have told her what had happened to the dog if she hadn't subconsciously wanted her to do something about it. She'd leave it a few days before she called her back, let her cool off a bit.

She flapped along the lane in her pink flip-flops, her long skirt trailing a little in the dirt. Owen had once said to her that he preferred earthy women, not like his ex-wife Miriam, with her blow-dried hair and her clicky court shoes. He liked women who were concerned with more important things than their appearance or, at least, the cost and label of their clothes. Real women. Women, he had intimated, like Katie, nurturing, maternal, soft. Today she had left her long hair down, curling round her shoulders. She wore the dangly silver and jade earrings he had admired once and a halter top with no bra, which was maybe pushing it a bit at her age but which was sure to get his attention. It was cold out so she put her baby pink hoody over the top. She could take it off just before she rounded the corner by Owen's bus stop.

As it was, she was early and he wasn't there, so she had to walk round the block in order to be casually passing when he arrived. The timing was crucial – too early and she would have to go round again, a minute late and he'd be on the bus and out of sight. As she came back round she caught sight of his green padded jacket and her heart jolted. God, she really had it bad. She took a couple of deep breaths to calm herself. Look casual, she thought.

Owen was gazing fixedly up the road in the direction the bus would be coming from. 'Hi,' she said, to get his attention, and he turned round slowly, not exactly looking, she thought, either surprised or pleased to see her.

'Hi,' he said, in a flat voice, and turned away again, obviously expecting her to keep walking.

OK, she thought, this might be harder than I was hoping. She sat down on the wooden bench next to him. 'How have you been?' she said.

Owen turned round to face her reluctantly. 'Fine.'

'I miss our sessions,' Katie said. 'I was wondering if you'd thought about coming back.'

'I don't have time.'

'I do evenings now. And weekends. I'm opening up a proper spa in the old vet's surgery.'

'Good for you,' he said, sounding genuine. 'I know that's what you've always wanted.'

He was definitely thawing, Katie thought, even if he hadn't bitten her hand off to come back for more acupuncture. The bus rounded the corner and Owen stood up. Katie stood too, change in hand.

'Well, 'bye then,' Owen said, as he boarded the bus.

Katie followed. 'Oh, I'm coming too. I've got something I need to do in town.' As soon as she'd said it she realized how lame it sounded. What in the world could she have to do in Lincoln at half past six in the morning? 'Swimming,' she added quickly. 'I'm going to the leisure centre. They open really early, these days, for people before they go to work, you know.'

Owen looked at her sceptically. 'With Stanley?'

'He waits outside. They have a bit where you can leave your dog . . .' She tailed off. It sounded ridiculous. She was so obviously lying. Owen sat at the back of the bus and she sat down next to him. She had him captive for eighteen minutes. She decided to go in for the kill.

'Actually, Owen, I was thinking I should take you up on that offer of dinner.'

'Dinner?'

She couldn't work out if he had really forgotten or if he was being deliberately obtuse. He was still angry with her, obviously. Maybe he just wanted to make her suffer a little.

'You said you wanted to take me out to dinner – don't you remember? To say thank you for being patient while you paid me back.' Owen had been pushing envelopes of cash through her door regularly – always when she was out – and only had another twenty pounds to go before his debt was cleared completely.

'You and James,' he said. 'I offered to take you and James out to dinner.'

God, he was being difficult. 'Well, obviously that's not going to happen now. So I thought you could just take me. It was me you owed anyway,' she added, sounding a bit sharper than she'd meant to. Why couldn't he just say yes?

'Sorry, Katie, I don't think my girlfriend would like it.'

Katie felt as if she'd been punched. She tried – almost successfully – to keep the shock from showing on her face. 'Your girlfriend?'

Owen smiled a smile so nervous that she knew he had worked out exactly how much this would hurt her and was worried by it. 'Danielle Robinson. She lives in the village. Do you know her?'

Katie did. Danielle Robinson was a plain, inoffensive

girl – well, woman actually, she was in her thirties – who worked at the doctor's surgery. Surely offered a choice between her and Katie, Owen wouldn't hesitate.

'Oh, well, I'm sure she'll understand. It's not like you're engaged or anything, is it? I mean, how long have you been seeing her for?'

'A couple of months,' Owen said, and Katie nearly fell off her seat. Two months? All this time she'd been getting up at half past five and prancing about in front of Owen at the bus stop he'd been seeing someone else? 'And yes,' he continued, 'she would understand because she's kind and caring and not at all possessive, but I still wouldn't feel right about it. Sorry.'

'But she's so . . . ordinary,' Katie blurted out. This was ridiculous. Owen had always had a massive crush on her, she knew it.

He looked at her pityingly. 'God, Katie, what's happened to you? I always thought you were such a sweet woman. I'm sorry for everything you've had to go through, I really am, but don't let it change who you are.'

They sat in silence for a few minutes and then Katie got up and rang the bell.

'I thought you were going to the leisure centre,' Owen called after her, as she made her way down the aisle.

'I've changed my mind,' she shouted back, pulling hard on Stanley's lead to make him hurry up.

Once off the bus she crossed the road looking for where she could get the bus to take her back to where she had come from. How dare he lecture her like that? What did Owen, of all people, know about how to be a good person? The man who had thrown his wife's

Moorcroft vase through her conservatory window and done God knows what to a joint of pork. The man who had confided in her that he was harbouring elaborate fantasies about how to get back at his wife and her lover. In an instant her crush on him had dissipated and she felt sick thinking of how she had chased after him so blatantly.

She reached into her pocket and pulled out her mobile. As soon as she turned it on it beeped. Another new message from Stephanie, saying, 'Call me.' It must have arrived after she had switched off the phone last night. Then it rang telling her it was her voicemail. She listened long enough to hear Stephanie's voice and then turned it off again. She didn't need this now.

49

Every time she finished a glass of champagne some passing waiter filled it again until Stephanie had absolutely no idea how many she'd had but what she did know was that the room was spinning and that she really needed to drink some water before she either passed out or made a fool of herself or both. Meredith had taken her by surprise when she'd asked to her go to the soap awards as her guest. Natasha would have had a field day going on and on about Stephanie being Meredith's new girlfriend and what should she wear to the wedding but, of course, Stephanie hadn't told her about it because she had been avoiding her, which hadn't been easy, given that they worked in the same office. Stephanie had spent the week working from home or visiting clients in their houses, leaving the occasional curt message on the office answerphone for Natasha, asking her to do something or other.

When Meredith had called, she had thought, What the hell? It wasn't as if her calendar was bursting with social engagements and she might pick up some new clients (she wasn't sure how, going up to people randomly and saying, 'You look awful, have you ever considered using a stylist' maybe). Besides, Michael was going to be there as one of the official photographers, snapping the happy winners with their trophies, so she could always sit backstage with him and pretend to be his assistant if she felt like it.

She had finally told him last night that she thought he was right – it was time they moved in together.

'Really?' Michael had said, his smile taking over his entire face. 'Really? Are you sure?'

'I just have to clear it with Finn,' Stephanie had said, smiling at his reaction.

'Of course. And, of course, if he feels it's too soon, we can wait. Whatever he wants.'

He wanted everything to be exactly right and everyone to be happy. He'd been ecstatic, ordering a bottle of champagne and squeezing her hand. It had felt good to be the person who had made him so happy.

She knew she would have to tell James sooner or later. She suspected he wasn't going to take it well – he was still clearly harbouring hopes of a reconciliation one day, however much she had made it clear that that was never going to happen. She just needed to pick her moment. God, everything was complex.

Today James was spending the day with Finn while she was supervising Meredith's hair and makeup. As soon as she had told him about Meredith's invitation he had said he would love to keep Finn overnight in his new tiny studio flat on Finchley Road. He had finally decided to rent while he waited to find something he could afford to buy and he had found this place in the local paper and moved in a week ago, after agreeing with the landlord that he could skip the first month's payment if he decorated it from top to bottom and did some minor repairs. Hardly a big job, considering the entire place measured fifteen by seventeen.

The bed, he had told her and Finn, folded back into being a sofa during the day; he had a two-ring cooker, a fridge and a microwave in one corner, with a tiny shower room and toilet off to one side. Small it might be, but now he had given it a lick of paint it was clean and private and it wasn't the Travel Motel.

James had told Finn that anytime he wanted to stay over he was welcome. He, James, would sleep on an air mattress on the floor, which he had bought specially. Finn had been nagging Stephanie ever since to be allowed to go. She had been unsure whether or not it was a good idea, but when she'd mentioned to James about her plans for the evening and he had offered yet again, she couldn't help thinking it was the most sensible option. Finn had nearly passed out with excitement.

She took a long drink of fizzy water and immediately her head felt clearer. She looked around for Meredith, who had almost certainly drunk even more than she had while celebrating her unexpected victory. She had made a gracious speech, thanking practically everyone she had ever met, including Stephanie, although she'd thankfully stopped short before she'd got to God. Now she was basking in the insincere compliments being showered on her by producers and directors, who wouldn't even have seen her for a casting yesterday, let alone hired her. Even Stephanie knew that their promissory notes of future jobs, should she ever leave the soap, were only redeemable for the next few weeks or until another of her cast mates took on the mantle of flavour of the month. But she was glad that Meredith was enjoying her moment in the spotlight.

Stephanie looked at her watch. It was already nearly midnight. The ceremony had gone on interminably and had finally finished at ten to ten. Dinner had followed, with copious amounts of wine. Stephanie had sat between one of the soap's directors and the wife of an actor who was up for something or other. They had both expressed an interest in using her services and had taken her number so it wasn't an entirely wasted evening. Michael had come through to say goodbye about an hour ago – he had to go and sort through his pictures, making the best ones available for tomorrow's morning newspapers. He had asked if she wanted to go with him and she should have said yes, but it had seemed rude to get up and leave when she was only halfway through her rack of lamb. She promised to call him once she was on her way home safely.

Now, though, they were encouraging people to move to the room next door for dancing and, no doubt, more drinking, and she had decided she had had enough. It was hard work making polite conversation with people you didn't know who probably had no interest in talking to you. She'd had a good time, it had been an experience – if only one that had taught her that events that look glamorous from the outside can often be fairly tedious once you're in – and she wanted her bed.

She drank another glass of water for good measure and made her way over to where Meredith was holding court to say goodbye. As Stephanie had anticipated she might, Meredith scooped her into her copious bosom and thanked her again for everything, as if Stephanie's dress sense had won her the award.

'He's a nice bloke,' Meredith said. Michael had photo-graphed Meredith with her trophy and had clearly man-aged to charm her more this time than he had when they had met previously.

'He is,' Stephanie said, hugging her again. 'I've decided to let him move in.'

Meredith smiled. 'Well, good for you. If you've decided that's the right thing to do then it is. I'm pleased for you both. How's your husband taking it?'

Stephanie's face fell. 'I haven't told him yet,' she said. 'He's having such a hard time of it at the moment. In fact, oh, God, I don't even know if I should tell you this . . .'

Meredith pulled Stephanie down into a chair and thrust another glass of champagne into her hand. 'What now?' she said.

And Stephanie found herself telling her the whole story: the plan to get back at James, how it had escalated, and how it had now got out of control. 'The thing is,' she found herself saying, 'I feel guilty. I never meant for it to go this far.'

'Revenge does strange things to people,' Meredith said, sounding like an agony aunt even though she was slurring. 'It can make you feel great or it can make you feel as low as the person you're exacting it on. Obviously this Katie's in the former camp.'

'I guess I'm in the latter. I thought it would make me feel stronger. To be honest, it did for a while.'

'But now you just feel shitty?'

'Exactly. You sound like you know from experi-ence.'

Meredith laughed. 'That person I told you I lived with once. It wasn't that I realized I'd made a mistake. It was actually that I came home one day and found her in bed with one of our friends.'

Stephanie paused, wine glass halfway to her lips. Had Meredith just said 'her'? She wanted to throw her arms round her and say, 'Thank you for confiding in me,' and then tell her to stop thinking she had to live a lie, that the world was a different place now, but she was worried that she had misheard or that Meredith would be embarrassed if she drew attention to it, so she merely sat and waited for what Meredith had to say next.

'Anyway, I decided to get her back. She was an actress, too, and I heard she had got a big break, a regular role in a long-running series. I rang the producer, pretending to be her agent, and told them she couldn't do it. And then I rang her agent, pretending to be someone from the production company, and said they'd changed their minds. I've always been good at accents.'

Stephanie laughed. 'It was ingenious, I'll give you that.'

'I know. And for a few months I felt wonderful. Empowered, even. Then, about a year later, I heard she was still out of work and I started to feel bad. Really bad. I'd affected her whole life, her whole career. OK, so she should never have done what she did, but me doing something wrong didn't make it better. It didn't take away what she'd done. It just meant there were two of us behaving badly.'

Stephanie sighed. 'I don't know what to do.'

'Well, the way I see it there are only two things you can do. You either convince Katie she has to stop or you tell James everything, allow him to arm himself against her.'

'Oh, God.'

'But first you need to go and sleep on it. Come on, I'll help you find your coat.'

When Stephanie's taxi eventually pulled up outside her house she noticed that most of the lights were off and silently cursed James for not thinking how unwelcoming that might be for her, coming home late. She had left him and Finn playing football in the garden with Finn's overnight bag packed and ready for him to go. James was bringing him back in the morning – not too early, they had agreed, in case Stephanie had a hangover and needed a lie-in. She let herself in and nearly tripped over Finn's rucksack on the hall floor. On top of it was a note: 'Stephanie,' it said, 'Finn couldn't settle in the flat. Said he was scared and wanted to go home so I brought him back here. I'm sleeping on the sofa. Sorry. Will leave first thing before you get up. Hope you had a good time. James.'

In the kitchen she found the remains of their dinner – pasta and tomato sauce, one of Finn's favourites – in a Tupperware container. The dishes and pans were stacked neatly in the dishwasher. Stephanie tiptoed to the living-room door and opened it softly. She could just make out a shape that must be James under a pile of blankets.

Without really knowing what she was doing she slipped off her shoes and walked into the room. She was over-whelmed by the urge to look at him while he was asleep and unaware of what she was doing. She felt as if she didn't know him any more. He didn't seem like the same man she had been married to for all those years – but then hadn't it turned out that she hadn't really known the man she was married to after all? The man she had been married to was successful, confident and handsome. He would never have grown a beard and worn the same clothes for days on end. He certainly would never have cooked his son homemade pasta and tomato sauce. She preferred this version, this strange man lying asleep on her sofa who took his responsibilities seriously, and whom she couldn't imagine ever having two women on the go at the same time, so burdened was he with the guilt of what he had done in his past. But then, she mentally cautioned herself, she had never imagined that the old James would have had two women on the go at the same time either. That was the whole point. He had deceived her. She had to remember that this man was capable of massive deception. She didn't want to hurt him any more, though. Hurting him hadn't made her feel better as she had thought it would. Meredith was right – now they were just two people who had behaved as badly as each other. What was the point in that?

He looked incredibly peaceful lying there, and Stephanie was seized with the desire to reach out and stroke his forehead, the way she always did with Finn when he was sick. James stirred and the noise shook Stephanie out of her reverie. What am I doing? she thought, and turned round quickly, nearly knocking over a picture frame. I've had way too much to drink and I need to go to bed.

James stirred again. 'Hello,' he said sleepily.

'I'm drunk,' Stephanie said, as if that was any kind of

an explanation for why she was standing over him. 'I was just . . . looking for something.'

James half sat up, and she was aware that she felt self-conscious with him sitting there bare-chested. 'Good for you. Did you have a good time?'

'Yes, great. I should go to bed, though.'

'Do you want a cup of tea?' he said, and she tried to remember the last time he had offered to do that for her late at night. There was no way she could bring herself to tell him she was responsible for everything that had been happening to him.

'No. Thanks. I really should go to bed.'

'Night, then,' he said, pulling the duvet up over himself again.

'Night.'

50

There were several things that Stephanie could think of that she would rather do than sit on a train for two and a bit hours travelling up to Lincoln to confront Katie. Included in them were ripping off her own arm and sitting through a Westlife concert sober. But the way she saw it she had no option. She had to get Katie to stop what she was doing – she just had no idea what she was going to say. Going back to Lower Shippingham was bad enough, running the risk of bumping into people she half knew who would want to offer their condolences for the wreck of her marriage. Funny that only a few months ago she had thought it would be a good idea – a twisted kind of fun, even – to turn up unannounced at James's birthday party. This time her plan was to get in and out as quickly as possible. If only she could work out how she was going to handle it.

She was walking through King's Cross towards the platform when her mobile rang. Pauline, her mother-in-law. Neither James nor Stephanie had yet had the courage to break the news of their separation to her and John. It would break their hearts. Twice Stephanie had intercepted Finn when he had started to say some-thing about Dad coming to visit or his room at the Travel Motel. She had ended up telling Pauline that it was best, these days, to call her on her mobile because she was so busy. She really didn't want to ask Finn to lie.

Now she thought about not answering – she wasn't in the mood for a cosy chat about how happy they all were and she was always afraid that Pauline would pick up on the fact that she was lying. She felt bad, though. She knew Pauline worried about the cost of making a call to a mobile phone, believing a five-minute conversation would cost her about the same as talking to someone in America for a couple of hours. If she went through to voicemail she would panic about whether or not to leave a message and how much that might cost.

Reluctantly Stephanie pressed the answer key. 'Hi, Pauline. I'll call you straight back,' she said, as she always did.

'OK dear,' Pauline said, and Stephanie thought she sounded a little shaky. She stopped herself from asking her if she was all right – she would do that on her own phone bill – and cut off the call without saying goodbye, redialling immediately.

'Is something wrong?' she said, as soon as Pauline answered.

'No. Well, as long as you and James are OK then nothing's wrong, no.'

Stephanie felt unaccountably nervous. 'Why wouldn't we be OK?' God, they really must get round to telling her. This was ridiculous. She had a faint suspicion that the real reason James had asked her not to say anything to his parents yet was because he was hoping the whole issue might go away and then they'd never have to know. It made her uneasy.

'It's just . . . I got this phone call. I had to go to the hairdresser's this morning . . .' Pauline could never just pass on a piece of information: she always had to give the recipient the whole story of the events leading up to it, what she was wearing, how she had felt. Stephanie had to hold herself back from screaming, 'Just tell me. Has something happened?'

'. . . you know I always go on a Thursday. It's half-price day if you go before ten o'clock and they open at eight, which really suits me because you know I get up early. Oh, and I was a bit late because I bumped into Mary Arthur on the way. You remember Mary? She came round one day when you and James were here. One Christmas, I think it was. Short woman. Quite round.'

Stephanie rolled her eyes. She looked up at the large clock on the station concourse. She still had ten minutes before the train to Lincoln left. 'Yes, I remember,' she said quickly, hoping that the tone of her voice said that she didn't want to get sidetracked into a conversation about Mary's virtues.

'She was taking her dog for a walk. Nice thing. Hairy. I don't know what breed it is. Anyway . . .'

Stephanie could stand it no longer. 'So, then what? After the hairdresser?'

'Well, the point is that I didn't get home until after half past nine. By the time I'd been to Morrisons, you know – it gets very busy in there in the mornings, people going in on their way to work.' She waited for Stephanie to add her agreement. She didn't, pausing instead in the hope that Pauline would get to the point.

'And when I got home there was a message on the

379

answerphone. Did I say that John had gone to the post office?'

'Who from?' Stephanie said, feeling sick. 'Who was the message from?'

'Well, that's why I'm ringing you, dear. It was from someone who said she was a friend of you and James. Said she needed to speak to one of us. And I thought something must have happened. An accident or something. Goodness, I need a brandy.'

'Did she say what her name was?' Stephanie asked, knowing the answer.

'Katie, I think. But you are OK, aren't you? Both of you?'

'We're fine,' Stephanie said. She needed to get off the phone. She needed to get hold of Katie fast.

'Well, I wonder why she was calling us. Do you know?'

'I have no idea. And listen, Pauline, don't worry about calling her back. She's not really a friend she's . . . well, she's just someone we know, but she's a bit crazy. Not dangerous, not like that,' she added quickly, suddenly worried that Pauline would have nightmares about an axe murderess, 'just a bit silly, a bit not quite right in the head.' As she said it, she thought maybe it was true; maybe Katie was a bit touched.

'And if she calls you again don't answer.' She thought about telling Pauline there and then, saying, 'Actually, James and I have separated and Katie was the other woman, but I don't want you to worry because we're fine,' but it wasn't up to her. It was James who had to come clean with his mother and, anyway, she didn't think she could take hearing the hurt and disappointment in her mother-in-law's voice.

'How will I know it's her?' Pauline asked nervously.

'Well, just don't talk to her, then. Tell her you're busy and you'll have to call her back. Meanwhile I'll get hold of her and find out what she wants. She's probably lost our numbers or something and she's trying to get hold of one of us,' she said, with a sudden burst of inspiration.

'I can give her your number. Or shall I give her James's?'

Oh, God. 'Just try not to get into conversation with her, Pauline. She has a funny sense of humour – she might say something that'd upset you. Like I said, she's a bit odd.'

There was no way Pauline wouldn't have twigged there was something wrong. For all her sweet-old-lady act she most definitely wasn't stupid. But as long as Stephanie could somehow stall her speaking to Katie, then she could tell James he had to go and see his parents and break the news to them right away.

'OK, if that's what you want,' Pauline said cautiously.

Stephanie ran for the train. She had no idea now if going up to Lincoln was the right thing to do, but if Katie was never going to answer her phone or return her calls then she had little option. She had no real hope that she could stop Katie doing whatever it was she was planning but she felt she had to do something. There was no getting round it: she needed James to help her. And asking him for help meant telling him the whole truth.

'Guess what,' he said cheerfully when he answered the

phone. 'I've got a job.' He paused triumphantly waiting for her reaction but Stephanie couldn't let herself be distracted and, besides, she had barely taken in what he'd said.

'James, I have something to tell you but I can't go into it now. I need you to ring your mum and keep her talking on the phone for as long as you can. Ideally for about two and a half hours,' she said, and almost laughed, it was so ridiculous. 'She just told me that someone called Katie is trying to ring her. I think she's going to tell her everything.'

'Jesus! How did she . . . I mean –'

'I'll tell you the details later. I'm going to try and call Katie, get her to change her mind.'

'Do you need her number?'

'Actually, I already have it. Oh, and I'm on my way up there. To Lower Shippingham. To talk to her.'

Stephanie heard James splutter in what would, under other circumstances, have been a comical way. This was clearly too much for him to take in all at once. 'I will explain everything later, I promise. The main thing now is that Pauline and John don't get caught up in the middle of our mess, OK? Just keep her on the phone for as long as you can and, hopefully, Katie'll get bored of trying. It's all we can do.'

'I'm going to meet you up there,' James said, and Stephanie found that she felt relieved. In truth, she didn't want to have to deal with this on her own. 'I'll call you later,' he said, and rang off.

Stephanie sat in the carriage and began the tedious process of dialling Katie's number over and over again, willing her to answer. She left endless messages, asking her not to stoop so low as to hurt Pauline and John. She had said to James weeks ago that she was happy to keep Katie's existence a secret from them for ever if that was what he thought best. They could tell them they had simply grown apart, that it was all perfectly amicable, preserve their son's saintly image. She was happy to do whatever would hurt Pauline and John the least. Why couldn't he have told them then? At least they would have got used to the news of the break-up by now. They would already have been picturing their son meeting other women. The whole thing would have been altogether less heart-attack-inducing.

51

After about half an hour Stephanie paused for a moment to allow her throbbing thumb to take a rest and almost immediately her phone rang and a voice told her that she had a new message.

'We're off the hook for a while,' James's voice said. 'I've persuaded them to go round to their friends for a couple of hours. Ring me back.'

Stephanie took a deep breath. Now that the possibility of Katie getting hold of Pauline and John had faded she had to face the fact that she was going to have to come clean with James. It wasn't that she thought he would be angry with her — he had no right, after all — it was just that she wasn't looking forward to having to tell him. She dialled his number reluctantly.

'I'm on the A1,' he shouted, when he answered. 'You don't have to get involved in this, you know, Steph. It's my mess. I'll sort it out.'

Stephanie closed her eyes. 'It's partly my mess too. I'll explain when I see you.'

She ignored his pleas to tell him what she meant. It was going to be hard enough as it was without being interrupted every couple of minutes because the train had gone into a tunnel or the man pushing the refreshment cart wanted to know if you would like a free bag of peanuts with your coffee.

They agreed that they would meet at Lincoln station and drive over to Lower Shippingham together. It was hardly a plan but it was all they had.

Katie had grown bored of dialling Pauline and John's number. It seemed to be permanently engaged. It had only been a whim, anyway. It wasn't that she was trying to hurt James's parents – that certainly hadn't been her primary aim, at least, and she was trying not to think about whether that might be one of the consequences – but she wanted to punish James for her humiliation with Owen. There was no doubt in her mind that if James hadn't behaved as he had then she wouldn't have thrown herself at the nearest available – well, unavailable, as it had turned out – man and subsequently been turned down flat. On a bus. At six thirty in the morning. While pretending to be going swimming.

She was assuming that James must have told his parents about his marriage ending by now. What she knew with absolute certainty was that he would never have come clean about the reasons behind it. He wasn't that courageous. All she was planning to do was to mention to his mother that she was a friend of her son's and she was trying to track him down and leave it there. Then get off the phone as quickly as she could, leaving that unexploded bomb ticking away in the background. She dialled the number again. This time it rang and rang and then went to answerphone again. She didn't bother to leave a second message. There was no point. She could try later. Even if she never managed to get through, she thought, smiling, at some point James's parents were bound to mention to him that someone called Katie, who had described herself as a friend of his, had left a message. That should finish him off. She wondered whether Pauline and John would put two and two together and remember that Katie was the name of the woman James had introduced them to in Lincoln all those weeks ago. That would get them thinking.

She went back to concentrating on her business plan. The bank had agreed to lend her a certain amount towards her start-up costs, providing she could show exactly how the money would be used and when she would be able to pay it back. Somehow she was finding her heart wasn't in it. She couldn't really feel excited about getting into debt and having to work all hours just to keep her head above water. The way she had worked before had suited her: life had come first and work second. If she hadn't felt like working, she had taken the day off. Now she had responsibilities and quotas and projections, and she wasn't sure she liked it.

It had been about the chase, she realized now. The important thing had been forcing James to sell her the surgery for a fraction of what it was really worth. That had been the victory. She had no real desire to be a businesswoman. Contracts had been exchanged, though. There was no pulling out now without losing her deposit, something which she could definitely not afford to do. She felt irrationally annoyed with James for putting her in the position where she would have to sacrifice her whole life to work.

She picked up the phone and dialled Pauline and John's number again. Answerphone.

*

By the time James arrived to collect Stephanie from the café in Lincoln station she was on her third cup of coffee and thinking seriously about getting on a train back to London. This was crazy. What were they going to do? Tie Katie to a chair to stop her calling? Actually, that wasn't such a bad idea. She certainly wasn't sure that turning up with James in tow would do any good. But there was something almost uplifting in the thought that soon everything would be out in the open. She had never quite understood Catholics with their love of confession – maybe because she had never had anything weighing so heavily on her that she had needed to confess – but now she could see it would be cathartic getting it all off her chest.

She was starting to feel like she had caffeine overload and was trying to ignore the impatient stares of the customers who were waiting for tables, hot cups of coffee in their hands, when James walked through the door and threw himself down in the seat opposite her. 'Have you been here long?' he said, as if they were meeting for a cup of tea and a friendly chat.

'It doesn't matter,' Stephanie said. 'We need to make a plan.'

They decided to head to Lower Shippingham and talk in the car. Once they were on the way, Stephanie took a deep breath and started at the beginning: how she had found the text message and contacted Katie, the fact that they had met, their plans to unravel James's life. James listened in silence. When she got to the part about Katie being responsible for the problems with the tax and the planning people, she forced herself to look at him to see how he was taking it. His face was flushed and she knew he was angry or embarrassed about the way he had treated Sally but that he wasn't about to say so.

'I'm sorry,' she said finally, when she had told him everything.

'It's fine,' he said. 'It's no more than I deserve.'

'Well, actually, I think maybe it is. A bit. You deserved most of it, I'll give you that.' She thought she saw a small smile forcing its way round the corners of his mouth. She decided to push her luck. 'Especially the dinner party. That was inspired.'

He actually laughed. 'Your idea?'

'Joint effort. It made me feel better, James. What can I say?'

'I can't believe I so wanted to impress those people, to be honest.'

'I can't believe a lot of things about you,' she said, and then wished she hadn't. They didn't need to rehash all his failings again. He clearly knew them all already. So, she tried to lighten the mood again. 'Like the fact you gave them bouillabaisse. You hate bouillabaisse.'

'It was all I could get. They really need to expand their range at the Joli Poulet.'

Stephanie smiled. 'So what are we going to do when we get there?'

'The Joli Poulet?'

'Very funny.'

James took his hand off the steering-wheel and wiped his forehead. 'I was hoping you might have a plan. I just don't want Mum and Dad to get dragged into this, that's all.'

'Neither do I,' Stephanie said.

'I can't believe she'd deliberately go out of her way to hurt them. It doesn't seem like Katie at all. Well, you know that, I guess.'

'I think she took it hard . . . what you did . . . And I think that getting her own back has made her feel better. She's definitely changed, I'll give you that.'

'Oh, God,' James said. 'What are we going to do?'

The roads were so familiar. Every junction, every potential bottleneck, every handy back route was hard-wired into his brain, which was just as well because he was completely unable to concentrate on where he was going. He hadn't thought twice about offering to drive up to Lincoln to meet Stephanie but as soon as he was on his way he had started to regret his decision. He had no idea really what was going on between Stephanie and Katie, although he had worked out that they seemed to have had some contact. Presumably Stephanie had found Katie's number in his phone and had called her, or maybe it had been Katie who had got in touch first, phoning and saying, 'I seem to be living with your husband.' Judging by how she was behaving now, that was more than possible. Maybe Katie had never been the sweet, naïve woman she had appeared to be. Somehow it made him feel better to think that that might be true.

Stephanie was looking pale and anxious when he spotted her sitting at a table in the corner of the café and his heart pounded for a couple of beats as if to remind him that it was her he really cared about. She smiled a half-smile at him when he caught her eye but then looked away quickly, like she didn't quite know what to say to him. He sat down.

It was hard to take in quite what Stephanie was telling him, especially since he was driving at the same time. He felt foolish, angry and humiliated all at once, as if he was the butt of an elaborate joke that everyone was in on except him. When she got to the part about the Inland Revenue he had nearly blurted out, 'But . . .' and then had stopped himself. Stephanie's point seemed to be that Katie had taken things way too far, had acted alone. And, anyway, what right did he have to complain that he had been badly treated? But he felt terrible about Sally. He felt himself colour up as he remembered the way he had spoken to her, the things he had said.

'I feel terrible about Sally,' Stephanie said, as if she could read his mind. 'She should never have ended up caught in the middle of all this.'

'I'll go and see her and explain. Apologize,' he said, and Stephanie offered to come with him, which made him feel a little better about the prospect.

'You can tell her she imagined the whole thing. It was all a dream, like on *Dallas*,' she said, and he laughed. Stephanie had a knack of always being able to make him laugh when he felt at his lowest.

By the time she opened the door and found her ex-boyfriend and his soon-to-be-ex-wife standing there together, Katie had forgotten all about phoning his parents. She had got bored of the idea quite quickly, once she had realized it was unlikely that anyone was ever going to answer, and then almost immediately had begun to feel bad about having left a message in the first place. Trying to hurt James was one thing, but upsetting his doting parents along the way was probably taking it too far. After all, they had seemed very sweet when she had met them, very vulnerable. Since when had she become the kind of person who would go out of her way to harm two seventy-five-year-olds? He had done this to her. He had made her like this. She tried to remember exactly what she had said into their answerphone: just that she was a friend of his and Stephanie's and was trying to get in touch. Enough that he would have a heart-attack if they mentioned it to him, but not enough that they would know something was wrong and worry about it. There was no need for her to do any more. Any more would tip over from justifiable revenge into something altogether darker, and she liked to think that somewhere deep inside her was still a nice person who was waiting to re-emerge once she had got James out of her system.

'Stephanie, hi,' she'd said, surprised as she'd opened the door. Then she'd noticed who else was there, standing slightly behind as if he was afraid of what the reception might be, and she'd added, 'What's he doing here?'

52

Katie didn't look her best, Stephanie thought, when the door opened. She looked older, more wary, less like something from a Disney cartoon. She did a definite double-take when she saw James, and who could blame her? Even Stephanie didn't understand what they were doing there together.

'Katie, we've come to ask you to stop. I realize this must seem a bit strange. Trust me, it's not just you who thinks that. But it's gone far enough now. Involving James's parents is a step too far.'

Katie looked nervously in James's direction. 'What are you talking about?' she asked unconvincingly.

'I've told him all about it. I've been trying to ring you all day. If you'd answered I would have explained – after I'd got you to promise to leave Pauline and John alone, that is.'

'You'd better come in,' Katie said, and backed into her front room just as Stanley, realizing exactly who was standing on the doorstep, came hurtling out and threw himself at James.

'Right,' Stephanie heard herself say. 'Of course, the dog.'

It was hard for her to imagine James living in the tiny feminine cottage. It was homely enough, quaint, even, but James's taste had always been for monochrome, stark, masculine lines and everything looking like it had come straight out of the pages of a magazine, something which had been hard to achieve once they had had Finn.

'Oh, you've painted,' James said, as they went in, speaking for the first time since they had got there.

Katie said nothing. Stephanie had noticed that she was avoiding even looking at James, if she could help it. Of course, she hadn't been in contact with him since it had all blown up. Stephanie, on the other hand, had got used to having to deal with him on a daily basis.

Katie banged around in the kitchen, making them coffee, which she hadn't even asked them if they wanted. James was sitting, head down, clearly wishing he wasn't there.

Stephanie decided to take matters into her own hands and followed Katie through to the tiny back room, pulling the door behind her to give them a semblance of privacy, although clearly James would be able to hear every word they were saying. Tough, she thought. I haven't come all this way just to worry about hurting his feelings.

'I'm really sorry to ambush you like this, Katie,' she said. 'It's just that it's all got out of hand. OK, so we wanted to pay him back –'

'You wanted to,' Katie said, and Stephanie was acutely aware that James would be all ears on the other side of the door.

'Yes, I wanted to. I know it was my idea and you would never have thought about revenge, not ever. It wasn't in your nature, I could see that. But the truth is that I've moved on, and I think you need to, maybe. And so does

James, for Finn's sake if no one else's. It's not good for a little boy to watch his father's life fall apart.'

Katie put down the mug she was holding. 'You were right. You said it would make me feel better and it did. And that's a good thing, isn't it?'

'Of course it is. But can you honestly say it's *still* making you feel better? Isn't it healthier to let things go?' she added, trying to think of a way to put it that would connect with Katie's New Age sensibilities. 'You need to ... purify or whatever. You've got the new business to think about. That's something good to have come out of all of this, isn't it?'

'I'm not really interested in the business,' Katie said petulantly. 'I liked things the way they were, just me and my clients, not worrying about staff and pension schemes and who's going to run reception. I just wanted him to have to sell it to me for a knock-down price. I wanted him to have to pay me back somehow, that's all.'

'Then do it up and sell it for a profit. You can be an aromatherapist who's a property magnate on the side.'

Katie shrugged.

'It's over anyway, Katie. Now that James knows everything it's over anyway. Just please don't hurt his parents. You're nicer than that. That was one of the first things that struck me about you, how nice you were. That's why I believed you as soon as you told me you were innocent in all this. That was why I liked you, which was, frankly, weird, if you think about it.'

'I never had any intention of telling them anything. I haven't changed that much.'

'So why call them?'

'To frighten him, I suppose.'

'Well, you achieved that. Now what?'

'What do you mean?' Katie said defensively.

'Is that it or are you planning anything else?'

Katie looked at her evenly. 'I didn't start this, Stephanie.'

'I know,' Stephanie said. 'I know it was all me. But now I'm asking you to stop. Please. Katie, you're better than this.'

'Being nice didn't get me far, did it?'

'Being nice made me like you despite everything that had happened,' Stephanie said. 'Being nice made me believe you when you said you'd been hurt as much as I had. It's what made you *you*.'

Katie sighed. 'OK, I'll stop. For your sake, though, not James's. You and Finn.'

Stephanie felt as if a weight had been lifted from her shoulders. She put her arms round Katie and hugged her. 'So, is that it now, then? We can all just try to get on with our lives?'

'I suppose,' Katie said, and hugged Stephanie back, which Stephanie took as a sign that she was telling the truth.

'We'll get out of your way,' she said, and moved to go back through to the living room. The sooner she was out of there, the sooner she could get home and just forget about this whole chapter of her life.

James, however, seemed to have other ideas. He was hovering just behind the door, looking purposeful, and as soon as she came through it, followed by Katie, he said, 'I want to say something.'

Oh, God, Stephanie thought. 'Everything's fine, James,' she said. 'Let's just go.'

'No,' he said. 'Not until I've said what I have to say.'

He hadn't planned to make a speech. He hadn't been intending to say anything at all, if he could help it, knowing that Katie was far more likely to listen to Stephanie than to him. He was just there for moral support, ballast in case Steph needed propping up. Over the past few months he had managed to put Katie completely out of his mind. It was as if she barely existed. She was a blip. A fairly large blip admittedly. He had wanted to forget about her for Stephanie's sake. Now, faced with the reality of her in front of him, he knew that he owed it to her to explain. He had fallen for her naïvety and her sweetness and her trusting nature and then he had destroyed those very things that he had thought he loved. As much as what he had done had been unkind to Stephanie, so it had been equally unkind to Katie, and if he was trying to be a better person, he had to acknowledge that and take full responsibility for what he had done to both women.

'Katie,' he began, 'I want to apologize, really sincerely and honestly apologize, for the way I treated you. It was unforgivable. I was weak and stupid and dishonest and, basically, an idiot. And a bastard. And whatever else you want to call me . . .'

Katie, in fact, was just looking at him impassively, as if to say, 'I know this already.'

Stephanie was just looking like she wanted to get out of there.

'The thing is,' he continued, determined to say his

piece, 'I made a terrible mistake. You see, the truth is that I never stopped loving Stephanie. I just couldn't see it.' He glanced at her to see if she had reacted to his declaration, but Stephanie was now studying the floor.

'I suppose it was a mid-life crisis, I don't know. I guess you'd be able to analyse my behaviour better than I can – you're good at that,' he said, looking back at Katie, who was now looking him straight in the eye as if challenging him to lie to her any more. 'And I used you to make me feel I was still young or attractive or something. It's pitiful, I know. And then, before I knew what was happening, I'd started to care for you. To love you, actually. I really thought I did – sorry, Steph . . .' Now he looked at Stephanie again. She was still admiring the carpet.

'Anyway, I wanted you to know that. I never meant to hurt you, either of you. I was a fool who thought he could have his cake and eat it, and then I realized that for me having what I really wanted meant having my marriage and my wife and my son. But by then it was too late. So, I want you both to know that I regret it all and I never meant to mess you around, Katie, but eventually I realized it was Stephanie who I had loved all along. And I still do. And I'd do anything if she'd take me back.'

No one said anything for a moment and James's statement stayed hanging there in the air. And then Katie turned to Stephanie and said, 'You're not taking him back, are you?'

When James had finished his speech, Katie realized she felt nothing for him. No attraction, no anger, no resentment. It had all gone and she was left with a big, empty sense of nothingness. If she was being honest, she would have admitted it felt good.

'You're not taking him back, are you?'

'No!' Stephanie said indignantly, looking up for the first time in ages. 'Of course not.' And then she had cast James a sideways look and added, 'In actual fact, I'm about to move in with someone else. Well, that is, he's moving in with me. Sorry,' she said, looking over at James again. 'I meant to tell you.'

James looked as if he had been hit by a large truck. 'Michael?' he said, and Stephanie nodded.

'Sorry,' she said again, and Katie started to wonder if she was hearing things.

'Why are you apologizing to him? And who's Michael?' She felt irritated with Stephanie. Not just because of the U-turn she seemed to have performed where James was concerned or the fact that she had chosen to reveal their whole plan to him without checking that that was an OK thing to do but because, she now realized, Stephanie had managed to move on to the extent that another man liked her enough to ask her to live with him. It was jealousy, pure and simple. Stephanie's life had worked out OK while Katie had merely humiliated herself by chasing after someone who wasn't interested. The old Katie – the real Katie – would have been delighted for her, would have taken pleasure simply from the fact that there were still happy endings to be had out there, whoever they were for. She had to try and get that other Katie back from wherever she had gone. That other Katie had been happy.

'Wow,' she forced herself to say when Stephanie told

her, and she thought she even sounded as if she meant it. 'I'm really pleased for you. That's great.'

James made a sort of grunting noise, kind of like an animal in pain and Katie saw that this news had devastated him. Had he really thought he'd had a chance of winning Stephanie back? After all that had happened? She realized she actually felt sorry for him. Now that she had let go of all the negative feelings, something of her old kind self was returning and she was able to feel bad for him in a way she had never imagined she could. Unrequited love was a terrible thing to suffer from, especially when you'd had it once and lost it. She managed a half-smile of sympathy for him and he responded with a look that contained so much relief, so much gratitude, that she instantly felt good about herself.

Stephanie was edging towards the door. 'I really need to get going,' she said. 'I've got to be back before Finn gets home.'

'Come back in the car with me,' James said. 'Or I can drive you to the station if you'd rather,' he added nervously.

Once Stephanie had agreed that it made no sense for her to get the train when he had his car right outside the front door, he went off to the bathroom, leaving her and Katie alone.

'What a mess, eh?'

Katie, buoyed up by the satisfaction that came from knowing she was being a good person, smiled. 'He's changed, I think. He sounds like he's learned his lesson.'

'Hey,' Stephanie said, smiling back at her warmly, 'Katie's back.'

53

Neither Stephanie nor James mentioned his outburst in the car on the way back. Stephanie decided that the only thing she could do if she was to survive the journey was to turn up the radio and pretend to be asleep. She didn't want to have to tell him there was no chance.

They had stopped off briefly at Sally O'Connell's house, and James had made a genuine and grovelling apology, which Sally had accepted with good grace.

'I could have sued you for wrongful dismissal apparently,' Sally had said, 'but I never would have done something like that.'

'That's because you're a nicer person than I am,' James had said. 'Or, at least, than I was. I'm trying.'

By three it was obvious that they weren't going to make it back by the time Cassie brought Finn home after school, so Stephanie called and asked her to stay on until they arrived, which luckily she agreed to do because Stephanie wasn't quite sure what she would have done otherwise. She really hadn't thought this through when she'd jumped on the train this morning.

By the time they got to the house she was exhausted, but James wanted to come in and say hello to Finn and she knew she had no right not to let him. Once Finn's tea was ready it seemed churlish not to offer James something, and it was only when they were all sitting round the big kitchen table that she remembered what he had said to her that morning. 'Did you say you had a new job?' she asked. The morning seemed like a year ago.

'I did!' He looked delighted with himself, his face lit up with enthusiasm in a way she hadn't seen for months, possibly years. 'It's only three days a week and it doesn't exactly pay brilliantly, but it's at the Cardew Rescue Centre in Kilburn. It's a charity and they see local people who can't afford vet's fees as well as taking in strays. No more dogs in handbags or cats that've had their claws removed in case they snag the silk cushions. Real stuff, you know.'

'That's great,' she said. 'I'm really pleased for you.'

'Can I get a dog?' Finn said, wide-eyed. 'One that someone brings in that no one else wants. An old one or one with three legs or something.'

James laughed. 'Maybe. Ask your mum.'

'Mu –'

'No,' Stephanie said, before he could finish. 'At least, not for a while.'

'Tell you what,' James said, 'if one comes in with *two* legs I promise you can have it.'

'One leg,' Stephanie said, 'and an eye missing. Then you have a deal.'

Stephanie had plans to make. Michael was supposed to be moving in next week and she still hadn't broached the subject with Finn, let alone cleared out cupboard space and thrown away anything embarrassing that Michael might stumble across, like haemorrhoid cream or support tights. She hadn't seen him for a few days as he'd been away photographing some band or other for a magazine.

She hadn't told him about her jaunt up to Lincoln with James or their encounter with Katie. She had a feeling he wouldn't understand. Natasha on the other hand would, if only they were speaking to each other, but Stephanie had made such a point of avoiding her friend lately that Natasha had cottoned on and had stopped trying to call her. They were still communicating by text messages and notes left around the office. Stephanie knew that, as the person who had created this whole situation, she was the one who would have to make the first move.

'I'm sorry, I'm sorry, I'm sorry, I'm sorry,' she said, as soon as Natasha answered the phone.

'I take it you're sorry,' Natasha said, and Stephanie could hear there was a smile in her voice.

'I should never have taken it out on you. I asked for your advice but because I didn't like what you said I got all defensive. It was stupid of me. And disloyal . . .'

'And childish.'

'. . . and childish, yes, thanks.'

'And ungrateful.'

'OK, you can stop now. I'm trying to be sincere for once. The point is that I fucked up and I'm sorry and I want to be friends again.'

'Accepted, obviously. How's Michael?'

'Fine. Moving in next week.'

'Great,' Natasha said, sounding as if she was trying to mean it.

'Is it?' Stephanie said. 'I'm not sure any more.'

'Well, don't expect me to give you any advice. Ever again. You're on your own in that department.'

*

402

In retrospect, Stephanie thought later, it would have been better to wait until after dinner to tell Michael her news. That way they wouldn't have had to sit there for twenty minutes chewing through their pasta and trying to think what to say to each other.

Michael had been very calm and reasonable, as she had known he would be: histrionics were not his style. He had been shocked, there was no doubt about it. He was telling her about a book he'd been reading about Afghanistan or Azerbaijan, she couldn't remember which because she hadn't been concentrating, so fixated was she on trying to work out how to steer the conversation round to their relationship. Finally she hadn't been able to wait any longer and as soon as he had paused to take a breath she'd heard herself say, 'I need to talk to you about something.'

He'd realized immediately that something was wrong, of course. Everyone knew that a sentence like that one was never the prelude to good news. He had put down his fork and wiped his mouth, waiting for the axe to fall.

Stephanie had gone over and over in her mind what she was intending to say. She'd even tried it out loud with Natasha, but Natasha had refused to take it seriously and had kept on acting Michael collapsing in hysterics, clutching his chest and shouting, 'Why? Why?' Eventually Stephanie had given up.

'Well, if it all goes wrong,' she'd said, laughing, 'it'll be your fault. I hope you'll be satisfied.'

Now she'd forgotten her well-practised words and could only think of platitudes, like 'It's not you, it's me,' and 'We should just be friends,' both of which she had

...ise not to say. So she'd settled for the blunt ...aightforward, 'I think we should stop seeing each ...ier,' then sat back and waited to see what he would say in response.

'OK,' he said quietly. 'Is there a reason?'

'Well,' she said, 'I think maybe I rushed into it.' This, she remembered, was the angle she had decided to take, part truth but leaving out the stuff about how she knew they'd never last because he didn't have much of a sense of humour. 'I should have dealt with everything that was going on with James before I let myself get involved with someone else. It was just that I met you and you were really nice and I was really flattered and before I knew it we were getting serious and I, well . . . I'm so sorry.'

She waited for him to accuse her of messing him around, of playing with his feelings, using him but, of course, being Michael, he just nodded sadly and said, 'Well, if that's your decision I have to accept it. I wish you'd change your mind, though.'

'If I'd met you a few months down the line . . .' she said, unable to stop the cliché as it forced its way out of her mouth '. . . things might have been different. But I feel like I need to be on my own for a while, sort myself out. Work out what I really want.'

'You're not going back to James?'

'No! Why do people keep asking me that?'

Michael ate a forkful of food, clearly weighing up what to say next. Even though he was making it easy for her, she wished that, just for once, he would get angry or even cry. He was so lacking in passion, she thought now, so strait-jacketed by politeness. It would drive you mad after a few years. She was doing the right thing.

'Well, obviously I'm upset,' he said, telling what he most definitely wasn't showing. 'I thought . . . Well, I thought we had something special. But I respect your honesty. Maybe in a few months, if you want to, we could try again. I'd like to be friends at least.'

Stephanie thought about the jazz nights and the gallery openings and the art films, and forced herself to say, 'Yes, I hope we can too.'

They finished their pasta and salad, making stilted but civilized conversation and then Stephanie yawned and said that she didn't think she could manage dessert, she was knackered and she had to get up early in the morning. Outside in the street they hugged and kissed each other on the cheek, and Michael said, 'I'll leave it up to you to call me. I don't want to push you.'

'OK, lovely,' she said, knowing that she probably wouldn't. She had never been any good at staying friends with her exes.

Back at home James was watching TV in the living room. He got up when he heard her come in.

'I didn't tell the taxi to wait,' she said. 'I thought maybe we could have a drink.'

James sat back down again. 'OK.' Stephanie looked as if she might have been crying.

'Are you all right?' he asked tentatively.

She sat down on the sofa. 'I've split up with Michael,' she said.

James's heart skipped a beat but he tried not to show

...s news had made him. 'I'm sorry. He ...ke a nice bloke.' Oh, yes, easy to be generous ...Michael was out of the picture.

'Don't be. It was my decision.'

There was his heart again, threatening to pound its way out of his chest. Play it cool, he told himself. 'Right.'

Stephanie looked at him as he held out a glass of wine for her. 'Don't go getting any ideas. It doesn't mean . . . you know. I just want to be on my own.'

James's heart screeched to a noisy halt. OK, so this wasn't yet the romantic happy ending he had been fantasizing about. 'Of course,' he said, managing to sound calm and mature. 'So,' he said, 'tell me all about it. Did he cry?'

Stephanie smiled, as he had hoped she would. 'No!'

'Did he threaten to throw himself off a tall building if you didn't change your mind?'

She laughed. 'No!'

'Doesn't sound like he was bothered, then. He was probably fed up with you anyway.' OK, so that last statement was taking a bit of a gamble. She would either take offence or find it hilarious.

She threw a cushion at him, laughing. 'Actually, he thought I was going back to you so he was obviously mentally impaired.'

James smiled. This was all he wanted, his old easy relationship with Stephanie back and the chance to prove to her that he could be a worthy husband. Hopefully, one day, even, to win her back. Making her laugh would do for now.

*

Stephanie waved to James as his taxi sped off, then closed the door. She was completely on her own for the first time in ten years. Well, on her own with Finn, which was fine by her. No husband, no Michael. It felt good. She was in no hurry to get into another relationship. She would spend some time sorting herself out first, making sure about what she really wanted. There was still one more hurdle she and James had to get across: telling Pauline and John that their marriage was over. She was in no rush to do that now either. She was just going to wait and see what happened.

Acknowledgements

With thanks to Louise Moore, Clare Pollock, Kate Cotton, Kate Burke and everyone at Penguin, Jonny Geller, Betsy Robbins, Alice Lutyens, Doug Kean and anyone I've forgotten at Curtis Brown, Charlotte Willow Edwards, for her invaluable research, and all the people who answered her questions, including Louise Riches, for her vet expertise, Jess Wilson, of Jess Wilson Stylists (www.threeshadesred.com/jesswilson), Jessica Kelly, Jeffery M. James and Steve Pamphilon.

GETTING RID OF MATTHEW

When Matthew, Helen's lover of the past four years, finally decides to leave his wife Sophie (and their two daughters) and move into Helen's flat, she should be over the moon. The only trouble is, she doesn't want him anymore. Now she has to figure out how to get rid of him …

PLAN A
Stop shaving your armpits. And your bikini line
Buy incontinence pads and leave them lying around
Stop having sex with him

PLAN B
Accidentally on purpose bump into his wife Sophie
Give yourself a fake name and identity
Befriend Sophie and actually begin to really like her
Snog Matthew's son (who's the same age as you by the way. You're not a paedophile)
Befriend Matthew's children. Unsuccessfully
Watch your whole plan go absolutely horribly wrong.

Getting Rid of Matthew isn't as easy as it seems, but along the way Helen will forge an unlikely friendship, find real love and realize that nothing ever goes exactly to plan…

Calling all girls!

It's the invitation of the season.

Penguin books would like to invite you to become a member of Bijoux – the exclusive club for anyone who loves to curl up with the hottest reads in fiction for women.

You'll get all the inside gossip on your favourite authors – what they're doing, where and when; we'll send you early copies of the latest reads months before they're on the High Street and you'll get the chance to attend fabulous launch parties!

And, of course, we realise that even while she's reading every girl wants to look her best, so we have heaps of beauty goodies to pamper you with too.

If you'd like to become a part of the exclusive world of Bijoux, email
bijoux@penguin.co.uk

Bijoux books for Bijoux girls

He just wanted a decent book to read ...

Not too much to ask, is it? It was in 1935 when Allen Lane, Managing Director of Bodley Head Publishers, stood on a platform at Exeter railway station looking for something good to read on his journey back to London. His choice was limited to popular magazines and poor-quality paperbacks – the same choice faced every day by the vast majority of readers, few of whom could afford hardbacks. Lane's disappointment and subsequent anger at the range of books generally available led him to found a company – and change the world.

'We believed in the existence in this country of a vast reading public for intelligent books at a low price, and staked everything on it'
Sir Allen Lane, 1902–1970, founder of Penguin Books

The quality paperback had arrived – and not just in bookshops. Lane was adamant that his Penguins should appear in chain stores and tobacconists, and should cost no more than a packet of cigarettes.

Reading habits (and cigarette prices) have changed since 1935, but Penguin still believes in publishing the best books for everybody to enjoy. We still believe that good design costs no more than bad design, and we still believe that quality books published passionately and responsibly make the world a better place.

So wherever you see the little bird – whether it's on a piece of prize-winning literary fiction or a celebrity autobiography, political tour de force or historical masterpiece, a serial-killer thriller, reference book, world classic or a piece of pure escapism – you can bet that it represents the very best that the genre has to offer.

Whatever you like to read – trust Penguin.

'So many wedding websites won't talk numbers – not so with **Whimsical Wonderland Wedings,** whose Budget real weddings spill all about their spends. But there's more to it than that: as well as all the fiddly little details and personal touches to inspire you, WWW lets you in on the love story behind the big days. Full disclosure: I have a slightly extra-soft spot for them since lovely Lou is featuring mine and Darren's wedding too!'

Social Networking
Come back! Come back! I've changed my mind! You know I love you, but just not enough to let you go. If you want to stay in the loop with all things High-Street Bride – including chic new dresses for less, sample sales and unusual big-day ideas – you can follow me on Twitter @HighStreetBride.

Please.

I need the validation...